VIRA
MODERN C
146

Edith Wharton

Edith Wharton was born in 1862, daughter of a distinguished and prosperous New York family. In 1885 she married a Boston socialite, Edward Robbins Wharton, and lived in Newport, Rhode Island. She became friendly with Henry James on her frequent trips to Europe. The Whartons' marriage was far from happy and she turned to writing, publishing her first novel, *The Valley of Decision*, in 1902. She was divorced in 1913 after she had moved to France permanently. By now, and for the rest of her life, she was publishing at least one book a year, her first popular success being *The House of Mirth* (1905). Her busy cosmopolitan and creative life was interrupted by energetic work during the 1914–18 war, for which she was awarded the Cross of the Legion d'Honneur and the Order of Leopold. In 1920 *The Age of Innocence* won the Pulitzer Prize; she was the first woman to receive a Doctorate of Letters from Yale University and in 1930 she became a member of the American Academy of Arts and letters. She died in France at the age of seventy-five.

Novels and short stories by Edith Wharton published by Virago

MADAME DE TREYMES
Four short novels

Edith
Wharton

With an Introduction by Janet Beer Goodwyn

Published by VIRAGO PRESS 1984
20 Vauxhall Bridge Road, London SW1V 2SA

Reprinted with new introduction 1995

This collection first published in New York by Charles Scribner's Sons 1970

'Madame de Treymes' and 'Bunner Sisters' were first published in
Scribner's Magazine 1906, 1916

Introduction Copyright © Janet Beer Goodwyn 1995

A CIP catalogue record for this book is available from the British Library

Printed and bound in Great Britain by
Cox & Wyman Ltd, Reading, Berkshire

Contents

Introduction

The four stories told in this volume are all in some way concerned with failures of communication between people, a theme which haunted Edith Wharton throughout her writing career. She returned repeatedly in her fiction to the tragic consequences of the misunderstandings which can arise as easily between lovers and friends as between strangers. The novellas collected together here have many common areas of interest, but these areas are given different treatments and different degrees of prominence in the telling of individual tales. All four are centrally focused on moral dilemmas and the guilt and shame which accompany the choices we make. They all treat the secondary role that women invariably play in society, regardless of capability or class, the conflicts between private and public spheres and, most poignantly, the inevitable failure of romantic love in a world full of competing individual appetites and ambitions.

In each instance the title of the novella is absolutely crucial in communicating a sense of the theme which will dominate the story; the titles resonate beyond the particular situation into a larger field of suggestion and meaning. *The Touchstone* is a metaphor for a test of superlative quality or worth which can, by its very nature, exist only in the abstract. So Margaret Aubyn's love – exposed to public view in the publication of her letters – reveals an emotional as well as an artistic sensibility which has reached a pitch of perfection, but, both her self and her writing are wasted on a lover who cannot respond. *Sanctuary* deals, quite literally, with places of safety, in both actual and figurative terms, as Kate Orme seeks to find a moral refuge for herself in the mission she undertakes. *Madame de Treymes* herself comes to embody all that is mysterious in the organisation of upper-class French society, particularly as it affects women, whilst *The Bunner Sisters* raises numerous questions about the nature of sisterhood in a world where marriage is the only intimate relationship that receives full endorsement from the wider culture.

In these novellas Wharton pays meticulous attention to her own language but also gives the failure of communication between people a large part to play in all the stories. Constant misunderstandings of words, signs and feelings distinguish her characters' dealings with each other. In *The Touchstone* Stephen Glennard can feel only 'inarticulate misery' when remembering his relationship with the writer Margaret Aubyn. The two Bunner sisters could scarcely live in more intimate circumstances, sharing a workplace, a single living room and bedroom, even the same bed; yet they conduct their lives constrained by 'habitually repressed emotion', divided by their failure to succeed in either the business of marriage or haberdashery. In *Sanctuary*, Kate Orme passes from co-habitation with one man to another – from father to husband to son – but can never say the things she means and be understood. Only as the story closes can she feel at last the response of a sympathetic intelligence but even then the understanding between her and her son is accomplished wordlessly by some sort of telepathic communion of a shared morality. In *Madame de Treymes*, a tale of cross-cultural confusions, the failure to understand the different uses to which two nations put their means of communication, whether words or signs, has the endlessly expansive American, John Durham, filling all the empty spaces of his native land with talk, and the French family of Malrive reserving their few words as a means of maintaining, unbroken, their ancestral line and age-old practices of mystification.

The Touchstone, the first novella in this collection, has received a good deal of attention from critics who are concerned with Wharton's biography as well as her fiction. The central concern of the story – the unsatisfactory nature of the private, emotional life of the woman who is known in the world to possess a superior intelligence – has resonances in Wharton's own history: she never found a long-term companion who could respond to her both romantically and intellectually. The tragic destiny of Margaret Aubyn in *The Touchstone* – in person or in writing – is to offer the inestimable gift of her love to a man who could only receive it as an insult: 'she made him feel his inferiority'. Her letters are wrenched out of their private significance into the public arena: 'The little broken phrases fled across the page like wounded animals in the open . . . helpless things driven savagely out of shelter'. They form the most literal representation of thwarted communication in a world where speech or writing habitually misses its intended audience and comes only to signify the collective failure to love, to respect, to respond to human need. The story is full of references to estrangement and separation expressed in a language which pertains to the territorial. Wharton offers the human soul as 'an unmapped region, a few acres of which we have cleared for our habitation; while of the nature of those nearest us we know but the boundaries that march with ours'; not only are people described in terms of their alien and alienating geographies but they have unexplored regions even within themselves. The novella chronicles a series of re-positionings and adjustments, a 'redistribution of meanings', brought about by a moral crisis which ends with the re-locating of a once-perfect relationship on a lower level of fulfilment. This lower level, however, is the place where both parties come to understand the compromises necessary to sustain a life together. The charting of such a process of disillusionment would become one of the most powerful and enduring themes in Edith Wharton's longer works.

There are no unqualified successes or happy endings in these stories, unless the moral triumph at the close of *Sanctuary* can be considered grounds for celebration of the human capacity to be scrupulous and decent. This novella has never received much praise from critics and Wharton's first biographer, R. W. B. Lewis, reports that during its composition she referred to it as *Sank* and, uncharacteristically, had very little to say about it once it had been written and published. Nevertheless the novella demonstrates further developments in a number of Wharton's recurrent themes and also establishes a structural principle, used repeatedly in her later work, where she draws powerful contrasts and imagery from language usually found in other contexts, like the law, commerce or the church, but which has a particular relevance to the tale she is telling. In *Sanctuary* she uses the words of the law and the church, incorporating them into the everyday speech of those involved in the working out of the central dramatic situation. This language not only extends and develops the central idea of sanctuary but helps to define what we attempt when we seek clarification of essential moral questions – those which are at the heart of our legal and religious systems – so as to make them of practical use in our own lives. Whilst the words denoting places of refuge or safety which punctuate the tale bring out the religious connotations of *Sanctuary* itself, it is in the struggle between the public and private uses of the idea of shelter that the story has most cogency. Both the law and the church, after all, are publicly accountable institutions which have dimensions which are intensely personal, as in the marriage contract. The moral dilemma which confronts Kate Orme – whether to marry a man whom she knows to be guilty of lies and denials that have resulted in the death of two innocent people – is made to carry the weight of an examination of the whole of the body politic as it is revealed to her through her own circumstances. Once she has 'begun to perceive that the fair surface of life was honeycombed by a vast system of moral sewage' she can no longer find refuge in innocence but must convert the meaning of 'sanctuary' to her own uses. In order to achieve this she must literally become the place of safety herself: in a 'vision of protecting maternity' she offers herself up as the physical sanctuary so that the sin can be expiated through her personal 'climax of effacement'. She uses the female body as the place wherein the seed of the sinner will be rehabilitated and transformed into a new life in whom the struggle between good and evil can be enacted. She is ultimately rewarded for this in the shape of her purified son, freed from the toils of the sophisticated and sophistical arguments of his lover, Clemence Verney, and ready, as he says, not to regard her morality as 'an obstacle any longer, but a refuge'.

When Kate Orme is first trying to come to terms with what she has learned about her fiancé, Denis Peyton, Wharton describes the position of ignorance and naïvety from which she starts: 'These were not things about which young girls were told'. Wharton forces Kate, however, to find a way of bringing her disillusionment, the knowledge which has been forced upon her, into the real world where she must engage with the complexities which arise from having to operate in the wider community. Such complexities are never approached nor even acknowledged by the hapless innocents who are *The Bunner Sisters*. Evelina and Ann Eliza Bunner know nothing of the world outside their shop window. They do not know how to read the simplest signs, the indications of Herman Ramy's enduring drug habit for one, the true object of his marital ambitions for another; they are hopelessly ill-equipped for life outside the boundaries of their basement.

The Bunner Sisters was the first of these novellas to be written, in 1892, but it was the last to be published, refused by *Scribner's* magazine on the grounds of its depressing nature and not appearing in print until 1916 when it was included in the volume of short stories, *Xingu*. Whilst all the novellas in this collection treat self-sacrifice in one form or another, 'the chill joy of renunciation' in the story of *The Bunner Sisters* is positioned as starkly as it can be between the choice of total isolation and a bitter parody of a marriage. The bleakness here is unmitigated; not even the renunciation which can be turned to positive moral effect in the other stories can do anything other than highlight the desperate nature of Ann Eliza's plight as she seeks to find a new place for herself in a city which 'seemed to throb with the stir of innumerable beginnings' for all its inhabitants except her.

The most sophisticated of these four novellas, *Madame de Treymes*, was Wharton's first extended venture into the 'International theme' and its opening pages are among the most resonant and seductive in her work. She offers us a delicate series of advances and withdrawals, implications and interpretations of the tiniest details of social conduct, in all its cross-cultural reverberations, as we are given to understand that there is a possibility that John Durham may be about to abandon the neutrality of the single man in committing himself to the wooing of Fanny de Malrive.

From the very beginning of *Madame de Treymes* Wharton sets in opposition the way in which French and American nations communicate, making their differences, not merely of language but of intent, meaning, and signification, the central point of both mystery and conflict. Like Wharton's later heroine, Ellen Olenska in *The Age of Innocence*, who also marries disastrously into the European aristocracy, Fanny believes in an America where everything is open, straightforward and spoken aloud, that there is a 'clear American air where there are no obscurities, no mysteries'. The world into which she has married, however, is closed to scrutiny or understanding, fuelled as it is by a 'mysterious solidarity' which defies the processes of reasonable argument and rational debate as proposed by John Durham with his American 'can-do' approach.

There is a strong sense in telling of this tale that the attractions of a Fanny de Malrive, so distinct from those of Fanny Frisbee, can be aligned in some respects with the mature and 'ordered beauty' of Paris itself. The words that Wharton repeatedly uses to describe the city are to do with its having been planned, informed by a larger spirit of both use and beauty but answering ultimately to the human need for continuity and support. She suggests that the grandeur of Paris somehow supplies much of the grandeur in its inhabitants' lives. Similarly Fanny Frisbee has been extended and matured by her European experience: 'Yes, it was the finish, the modelling, which Madame de Malrive's experience had given her that set her apart from the fresh uncomplicated personalities of which she had once been simply the most charming type. The influences that had lowered her voice, regulated her gestures, toned her down to harmony with the warm dim background of a long social past – these influences had lent to her natural fineness of perception a command of expression adapted to complex conditions'. What John Durham sees before him is a woman who has been, on the European plan, matured and made more complex and interesting by marriage rather than, as in American nuptials, 'cut off from men's society in all but the most formal and intermittent ways', as Wharton says in her later book, *French Ways and Their Meaning*. Durham is drawn by 'the sense of unprobed depths of initiation', not by the naïvety and innocence which had made her once interchangeable with all other American girls. The tragedy of *Madame de Treymes* is that having once recognized the superior complications of the older civilization Durham is left with only his adherence to an 'abstract standard of truth' in return for renouncing his love. For him, as for Kate Orme, Stephen and Alexa Glennard and Ann Eliza Bunner, between initiation and disillusion there is no space for the individual to flourish, for intentions or desires to be fulfilled or for an understanding to be reached which would ameliorate the 'great moral loneliness' at the heart of every story told here.

Janet Beer Goodwyn, London 1995

The Touchstone

❦[1900]❧

※ I ※

Professor Joslin, who, as our readers are doubtless aware, is engaged in writing the life of Mrs. Aubyn, asks us to state that he will be greatly indebted to any of the famous novelist's friends who will furnish him with information concerning the period previous to her coming to England. Mrs. Aubyn had so few intimate friends, and consequently so few regular correspondents, that letters will be of special value. Professor Joslin's address is 10 Augusta Gardens, Kensington, and he begs us to say that he will promptly return any documents entrusted to him.

G LENNARD dropped the *Spectator* and sat looking into the fire. The club was filling up, but he still had to himself the small inner room with its darkening outlook down the rain-streaked prospect of Fifth Avenue. It was all dull and dismal enough, yet a moment earlier his boredom had been perversely tinged by a sense of resentment at the thought that, as things were going, he might in time have to surrender even the despised privilege of boring himself within those particular four walls. It was not that he cared much for the club, but that the remote contingency of having to give it up stood to him, just then, perhaps by very reason of its insignificance and remoteness, for the symbol of his increasing abnegations; of that perpetual paring-off that was gradually reducing existence to the naked business of keeping himself alive. It was the futility of his multiplied shifts and privations that made them seem unworthy of a high attitude—the sense that, however rapidly he eliminated the superfluous, his cleared horizon was likely to offer no nearer view of the one prospect toward which he strained. To give up things in order to marry the woman one loves is easier than to give them up without being brought appreciably nearer to such a conclusion.

3

Through the open door he saw young Hollingsworth rise with a yawn from the ineffectual solace of a brandy-and-soda and transport his purposeless person to the window. Glennard measured his course with a contemptuous eye. It was so like Hollingsworth to get up and look out of the window just as it was growing too dark to see anything! There was a man rich enough to do what he pleased—had he been capable of being pleased— yet barred from all conceivable achievement by his own impervious dulness; while, a few feet off, Glennard, who wanted only enough to keep a decent coat on his back and a roof over the head of the woman he loved—Glennard, who had sweated, toiled, denied himself for the scant measure of opportunity that his zeal would have converted into a kingdom—sat wretchedly calculating that, even when he had resigned from the club, and knocked off his cigars, and given up his Sundays out of town, he would still be no nearer to attainment.

The *Spectator* had slipped to his feet, and as he picked it up his eye fell again on the paragraph addressed to the friends of Mrs. Aubyn. He had read it for the first time with a scarcely perceptible quickening of attention: her name had so long been public property that his eye passed it unseeingly, as the crowd in the street hurries without a glance by some familiar monument.

"Information concerning the period previous to her coming to England. . . ." The words were an evocation. He saw her again as she had looked at their first meeting, the poor woman of genius with her long pale face and short-sighted eyes, softened a little by the grace of youth and inexperience, but so incapable even then of any hold upon the pulses. When she spoke, indeed, she was wonderful, more wonderful, perhaps, than when later, to Glennard's fancy at least, the consciousness of memorable things uttered seemed to take from even her most intimate speech the perfect bloom of privacy. It was in those earliest days, if ever, that he had come near loving her; though even then his sentiment had lived only in the intervals of its expression. Later, when to be loved by her had been a state to touch any man's imagination, the physical reluctance had, inexplicably, so overborne the intellectual attraction, that the last years had been, to both of them, an agony of conflicting impulses. Even now, if, in turning over old papers his hand lit on her letters, the touch filled him with inarticulate misery.

"She had so few intimate friends . . . that letters will be of special value." So few intimate friends! For years she had had but one; one who in the last years had requited her wonderful pages, her tragic outpourings of love, humility and pardon, with the scant phrases by which a man evades the vulgarest of sentimental importunities. He had been a brute in spite of himself, and sometimes, now that the remembrance of her face had faded, and only her voice and words remained with him, he chafed at his own inadequacy, his stupid inability to rise to the height of her passion. His egoism was not of a kind to mirror its complacency in the adventure. To have been loved by the most brilliant woman of her day, and to have been incapable of loving her, seemed to him, in looking back, derisive evidence of his limitations; and his remorseful tenderness for her memory was complicated with a sense of irritation against her for having given him once for all the measure of his emotional capacity. It was not often, however, that he thus probed the past. The public, in taking possession of Mrs. Aubyn, had eased his shoulders of their burden. There was something fatuous in an attitude of sentimental apology toward a memory already classic: to reproach one's self for not having loved Margaret Aubyn was a good deal like being disturbed by an inability to admire the Venus of Milo. From her cold niche of fame she looked down ironically enough on his self-flagellations. . . . It was only when he came on something that belonged to her that he felt a sudden renewal of the old feeling, the strange dual impulse that drew him to her voice but drove him from her hand, so that even now, at sight of anything she had touched, his heart contracted painfully. It happened seldom nowadays. Her little presents, one by one, had disappeared from his room, and her letters, kept from some unacknowledged puerile vanity in the possession of such treasures, seldom came beneath his hand.

"Her letters will be of special value—" Her letters! Why, he must have hundreds of them—enough to fill a volume. Sometimes it used to seem to him that they came with every post—he used to avoid looking in his letter-box when he came home to his rooms—but her writing seemed to spring out at him as he put his key in the door.

He stood up and strolled into the other room. Hollingsworth, lounging away from the window, had joined himself to a languidly convivial group of men, to whom, in phrases as halting as though they struggled to define an ultimate idea, he was expounding the cursed nuisance of living in a hole with such a damned climate that one had to get out of it by February, with the contingent difficulty of there being no place to take one's yacht to in winter but that other played-out hole, the Riviera. From the outskirts of this group Glennard wandered to another, where a voice as different as possible from Hollingsworth's colorless organ dominated another circle of languid listeners.

"Come and hear Dinslow talk about his patent: admission free," one of the men sang out in a tone of mock resignation.

Dinslow turned to Glennard the confident pugnacity of his smile. "Give it another six months and it'll be talking about itself," he declared. "It's pretty nearly articulate now."

"Can it say papa?" someone else inquired.

Dinslow's smile broadened. "You'll be deuced glad to say papa to *it* a year from now," he retorted. "It'll be able to support even you in affluence. Look here, now, just let me explain to you—"

Glennard moved away impatiently. The men at the club—all but those who were "in it"—were proverbially "tired" of Dinslow's patent, and none more so than Glennard, whose knowledge of its merits made it loom large in the depressing catalogue of lost opportunities. The relations between the two men had always been friendly, and Dinslow's urgent offers to "take him in on the ground floor" had of late intensified Glennard's sense of his own inability to meet good luck half-way. Some of the men who had paused to listen were already in evening clothes, others on their way home to dress; and Glennard, with an accustomed twinge of humiliation, said to himself that if he lingered among them it was in the miserable hope that one of the number might ask him to dine. Miss Trent had told him that she was to go to the opera that evening with her rich aunt; and if he should have the luck to pick up a dinner invitation he might join her there without extra outlay.

He moved about the room, lingering here and there in a tentative affectation of interest; but though the men greeted him pleasantly, no one asked him to dine. Doubtless they were all engaged, these men who could afford to pay for their dinners, who did not have to hunt for invitations as a beggar rummages for a crust in an ash-barrel! But no—as Hollingsworth left the lessening circle about the table, an admiring youth called out, "Holly, stop and dine!"

Hollingsworth turned on him the crude countenance that looked like the wrong side of a more finished face. "Sorry I can't. I'm in for a beastly banquet."

Glennard threw himself into an armchair. Why go home in the rain to dress? It was folly to take a cab to the opera, it was worse folly to go there at all. His perpetual meetings with Alexa Trent were as unfair to the girl as they were unnerving to himself. Since he couldn't marry her, it was time to stand aside and give a better man the chance—and his thought admitted the ironical implication that in the terms of expediency the phrase might stand for Hollingsworth.

※ II ※

He dined alone and walked home to his rooms in the rain. As he turned into Fifth Avenue he caught the wet gleam of carriages on their way to the opera, and he took the first side street, in a moment of irritation against the petty restrictions that thwarted every impulse. It was ridiculous to give up the opera, not because one might possibly be bored there, but because one must pay for the experiment.

In his sitting-room, the tacit connivance of the inanimate had centred the lamplight on a photograph of Alexa Trent, placed, in the obligatory silver frame, just where, as memory officiously reminded him, Margaret Aubyn's picture had long throned in its stead. Miss Trent's features cruelly justified the usurpation. She had the kind of beauty that comes of a happy accord of face and spirit. It is not given to many to have the lips and eyes of their rarest mood, and some women go through life behind a mask expressing only their anxiety about the butcher's bill or their inability to see a joke. With Miss Trent, face and mind had the same high serious contour. She looked like a throned Justice by some grave Florentine painter; and it seemed to Glennard that her most salient attribute, or that at least to which her conduct gave most consistent expression, was a kind of passionate justness—the intuitive feminine justness that is so much rarer than a reasoned impartiality. Circumstances had tragically combined to develop this instinct into a conscious habit. She had seen more than most girls of the shabby side of life, of the perpetual tendency of want to cramp the noblest attitude. Poverty and misfortune had overhung her childhood, and she had none of the pretty delusions about life that are supposed to be the crowning grace of girlhood. This very competence, which gave her a touching reasonableness, made Glennard's situation more difficult than if he had aspired to a princess. Between them they asked so little—they knew so well how to make that little do; but they understood also, and she especially did not for a moment let him forget, that without that little the future they dreamed of was impossible.

The sight of her photograph quickened Glennard's exasperation. He was sick and ashamed of the part he was playing. He had loved her now for two years, with the tranquil tenderness that gathers depth and volume as it nears fulfilment; he knew that she would wait for him—but the certitude was an added pang. There are times when the constancy of the woman one cannot marry is almost as trying as that of the woman one does not want to.

Glennard turned up his reading-lamp and stirred the fire. He had a long evening before him, and he wanted to crowd out thought with action. He had brought some papers from his office and he spread them out on his table and squared himself to the task.

It must have been an hour later that he found himself automatically fitting a key into a locked drawer. He had no more notion than a somnambulist of the mental process that had led up to this action. He was just dimly aware of having pushed aside the papers and the heavy calf volumes that a moment before had bounded his horizon, and of laying in their place, without a trace of conscious volition, the parcel he had taken from the drawer.

The letters were tied in packets of thirty or forty. There were a great many packets. On some of the envelopes the ink was fading; on others, which bore the English postmark, it was still fresh. She had been dead hardly three years, and she had written, at lengthening intervals, to the last.

He undid one of the early packets—little notes written during their first acquaintance at Hillbridge. Glennard, on leaving college, had begun life in his uncle's law office in the old university town. It was there that, at the house of her father, Professor Forth, he had first met the young lady then chiefly distinguished for having, after two years of a conspicuously unhappy marriage, returned to the protection of the paternal roof.

Mrs. Aubyn was at that time an eager and somewhat tragic young woman, of complex mind and undeveloped manners, whom her crude experience of matrimony had fitted out with a stock of generalizations that exploded like bombs in the academic air of Hillbridge. In her choice of a husband she had been fortunate enough, if the paradox be permitted, to light on one so signally gifted with the faculty of putting himself in the wrong that her leaving him had the dignity of a manifesto—made her, as it were, the spokeswoman of outraged wifehood. In this light she was cherished by that dominant portion of Hillbridge society which was least indulgent to conjugal differences, and which found a proportionate pleasure in being for once able to feast openly on a dish liberally seasoned with the outrageous. So much did this endear Mrs. Aubyn to the university ladies, that they were disposed from the first to allow her more latitude of speech and action than the ill-used wife was generally accorded in Hillbridge, where misfortune was still regarded as a visitation designed to put people in their proper place and make them feel the superiority of their neighbors. The young woman so privileged combined with a kind of personal shyness an intellectual audacity that was like a deflected impulse of coquetry: one felt that if she had been prettier she would have had emotions instead of ideas. She was in fact even then what she had always remained: a genius capable of the acutest generalizations, but curiously undiscerning where her personal susceptibilities were concerned. Her psychology failed her just where it serves most women, and one felt that her brains would never be a guide to her heart. Of all this, however, Glennard thought little in the first year of their acquaintance. He was at an age when all the gifts and graces are but so much undiscriminated food to the ravening egoism of youth. In seeking Mrs. Aubyn's company he was prompted by an intuitive taste for the best as a pledge of his own superiority. The sympathy of the cleverest woman in Hillbridge was balm to his craving for distinction; it was public confirmation of his secret sense that he was cut out for a bigger place. It must not be understood that Glennard was vain. Vanity contents itself with the coarsest diet; there is no palate so fastidious as that of self-distrust. To a youth of Glennard's aspirations the encouragement of a clever woman stood for the symbol of all success. Later, when he had begun to feel his way, to gain a foothold, he would not need such support; but it served to carry him lightly and easily over what is often a period of insecurity and discouragement.

It would be unjust, however, to represent his interest in Mrs. Aubyn as a matter of calculation. It was as instinctive as love, and it missed being love by just such a hair-breadth deflection from the line of beauty as had determined the curve of Mrs. Aubyn's lips. When they met she had just published her first novel, and Glennard, who afterward had an ambitious man's impatience of distinguished women, was young enough to be dazzled by the semi-publicity it gave her. It was the kind of book that makes elderly ladies lower their voices and call each other "my dear" when they furtively discuss it; and Glennard exulted in the superior knowledge of the world that enabled him to take as a matter of course sentiments over which the university shook its head. Still more delightful was it to hear Mrs. Aubyn waken the echoes of academic drawing-rooms with audacities surpassing those of her printed page. Her intellectual independence gave a touch of comradeship to their intimacy, prolonging the illusion of college friendships based on a joyous interchange of heresies. Mrs. Aubyn and Glennard represented to each other the augur's wink behind the Hillbridge idol: they walked together in that light of young omniscience from which fate so curiously excludes one's elders.

Husbands, who are notoriously inopportune, may even die inopportunely, and this was the revenge that Mr. Aubyn, some two years after her return to Hillbridge, took upon his injured wife. He died precisely at the moment when Glennard was beginning to criticise her. It was not that she bored him; she did what was infinitely worse—she made him feel his inferiority. The sense of mental equality had been gratifying to his raw ambition; but as his self-knowledge defined itself, his understanding of her also increased; and if man is at times indirectly flattered by the moral superiority of woman, her mental ascendency is extenuated by no such oblique tribute to his powers. The attitude of

looking up is a strain on the muscles; and it was becoming more
and more Glennard's opinion that brains, in a woman, should be
merely the obverse of beauty. To beauty Mrs. Aubyn could lay
no claim; and while she had enough prettiness to exasperate him
by her incapacity to make use of it, she seemed invincibly ignorant of any of the little artifices whereby women contrive to hide
their defects and even to turn them into graces. Her dress never
seemed a part of her; all her clothes had an impersonal air, as
though they had belonged to someone else and been borrowed in
an emergency that had somehow become chronic. She was conscious enough of her deficiencies to try to amend them by rash
imitations of the most approved models; but no woman who does
not dress well intuitively will ever do so by the light of reason,
and Mrs. Aubyn's plagiarisms, to borrow a metaphor of her
trade, somehow never seemed to be incorporated with the text.

Genius is of small use to a woman who does not know how
to do her hair. The fame that came to Mrs. Aubyn with her second book left Glennard's imagination untouched, or had at most
the negative effect of removing her still farther from the circle of
his contracting sympathies. We are all the sport of time; and fate
had so perversely ordered the chronology of Margaret Aubyn's
romance that when her husband died Glennard felt as though he
had lost a friend.

It was not in his nature to be needlessly unkind; and though
he was in the impregnable position of the man who has given a
woman no more definable claim on him than that of letting her
fancy that he loves her, he would not for the world have accen-
tuated his advantage by any betrayal of indifference. During the
first year of her widowhood their friendship dragged on with
halting renewals of sentiment, becoming more and more a banquet of empty dishes from which the covers were never removed;
then Glennard went to New York to live and exchanged the
faded pleasures of intercourse for the comparative novelty of correspondence. Her letters, oddly enough, seemed at first to bring
her nearer than her presence. She had adopted, and she success-

fully maintained, a note as affectionately impersonal as his own; she wrote ardently of her work, she questioned him about his, she even bantered him on the inevitable pretty girl who was certain before long to divert the current of his confidences. To Glennard, who was almost a stranger in New York, the sight of Mrs. Aubyn's writing was like a voice of reassurance in surroundings as yet insufficiently aware of him. His vanity found a retrospective enjoyment in the sentiment his heart had rejected, and this factitious emotion drove him once or twice to Hillbridge, whence, after scenes of evasive tenderness, he returned dissatisfied with himself and her. As he made room for himself in New York and peopled the space he had cleared with the sympathies at the disposal of agreeable and self-confident young men, it seemed to him natural to infer that Mrs. Aubyn had refurnished in the same manner the void he was not unwilling his departure should have left. But in the dissolution of sentimental partnerships it is seldom that both associates are able to withdraw their funds at the same time; and Glennard gradually learned that he stood for the venture on which Mrs. Aubyn had irretrievably staked her all. It was not the kind of figure he cared to cut. He had no fancy for leaving havoc in his wake and would have preferred to sow a quick growth of oblivion in the spaces wasted by his unconsidered inroads; but if he supplied the seed, it was clearly Mrs. Aubyn's business to see to the raising of the crop. Her attitude seemed indeed to throw his own reasonableness into distincter relief; so that they might have stood for thrift and improvidence in an allegory of the affections.

It was not that Mrs. Aubyn permitted herself to be a pensioner on his bounty. He knew she had no wish to keep herself alive on the small change of sentiment; she simply fed on her own funded passion, and the luxuries it allowed her made him, even then, dimly aware that she had the secret of an inexhaustible alchemy.

Their relations remained thus negatively tender till she suddenly wrote him of her decision to go abroad to live. Her father had died, she had no near ties in Hillbridge, and London offered more scope than New York to her expanding personality. She was already famous, and her laurels were yet unharvested.

For a moment the news roused Glennard to a jealous sense of lost opportunities. He wanted, at any rate, to reassert his power before she made the final effort of escape. They had not met for over a year, but of course he could not let her sail without seeing her. She came to New York the day before her departure, and they spent its last hours together. Glennard had planned no course of action—he simply meant to let himself drift. They both drifted, for a long time, down the languid current of reminiscence; she seemed to sit passive, letting him push his way back through the overgrown channels of the past. At length she reminded him that they must bring their explorations to an end. He rose to leave, and stood looking at her with the same uncertainty in his heart. He was tired of her already— he was always tired of her—yet he was not sure that he wanted her to go.

"I may never see you again," he said, as though confidently appealing to her compassion.

Her look enveloped him. "And I shall see you always— always!"

"Why go then—?" escaped him.

"To be nearer you," she answered; and the words dismissed him like a closing door.

The door was never to reopen; but through its narrow crack Glennard, as the years went on, became more and more conscious of an inextinguishable light directing its small ray toward the past which consumed so little of his own commemorative oil. The reproach was taken from this thought by Mrs. Aubyn's gradual translation into terms of universality. In becoming a personage she so naturally ceased to be a person that Glennard could almost look back to his explorations of her spirit as on a visit to some famous shrine, immortalized, but in a sense desecrated, by popular veneration.

Her letters from London continued to come with the same tender punctuality; but the altered conditions of her life, the vistas of new relationships disclosed by every phrase, made her communications as impersonal as a piece of journalism. It was as though the state, the world, indeed, had taken her off his hands, assuming the maintenance of a temperament that had long exhausted his slender store of reciprocity.

In the retrospective light shed by the letters he was blinded to their specific meaning. He was not a man who concerned himself with literature, and they had been to him, at first, simply the extension of her brilliant talk, later the dreaded vehicle of a tragic importunity. He knew, of course, that they were wonderful; that, unlike the authors who give their essence to the public and keep only a dry rind for their friends, Mrs. Aubyn had stored of her rarest vintage for this hidden sacrament of tenderness. Sometimes, indeed, he had been oppressed, humiliated almost, by the multiplicity of her allusions, the wide scope of her interests, her persistence in forcing her superabundance of thought and emotion into the shallow receptacle of his sympathy; but he had never thought of the letters objectively, as the production of a distinguished woman; had never measured the literary significance of her oppressive prodigality. He was almost frightened now at the wealth in his hands; the obligation of her love had never weighed on him like this gift of her imagination: it was as though he had accepted from her something to which even a reciprocal tenderness could not have justified his claim.

He sat a long time staring at the scattered pages on his desk; and in the sudden realization of what they meant he could almost fancy some alchemistic process changing them to gold as he stared.

He had the sense of not being alone in the room, of the presence of another self observing from without the stirring of subconscious impulses that sent flushes of humiliation to his forehead. At length he stood up, and with the gesture of a man who wishes to give outward expression to his purpose—to establish, as it were, a moral alibi—swept the letters into a heap and carried them toward the grate. But it would have taken too long to burn all the packets. He turned back to the table and one by one fitted the pages into their envelopes; then he tied up the letters and put them back into the locked drawer.

※ III ※

IT was one of the laws of Glennard's intercourse with Miss Trent that he always went to see her the day after he had resolved to give her up. There was a special charm about the moments thus snatched from the jaws of renunciation; and his sense of their significance was on this occasion so keen that he hardly noticed the added gravity of her welcome.

His feeling for her had become so vital a part of him that her nearness had the quality of imperceptibly readjusting his point of view, of making the jumbled phenomena of experience fall at once into a rational perspective. In this redistribution of values the sombre retrospect of the previous evening shrank to a mere cloud on the edge of consciousness. Perhaps the only service an unloved woman can render the man she loves is to enhance and prolong his illusions about her rival. It was the fate of Margaret Aubyn's memory to serve as a foil to Miss Trent's presence, and never had the poor lady thrown her successor into more vivid relief.

Miss Trent had the charm of still waters that are felt to be renewed by rapid currents. Her attention spread a tranquil surface to the demonstrations of others, and it was only in days of storm that one felt the pressure of the tides. This inscrutable composure was perhaps her chief grace in Glennard's eyes. Reserve, in some natures, implies merely the locking of empty rooms or the dissimulation of awkward encumbrances; but Miss Trent's reticence was to Glennard like the closed door to the sanctuary, and his certainty of divining the hidden treasure made him content to remain outside in the happy expectancy of the neophyte.

"You didn't come to the opera last night," she began, in the tone that seemed always rather to record a fact than to offer a reflection on it.

He answered with a discouraged gesture. "What was the use? We couldn't have talked."

"Not as well as here," she assented; adding, after a meditative pause, "As you didn't come I talked to Aunt Virginia instead."

"Ah!" he returned, the fact being hardly striking enough to detach him from the contemplation of her hands, which had fallen, as was their wont, into an attitude full of plastic possibilities. One felt them to be hands that, moving only to some purpose, were capable of intervals of serene inaction.

"We had a long talk," Miss Trent went on; and she waited again before adding, with the increased absence of stress that marked her graver communications, "Aunt Virginia wants me to go abroad with her."

Glennard looked up with a start. "Abroad? When?"

"Now—next month. To be gone two years."

He permitted himself a movement of tender derision. "Does she really? Well, I want you to go abroad with *me*—for any number of years. Which offer do you accept?"

"Only one of them seems to require immediate consideration," she returned with a smile.

Glennard looked at her again. "You're not thinking of it?"

Her gaze dropped and she unclasped her hands. Her movements were so rare that they might have been said to italicize her words. "Aunt Virginia talked to me very seriously. It will be a great relief to mother and the others to have me provided for in that way for two years. I must think of that, you know." She glanced down at her gown, which, under a renovated surface, dated back to the first days of Glennard's wooing. "I try not to cost much—but I do."

"Good Lord!" Glennard groaned.

They sat silent till at length she gently took up the argument. "As the eldest, you know, I'm bound to consider these things. Women are such a burden. Jim does what he can for mother, but with his own children to provide for it isn't very much. You see we're all poor together."

"Your aunt isn't. She might help your mother."

"She does—in her own way."

"Exactly—that's the rich relation all over! You may be miserable in any way you like, but if you're to be happy, you must be so in her way—and in her old gowns."

"I could be very happy in Aunt Virginia's old gowns," Miss Trent interposed.

"Abroad, you mean?"

"I mean wherever I felt that I was helping. And my going abroad will help."

"Of course—I see that. And I see your considerateness in putting its advantages negatively."

"Negatively?"

"In dwelling simply on what the going will take you from, not on what it will bring you to. It means a lot to a woman, of course, to get away from a life like this." He summed up in a disparaging glance the background of indigent furniture. "The question is how you'll like coming back to it."

She seemed to accept the full consequences of his thought. "I only know I don't like leaving it."

He flung back sombrely, "You don't even put it conditionally then?"

Her gaze deepened. "On what?"

He stood up and walked across the room. Then he came back and paused before her. "On the alternative of marrying me."

The slow color—even her blushes seemed deliberate—rose to her lower lids; her lips stirred, but the words resolved themselves into a smile and she waited.

He took another turn, with the thwarted step of the man whose nervous exasperation escapes through his muscles.

"And to think that in fifteen years I shall have a big practice!"

Her eyes triumphed for him. "In less!"

"The cursed irony of it! What do I care for the man I shall be then? It's slaving one's life away for a stranger!" He took her hands abruptly. "You'll go to Cannes, I suppose, or Monte Carlo? I heard Hollingsworth say today that he meant to take his yacht over to the Mediterranean—"

She released herself. "If you think that—"

"I don't. I almost wish I did. It would be easier, I mean." He broke off incoherently. "I believe your Aunt Virginia does, though. She somehow connotes Hollingsworth and the Mediterranean." He caught her hands again. "Alexa—if we could manage a little hole somewhere out of town?"

"Could we?" she sighed, half yielding.

"In one of those places where they make jokes about the mosquitoes," he pressed her. "Could you get on with one servant?"

"Could you get on without varnished boots?"

"Promise me you won't go, then!"

"What are you thinking of, Stephen?"

"I don't know," he stammered, the question giving unexpected form to his intention. "It's all in the air yet, of course; but I picked up a tip the other day—"

"You're not speculating?" she cried, with a kind of superstitious terror.

"Lord, no. This is a sure thing—I almost wish it wasn't: I mean if I can work it—" He had a sudden vision of the comprehensiveness of the temptation. If only he had been less sure of Dinslow! His assurance gave the situation the base element of safety.

"I don't understand you," she faltered.

"Trust me, instead!" he adjured her with sudden energy; and

turning on her abruptly, "If you go, you know, you go free," he concluded.

She drew back, paling a little. "Why do you make it harder for me?"

"To make it easier for myself," he retorted.

※ IV ※

THE next afternoon Glennard, leaving his office earlier than usual, turned, on his way home, into one of the public libraries.

He had the place to himself at that closing hour, and the librarian was able to give an undivided attention to his tentative request for letters—collections of letters. The librarian suggested Walpole.

"I meant women—women's letters."

The librarian proffered Hannah More and Miss Martineau.

Glennard cursed his own inarticulateness. "I mean letters to —to some one person—a man: their husband—or—"

"Ah," said the inspired librarian. "Eloise and Abelard."

"Well—something a little nearer, perhaps," said Glennard, with lightness. "Didn't Mérimée—

"The lady's letters, in that case, were not published."

"Of course not," said Glennard, vexed at his blunder.

"There are George Sand's letters to Flaubert."

"Ah!" Glennard hesitated. "Was she—were they—?" He chafed at his own ignorance of the sentimental by-paths of literature.

"If you want love-letters, perhaps some of the French eighteenth-century correspondences might suit you better—Mlle. Aïssé or Madame de Sabran—"

But Glennard insisted. "I want something modern—English or American. I want to look something up," he lamely concluded.

The librarian could only suggest George Eliot.

"Well, give me some of the French things, then—and I'll

have Mérimée's letters. It was the woman who published them, wasn't it?"

He caught up his armful, transferring it, on the doorstep, to a cab which carried him to his rooms. He dined alone, hurriedly, at a small restaurant nearby, and returned at once to his books.

Late that night, as he undressed, he wondered what contemptible impulse had forced from him his last words to Alexa Trent. It was bad enough to interfere with the girl's chances by hanging about her to the obvious exclusion of other men, but it was worse to seem to justify his weakness by dressing up the future in delusive ambiguities. He saw himself sinking from depth to depth of sentimental cowardice in his reluctance to renounce his hold on her; and it filled him with self-disgust to think that the highest feeling of which he supposed himself capable was blent with such base elements.

His awakening was hardly cheered by the sight of her writing. He tore her note open and took in the few lines—she seldom exceeded the first page—with the lucidity of apprehension that is the forerunner of evil.

"My aunt sails on Saturday and I must give her my answer the day after tomorrow. Please don't come till then—I want to think the question over by myself. I know I ought to go. Won't you help me to be reasonable?"

It was settled, then. Well, he would help her to be reasonable; he wouldn't stand in her way; he would let her go. For two years he had been living some other, luckier man's life; the time had come when he must drop back into his own. He no longer tried to look ahead, to grope his way through the endless labyrinth of his material difficulties; a sense of dull resignation closed in on him like a fog.

"Hullo, Glennard!" a voice said, as an electric car, late that afternoon, dropped him at an uptown corner.

He looked up and met the interrogative smile of Barton Flamel, who stood on the curbstone watching the retreating car with the eye of a man philosophic enough to remember that it will be followed by another.

Glennard felt his usual impulse of pleasure at meeting Flamel; but it was not in this case curtailed by the reaction of contempt that habitually succeeded it. Probably even the few men who had known Flamel since his youth could have given no good reason for the vague mistrust that he inspired. Some people are judged by their actions, others by their ideas; and perhaps the shortest way of defining Flamel is to say that his well-known leniency of view was vaguely divined to include himself. Simple minds may have resented the discovery that his opinions were based on his perceptions; but there was certainly no more definite charge against him than that implied in the doubt as to how he would behave in an emergency, and his company was looked upon as one of those mildly unwholesome dissipations to which the prudent may occasionally yield. It now offered itself to Glennard as an easy escape from the obsession of moral problems, which somehow could no more be worn in Flamel's presence than a surplice in the street.

"Where are you going? To the club?" Flamel asked, adding, as the younger man assented, "Why not come to my studio instead? You'll see one bore instead of twenty."

The apartment which Flamel described as his studio showed, as its one claim to the designation, a perennially empty easel, the rest of its space being filled with the evidences of a comprehensive dilettantism. Against this background, which seemed the visible expression of its owner's intellectual tolerance, rows of fine books detached themselves with a prominence showing them to be Flamel's chief care.

Glennard glanced with the eye of untrained curiosity at the lines of warm-toned morocco, while his host busied himself with the uncorking of Apollinaris.

"You've got a splendid lot of books," he said.

"They're fairly decent," the other assented, in the curt tone of the collector who will not talk of his passion for fear of talking of nothing else; then, as Glennard, his hands in his pockets, began to stroll perfunctorily down the long line of bookcases— "Some men," Flamel irresistibly added, "think of books merely as tools, others as tooling. I'm between the two; there are days when I use them as scenery, other days when I want them as society; so that, as you see, my library represents a makeshift compromise between looks and brains, and the collectors look down on me almost as much as the students."

Glennard, without answering, was mechanically taking one book after another from the shelves. His hands slipped curiously over the smooth covers and the noiseless subsidence of opening pages. Suddenly he came on a thin volume of faded manuscript. "What's this?" he asked with a listless sense of wonder.

"Ah, you're at my manuscript shelf. I've been going in for that sort of thing lately." Flamel came up and looked over his shoulders. "That's a bit of Stendhal—one of the Italian stories— and here are some letters of Balzac to Madame Surville."

Glennard took the book with sudden eagerness. "Who was Madame Surville?"

"His sister." He was conscious that Flamel was looking at him with the smile that was like an interrogation point. "I didn't know you cared for this kind of thing."

"I don't—at least I've never had the chance. Have you many collections of letters?"

"Lord, no—very few. I'm just beginning, and most of the interesting ones are out of my reach. Here's a queer little collection, though—the rarest thing I've got—half a dozen of Shelley's letters to Harriet Westbrook. I had a devil of a time getting them —a lot of collectors were after them."

Glennard, taking the volume from his hand, glanced with a kind of repugnance at the interleaving of yellow crisscrossed sheets. "She was the one who drowned herself, wasn't she?"

Flamel nodded. "I suppose that little episode adds about fifty per cent to their value," he said meditatively.

Glennard laid the book down. He wondered why he had

joined Flamel. He was in no humor to be amused by the older man's talk, and a recrudescence of personal misery rose about him like an icy tide.

"I believe I must take myself off," he said. "I'd forgotten an engagement."

He turned to go; but almost at the same moment he was conscious of a duality of intention wherein his apparent wish to leave revealed itself as a last effort of the will against the overmastering desire to stay and unbosom himself to Flamel.

The older man, as though divining the conflict, laid a detaining pressure on his arm.

"Won't the engagement keep? Sit down and try one of these cigars. I don't often have the luck of seeing you here."

"I'm rather driven just now," said Glenard vaguely. He found himself seated again, and Flamel had pushed to his side a low stand holding a bottle of Apollinaris and a decanter of cognac.

Flamel, thrown back in his capacious armchair, surveyed him through a cloud of smoke with the comfortable tolerance of the man to whom no inconsistencies need be explained. Connivance was implicit in the air. It was the kind of atmosphere in which the outrageous loses its edge. Glennard felt a gradual relaxing of his nerves.

"I suppose one has to pay a lot for letters like that?" he heard himself asking, with a glance in the direction of the volume he had laid aside.

"Oh, so-so—depends on circumstances." Flamel viewed him thoughtfully. "Are you thinking of collecting?"

Glennard laughed. "Lord, no. The other way round."

"Selling?"

"Oh, I hardly know. I was thinking of a poor chap—"

Flamel filled the pause with a nod of interest.

"A poor chap I used to know—who died—he died last year —and who left me a lot of letters, letters he thought a great deal of—he was fond of me and left 'em to me outright with the idea,

I suppose, that they might benefit me somehow—I don't know—I'm not much up on such things—" He reached his hand to the tall glass his host had filled.

"A collection of autograph letters, eh? Any big names?"

"Oh, only one name. They're all letters written to him—by one person, you understand; a woman, in fact—"

"Oh, a woman," said Flamel negligently.

Glennard was nettled by his obvious loss of interest. "I rather think they'd attract a good deal of notice if they were published."

Flamel still looked uninterested. "Love-letters, I suppose?"

"Oh, just—the letters a woman would write to a man she knew well. They were tremendous friends, he and she."

"And she wrote a clever letter?"

"Clever? It was Margaret Aubyn."

A great silence filled the room. It seemed to Glennard that the words had burst from him as blood gushes from a wound.

"Great Scott!" said Flamel sitting up. "A collection of Margaret Aubyn's letters? Did you say *you* had them?"

"They were left me—by my friend."

"I see. Was he—well, no matter. You're to be congratulated, at any rate. What are you going to do with them?"

Glennard stood up with a sense of weariness in all his bones. "Oh, I don't know. I haven't thought much about it. I just happened to see that some fellow was writing her life—"

"Joslin; yes. You didn't think of giving them to him?"

Glennard lounged across the room and stood staring up at a bronze Bacchus who drooped his garlanded head above the pediment of an Italian cabinet. "What ought I to do? You're just the fellow to advise me." He felt the blood in his cheek as he spoke.

Flamel sat with meditative eye. "What do you *want* to do with them?" he asked.

"I want to publish them," said Glennard, swinging round with sudden energy—"If I can—"

"If you can? They're yours, you say?"

"They're mine fast enough. There's no one to prevent—I mean there are no restrictions—" he was arrested by the sense that these accumulated proofs of impunity might precisely stand as the strongest check on his action.

"And Mrs. Aubyn had no family, I believe?"

"No."

"Then I don't see who's to interfere," said Flamel, studying his cigar-tip.

Glennard had turned his unseeing stare on an ecstatic Saint Catherine framed in tarnished gilding.

"It's just this way," he began again, with an effort. "When letters are as personal as—as these of my friend's. . . . Well, I don't mind telling you that the cash would make a heap of difference to me; such a lot that it rather obscures my judgment— the fact is, if I could lay my hand on a few thousands now I could get into a big thing, and without appreciable risk; and I'd like to know whether you think I'd be justified—under the circumstances. . . ." He paused with a dry throat. It seemed to him at the moment that it would be impossible for him ever to sink lower in his own estimation. He was in truth less ashamed of weighing the temptation than of submitting his scruples to a man like Flamel, and affecting to appeal to sentiments of delicacy on the absence of which he had consciously reckoned. But he had reached a point where each word seemed to compel another, as each wave in a stream is forced forward by the pressure behind it; and before Flamel could speak he had faltered out—"You don't think people could say . . . could criticise the man. . . ."

"But the man's dead, isn't he?"

"He's dead—yes; but can I assume the responsibility without—"

Flamel hesitated; and almost immediately Glennard's scruples gave way to irritation. If at this hour Flamel were to affect an inopportune reluctance—!

The older man's answer reassured him. "Why need you assume any responsibility? Your name won't appear, of course; and as to your friend's, I don't see why his should either. He wasn't a celebrity himself, I suppose?"

"No, no."

"Then the letters can be addressed to Mr. Blank. Doesn't that make it all right?"

Glennard's hesitation revived. "For the public, yes. But I don't see that it alters the case for me. The question is, ought I to publish them at all?"

"Of course you ought to." Flamel spoke with invigorating emphasis. "I doubt if you'd be justified in keeping them back. Anything of Margaret Aubyn's is more or less public property by this time. She's too great for any one of us. I was only wondering how you could use them to the best advantage—to yourself, I mean. How many are there?"

"Oh, a lot; perhaps a hundred—I haven't counted. There may be more. . . ."

"Gad! What a haul! When were they written?"

"I don't know—that is—they corresponded for years. What's the odds?" He moved toward his hat with a vague impulse of flight.

"It all counts," said Flamel imperturbably. "A long correspondence—one, I mean, that covers a great deal of time—is obviously worth more than if the same number of letters had been written within a year. At any rate, you won't give them to Joslin? They'd fill a book, wouldn't they?"

"I suppose so. I don't know how much it takes to fill a book."

"Not love-letters, you say?"

"Why?" flashed from Glennard.

"Oh, nothing—only the big public is sentimental, and if they *were*—why, you could get any money for Margaret Aubyn's love-letters."

Glennard was silent.

"Are the letters interesting in themselves? I mean apart from the association with her name?"

"I'm no judge." Glennard took up his hat and thrust himself

into his overcoat. "I dare say I shan't do anything about it. And, Flamel—you won't mention this to any one?"

"Lord, no. Well, I congratulate you. You've got a big thing." Flamel was smiling at him from the hearth.

Glennard, on the threshold, forced a response to the smile, while he questioned with loitering indifference—"Financially, eh?"

"Rather; I should say so."

Glennard's hand lingered on the knob. "How much—should you say? You know about such things."

"Oh, I should have to see the letters; but I should say—well, if you've got enough to fill a book and they're fairly readable, and the book is brought out at the right time—say ten thousand down from the publisher, and possibly one or two more in royalties. If you got the publishers bidding against each other you might do even better; but of course I'm talking in the dark."

"Of course," said Glennard, with sudden dizziness. His hand had slipped from the knob and he stood staring down at the exotic spirals of the Persian rug beneath his feet.

"I'd have to see the letters," Flamel repeated.

"Of course—you'd have to see them. . . ." Glennard stammered; and, without turning, he flung over his shoulder an inarticulate "Good-bye. . . ."

※ V ※

THE little house, as Glennard strolled up to it between the trees, seemed no more than a gay tent pitched against the sunshine. It had the crispness of a freshly starched summer gown, and the geraniums on the veranda bloomed as simultaneously as the flowers in a bonnet. The garden was prospering absurdly. Seed they had sown at random—amid laughing countercharges of incompetence—had shot up in fragrant defiance of their blunders. He smiled to see the clematis unfolding its punctual wings about the porch. The tiny lawn was smooth as a shaven cheek, and a crimson rambler mounted to the nursery window of a baby who never cried. A breeze shook the awning above the tea-table, and his wife, as he drew near, could be seen bending above a kettle that was just about to boil. So vividly did the whole scene suggest the painted bliss of a stage setting, that it would have been hardly surprising to see her step forward among the flowers and trill out her virtuous happiness from the veranda rail.

The stale heat of the long day in town, the dusty promiscuity of the suburban train, were now but the requisite foil to an evening of scented breezes and tranquil talk. They had been married more than a year, and each homecoming still reflected the freshness of their first day together. If, indeed, their happiness had a flaw, it was in resembling too closely the bright impermanence of their surroundings. Their love as yet was but the gay tent of holiday-makers.

His wife looked up with a smile. The country life suited her, and her beauty had gained depth from a stillness in which certain faces might have grown opaque.

"Are you very tired?" she asked, pouring his tea.

"Just enough to enjoy this." He rose from the chair in which he had thrown himself and bent over the tray for his cream. "You've had a visitor?" he commented, noticing a half-empty cup beside her own.

"Only Mr. Flamel," she said indifferently.

"Flamel? Again?"

She answered without show of surprise. "He left just now. His yacht is down at Laurel Bay and he borrowed a trap of the Dreshams to drive over here."

Glennard made no comment, and she went on, leaning her head back against the cushions of her bamboo seat, "He wants us to go for a sail with him next Sunday."

Glennard meditatively stirred his tea. He was trying to think of the most natural and unartificial thing to say, and his voice seemed to come from the outside, as though he were speaking behind a marionette. "Do you want to?"

"Just as you please," she said compliantly. No affectation of indifference could have been as baffling as her compliance. Glennard, of late, was beginning to feel that the surface which, a year ago, he had taken for a sheet of clear glass, might, after all, be a mirror reflecting merely his own conception of what lay behind it.

"Do you like Flamel?" he suddenly asked; to which, still engaged with her tea, she returned the feminine answer—"I thought you did."

"I do, of course," he agreed, vexed at his own incorrigible tendency to magnify Flamel's importance by hovering about the topic. "A sail would be rather jolly; let's go."

She made no reply and he drew forth the rolled-up evening papers which he had thrust into his pocket on leaving the train. As he smoothed them out his own countenance seemed to undergo the same process. He ran his eye down the list of stocks, and Flamel's importunate personality receded behind the rows of figures pushing forward into notice like so many bearers of good news. Glennard's investments were flowering like his garden: the dryest shares blossomed into dividends and a golden harvest awaited his sickle.

He glanced at his wife with the tranquil air of a man who digests good luck as naturally as the dry ground absorbs a shower. "Things are looking uncommonly well. I believe we shall be able to go to town for two or three months next winter if we can find something cheap."

She smiled luxuriously: it was pleasant to be able to say, with an air of balancing relative advantages, "Really, on the baby's account I shall be almost sorry; but if we do go, there's Kate Erskine's house . . . she'll let us have it for almost nothing. . . ."

"Well, write her about it," he recommended, his eye travelling on in search of the weather report. He had turned to the wrong page; and suddenly a line of black characters leapt out at him as from an ambush.

MARGARET AUBYN'S LETTERS

Two volumes. Out Today. First Edition of five thousand sold out before leaving the press. Second Edition ready next week. The Book of the Year. . . .

He looked up stupidly. His wife still sat with her head thrown back, her pure profile detached against the cushions. She was smiling a little over the prospect his last words had opened. Behind her head shivers of sun and shade ran across the striped awning. A row of maples and a privet hedge hid their neighbor's gables, giving them undivided possession of their leafy half-acre; and life, a moment before, had been like their plot of ground, shut off, hedged in from importunities, impenetrably his and hers. Now it seemed to him that every maple-leaf, every privet-bud, was a relentless human gaze, pressing close upon their privacy. It was as though they sat in a brightly lit room, uncurtained from a darkness full of hostile watchers. . . . His wife still smiled; and her unconsciousness of danger seemed in some horrible way to put her beyond the reach of rescue.

He had not known that it would be like this. After the first odious weeks, spent in preparing the letters for publication, in submitting them to Flamel, and in negotiating with the publishers, the transaction had dropped out of his consciousness into that unvisited limbo to which we relegate the deeds we would rather not have done but have no notion of undoing. From the moment he had obtained Miss Trent's promise not to sail with her aunt he had tried to imagine himself irrevocably committed. After that, he argued, his first duty was to her—she had become his conscience. The sum obtained from the publishers by Flamel's manipulations, and opportunely transferred to Dinslow's successful venture, already yielded a return which, combined with Glennard's professional earnings, took the edge of compulsion from their way of living, making it appear the expression of a graceful preference for simplicity. It was the mitigated poverty which can subscribe to a review or two and have a few flowers on the dinner-table. And already in a small way Glennard was beginning to feel the magnetic quality of prosperity. Clients who had passed his door in the hungry days sought it out now that it bore the name of a successful man. It was understood that a small inheritance, cleverly invested, was the source of his fortune; and there was a feeling that a man who could do so well for himself was likely to know how to turn over other people's money.

But it was in the more intimate reward of his wife's happiness that Glennard tasted the full flavor of success. Coming out of conditions so narrow that those he offered her seemed spacious, she fitted into her new life without any of those manifest efforts at adjustment that are as sore to a husband's pride as the critical rearrangement of the bridal furniture. She had given him, instead, the delicate pleasure of watching her expand like a sea-creature restored to its element, stretching out the atrophied tentacles of girlish vanity and enjoyment to the rising tide of opportunity. And somehow—in the windowless inner cell of his consciousness where self-criticism cowered—Glennard's course seemed justified by its merely material success. How could such a crop of innocent blessedness have sprung from tainted soil?

Now he had the injured sense of a man entrapped into a disadvantagous bargain. He had not known it would be like this; and a dull anger gathered at his heart. Anger against whom? Against his wife, for not knowing what he suffered? Against Flamel, for being the unconscious instrument of his wrong-doing? Or against that mute memory to which his own act had suddenly given a voice of accusation? Yes, that was it; and his punishment henceforth would be the presence, the unescapable presence, of the woman he had so persistently evaded. She would always be there now. It was as though he had married her instead of the other. It was what she had always wanted—to be with him—and she had gained her point at last.

He sprang up, as though in an impulse of flight. The sudden movement lifted his wife's lids, and she asked, in the incurious voice of the woman whose life is enclosed in a magic circle of prosperity—"Any news?"

"No—none—" he said, roused to a sense of immediate peril. The papers lay scattered at his feet—what if she were to see them? He stretched his arm to gather them up, but his next thought showed him the futility of such concealment. The same advertisement would appear every day, for weeks to come, in every newspaper; how could he prevent her seeing it? He could not always be hiding the papers from her. . . . Well, and what if she did see it? It would signify nothing to her; the chances were that she would never even read the book. . . . As she ceased to be an element of fear in his calculations the distance between them seemed to lessen and he took her again, as it were, into the circle of his conjugal protection. . . . Yet a moment before he had almost hated her! . . . He laughed aloud at his senseless terrors. . . . He was off his balance, decidedly.

"What are you laughing at?" she asked.

He explained, elaborately, that he was laughing at the recollection of an old woman in the train, an old woman with a lot of bundles, who couldn't find her ticket. . . . But somehow, in the telling, the humor of the story seemed to evaporate, and he felt the conventionality of her smile. He glanced at his watch. "Isn't it time to dress?"

She rose with serene reluctance. "It's a pity to go in. The garden looks so lovely."

They lingered side by side, surveying their domain. There was not space in it, at this hour, for the shadow of the elm tree in the angle of the hedge: it crossed the lawn, cut the flower-border in two, and ran up the side of the house to the nursery window. She bent to flick a caterpillar from the honeysuckle; then, as they turned indoors, "If we mean to go on the yacht next Sunday," she suggested, "oughtn't you to let Mr. Flamel know?"

Glennard's exasperation deflected suddenly. "Of course I

shall let him know. You always seem to imply that I'm going to do something rude to Flamel."

The words reverberated through her silence; she had a way of thus leaving one space in which to contemplate one's folly at arm's length. Glennard turned on his heel and went upstairs. As he dropped into a chair before his dressing-table, he said to himself that in the last hour he had sounded the depths of his humiliation, and that the lowest dregs of it, the very bottom-slime, was the hateful necessity of having always, as long as the two men lived, to be civil to Barton Flamel.

※ VI ※

THE week in town had been sultry, and the men, in the Sunday emancipation of white flannel and duck, filled the deck chairs of the yacht with their outstretched apathy, following, through a mist of cigarette smoke, the flitting inconsequences of the women. The party was a small one—Flamel had few intimate friends—but composed of more heterogeneous atoms than the little pools into which society usually runs. The reaction from the chief episode of his earlier life had bred in Glennard an uneasy distaste for any kind of personal saliency. Cleverness was useful in business; but in society it seemed to him as futile as the sham cascades formed by a stream that might have been used to drive a mill. He liked the collective point of view that goes with the civilized uniformity of dress clothes, and his wife's attitude implied the same preference; yet they found themselves slipping more and more into Flamel's intimacy. Alexa had once or twice said that she enjoyed meeting clever people; but her enjoyment took the negative form of a smiling receptivity; and Glennard felt a growing preference for the kind of people who have their thinking done for them by the community.

Still, the deck of the yacht was a pleasant refuge from the heat on shore, and his wife's profile, serenely projected against the changing blue, lay on his retina like a cool hand on the nerves. He had never been more impressed by the kind of absoluteness that lifted her beauty above the transient effects of other women, making the most harmonious face seem an accidental collocation of features.

The ladies who directly suggested this comparison were of a kind accustomed to take similar risks with more gratifying results. Mrs. Armiger had in fact long been the triumphant alternative of those who couldn't "see" Alexa Glennard's looks; and Mrs. Touchett's claims to consideration were founded on that distribution of effects which is the wonder of those who admire a highly cultivated country. The third lady of the trio which Glennard's fancy had put to such unflattering uses was bound by circumstances to support the claims of the other two. This was Mrs. Dresham, the wife of the editor of the *Radiator*. Mrs. Dresham was a lady who had rescued herself from social obscurity by assuming the role of her husband's exponent and interpreter; and Dresham's leisure being devoted to the cultivation of remarkable women, his wife's attitude committed her to the public celebration of their remarkableness. For the conceivable tedium of this duty, Mrs. Dresham was repaid by the fact that there were people who took *her* for a remarkable woman; and who in turn probably purchased similar distinction with the small change of her reflected importance. As to the other ladies of the party, they were simply the wives of some of the men—the kind of women who expect to be talked to collectively and to have their questions left unanswered.

Mrs. Armiger, the latest embodiment of Dresham's instinct for the remarkable, was an innocent beauty who for years had distilled dulness among a set of people now self-condemned by their inability to appreciate her. Under Dresham's tutelage she had developed into a "thoughtful woman," who read his leaders in the *Radiator* and bought the works he recommended. When a new book appeared, people wanted to know what Mrs. Armiger thought of it; and a young gentleman who had made a trip in

Touraine had recently inscribed to her the wide-margined result of his explorations.

Glennard, leaning back with his head against the rail and a slit of fugitive blue between his half-closed lids, vaguely wished she wouldn't spoil the afternoon by making people talk; though he reduced his annoyance to the minimum by not listening to what was said, there remained a latent irritation against the general futility of words.

His wife's gift of silence seemed to him the most vivid commentary on the clumsiness of speech as a means of intercourse, and his eyes had turned to her in renewed appreciation of this finer faculty when Mrs. Armiger's voice abruptly brought home to him the underrated potentialities of language.

"You've read them, of course, Mrs. Glennard?" he heard her ask: and, in reply to Alexa's vague interrogation—"Why, the *Aubyn Letters*—it's the only book people are talking of this week."

Mrs. Dresham immediately saw her advantage. "You *haven't* read them? How very extraordinary! As Mrs. Armiger says, the book's in the air: one breathes it in like the influenza."

Glennard sat motionless, watching his wife.

"Perhaps it hasn't reached the suburbs yet," she said with her unruffled smile.

"Oh, *do* let me come to you, then!" Mrs. Touchett cried; "anything for a change of air! I'm positively sick of the book and I can't put it down. Can't you sail us beyond its reach, Mr. Flamel?"

Flamel shook his head. "Not even with this breeze. Literature travels faster than steam nowadays. And the worst of it is that we can't any of us give up reading: it's as insidious as a vice and as tiresome as a virtue."

"I believe it *is* a vice, almost, to read such a book as the *Letters*," said Mrs. Touchett. "It's the woman's soul, absolutely torn up by the roots—her whole self laid bare; and to a man who evidently didn't care; who couldn't have cared. I don't mean to read another line: it's too much like listening at a keyhole."

"But if she wanted it published?"

"Wanted it? How do we know she did?"

"Why, I heard she'd left the letters to the man—whoever he is—with directions that they should be published after his death—"

"I don't believe it," Mrs. Touchett declared.

"He's dead then, is he?" one of the men asked.

"Why, you don't suppose if he were alive he could ever hold up his head again, with these letters being read by everybody?" Mrs. Touchett protested. "It must have been horrible enough to know they'd been written to him; but to publish them! No man could have done it and no woman could have told him to—"

"Oh, come, come," Dresham judicially interposed; "after all, they're not love-letters."

"No—that's the worst of it; they're unloved letters," Mrs. Touchett retorted.

"Then, obviously, she needn't have written them; whereas the man, poor devil, could hardly help receiving them."

"Perhaps he counted on the public to save him the trouble of reading them," said young Hartly, who was in the cynical stage.

Mrs. Armiger turned her reproachful loveliness to Dresham. "From the way you defend him I believe you know who he is."

Everyone looked at Dresham, and his wife smiled with the superior air of the woman who is in her husband's professional secrets. Dresham shrugged his shoulders.

"What have I said to defend him?"

"You called him a poor devil—you pitied him."

"A man who could let Margaret Aubyn write to him in that way? Of course I pity him."

"Then you *must* know who he is," cried Mrs. Armiger with a triumphant air of penetration.

Hartly and Flamel laughed and Dresham shook his head.

"No one knows; not even the publishers; so they tell me at least."

"So they tell you to tell us," Hartly astutely amended; and Mrs. Armiger added, with the appearance of carrying the argument a point farther, "But even if *he's* dead and *she's* dead, somebody must have given the letters to the publishers."

"A little bird, probably," said Dresham, smiling indulgently on her deduction.

"A little bird of prey then—a vulture, I should say—" another man interpolated.

"Oh, I'm not with you there," said Dresham easily. "Those letters belonged to the public."

"How can any letters belong to the public that weren't written to the public?" Mrs. Touchett interposed.

"Well, these were, in a sense. A personality as big as Margaret Aubyn's belongs to the world. Such a mind is part of the general fund of thought. It's the penalty of greatness—one becomes a *monument historique*. Posterity pays the cost of keeping one up, but on condition that one is always open to the public."

"I don't see that that exonerates the man who gives up the keys of the sanctuary, as it were."

"Who *was* he?" another voice inquired.

"Who was he? Oh, nobody, I fancy—the letter-box, the slit in the wall through which the letters passed to posterity. . . ."

"But she never meant them for posterity!"

"A woman shouldn't write such letters if she doesn't mean them to be published. . . ."

"She shouldn't write them to such a man!" Mrs. Touchett scornfully corrected.

"I never keep letters," said Mrs. Armiger, under the obvious impression that she was contributing a valuable point to the discussion.

There was a general laugh, and Flamel, who had not spoken, said lazily, "You women are too incurably subjective. I venture to say that most men would see in those letters merely their immense literary value, their significance as documents. The personal side doesn't count where there's so much else."

"Oh, we all know you haven't any principles," Mrs. Armiger declared; and Alexa Glennard, lifting an indolent smile, said: "I shall never write you a love-letter, Mr. Flamel."

Glennard moved away impatiently. Such talk was as tedious as the buzzing of gnats. He wondered why his wife had wanted to drag him on such a senseless expedition. . . . He hated Flamel's crowd—and what business had Flamel himself to interfere in that way, standing up for the publication of the letters as though Glennard's needed his defence?

Glennard turned his head and saw that Flamel had drawn a seat to Alexa's elbow and was speaking to her in a low tone. The other groups had scattered, straying in twos along the deck. It came over Glennard that he should never again be able to see Flamel speaking to his wife without the sense of sick mistrust that now loosened his joints.

Alexa, the next morning, over their early breakfast, surprised her husband by an unexpected request.

"Will you bring me those letters from town?" she asked.

"What letters?" he said, putting down his cup. He felt himself as vulnerable as a man who is lunged at in the dark.

"Mrs. Aubyn's. The book they were all talking about yesterday."

Glennard, carefully measuring his second cup of tea, said with deliberation, "I didn't know you cared about that sort of thing."

She was, in fact, not a great reader, and a new book seldom reached her till it was, so to speak, on the home stretch; but she replied with a gentle tenacity, "I think it would interest me because I read her life last year."

"Her life? Where did you get that?"

"Someone lent it to me when it came out—Mr. Flamel, I think."

His first impulse was to exclaim, "Why the devil do you borrow books of Flamel? I can buy you all you want—" but he felt himself irresistibly forced into an attitude of smiling compliance. "Flamel always has the newest books going, hasn't he? You must be careful, by the way, about returning what he lends you. He's rather crotchety about his library."

"Oh, I'm always very careful," she said, with a touch of competence that struck him; and she added, as he caught up his hat: "Don't forget the letters."

Why had she asked for the book? Was her sudden wish to see it the result of some hint of Flamel's? The thought turned Glennard sick, but he preserved sufficient lucidity to tell himself, a moment later, that his last hope of self-control would be lost if he yielded to the temptation of seeing a hidden purpose in everything she said and did. How much Flamel guessed, he had no means of divining; nor could he predicate, from what he knew of the man, to what use his inferences might be put. The very qualities that had made Flamel a useful adviser made him the most dangerous of accomplices. Glennard felt himself agrope among alien forces that his own act had set in motion.

Alexa was a woman of few requirements; but her wishes, even in trifles, had a definiteness that distinguished them from the fluid impulses of her kind. He knew that, having once asked for the book, she would not forget it; and he put aside, as an ineffectual expedient, his momentary idea of applying for it at the circulating library and telling her that all the copies were out. If the book was to be bought, it had better be bought at once. He left his office earlier than usual and turned in at the first bookshop on his way to the train. The show-window was stacked with conspicuously lettered volumes. *Margaret Aubyn* flashed back at him in endless iteration. He plunged into the shop and came on a counter where the name repeated itself on row after row of bindings. It seemed to have driven the rest of literature to the back shelves. He caught up a copy, tossing the money to an astonished clerk, who pursued him to the door with the unheeded offer to wrap up the volumes.

In the street he was seized with a sudden apprehension. What if he were to meet Flamel? The thought was intolerable. He called a cab and drove straight to the station, where, amid the palm-leaf fans of a perspiring crowd, he waited a long half-hour for his train to start.

He had thrust a volume in either pocket, and in the train he dared not draw them out; but the detested words leaped at him from the folds of the evening paper. The air seemed full of Margaret Aubyn's name; the motion of the train set it dancing up and down on the page of a magazine that a man in front of him was reading.

At the door he was told that Mrs. Glennard was still out, and he went upstairs to his room and dragged the books from his pocket. They lay on the table before him like live things that he feared to touch. . . . At length he opened the first volume. A familiar letter sprang out at him, each word quickened by its glaring garb of type. The little broken phrases fled across the page like wounded animals in the open. . . . It was a horrible sight . . . a *battue* of helpless things driven savagely out of shelter. He had not known it would be like this.

He understood now that, at the moment of selling the letters, he had viewed the transaction solely as it affected himself: as an unfortunate blemish on an otherwise presentable record. He had scarcely considered the act in relation to Margaret Aubyn; for death, if it hallows, also makes innocuous. Glennard's God was a god of the living, of the immediate, the actual, the tangible; all his days he had lived in the presence of that god, heedless of the divinities who, below the surface of our deeds and passions, silently forge the fatal weapons of the dead.

※ VII ※

A KNOCK roused him, and looking up he saw his wife. He met her glance in silence, and she faltered out, "Are you ill?"

The words restored his self-possession. "Ill? Of course not. They told me you were out and I came upstairs."

The books lay between them on the table; he wondered when she would see them. She lingered tentatively on the threshold, with the air of leaving his explanation on his hands. She was not the kind of woman who could be counted on to fortify an excuse by appearing to dispute it.

"Where have you been?" Glennard asked, moving forward so that he obstructed her vision of the books.

"I walked over to the Dreshams' for tea."

"I can't think what you see in those people," he said with a shrug; adding, uncontrollably—"I suppose Flamel was there?"

"No; he left on the yacht this morning."

An answer so obstructing to the natural escape of his irritation left Glennard with no momentary resource but that of strolling impatiently to the window. As her eyes followed him they lit on the books.

"Ah, you've brought them! I'm so glad," she said.

He answered over his shoulder, "For a woman who never reads you make the most astounding exceptions!"

Her smile was an exasperating concession to the probability that it had been hot in town or that something had bothered him.

"Do you mean it's not nice to want to read the book?" she asked. "It was not nice to publish it, certainly; but after all, I'm not responsible for that, am I?" She paused, and, as he made no answer, went on, still smiling, "I do read sometimes, you know; and I'm very fond of Margaret Aubyn's books. I was reading *Pomegranate Seed* when we first met. Don't you remember? It was then you told me all about her."

Glennard had turned back into the room and stood staring at his wife. "All about her?" he repeated, and with the words remembrance came to him. He had found Miss Trent one afternoon with the novel in her hand, and moved by the lover's fatuous impulse to associate himself in some way with whatever fills the mind of the beloved, had broken through his habitual silence about the past. Rewarded by the consciousness of figuring impressively in Miss Trent's imagination, he had gone on from one anecdote to another, reviving dormant details of his old Hillbridge life, and pasturing his vanity on the eagerness with which she listened to his reminiscences of a being already clothed in the impersonality of greatness.

The incident had left no trace in his mind; but it sprang up now like an old enemy, the more dangerous for having been forgotten. The instinct of self-preservation—sometimes the most perilous that man can exercise—made him awkwardly declare: "Oh, I used to see her at people's houses, that was all," and her silence as usual leaving room for a multiplication of blunders, he added, with increased indifference, "I simply can't see what you can find to interest you in such a book."

She seemed to consider this intently. "You've read it, then?"

"I glanced at it—I never read such things."

"Is it true that she didn't wish the letters to be published?"

Glennard felt the sudden dizziness of the mountaineer on a narrow ledge, and with it the sense that he was lost if he looked more than a step ahead.

"I'm sure I don't know," he said; then, summoning a smile, he passed his hand through her arm. "*I* didn't have tea at the Dreshams', you know; won't you give me some now?" he suggested.

That evening Glennard, under pretext of work to be done, shut himself into the small study opening off the drawing-room. As he gathered up his papers he said to his wife: "You're not going to sit indoors on such a night as this? I'll join you presently outside."

But she had drawn her armchair to the lamp. "I want to look at my book," she said, taking up the first volume of the *Letters*.

Glennard, with a shrug, withdrew into the study. "I'm going to shut the door; I want to be quiet," he explained from the threshold; and she nodded without lifting her eyes from the book.

He sank into a chair, staring aimlessly at the outspread papers. How was he to work, while on the other side of the door she sat with that volume in her hand? The door did not shut her out—he saw her distinctly, felt her close to him in a contact as painful as the pressure on a bruise.

The sensation was part of the general strangeness that made him feel like a man waking from a long sleep to find himself in an unknown country among people of alien tongue. We live in our own souls as in an unmapped region, a few acres of which we have cleared for our habitation; while of the nature of those nearest us we know but the boundaries that march with ours. Of the points in his wife's character not in direct contact with his own, Glennard now discerned his ignorance; and the baffling sense of her remoteness was intensified by the discovery that, in one way, she was closer to him than ever before. As one may live for years in happy unconsciousness of the possession of a sensitive nerve, he had lived beside his wife unaware that her individuality had become a part of the texture of his life, ineradicable as some growth on a vital organ; and he now felt himself at once incapable of forecasting her judgment and powerless to evade its effects.

To escape, the next morning, the confidences of the breakfast-table, he went to town earlier than usual. His wife, who read slowly, was given to talking over what she read, and at present his first object in life was to postpone the inevitable discussion of the letters. This instinct of protection, in the afternoon, on his way up town, guided him to the club in search of a man who might be persuaded to come out to the country to dine. The only man in the club was Flamel.

Glennard, as he heard himself almost involuntarily pressing Flamel to come and dine, felt the full irony of the situation. To use Flamel as a shield against his wife's scrutiny was only a shade less humiliating than to reckon on his wife as a defence against Flamel.

He felt a contradictory movement of annoyance at the latter's ready acceptance, and the two men drove in silence to the station. As they passed the bookstall in the waiting-room Flamel lingered a moment, and the eyes of both fell on Margaret Aubyn's name, conspicuously displayed above a counter stacked with the familiar volumes.

"We shall be late, you know," Glennard remonstrated, pulling out his watch.

"Go ahead," said Flamel imperturbably. "I want to get something—"

Glennard turned on his heel and walked down the platform. Flamel rejoined him with an innocent-looking magazine in his hand; but Glennard dared not even glance at the cover, lest it should show the syllables he feared.

The train was full of people they knew, and they were kept apart till it dropped them at the little suburban station. As they strolled up the shaded hill, Glennard talked volubly, pointing out the improvements in the neighborhood, deploring the threatened approach of an electric railway, and screening himself by a series of reflex adjustments from the risk of any allusion to the *Letters*. Flamel suffered his discourse with the bland inattention that we accord to the affairs of someone else's suburb, and they reached the shelter of Alexa's tea-table without a perceptible turn toward the dreaded topic.

The dinner passed off safely. Flamel, always at his best in Alexa's presence, gave her the kind of attention which is like a becoming light thrown on the speaker's words: his answers seemed to bring out a latent significance in her phrases, as the sculptor draws his statue from the block. Glennard, under his wife's composure, detected a sensibility to this manœuvre, and the discovery was like the lightning-flash across a nocturnal landscape. Thus far these momentary illuminations had served only to reveal the strangeness of the intervening country: each fresh observation seemed to increase the sum-total of his ignorance. Her simplicity of outline was more puzzling than a complex surface. One may conceivably work one's way through a labyrinth; but Alexa's candor was like a snow-covered plain, where, the road once lost, there are no landmarks to travel by.

Dinner over, they returned to the veranda, where a moon, rising behind the old elm, was combining with that complaisant tree a romantic enlargement of their borders. Glennard had forgotten the cigars. He went to his study to fetch them, and in passing through the drawing-room he saw the second volume of the *Letters* lying open on his wife's table. He picked up the book and looked at the date of the letter she had been reading. It was one of the last . . . he knew the few lines by heart. He dropped the book and leaned against the wall. Why had he included that one among the others? Or was it possible that now they would all seem like that?

Alexa's voice came suddenly out of the dusk. "May Touchett was right—it *is* like listening at a keyhole. I wish I hadn't read it!"

Flamel returned, in the leisurely tone of the man whose phrases are punctuated by a cigarette, "It seems so to us, perhaps; but to another generation the book will be a classic."

"Then it ought not to have been published till it had time to become a classic. It's horrible, it's degrading almost, to read the secrets of a woman one might have known." She added, in a lower tone, "Stephen *did* know her—"

"Did he?" came from Flamel.

"He knew her very well, at Hillbridge, years ago. The book has made him feel dreadfully . . . he wouldn't read it . . . he didn't want me to read it. I didn't understand at first, but now I can see how horribly disloyal it must seem to him. It's so much worse to surprise a friend's secrets than a stranger's."

"Oh, Glennard's such a sensitive chap," Flamel said easily; and Alexa almost rebukingly rejoined, "If you'd known her I'm sure you'd feel as he does. . . ."

Glennard stood motionless, overcome by the singular infelicity with which he had contrived to put Flamel in possession of the two points most damaging to his case: the fact that he had been a friend of Margaret Aubyn's and that he had concealed from Alexa his share in the publication of the letters. To a man of less than Flamel's astuteness it must now be clear to whom the letters were addressed; and the possibility once suggested, nothing could be easier than to confirm it by discreet research. An impulse of self-accusal drove Glennard to the window. Why not anticipate betrayal by telling his wife the truth in Flamel's presence? If the man had a drop of decent feeling in him, such a course would be the surest means of securing his silence; and above all, it would rid Glennard of the necessity of defending himself against the perpetual criticism of his wife's belief in him.

The impulse was strong enough to carry him to the window; but there a reaction of defiance set in. What had he done, after all, to need defence and explanation? Both Dresham and Flamel had, in his hearing, declared the publication of the letters to be not only justifiable but obligatory; and if the disinterestedness of Flamel's verdict might be questioned, Dresham's at least represented the impartial view of the man of letters. As to Alexa's words, they were simply the conventional utterance of the "nice" woman on a question already decided for her by other "nice" women. She had said the proper thing as mechanically as she would have put on the appropriate gown or written the correct form of dinner invitation. Glennard had small faith in the abstract judgments of the other sex: he knew that half the women who were horrified by the publication of Mrs. Aubyn's letters would have betrayed her secrets without a scruple.

The sudden lowering of his emotional pitch brought a proportionate relief. He told himself that now the worst was over and things would fall into perspective again. His wife and Flamel had turned to other topics, and coming out on the veranda, he handed the cigars to Flamel, saying cheerfully—and yet he could have sworn they were the last words he meant to utter!—"Look here, old man, before you go down to Newport you must come out and spend a few days with us—mustn't he, Alexa?"

※ VIII ※

GLENNARD, perhaps unconsciously, had counted on the continuance of this easier mood. He had always taken pride in a certain robustness of fibre that enabled him to harden himself against the inevitable, to convert his failures into the building materials of success. Though it did not even now occur to him that what he called the inevitable had hitherto been the alternative he happened to prefer, he was yet obscurely aware that his present difficulty was one not to be conjured by any affectation of indifference. Some griefs build the soul a spacious house, but in this misery of Glennard's he could not stand upright. It pressed against him at every turn. He told himself that this was because there was no escape from the visible evidences of his act. The *Letters* confronted him everywhere. People who had never opened a book discussed them with critical reservations; to have read them had become a social obligation in circles to which literature never penetrates except in a personal guise.

Glennard did himself injustice. It was from the unexpected discovery of his own pettiness that he chiefly suffered. Our self-esteem is apt to be based on the hypothetical great act we have never had occasion to perform; and even the most self-scrutinizing modesty credits itself negatively with a high standard of conduct. Glennard had never thought himself a hero; but he had been certain that he was incapable of baseness. We all like our wrong-doings to have a becoming cut, to be made to order, as it were; and Glennard found himself suddenly thrust into a garb of dishonor surely meant for a meaner figure.

The immediate result of his first weeks of wretchedness was the resolve to go to town for the winter. He knew that such a course was just beyond the limit of prudence; but it was easy to allay the fears of Alexa, who, scrupulously vigilant in the management of the household, preserved the American wife's usual aloofness from her husband's business cares. Glennard felt that he could not trust himself to a winter's solitude with her. He had an unspeakable dread of her learning the truth about the letters, yet could not be sure of steeling himself against the suicidal impulse of avowal. His very soul was parched for sympathy; he thirsted for a voice of pity and comprehension. But would his wife pity? Would she understand? Again he found himself brought up abruptly against his incredible ignorance of her nature. The fact that he knew well enough how she would behave in the ordinary emergencies of life, that he could count, in such contingencies, on the kind of high courage and directness he had always divined in her, made him the more hopeless of her entering into the tortuous psychology of an act that he himself could no longer explain or understand. It would have been easier had she been more complex, more feminine—if he could have counted on her imaginative sympathy or her moral obtuseness—but he was sure of neither. He was sure of nothing but that, for a time, he must avoid her. Glennard could not rid himself of the delusion that by and by his action would cease to make its consequences felt. He would not have cared to own to himself that he counted on the dulling of his sensibilities: he preferred to indulge the vague hypothesis that extraneous circumstances would somehow efface the blot upon his conscience. In his worst moments of self-abasement he tried to find solace in the thought that Flamel had sanctioned his course. Flamel, at the outset, must have guessed to whom the letters were addressed; yet neither then nor afterward had he hesitated to advise their publication. This thought drew Glennard to him in fitful impulses of friendliness, from each of which there was a sharper reaction of distrust and aversion. When Flamel was not at the house, he missed the support of his tacit connivance; when he was there, his presence seemed the assertion of an intolerable claim.

Early in the winter the Glennards took possession of the little house that was to cost them almost nothing. The change brought Glennard the relief of seeing less of his wife, and of being protected, in her presence, by the multiplied preoccupations of town life. Alexa, who could never appear hurried, showed the smiling abstraction of a pretty woman to whom the social side of married life has not lost its novelty. Glennard, with the recklessness of a man fresh from his first financial imprudence, encouraged her in such little extravagances as her good sense at first resisted. Since they had come to town, he argued, they might as well enjoy themselves. He took a sympathetic view of the necessity of new gowns, he gave her a set of furs at Christmas, and before the New Year they had agreed on the necessity of adding a parlormaid to their small establishment.

Providence the very next day hastened to justify this measure by placing on Glennard's breakfast-plate an envelope bearing the name of the publishers to whom he had sold Mrs. Aubyn's letters. It happened to be the only letter the early post had brought, and he glanced across the table at his wife, who had come down before him and had probably laid the envelope on his plate. She was not the woman to ask awkward questions, but he felt the conjecture of her glance, and he was debating whether to affect surprise at the receipt of the letter, or to pass it off as a business communication that had strayed to his house, when a check fell from the envelope. It was the royalty on the first edition of the letters. His first feeling was one of simple satisfaction. The money had come with such infernal opportuneness that he could not help welcoming it. Before long, too, there would be more; he knew the book was still selling far beyond the publishers' previsions. He put the check in his pocket and left the room without looking at his wife.

On the way to his office the habitual reaction set in. The money he had received was the first tangible reminder that he was living on the sale of his self-esteem. The thought of material benefit had been overshadowed by his sense of the intrinsic baseness of making the letters known: now he saw what an element of sordidness it added to the situation and how the fact that he needed the money, and must use it, pledged him more irrevocably than ever to the consequences of his act. It seemed to him, in that first hour of misery, that he had betrayed his friend anew.

When, that afternoon, he reached home earlier than usual, Alexa's drawing-room was full of a gayety that overflowed to the stairs. Flamel, for a wonder, was not there; but Dresham and young Hartly, grouped about the tea-table, were receiving with resonant mirth a narrative delivered in the fluttered staccato that made Mrs. Armiger's conversation like the ejaculations of a startled aviary.

She paused as Glennard entered, and he had time to notice that his wife, who was busied about the tea-tray, had not joined in the laughter of the men.

"Oh, go on, go on," young Hartly rapturously groaned; and Mrs. Armiger met Glennard's inquiry with the deprecating cry that really she didn't see what there was to laugh at. "I'm sure I feel more like crying. I don't know what I should have done if Alexa hadn't been at home to give me a cup of tea. My nerves are in shreds—yes, another, dear, please—" and as Glennard looked his perplexity, she went on, after pondering on the selection of a second lump of sugar, "Why, I've just come from the reading, you know—the reading at the Waldorf."

"I haven't been in town long enough to know anything," said Glennard, taking the cup his wife handed him. "Who has been reading what?"

"That lovely girl from the South—Georgie—Georgie

What's-her-name—Mrs. Dresham's protégée—unless she's *yours,*
Mr. Dresham! Why, the big ballroom was *packed,* and all the
women were crying like idiots—it was the most harrowing thing
I ever heard—"

"What *did* you hear?" Glennard asked; and his wife interposed: "Won't you have another bit of cake, Julia? Or, Stephen,
ring for some hot toast, please." Her tone betrayed a polite weariness of the topic under discussion. Glennard turned to the bell,
but Mrs. Armiger pursued him with her lovely amazement.

"Why, the *Aubyn Letters*—didn't you know about it? She
read them so beautifully that it was quite horrible—I should
have fainted if there'd been a man near enough to carry me out."

Hartly's glee redoubled, and Dresham said jovially, "How
like you women to raise a shriek over the book and then do all
you can to encourage the blatant publicity of the readings!"

Mrs. Armiger met him more than half-way on a torrent of
self-accusal. "It *was* horrid; it was disgraceful. I told your wife
we ought all to be ashamed of ourselves for going, and I think
Alexa was quite right to refuse to take any tickets—even if it was
for a charity."

"Oh," her hostess murmured indifferently, "with me charity
begins at home. I can't afford emotional luxuries."

"A charity? A charity?" Hartly exulted. "I hadn't seized the
full beauty of it. Reading poor Margaret Aubyn's love-letters at
the Waldorf before five hundred people for a charity! *What* charity, dear Mrs. Armiger?"

"Why, the Home for Friendless Women——"

"It was well chosen," Dresham commented; and Hartly buried his mirth in the sofa cushions.

When they were alone Glennard, still holding his untouched
cup of tea, turned to his wife, who sat silently behind the kettle.
"Who asked you to take a ticket for that reading?"

"I don't know, really—Kate Dresham, I fancy. It was she
who got it up."

"It's just the sort of damnable vulgarity she's capable of! It's loathsome—it's monstrous—"

His wife, without looking up, answered gravely, "I thought so too. It was for that reason I didn't go. But you must remember that very few people feel about Mrs. Aubyn as you do—"

Glennard managed to set down his cup with a steady hand, but the room swung round with him and he dropped into the nearest chair. "As I do?" he repeated.

"I mean that very few people knew her when she lived in New York. To most of the women who went to the reading she was a mere name, too remote to have any personality. With me, of course, it was different—"

Glennard gave her a startled look. "Different? Why different?"

"Since you were her friend—"

"Her friend!" He stood up. "You speak as if she had had only one—the most famous woman of her day!" He moved vaguely about the room, bending down to look at some books on the table. "I hope," he added, "you didn't give that as a reason?"

"A reason?"

"For not going. A woman who gives reasons for getting out of social obligations is sure to make herself unpopular or ridiculous."

The words were uncalculated; but in an instant he saw that they had strangely bridged the distance between his wife and himself. He felt her close on him, like a panting foe, and her answer was a flash that showed the hand on the trigger.

"I seem," she said from the threshold, "to have done both in giving my reason to you."

The fact that they were dining out that evening made it easy for him to avoid Alexa till she came downstairs in her opera-cloak. Mrs. Touchett, who was going to the same dinner, had offered to call for her, and Glennard, refusing a precarious seat between the ladies' draperies, followed on foot. The evening was interminable. The reading at the Waldorf, at which all the women had been present, had revived the discussion of the *Aubyn Letters,* and Glennard, hearing his wife questioned as to her absence, felt himself miserably wishing that she had gone, rather than that her staying away should have been remarked. He was rapidly losing all sense of proportion where the *Letters* were concerned. He could no longer hear them mentioned without suspecting a purpose in the allusion; he even yielded himself for a moment to the extravagance of imagining that Mrs. Dresham, whom he disliked, had organized the reading in the hope of making him betray himself—for he was already sure that Dresham had divined his share in the transaction.

The attempt to keep a smooth surface on this inner tumult was as endless and unavailing as efforts made in a nightmare. He lost all sense of what he was saying to his neighbors; and once when he looked up his wife's glance struck him cold.

She sat nearly opposite him, at Flamel's side, and it appeared to Glennard that they had built about themselves one of those airy barriers of talk behind which two people can say what they please. While the reading was discussed they were silent. Their silence seemed to Glennard almost cynical—it stripped the last disguise from their complicity. A throb of anger rose in him, but suddenly it fell, and he felt, with a curious sense of relief, that at bottom he no longer cared whether Flamel had told his wife or not. The assumption that Flamel knew about the letters had become a fact to Glennard; and it now seemed to him better that Alexa should know too.

He was frightened at first by the discovery of his own indifference. The last barriers of his will seemed to be breaking down before a flood of moral lassitude. How could he continue to play his part, how keep his front to the enemy, with this poison of indifference stealing through his veins? He tried to brace himself with the remembrance of his wife's scorn. He had not forgotten the note on which their conversation had closed. If he had ever wondered how she would receive the truth he wondered no longer—she would despise him. But this lent a new insidiousness to his temptation, since her contempt would be a refuge from his own. He said to himself that, since he no longer cared for the consequences, he could at least acquit himself of speaking in self-defence. What he wanted now was not immunity but castigation: his wife's indignation might still reconcile him to himself. Therein lay his one hope of regeneration; her scorn was the moral antiseptic that he needed, her comprehension the one balm that could heal him.

When they left the dinner he was so afraid of speaking that he let her drive home alone, and went to the club with Flamel.

※ IX ※

HE rose next morning with the resolve to know what Alexa thought of him. It was not anchoring in a haven but lying to in a storm—he felt the need of a temporary lull in the turmoil of his sensations.

He came home late, for they were dining alone and he knew that they would have the evening together. When he followed her to the drawing-room after dinner he thought himself on the point of speaking; but as she handed him his coffee he said involuntarily: "I shall have to carry this off to the study; I've got a lot of work tonight."

Alone in the study he cursed his cowardice. What was it that had withheld him? A certain bright unapproachableness seemed to keep him at arm's length. She was not the kind of woman whose compassion could be circumvented; there was no chance of slipping past the outposts—he would never take her by surprise. Well—why not face her, then? What he shrank from could be no worse than what he was enduring. He had pushed back his chair and turned to go upstairs when a new expedient presented itself. What if, instead of telling her, he were to let her find out for herself and watch the effect of the discovery before speaking?

In this way he made over to chance the burden of the revelation.

The idea had been suggested by the sight of the formula enclosing the publisher's check. He had deposited the money, but the notice accompanying it dropped from his note-case as he cleared his table for work. It was the formula usual in such cases, and revealed clearly enough that he was the recipient of a royalty on Margaret Aubyn's letters. It would be impossible for Alexa to read it without understanding at once that the letters had been written to him and that he had sold them.

He sat downstairs till he heard her ring for the parlormaid to put out the lights; then he went up to the drawing-room with a bundle of papers in his hand. Alexa was just rising from her seat, and the lamplight fell on the deep roll of hair that overhung her brow like the eaves of a temple. Her face had often the high secluded look of a shrine; and it was this touch of awe in her beauty that now made him feel himself on the brink of sacrilege.

Lest the feeling should control him, he spoke at once. "I've brought you a piece of work—a lot of old bills and things that I want you to sort for me. Some are not worth keeping—but you'll be able to judge of that. There may be a letter or two among them—nothing of much account; but I don't like to throw away the whole lot without having them looked over, and I haven't time to do it myself."

He held out the papers, and she took them with a smile that seemed to recognize in the service he asked the tacit intention of making amends for the incident of the previous day.

"Are you sure I shall know which to keep?"

"Oh, quite sure," he answered easily; "and besides, none are of much importance."

The next morning he invented an excuse for leaving the house without seeing her, and when he returned, just before dinner, he found a visitor's hat and stick in the hall. The visitor was Flamel, who was just taking leave.

He had risen, but Alexa remained seated; and their attitude gave the impression of a colloquy that had prolonged itself beyond the limits of speech. Both turned a surprised eye on Glennard, and he had the sense of walking into a room grown suddenly empty, as though their thoughts were conspirators dispersed by his approach. He felt the clutch of his old fear. What if his wife had already sorted the papers and had told Flamel of her discovery? Well, it was no news to Flamel that Glennard was in receipt of a royalty on the *Aubyn Letters*.

A sudden resolve to know the worst made him lift his eyes to his wife as the door closed on Flamel. But Alexa had risen also, and bending over her writing-table, with her back to Glennard, was beginning to speak precipitately.

"I'm dining out tonight—you don't mind my deserting you? Julia Armiger sent me word just now that she had an extra ticket for the last Ambrose concert. She told me to say how sorry she was that she hadn't two, but I knew *you* wouldn't be sorry!" She ended with a laugh that had the effect of being a strayed echo of Mrs. Armiger's; and before Glennard could speak she had added, with her hand on the door, "Mr. Flamel stayed so late that I've hardly time to dress. The concert begins ridiculously early, and Julia dines at half-past seven."

Glennard stood alone in the empty room that seemed somehow full of an ironical consciousness of what was happening. "She hates me," he murmured. "She hates me . . ."

The next day was Sunday, and Glennard purposely lingered late in his room. When he came downstairs his wife was already seated at the breakfast-table. She lifted her usual smile to his entrance and they took shelter in the nearest topic, like wayfarers overtaken by a storm. While he listened to her account of the concert he began to think that, after all, she had not yet sorted the papers, and that her agitation of the previous day must be ascribed to another cause, in which perhaps he had but an indirect concern. He wondered it had never before occurred to him that Flamel was the kind of man who might very well please a woman at his own expense, without need of fortuitous assistance.

If this possibility cleared the outlook it did not brighten it. Glennard merely felt himself left alone with his baseness.

Alexa left the breakfast-table before him, and when he went up to the drawing-room he found her dressed to go out.

"Aren't you a little early for church?" he asked.

She replied that, on the way there, she meant to stop a moment at her mother's; and while she drew on her gloves he fumbled among the knickknacks on the mantelpiece for a match to light his cigarette.

"Well, goodbye," she said, turning to go; and from the threshold she added: "By the way, I've sorted the papers you gave me. Those that I thought you would like to keep are on your study table." She went downstairs and he heard the door close behind her.

She had sorted the papers—she knew, then—she *must* know —and she had made no sign!

Glennard, he hardly knew how, found himself once more in the study. On the table lay the packet he had given her. It was much smaller—she had evidently gone over the papers with care, destroying the greater number. He loosened the elastic band and spread the remaining envelopes on his desk. The publisher's notice was among them.

※ X ※

His wife knew and she made no sign. Glennard found himself in the case of the seafarer who, closing his eyes at nightfall on a scene he thinks to put leagues behind him before day, wakes to a porthole framing the same patch of shore. From the kind of exaltation to which his resolve had lifted him he dropped to an unreasoning apathy. His impulse of confession had acted as a drug to self-reproach. He had tried to shift a portion of his burden to his wife's shoulders; and now that she had tacitly refused to carry it, he felt the load too heavy to be taken up.

A fortunate interval of hard work brought respite from this phase of sterile misery. He went West to argue an important case, won it, and came back to fresh preoccupations. His own affairs were thriving enough to engross him in the pauses of his professional work, and for over two months he had little time to look himself in the face. Not unnaturally—for he was as yet unskilled in the subtleties of introspection—he mistook his temporary insensibility for a gradual revival of moral health.

He told himself that he was recovering his sense of proportion, getting to see things in their true light; and if he now thought of his rash appeal to his wife's sympathy it was as an act of folly from the consequences of which he had been saved by the providence that watches over madmen. He had little leisure to observe Alexa; but he concluded that the common sense momentarily denied him had counselled her silent acceptance of the inevitable. If such a quality was a poor substitute for the passionate justness that had once seemed to distinguish her, he accepted the alternative as a part of that general lowering of the key that seems needful to the maintenance of the matrimonial duet. What woman ever retained her abstract sense of justice where another woman was concerned? Possibly the thought that he had profited by Mrs. Aubyn's tenderness was not wholly disagreeable to his wife.

When the pressure of work began to lessen, and he found himself, in the lengthening afternoons, able to reach home somewhat earlier, he noticed that the little drawing-room was always full and that he and his wife seldom had an evening alone together. When he was tired, as often happened, she went out alone; the idea of giving up an engagement to remain with him seemed not to occur to her. She had shown, as a girl, little fondness for society, nor had she seemed to regret it during the year they had spent in the country. He reflected, however, that he was sharing the common lot of husbands, who proverbially mistake the early ardors of housekeeping for a sign of settled domesticity. Alexa, at any rate, was refuting his theory as inconsiderately as a

seedling defeats the gardener's expectations. An undefinable
change had come over her. In one sense it was a happy one, since
she had grown, if not handsomer, at least more vivid and expressive; her beauty had become more communicable: it was as
though she had learned the conscious exercise of intuitive attributes and now used her effects with the discrimination of an
artist skilled in values. To a dispassionate critic (as Glennard
now rated himself) the art may at times have been a little too
obvious. Her attempts at lightness lacked spontaneity, and she
sometimes rasped him by laughing like Julia Armiger; but he had
enough imagination to perceive that, in respect of his wife's social arts, a husband necessarily sees the wrong side of the tapes-
try.

In this ironical estimate of their relation Glennard found
himself strangely relieved of all concern as to his wife's feelings
for Flamel. From an Olympian pinnacle of indifference he calmly
surveyed their inoffensive antics. It was surprising how his
cheapening of his wife put him at ease with himself. Far as he
and she were from each other they had yet had, in a sense, the
tacit nearness of complicity. Yes, they were accomplices; he could
no more be jealous of her than she could despise him. The jealousy that would once have seemed a blur on her whiteness now
appeared like a tribute to ideals in which he no longer believed.

Glennard was little given to exploring the outskirts of literature. He always skipped the "literary notices" in the papers, and
he had small leisure for the intermittent pleasures of the periodi-
cal. He had therefore no notion of the prolonged reverberations
which the *Aubyn Letters* had awakened. When the book ceased
to be talked about he supposed it had ceased to be read; and
this apparent subsidence of the agitation about it brought the reassuring sense that he had exaggerated its vitality. The conviction, if it did not ease his conscience, at least offered him the relative relief of obscurity; he felt like an offender taken down from
the pillory and thrust into the soothing darkness of a cell.

But one evening, when Alexa had left him to go to a dance, he chanced to turn over the magazines on her table, and the copy of the *Horoscope* to which he settled down with his cigar confronted him, on its first page, with a portrait of Margaret Aubyn. It was a reproduction of the photograph that had stood so long on his desk. The desiccating air of memory had turned her into the mere abstraction of a woman, and this unexpected evocation seemed to bring her nearer than she had ever been in life. Was it because he understood her better? He looked long into her eyes; little personal traits reached out to him like caresses—the tired droop of her lids, her quick way of leaning forward as she spoke, the movements of her long expressive hands. All that was feminine in her, the quality he had always missed, stole toward him from her unreproachful gaze; and now that it was too late, life had developed in him the subtler perceptions which could detect it in even this poor semblance of herself. For a moment he found consolation in the thought that, at any cost, they had thus been brought together; then a sense of shame rushed over him. Face to face with her, he felt himself laid bare to the inmost fold of consciousness. The shame was deep, but it was a renovating anguish: he was like a man whom intolerable pain has roused from the creeping lethargy of death.

He rose next morning to as fresh a sense of life as though his hour of communion with Margaret Aubyn had been a more exquisite renewal of their earlier meetings. His waking thought was that he must see her again; and as consciousness affirmed itself he felt an intense fear of losing the sense of her nearness. But she was still close to him: her presence remained the one reality in a world of shadows. All through his working hours he was re-living with incredible minuteness every incident of their obliterated past: as a man who has mastered the spirit of a foreign tongue turns with renewed wonder to the pages his youth has plodded over. In this lucidity of retrospection the most trivial detail had its meaning, and the joy of recovery was embittered to Glennard by the perception of all that he had missed. He had been pitiably, grotesquely stupid; and there was irony in the thought that, but for the crisis through which he was passing, he might have lived on in complacent ignorance of his loss. It was as though she had bought him with her blood.

That evening he and Alexa dined alone. After dinner he followed her to the drawing-room. He no longer felt the need of avoiding her; he was hardly conscious of her presence. After a few words they lapsed into silence, and he sat smoking with his eyes on the fire. It was not that he was unwilling to talk to her; he felt a curious desire to be as kind as possible; but he was always forgetting that she was there. Her full bright presence, through which the currents of life flowed so warmly, had grown as tenuous as a shadow, and he saw so far beyond her.

Presently she rose and began to move about the room. She seemed to be looking for something, and he roused himself to ask what she wanted.

"Only the last number of the *Horoscope*. I thought I'd left it on this table." He said nothing, and she went on: "You haven't seen it?"

"No," he returned coldly. The magazine was locked in his desk.

His wife had moved to the mantelpiece. She stood facing him, and as he looked up he met her tentative gaze. "I was reading an article in it—a review of Mrs. Aubyn's *Letters*," she added slowly, with her deep deliberate blush.

Glennard stooped to toss his cigar into the fire. He felt a savage wish that she would not speak the other woman's name; nothing else seemed to matter.

"You seem to do a lot of reading," he said.

She still confronted him. "I was keeping this for you—I thought it might interest you," she said with an air of gentle insistence.

He stood up and turned away. He was sure she knew that he

had taken the review, and he felt that he was beginning to hate her again.

"I haven't time for such things," he said indifferently. As he moved to the door he heard her take a hurried step forward; then she paused, and sank without speaking into the chair from which he had risen.

❊ XI ❊

As Glennard, in the raw February sunlight, mounted the road to the cemetery, he felt the beatitude that comes with an abrupt cessation of physical pain. He had reached the point where self-analysis ceases; the impulse that moved him was purely intuitive. He did not even seek a reason for it, beyond the obvious one that his desire to stand by Margaret Aubyn's grave was prompted by no attempt at a sentimental reparation, but rather by the need to affirm in some way the reality of the tie between them.

The ironical promiscuity of death had brought Mrs. Aubyn back to share the hospitality of her husband's last lodging; but though Glennard knew she had been buried near New York he had never visited her grave. He was oppressed, as he now threaded the long avenues, by a chilling vision of her return. There was no family to follow her hearse; she had died alone, as she had lived; and the "distinguished mourners" who had formed the escort of the famous writer knew nothing of the woman they were committing to the grave. Glennard could not even remember at what season she had been buried; but his mood indulged the fancy that it must have been on some such day of harsh sunlight, the incisive February brightness that gives perspicuity without warmth. The white avenues stretched before him interminably, lined with stereotyped emblems of affliction, as though all the platitudes ever uttered had been turned to marble and set up over the unresisting dead. Here and there, no doubt, a frigid urn or an insipid angel imprisoned some fine-fibred grief, as the most hackneyed words may become the vehicle of rare meanings; but for the most part the endless alignment of monuments seemed to embody those easy generalizations about death that do not disturb the repose of the living. Glennard's eye, as he followed the way pointed out to him, had instinctively sought some low mound with a quiet headstone. He had forgotten that the dead seldom plan their own houses, and with a pang he discovered the name he sought on the cyclopean base of a shaft rearing its aggressive height at the angle of two avenues.

"How she would have hated it!" he murmured.

A bench stood near and he seated himself. The monument rose before him like some pretentious uninhabited dwelling: he could not believe that Margaret Aubyn lay there. It was a Sunday morning, and black figures moved among the paths, placing flowers on the frost-bound hillocks. Glennard noticed that the neighboring graves had been thus newly dressed, and he fancied a blind stir of expectancy through the sod, as though the bare mounds spread a parched surface to that commemorative rain. He rose presently and walked back to the entrance of the cemetery. Several greenhouses stood near the gates, and turning in at the first he asked for some flowers.

"Anything in the emblematic line?" asked the anæmic man behind the dripping counter.

Glennard shook his head.

"Just cut flowers? This way then." The florist unlocked a glass door and led him down a moist green aisle. The hot air was choked with the scent of white azaleas, white lilies, white lilacs; all the flowers were white: they were like a prolongation, a mystic efflorescence, of the long rows of marble tombstones, and their perfume seemed to cover an odor of decay. The rich atmosphere made Glennard dizzy. As he leaned in the doorway, waiting for the flowers, he had a penetrating sense of Margaret Aubyn's nearness—not the imponderable presence of his inner vision, but a life that beat warm in his arms.

The sharp air caught him as he stepped out into it again. He walked back and scattered the flowers over the grave. The edges of the white petals shrivelled like burnt paper in the cold; and as he watched them the illusion of her nearness faded, shrank back frozen.

※ XII ※

THE motive of his visit to the cemetery remained undefined save as a final effort of escape from his wife's inexpressive acceptance of his shame. It seemed to him that as long as he could keep himself alive to that shame he would not wholly have succumbed to its consequences. His chief fear was that he should become the creature of his act. His wife's indifference degraded him: it seemed to put him on a level with his dishonor. Margaret Aubyn would have abhorred the deed in proportion to her pity for the man. The sense of her potential pity drew him back to her. The one woman knew but did not understand; the other, it sometimes seemed, understood without knowing.

In its last disguise of retrospective remorse, his self-pity affected a desire for solitude and meditation. He lost himself in morbid musings, in futile visions of what life with Margaret Aubyn might have been. There were moments when, in the strange dislocation of his view, the wrong he had done her seemed a tie between them.

To indulge these emotions he fell into the habit, on Sunday afternoons, of solitary walks prolonged till after dusk. The days were lengthening, there was a touch of spring in the air, and his wanderings now usually led him to the Park and its outlying regions.

One Sunday, tired of aimless locomotion, he took a cab at the Park gates and let it carry him out to the Riverside Drive. It was a gray afternoon streaked with east wind. Glennard's cab advanced slowly, and as he leaned back, gazing with absent intent-

ness at the deserted paths that wound under bare boughs between grass banks of premature vividness, his attention was
arrested by two figures walking ahead of him. This couple, who
had the path to themselves, moved at an uneven pace, as though
adapting their gait to a conversation marked by meditative intervals. Now and then they paused, and in one of these pauses the
lady, turning toward her companion, showed Glennard the outline of his wife's profile. The man was Flamel.

The blood rushed to Glennard's forehead. He sat up with a
jerk and pushed back the lid in the roof of the hansom; but when
the cabman bent down he dropped into his seat without speaking. Then, becoming conscious of the prolonged interrogation of
the lifted lid, he called out—"Turn—drive back—anywhere—
I'm in a hurry—"

As the cab swung round he caught a last glimpse of the two
figures. They had not moved; Alexa, with bent head, stood listening.

"My God, my God—" he groaned.

It was hideous—it was abominable—he could not understand it. The woman was nothing to him—less than nothing—yet
the blood hummed in his ears and hung a cloud before him. He
knew it was only the stirring of the primal instinct, that it had no
more to do with his reasoning self than any reflex impulse of the
body; but that merely lowered anguish to disgust. Yes, it was disgust he felt—almost a physical nausea. The poisonous fumes of
life were in his lungs. He was sick, unutterably sick.

He drove home and went to his room. They were giving a
little dinner that night, and when he came down the guests were
arriving. He looked at his wife: her beauty was extraordinary,
but it seemed to him the beauty of a smooth sea along an unlit
coast. She frightened him.

He sat late in his study. He heard the parlormaid lock the
front door; then his wife went upstairs and the lights were put
out. His brain was like some great empty hall with an echo in it:
one thought reverberated endlessly. . . . At length he drew his

chair to the table and began to write. He addressed an envelope and then slowly re-read what he had written.

My dear Flamel

Many apologies for not sending you sooner the enclosed check, which represents the customary percentage on the sale of the "Letters."

Trusting you will excuse the oversight.

Yours truly

Stephen Glennard.

He let himself out of the darkened house and dropped the letter in the post-box at the corner.

The next afternoon he was detained late at his office, and as he was preparing to leave he heard someone asking for him in the outer room. He seated himself again and Flamel was shown in.

The two men, as Glennard pushed aside an obstructive chair, had a moment to measure each other; then Flamel advanced, and drawing out his note-case, laid a slip of paper on the desk.

"My dear fellow, what on earth does this mean?"

Glennard recognized his check.

"That I was remiss, simply. It ought to have gone to you before."

Flamel's tone had been that of unaffected surprise, but at this his accent changed and he asked quickly: "On what ground?"

Glennard had moved away from the desk and stood leaning against the calf-backed volumes of the bookcase. "On the ground that you sold Mrs. Aubyn's letters for me, and that I find the intermediary in such cases is entitled to a percentage on the sale."

Flamel paused before answering. "You find, you say. It's a recent discovery?"

"Obviously, from my not sending the check sooner. You see I'm new to the business."

"And since when have you discovered that there was any question of business, as far as I was concerned?"

Glennard flushed and his voice rose slightly. "Are you reproaching me for not having remembered it sooner?"

Flamel, who had spoken in the rapid repressed tone of a man on the verge of anger, stared a moment at this and then, in his natural voice, rejoined good-humoredly, "Upon my soul, I don't understand you!"

The change of key seemed to disconcert Glennard. "It's simple enough," he muttered.

"Simple enough—your offering me money in return for a friendly service? I don't know what your other friends expect!"

"Some of my friends wouldn't have undertaken the job. Those who would have done so would probably have expected to be paid."

He lifted his eyes to Flamel and the two men looked at each other. Flamel had turned white and his lips stirred, but he held his temperate note. "If you mean to imply that the job was not a nice one you lay yourself open to the retort that you proposed it. But for my part I've never seen, I never shall see, any reason for not publishing the letters."

"That's just it!"

"What—?"

"The certainty of your not seeing was what made me go to you. When a man's got stolen goods to pawn he doesn't take them to the police-station."

"Stolen?" Flamel echoed. "The letters were stolen?"

Glennard burst into a laugh. "How much longer do you expect me to keep up that pretence about the letters? You know well enough they were written to me."

Flamel looked at him in silence. "Were they?" he said at length. "I didn't know it."

"And didn't suspect it, I suppose," Glennard sneered.

The other was again silent; then he said, "I may remind you that, supposing I had felt any curiosity about the matter, I had no way of finding out that the letters were written to you. You never showed me the originals."

"What does that prove? There were fifty ways of finding out. It's the kind of thing one can easily do."

Flamel glanced at him with contempt. "Our ideas probably differ as to what a man can easily do. It would not have been easy for me."

Glennard's anger vented itself in the words uppermost in his thought. "It may, then, interest you to hear that my wife *does* know about the letters—has known for some months. . . ."

"Ah," said the other, slowly.

Glennard saw that, in his blind clutch at a weapon, he had seized the one most apt to wound. Flamel's muscles were under control, but his face showed the undefinable change produced by the slow infiltration of poison. Every implication that the words contained had reached its mark; but Glennard felt that their obvious intent was lost in the anguish of what they suggested. He was sure now that Flamel would never have betrayed him, but the inference only made a wider outlet for his anger. He paused breathlessly for Flamel to speak.

"If she knows it's not through me." It was what Glennard had waited for.

"Through you, by God? Who said it was through you? Do you suppose I leave it to you, or to anybody else, for that matter, to keep my wife informed of my actions? I didn't suppose even such egregious conceit as yours could delude a man to that degree!" Struggling for a foothold in the landslide of his dignity, he added in a steadier tone, "My wife learned the facts from me."

Flamel received this in silence. The other's outbreak seemed to have restored his self-control, and when he spoke it was with a deliberation implying that his course was chosen. "In that case I understand still less—"

"Still less—?"

"The meaning of this." He pointed to the check. "When you began to speak I supposed you had meant it as a bribe; now I can only infer it was intended as a random insult. In either case, here's my answer."

He tore the slip of paper in two and tossed the fragments across the desk to Glennard. Then he turned and walked out of the office.

Glennard dropped his head on his hands. If he had hoped to restore his self-respect by the simple expedient of assailing Flamel's, the result had not justified his expectation. The blow he had struck had blunted the edge of his anger, and the unforeseen extent of the hurt inflicted did not alter the fact that his weapon had broken in his hands. He now saw that his rage against Flamel was only the last projection of a passionate self-disgust. This consciousness did not dull his dislike of the man; it simply made reprisals ineffectual. Flamel's unwillingness to quarrel with him was the last stage of his abasement.

In the light of this final humiliation his assumption of his wife's indifference struck him as hardly so fatuous as the sentimental resuscitation of his past. He had been living in a factitious world wherein his emotions were the sycophants of his vanity, and it was with instinctive relief that he felt its ruins crash about his head.

It was nearly dark when he left his office, and he walked slowly homeward in the complete mental abeyance that follows on such a crisis. He was not aware that he was thinking of his wife; yet when he reached his own door he found that, in the involuntary readjustment of his vision, she had once more become the central point of consciousness.

❊ XIII ❊

IT had never before occurred to him that she might, after all, have missed the purport of the document he had put in her way. What if, in her hurried inspection of the papers, she had passed it over as related to the private business of some client? What, for instance, was to prevent her concluding that Glennard was the counsel of the unknown person who had sold the *Aubyn Letters?* The subject was one not likely to fix her attention—she was not a curious woman.

Glennard at this point laid down his fork and glanced at her between the candle-shades. The alternative explanation of her indifference was not slow in presenting itself. Her head had the same listening droop as when he had caught sight of her the day before in Flamel's company; the attitude revived the vividness of his impression. It was simple enough, after all. She had ceased to care for him because she cared for someone else.

As he followed her upstairs he felt a sudden stirring of his dormant anger. His sentiments had lost their artificial complexity. He had already acquitted her of any connivance in his baseness, and he felt only that he loved her and that she had escaped him. This was now, strangely enough, his dominant thought: the sense that he and she had passed through the fusion of love and had emerged from it as incommunicably apart as though the transmutation had never taken place. Every other passion, he mused, left some mark upon the nature, but love passed like the flight of a ship across the waters.

She dropped into her usual seat near the lamp, and he leaned against the chimney, moving about with an inattentive hand the knickknacks on the mantel.

Suddenly he caught sight of her reflection in the mirror. She was looking at him. He turned and their eyes met.

He moved across the room.

"There's something that I want to say to you," he began.

She held his gaze, but her color deepened. He noticed again, with a jealous pang, how her beauty had gained in warmth and meaning. It was as though a transparent cup had been filled with wine. He looked at her ironically.

"I've never prevented your seeing your friends here," he broke out. "Why do you meet Flamel in out-of-the-way places? Nothing makes a woman so cheap—"

She rose abruptly and they faced each other a few feet apart.

"What do you mean?" she asked.

"I saw you with him last Sunday on the Riverside Drive," he went on, the utterance of the charge reviving his anger.

"Ah," she murmured. She sank into her chair again and began to play with a paper-knife that lay on the table at her elbow.

Her silence exasperated him.

"Well?" he burst out. "Is that all you have to say?"

"Do you wish me to explain?" she asked proudly.

"Do you imply I haven't the right to?"

"I imply nothing. I will tell you whatever you wish to know. I went for a walk with Mr. Flamel because he asked me to."

"I didn't suppose you went uninvited. But there are certain things a sensible woman doesn't do. She doesn't slink about in out-of-the-way streets with men. Why couldn't you have seen him here?"

She hesitated. "Because he wanted to see me alone."

"Did he indeed? And may I ask if you gratify all his wishes with equal alacrity?"

"I don't know that he has any others where I am concerned." She paused again and then continued, in a voice that somehow had an under-note of warning, "He wished to bid me good-bye. He's going away."

Glennard turned on her a startled glance. "Going away?"

"He's going to Europe tomorrow. He goes for a long time. I supposed you knew."

The last phrase revived his irritation. "You forget that I depend on you for my information about Flamel. He's your friend and not mine. In fact, I've sometimes wondered at your going out of your way to be so civil to him when you must see plainly enough that I don't like him."

Her answer to this was not immediate. She seemed to be choosing her words with care, not so much for her own sake as for his, and his exasperation was increased by the suspicion that she was trying to spare him.

"He was your friend before he was mine. I never knew him till I was married. It was you who brought him to the house and who seemed to wish me to like him."

Glennard gave a short laugh. The defence was feebler than he had expected: she was certainly not a clever woman.

"Your deference to my wishes is really beautiful; but it's not the first time in history that a man had made a mistake in introducing his friends to his wife. You must, at any rate, have seen since then that my enthusiasm had cooled; but so, perhaps, has your eagerness to oblige me."

She met this with a silence that seemed to rob the taunt of half its efficacy.

"Is that what you imply?" he pressed her.

"No," she answered with sudden directness. "I noticed some time ago that you seemed to dislike him, but since then—"

"Well—since then?"

"I've imagined that you had reasons for still wishing me to be civil to him, as you call it."

"Ah," said Glennard with an effort at lightness; but his irony dropped, for something in her voice made him feel that he and she stood at last in that naked desert of apprehension where meaning skulks vainly behind speech.

"And why did you imagine this?" The blood mounted to his forehead. "Because he told you that I was under obligations to him?"

She turned pale. "Under obligations?"

"Oh, don't let's beat about the bush. Didn't he tell you it was I who published Mrs. Aubyn's letters? Answer me that."

"No," she said; and after a moment which seemed given to the weighing of alternatives, she added: "No one told me."

"You didn't know, then?"

She seemed to speak with an effort. "Not until—not until—"

"Till I gave you those papers to sort?"

Her head sank.

"You understood then?"

"Yes."

He looked at her immovable face. "Had you suspected—before?" was slowly wrung from him.

"At times—yes—." Her voice dropped to a whisper.

"Why? From anything that was said—?"

There was a shade of pity in her glance. "No one said anything—no one told me anything." She looked away from him. "It was your manner—"

"My manner?"

"Whenever the book was mentioned. Things you said—once or twice—your irritation—I can't explain."

Glennard, unconsciously, had moved nearer. He breathed like a man who has been running. "You knew, then, you knew—" he stammered. The avowal of her love for Flamel would have hurt him less, would have rendered her less remote. "You knew—you knew—" he repeated, and suddenly his anguish gathered voice. "My God!" he cried, "you suspected it first, you say—and then you knew it—this damnable, this accursed thing; you knew it months ago—it's months since I put that paper in your way—and yet you've done nothing, you've said nothing, you've made no sign, you've lived alongside of me as if it had made no difference—no difference in either of our lives. What are you made of, I wonder? Don't you see the hideous ignominy of it? Don't you see how you've shared in my disgrace? Or haven't you any sense of shame?"

He preserved sufficient lucidity, as the words poured from him, to see how fatally they invited her derision; but something told him they had both passed beyond the phase of obvious retaliations, and that if any chord in her responded it would not be that of scorn.

He was right. She rose slowly and moved toward him.

"Haven't you had enough—without that?" she said in a strange voice of pity.

He stared at her. "Enough—?"

"Of misery . . ."

An iron band seemed loosened from his temples. "You saw then . . ?" he whispered.

"Oh, God—oh, God—" she sobbed. She dropped beside him and hid her anguish against his knees. They clung thus in silence a long time, driven together down the same fierce blast of shame.

When at length she lifted her face he averted his. Her scorn would have hurt him less than the tears on his hands.

She spoke languidly, like a child emerging from a passion of weeping. "It was for the money—?"

His lips shaped an assent.

"That was the inheritance—that we married on?"

"Yes."

She drew back and rose to her feet. He sat watching her as she wandered away from him.

"You hate me," broke from him.

She made no answer.

"Say you hate me!" he persisted.

"That would have been so simple," she answered with a strange smile. She dropped into a chair near the writing-table and rested a bowed forehead on her hand.

"Was it much—?" she began at length.

"Much—?" he returned vaguely.

"The money."

"The money?" That part of it seemed to count so little that for a moment he did not follow her thought.

"It must be paid back," she insisted. "Can you do it?"

"Oh, yes," he returned listlessly. "I can do it."

"I would make any sacrifice for that!" she urged.

He nodded. "Of course." He sat staring at her in dry-eyed self-contempt. "Do you count on its making much difference?"

"Much difference?"

"In the way I feel—or you feel about me?"

She shook her head.

"It's the least part of it," he groaned.

"It's the only part we can repair."

"Good heavens! If there were any reparation—" He rose quickly and crossed the space that divided them. "Why did you never speak?"

"Haven't you answered that yourself?"

"Answered it?"

"Just now—when you told me you did it for me."

She paused a moment and then went on with a deepening note—"I would have spoken if I could have helped you."

"But you must have despised me."

"I've told you that would have been simpler."

"But how could you go on like this—hating the money?"

"I knew you'd speak in time. I wanted you, first, to hate it as I did."

He gazed at her with a kind of awe. "You're wonderful," he murmured. "But you don't yet know the depths I've reached."

She raised an entreating hand. "I don't want to!"

"You're afraid, then, that you'll hate me?"

"No—but that you'll hate *me*. Let me understand without your telling me."

"You can't. It's too base. I thought you didn't care because you loved Flamel."

She blushed deeply. "Don't—don't—" she warned him.

"I haven't the right to, you mean?"

"I mean that you'll be sorry."

He stood imploringly before her. "I want to say something worse—something more outrageous. If you don't understand *this* you'll be perfectly justified in ordering me out of the house."

She answered him with a glance of divination. "I shall understand—but you'll be sorry."

"I must take my chance of that." He moved away and tossed the books about the table. Then he swung round and faced her. "Does Flamel care for you?" he asked.

Her flush deepened, but she still looked at him without anger. "What would be the use?" she said with a note of sadness.

"Ah, I didn't ask *that*," he penitently murmured.

"Well, then—"

To this adjuration he made no response beyond that of gazing at her with an eye which seemed now to view her as a mere factor in an immense redistribution of meanings.

"I insulted Flamel today. I let him see that I suspected him of having told you. I hated him because he knew about the letters."

He caught the spreading horror of her eyes, and for an instant he had to grapple with the new temptation they lit up. Then he said with an effort—"Don't blame him—he's impeccable. He helped me to get them published; but I lied to him too; I pretended they were written to another man . . . a man who was dead . . ."

She raised her arms in a gesture that seemed to ward off his blows.

"You *do* despise me!" he insisted.

"Ah, that poor woman—that poor woman—" he heard her murmur.

"I spare no one, you see!" he triumphed over her. She kept her face hidden.

"You do hate me, you do despise me!" he strangely exulted.

"Be silent!" she commanded him; but he seemed no longer conscious of any check on his gathering purpose.

"He cared for you—he cared for you," he repeated, "and he never told you of the letters—"

She sprang to her feet. "How can you?" she flamed. "How dare you? *That—!*"

Glennard was ashy pale. "It's a weapon . . . like another . . ."

"A scoundrel's!"

He smiled wretchedly. "I should have used it in his place."

"Stephen! Stephen!" she cried, as though to drown the blasphemy on his lips. She swept to him with a rescuing gesture. "Don't say such things. I forbid you! It degrades us both."

He put her back with trembling hands. "Nothing that I say of myself can degrade you. We're on different levels."

"I'm on yours, wherever it is!"

He lifted his head and their gaze flowed together.

❈ XIV ❈

THE great renewals take effect as imperceptibly as the first workings of spring. Glennard, though he felt himself brought nearer to his wife, was still, as it were, hardly within speaking distance. He was but laboriously acquiring the rudiments of a new language, and he had to grope for her through the dense fog of his humiliation, the distorting vapor against which her personality loomed grotesque and mean.

Only the fact that we are unaware how well our nearest know us enables us to live with them. Love is the most impregnable refuge of self-esteem, and we hate the eye that reaches to our nakedness. If Glennard did not hate his wife it was slowly, sufferingly, that there was born in him that profounder passion which made his earlier feeling seem a mere commotion of the blood. He was like a child coming back to the sense of an enveloping presence: her nearness was a breast on which he leaned.

They did not, at first, talk much together, and each beat a devious track about the outskirts of the subject that lay between them like a haunted wood. But every word, every action, seemed to glance at it, to draw toward it, as though a fount of healing sprang in its poisoned shade. If only they might cut a way through the thicket to that restoring spring!

Glennard, watching his wife with the intentness of a wanderer to whom no natural sign is negligible, saw that she had taken temporary refuge in the purpose of renouncing the money. If both, theoretically, owned the inefficacy of such amends, the woman's instinctive subjectiveness made her find relief in this crude form of penance. Glennard saw that she meant to live as frugally as possible till what she deemed their debt was discharged, and he prayed she might not discover how far-reaching, in its merely material sense, was the obligation she thus hoped to acquit. Her mind was fixed on the sum originally paid for the letters, and this he knew he could lay aside in a year or two. He was touched, meanwhile, by the spirit that made her discard the petty luxuries which she regarded as the sign of their bondage. Their shared renunciations drew her nearer to him, helped, in their evidence of her helplessness, to restore the full protecting stature of his love. And still they did not speak.

It was several weeks later that, one afternoon by the drawing-room fire, she handed him a letter that she had been reading when he entered.

"I've heard from Mr. Flamel," she said.

It was as though a latent presence had become visible to both. Glennard took the letter mechanically.

"It's from Smyrna," she said. "Won't you read it?"

He handed it back. "You can tell me about it—his hand's so illegible." He wandered to the other end of the room and then turned and stood before her. "I've been thinking of writing to Flamel," he said.

She looked up.

"There's one point," he continued slowly, "that I ought to clear up. I told him you'd known about the letters all along; for a long time, at least; and I saw how it hurt him. It was just what I meant to do, of course; but I can't leave him to that false impression; I must write him."

She received this without outward movement, but he saw that the depths were stirred. At length she returned in a hesitating tone, "Why do you call it a false impression? I did know."

"Yes, but I implied you didn't care."

"Ah!"

He still stood looking down on her. "Don't you want me to set that right?" he pursued.

She lifted her head and fixed him bravely. "It isn't necessary," she said.

Glennard flushed with the shock of the retort, then, with a gesture of comprehension, "No," he said, "with you it couldn't be; but I might still set myself right."

She looked at him gently. "Don't I," she murmured, "do that?"

"In being yourself merely? Alas, the rehabilitation's too complete! You make me seem—to myself even—what I'm not; what I can never be. I can't, at times, defend myself from the delusion; but I can at least enlighten others."

The flood was loosened, and kneeling by her he caught her hands. "Don't you see that it's become an obsession with me? That if I could strip myself down to the last lie—only there'd always be another one left under it!—and do penance naked in the market-place, I should at least have the relief of easing one anguish by another? Don't you see that the worst of my torture is the impossibility of such amends?"

Her hands lay in his without returning pressure. "Ah, poor woman, poor woman," he heard her sigh.

"Don't pity her, pity me! What have I done to her or to you, after all? You're both inaccessible! It was myself I sold."

He took an abrupt turn away from her; then halted before her again. "How much longer," he burst out, "do you suppose you can stand it? You've been magnificent, you've been inspired, but what's the use? You can't wipe out the ignominy of it. It's miserable for you and it does *her* no good!"

She lifted a vivid face. "That's the thought I can't bear!" she cried.

"What thought?"

"That it does her no good—all you're feeling, all you're suffering. Can it be that it makes no difference?"

He avoided her challenging glance. "What's done is done," he muttered.

"Is it ever, quite, I wonder?" she mused. He made no answer and they lapsed into one of the pauses that are a subterranean channel of communication.

It was she who, after a while, began to speak, with a new suffusing diffidence that made him turn a roused eye on her.

"Don't they say," she asked, feeling her way as in a kind of tender apprehensiveness, "that the early Christians, instead of pulling down the heathen temples—the temples of the unclean gods—purified them by turning them to their own uses? I've always thought one might do that with one's actions—the actions one loathes but can't undo. One can make, I mean, a wrong the door to other wrongs or an impassable wall against them . . ." Her voice wavered on the word. "We can't always tear down the temples we've built to the unclean gods, but we can put good spirits in the house of evil—the spirits of mercy and shame and understanding, that might never have come to us if we hadn't been in such great need . . ."

She moved over to him and laid a hand on his. His head was bent and he did not change his attitude. She sat down beside him without speaking; but their silences were now fertile as rainclouds—they quickened the seeds of understanding.

At length he looked up. "I don't know," he said, "what spirits have come to live in the house of evil that I built—but you're there and that's enough. It's strange," he went on after another pause, "she wished the best for me so often, and now, at last, it's through her that it's come to me. But for her I shouldn't have known you—it's through her that I've found you. Sometimes—do you know?—that makes it hardest—makes me most intolerable to myself. Can't you see that it's the worst thing I've got to face? I sometimes think I could have borne it better if you hadn't understood! I took everything from her—everything—even to the poor shelter of loyalty she's trusted in—the only thing I *could* have left her!—I took everything from her, I deceived her, I despoiled her, I destroyed her—and she's given me *you* in return!"

His wife's cry caught him up. "It isn't that she's given *me* to you—it is that she's given you to yourself." She leaned to him as though swept forward on a wave of pity. "Don't you see," she went on, as his eyes hung on her, "that that's the gift you can't escape from, the debt you're pledged to acquit? Don't you see that you've never before been what she thought you, and that now, so wonderfully, she's made you into the man she loved? *That's* worth suffering for, worth dying for, to a woman—that's the gift she would have wished to give!"

"Ah," he cried, "but woe to him by whom it cometh. What did I ever give her?"

"The happiness of giving," she said.

Sanctuary

❧[1903]❧

PART I

❋ I ❋

I T IS not often that youth allows itself to feel undividedly happy: the sensation is too much the result of selection and elimination to be within reach of the awakening clutch on life. But Kate Orme, for once, had yielded herself to happiness, letting it permeate every faculty as a spring rain soaks into a germinating meadow. There was nothing to account for this sudden sense of beatitude; but was it not this precisely which made it so irresistible, so overwhelming? There had been, within the last two months—since her engagement to Denis Peyton—no distinct addition to the sum of her happiness, and no possibility, she would have affirmed, of adding perceptibly to a total already incalculable. Inwardly and outwardly the conditions of her life were unchanged; but whereas, before, the air had been full of flitting wings, now they seemed to pause over her and she could trust herself to their shelter.

Many influences had combined to build up the centre of brooding peace in which she found herself. Her nature answered to the finest vibrations, and at first her joy in loving had been too great not to bring with it a certain confusion, a readjusting of the whole scenery of life. She found herself in a new country, wherein he who had led her there was least able to be her guide. There were moments when she felt that the first stranger in the street could have interpreted her happiness for her more easily than Denis. Then, as her eye adapted itself, as the lines flowed into each other, opening deep vistas upon new horizons, she began to enter into possession of her kingdom, to entertain the actual sense of its belonging to her. But she had never before felt that she also belonged to it; and this was the feeling which now came to complete her happiness, to give it the hallowing sense of permanence.

She rose from the writing-table where, list in hand, she had been going over the wedding-invitations, and walked toward the drawing-room window. Everything about her seemed to contribute to that rare harmony of feeling which levied a tax on every sense. The large coolness of the room, its fine traditional air of spacious living, its outlook over field and woodland toward the lake lying under the silver bloom of September; the very scent of the late violets in a glass on the writing-table; the rosy-mauve masses of hydrangea in tubs along the terrace; the fall, now and then, of a leaf through the still air—all, somehow, were mingled in the suffusion of well-being that yet made them seem but so much dross upon its current.

The girl's smile prolonged itself at the sight of a figure approaching from the lower slopes above the lake. The path was a short cut from the Peyton place, and she had known that Denis would appear in it at about that hour. Her smile, however, was prolonged not so much by his approach as by her sense of the impossibility of communicating her mood to him. The feeling did not disturb her. She could not imagine sharing her deepest moods with any one, and the world in which she lived with Denis was too bright and spacious to admit of any sense of constraint. Her smile was in truth a tribute to that clear-eyed directness of his which was so often a refuge from her own complexities.

Denis Peyton was used to being met with a smile. He might have been pardoned for thinking smiles the habitual wear of the human countenance; and his estimate of life and of himself was necessarily tinged by the cordial terms on which they had always met each other. He had in fact found life, from the start, an uncommonly agreeable business, culminating fitly enough in his engagement to the only girl he had ever wished to marry, and the inheritance, from his unhappy step-brother, of a fortune which agreeably widened his horizon. Such a combination of circumstances might well justify a young man in thinking himself of some account in the universe; and it seemed the final touch of fitness that the mourning which Denis still wore for poor Arthur should lend a new distinction to his somewhat florid good looks.

Kate Orme was not without an amused perception of her future husband's point of view; but she could enter into it with the tolerance which allows for the inconscient element in all our judgments. There was, for instance, no one more sentimentally humane than Denis's mother, the second Mrs. Peyton, a scented silvery person whose lavender silks and neutral-tinted manner expressed a mind with its blinds drawn down toward all the unpleasantness of life; yet it was clear that Mrs. Peyton saw a "dispensation" in the fact that her step-son had never married, and that his death had enabled Denis, at the right moment, to step gracefully into affluence. Was it not, after all, a sign of healthy-mindedness to take the gifts of the gods in this religious spirit, discovering fresh evidence of "design" in what had once seemed the sad fact of Arthur's inaccessibility to correction? Mrs. Peyton, beautifully conscious of having done her "best" for Arthur, would have thought it unchristian to repine at the providential failure of her efforts. Denis's deductions were, of course, a little less direct than his mother's. He had, besides, been fond of Arthur, and his efforts to keep the poor fellow straight had been less didactic and more spontaneous. Their result read itself, if not in any change in Arthur's character, at least in the revised wording of his will; and Denis's moral sense was pleasantly fortified by the discovery that it very substantially paid to be a good fellow.

The sense of general providentialness on which Mrs. Peyton reposed had in fact been confirmed by events which reduced Denis's mourning to a mere tribute of respect—since it would have been a mockery to deplore the disappearance of anyone who had left behind him such an unsavory wake as poor Arthur. Kate did not quite know what had happened: her father was as firmly convinced as Mrs. Peyton that young girls should not be admitted to any open discussion of life. She could only gather, from the silences and evasions amid which she moved, that a woman had turned up—a woman who was of course "dreadful," and whose dreadfulness appeared to include a sort of shadowy claim upon Arthur. But the claim, whatever it was, had been promptly discredited. The whole question had vanished and the woman with it. The blinds were drawn again on the ugly side of things, and life was resumed on the usual assumption that no such side existed. Kate knew only that a darkness had crossed her sky and left it as unclouded as before.

Was it, perhaps, she now asked herself, the very lifting of the cloud—remote, unthreatening as it had been—which gave such new serenity to her heaven? It was horrible to think that one's deepest security was a mere sense of escape—that happiness was no more than a reprieve. The perversity of such ideas was emphasized by Peyton's approach. He had the gift of restoring things to their normal relations, of carrying one over the chasms of life through the closed tunnel of an incurious cheerfulness. All that was restless and questioning in the girl subsided in his presence, and she was content to take her love as a gift of grace, which began just where the office of reason ended. She was more than ever, today, in this mood of charmed surrender. More than ever he seemed the keynote of the accord between herself and life, the centre of a delightful complicity in every surrounding circumstance. One could not look at him without seeing that there was always a fair wind in his sails.

It was carrying him toward her, as usual, at a quick confident pace, which nevertheless lagged a little, she noticed, as he emerged from the beech-grove and struck across the lawn. He walked as though he were tired. She had meant to wait for him on the terrace, held in check by her usual inclination to linger on the threshold of her pleasures; but now something drew her toward him, and she went quickly down the steps and across the lawn.

"Denis, you look tired. I was afraid something had happened."

She had slipped her hand through his arm, and as they moved forward she glanced up at him, struck not so much by any new look in his face as by the fact that her approach had made no change in it.

"I am rather tired.—Is your father in?"

"Papa?" She looked up in surprise. "He went to town yesterday. Don't you remember?"

"Of course—I'd forgotten. You're alone, then?" She dropped his arm and stood before him. He was very pale now, with the furrowed look of extreme physical weariness.

"Denis—are you ill? *Has* anything happened?"

He forced a smile. "Yes—but you needn't look so frightened."

She drew a deep breath of reassurance. *He* was safe, after all! And all else, for a moment, seemed to swing below the rim of her world.

"Your mother—?" she then said, with a fresh start of fear.

"It's not my mother." They had reached the terrace, and he moved toward the house. "Let us go indoors. There's such a beastly glare out here."

He seemed to find relief in the cool obscurity of the drawing-room, where, after the brightness of the afternoon light, their faces were almost indistinguishable to each other. She sat down, and he moved a few paces away. Before the writing-table he paused to look at the neatly sorted heaps of wedding-cards.

"They are to be sent out to-morrow?"

"Yes."

He turned back and stood before her.

"It's about the woman," he began abruptly—"the woman who pretended to be Arthur's wife."

Kate started as at the clutch of an unacknowledged fear.

"She *was* his wife, then?"

Peyton made an impatient movement of negation. "If she was, why didn't she prove it? She hadn't a shred of evidence. The courts rejected her appeal."

"Well, then—?"

"Well, she's dead." He paused, and the next words came with difficulty. "She and the child."

"The child? There was a child?"

"Yes."

Kate started up and then sank down. These were not things about which young girls were told. The confused sense of horror had been nothing to this first sharp edge of fact.

"And both are dead?"

"Yes."

"How do you know? My father said she had gone away—gone back to the West—"

"So we thought. But this morning we found her."

"Found her?"

He motioned toward the window. "Out there—in the lake."

"Both?"

"Both."

She drooped before him shudderingly, her eyes hidden, as though to exclude the vision. "She had drowned herself?"

"Yes."

"Oh, poor thing—poor thing!"

They paused awhile, the minutes delving an abyss between them till he threw a few irrelevant words across the silence.

"One of the gardeners found them."

"Poor thing!"

"It was sufficiently horrible."

"Horrible—oh!" She had swung round again to her pole. "Poor Denis! *You* were not there—*you* didn't have to—?"

"I had to see her." She felt the instant relief in his voice. He could talk now, could distend his nerves in the warm air of her sympathy. "I had to identify her." He rose nervously and began to pace the room. "It's knocked the wind out of me. I—my God!

I couldn't foresee it, could I?" He halted before her with out-stretched hands of argument. "I did all I could—it's not *my* fault, is it?"

"Your fault? Denis!"

"She wouldn't take the money—" He broke off, checked by her awakened glance.

"The money? What money?" Her face changed, hardening as his relaxed. "Had you offered her *money* to give up the case?"

He stared a moment, and then dismissed the implication with a laugh.

"No—no; after the case was decided against her. She seemed hard up, and I sent Hinton to her with a cheque."

"And she refused it?"

"Yes."

"What did she say?"

"Oh, I don't know—the usual thing. That she'd only wanted to prove she was his wife—on the child's account. That she'd never wanted his money. Hinton said she was very quiet—not in the least excited—but she sent back the cheque."

Kate sat motionless, her head bent, her hands clasped about her knees. She no longer looked at Peyton.

"Could there have been a mistake?" she asked slowly.

"A mistake?"

She raised her head now, and fixed her eyes on his, with a strange insistence of observation. "Could they have been married?"

"The courts didn't think so."

"Could the courts have been mistaken?"

He started up again, and threw himself into another chair. "Good God, Kate! We gave her every chance to prove her case—why didn't she do it? You don't know what you're talking about —such things are kept from girls. Why, whenever a man of Arthur's kind dies, such—such women turn up. There are lawyers who live on such jobs—ask your father about it. Of course, this woman expected to be bought off—"

"But if she wouldn't take your money?"

"She expected a big sum, I mean, to drop the case. When she found we meant to fight it, she saw the game was up. I suppose it was her last throw, and she was desperate; we don't know how many times she may have been through the same thing before. That kind of woman is always trying to make money out of the heirs of any man who—who has been about with them."

Kate received this in silence. She had a sense of walking along a narrow ledge of consciousness above a sheer hallucinating depth into which she dared not look. But the depth drew her, and she plunged one terrified glance into it.

"But the child—the child was Arthur's?"

Peyton shrugged his shoulders. "There again—how can we tell? Why, I don't suppose the woman herself—I wish to heaven your father were here to explain!"

She rose and crossed over to him, laying her hands on his shoulders with a gesture almost maternal.

"Don't let us talk of it," she said. "You did all you could. Think what a comfort you were to poor Arthur."

He let her hands lie where she had placed them, without response or resistance.

"I tried—I tried hard to keep him straight!"

"We all know that—everyone knows it. And we know how grateful he was—what a difference it made to him in the end. It would have been dreadful to think of his dying out there alone."

She drew him down on a sofa and seated herself by his side. A deep lassitude was upon him, and the hand she had possessed herself of lay in her hold inert.

"It was splendid of you to travel day and night as you did. And then that dreadful week before he died! But for you he would have died alone among strangers."

He sat silent, his head dropping forward, his eyes fixed. "Among strangers," he repeated absently.

She looked up, as if struck by a sudden thought. "That poor woman—did you ever see her while you were out there?"

He drew his hand away and gathered his brows together as if in an effort of remembrance.

"I saw her—oh, yes, I saw her." He pushed the tumbled hair from his forehead and stood up. "Let us go out," he said. "My head is in a fog. I want to get away from it all."

A wave of compunction drew her to her feet.

"It was my fault! I ought not to have asked so many questions." She turned and rang the bell. "I'll order the ponies—we shall have time for a drive before sunset."

※ II ※

WITH the sunset in their faces they swept through the keen-scented autumn air at the swiftest pace of Kate's ponies. She had given the reins to Peyton, and he had turned the horses' heads away from the lake, rising by woody upland lanes to the high pastures which still held the sunlight. The horses were fresh enough to claim his undivided attention, and he drove in silence, his smooth fair profile turned to his companion, who sat silent also.

Kate Orme was engaged in one of those rapid mental excursions which were forever sweeping her from the straight path of the actual into uncharted regions of conjecture. Her survey of life had always been marked by the tendency to seek out ultimate relations, to extend her researches to the limit of her imaginative experience. But hitherto she had been like some young captive brought up in a windowless palace whose painted walls she takes for the actual world. Now the palace had been shaken to its base, and through a cleft in the walls she looked out upon life. For the first moment all was indistinguishable blackness; then she began to detect vague shapes and confused gestures in the depths. There were people below there, men like Denis, girls like herself—for under the unlikeness she felt the strange affinity

—all struggling in that awful coil of moral darkness, with agonized hands reaching up for rescue. Her heart shrank from the horror of it, and then, in a passion of pity, drew back to the edge of the abyss. Suddenly her eyes turned toward Denis. His face was grave, but less disturbed. And men knew about these things! They carried this abyss in their bosoms, and went about smiling, and sat at the feet of innocence. Could it be that Denis—Denis even—Ah, no! She remembered what he had been to poor Arthur; she understood, now, the vague allusions to what he had tried to do for his brother. He had seen Arthur down there, in that coiling blackness, and had leaned over and tried to drag him out. But Arthur was too deep down, and his arms were interlocked with other arms—they had dragged each other deeper, poor souls, like drowning people who fight together in the waves! Kate's visualizing habit gave a hateful precision and persistency to the image she had evoked—she could not rid herself of the vision of anguished shapes striving together in the darkness. The horror of it took her by the throat—she drew a choking breath, and felt the tears on her face.

Peyton turned to her. The horses were climbing a hill, and his attention had strayed from them.

"This has done me good," he began; but as he looked his voice changed. "Kate! What is it? Why are you crying? Oh, for God's sake, *don't!*" he ended, his hand closing on her wrist.

She steadied herself and raised her eyes to his.

"I—I couldn't help it," she stammered, struggling in the sudden release of her pent compassion. "It seems so awful that we should stand so close to this horror—that it might have been you who—"

"I who—what on earth do you mean?" he broke in stridently.

"Oh, don't you see? I found myself exulting that you and I were so far from it—above it—safe in ourselves and each other— and then the other feeling came—the sense of selfishness, of going by on the other side; and I tried to realize that it might

have been you and I who—who were down there in the night
and the flood—"

Peyton let the whip fall on the ponies' flanks. "Upon my
soul," he said with a laugh, "you must have a nice opinion of
both of us."

The words fell chillingly on the blaze of her self-immolation.
Would she never learn to remember that Denis was incapable of
mounting such hypothetical pyres? He might be as alive as herself to the direct demands of duty, but of its imaginative claims
he was robustly unconscious. The thought brought a wholesome
reaction of thankfulness.

"Ah, well," she said, the sunset dilating through her tears,
"don't you see that I can bear to think such things only because
they're impossibilities? It's easy to look over into the depths if
one has a rampart to lean on. What I most pity poor Arthur for is
that, instead of that woman lying there, so dreadfully dead, there
might have been a girl like me, so exquisitely alive because of
him; but it seems cruel, doesn't it, to let what he was *not* add
ever so little to the value of what you are? To let him contribute
ever so little to my happiness by the difference there is between
you?"

She was conscious, as she spoke, of straying again beyond
his reach, through intricacies of sensation new even to her exploring susceptibilities. A happy literalness usually enabled him
to strike a short cut through such labyrinths, and rejoin her smiling on the other side; but now she became wonderingly aware
that he had been caught in the thick of her hypothesis.

"It's the difference that makes you care for me, then?" he
broke out, with a kind of violence which seemed to renew his
clutch on her wrist.

"The difference?"

He lashed the ponies again, so sharply that a murmur escaped her, and he drew them up, quivering, with an
inconsequent "Steady, boys," at which their back-laid ears protested.

"It's because I'm moral and respectable, and all that, that you're fond of me," he went on; "you're—you're simply in love with my virtues. You couldn't imagine caring if I were down there in the ditch, as you say, with Arthur?"

The question fell on a silence which seemed to deepen suddenly within herself. Every thought hung bated on the sense that something was coming: her whole consciousness became a void to receive it.

"Denis!" she cried.

He turned on her almost savagely. "I don't want your pity, you know," he burst out. "You can keep that for Arthur. I had an idea women loved men for themselves—through everything, I mean. But I wouldn't steal your love—I don't want it on false pretenses, you understand. Go and look into other men's lives, that's all I ask of you. I slipped into it—it was just a case of holding my tongue when I ought to have spoken—but I—I—for God's sake, don't sit there staring! I suppose you've seen all along that I knew he was married to the woman."

※ III ※

THE housekeeper's reminding her that Mr. Orme would be at home the next day for dinner, and did she think he would like the venison with claret sauce or jelly, roused Kate to the first consciousness of her surroundings. Her father would return on the morrow: he would give to the dressing of the venison such minute consideration as, in his opinion, every detail affecting his comfort or convenience quite obviously merited. And if it were not the venison it would be something else; if it were not the housekeeper it would be Mr. Orme, charged with the results of a conference with his agent, a committee-meeting at his club, or any of the other incidents which, by happening to himself, became events. Kate found herself caught in the inexorable continuity of life, found herself gazing over a scene of ruin lit up by the punctual recurrence of habit as nature's calm stare lights the morrow of a whirlwind.

Life was going on, then, and dragging her at its wheels. She could neither check its rush nor wrench loose from it and drop out—oh, how blessedly—into darkness and cessation. She must go bounding on, racked, broken, but alive in every fibre. The most she could hope was a few hours' respite, not from her own terrors, but from the pressure of outward claims: the midday halt, during which the victim is unbound while his torturers rest from their efforts. Till her father's return she would have the house to herself, and, the question of the venison despatched, could give herself to long lonely pacings of the empty rooms, and shuddering subsidences upon her pillow.

Her first impulse, as the mist cleared from her brain, was the habitual one of reaching out for ultimate relations. She wanted to know the worst; and for her, as she saw in a flash, the worst of it was the core of fatality in what had happened. She shrank from her own way of putting it—nor was it even figuratively true that she had ever felt, under faith in Denis, any such doubt as the perception implied. But that was merely because her imagination had never put him to the test. She was fond of exposing herself to hypothetical ordeals, but somehow she had never carried Denis with her on these adventures. What she saw now was that, in a world of strangeness, he remained the object least strange to her. She was not in the tragic case of the girl who suddenly sees her lover unmasked. No mask had dropped from Denis's face: the pink shades had simply been lifted from the lamps, and she saw him for the first time in an unmitigated glare.

Such exposure does not alter the features, but it lays an ugly emphasis on the most charming lines, pushing the smile to a grin, the curve of good-nature to the droop of slackness. And it was precisely into the flagging lines of extreme weakness that Denis's graceful contour flowed. In the terrible talk which had followed his avowal, and wherein every word flashed a light on his moral processes, she had been less startled by what he had done than by the way in which his conscience had already become a passive surface for the channelling of consequences. He was like a child who had put a match to the curtains, and stands agape at the blaze. It was horribly naughty to put the match—but beyond that the child's responsibility did not extend. In this business of Arthur's, where all had been wrong from the beginning—where self-defence might well find a plea for its casuistries in the absence of a definite right to be measured by—it had been easy, after the first slip, to drop a little lower with each struggle. The woman—oh, the woman was—well, of the kind who prey on such men. Arthur, out there, at his lowest ebb, had drifted into living with her as a man drifts into drink or opium. He knew what she was—he knew where she had come from. But he had fallen ill, and she had nursed him—nursed him devotedly, of course. That was her chance, and she knew it. Before he was out of the fever she had the noose around him—he came to and found himself married. Such cases were common enough—if the man recovered he bought off the woman and got a divorce. It was all a part of the business—the marriage, the bribe, the divorce. Some of those women made a big income out of it—they were married and divorced once a year. If Arthur had only got well—but, instead, he had a relapse and died. And there was the woman, made his widow by mischance as it were, with her child on her arm—whose child?—and a scoundrelly blackmailing lawyer to work up her case for her. Her claim was clear enough—the right of dower, a third of his estate. But if he had never meant to marry her? If he had been trapped as patently as a rustic fleeced in a gambling-hell? Arthur, in his last hours, had confessed to the marriage, but had also acknowledged its folly. And after his death, when Denis came to look about him and make inquiries, he found that the witnesses, if there had been any, were dispersed and undiscoverable. The whole question hinged on Arthur's statement to his brother. Suppress that statement, and the claim vanished, and with it the scandal, the humiliation, the life-long burden of the woman and child dragging the name of Peyton through heaven knew what depths. He had thought of that first, Denis swore, rather than of the money. The money, of course, had made a difference,—he was too honest not to own it —but not till afterward, he declared—would have declared on his honour, but that the word tripped him up, and sent a flush to his forehead.

Thus, in broken phrases, he flung his defence at her: a defence improvised, pieced together as he went along, to mask the crude instinctiveness of his act. For with increasing clearness Kate saw, as she listened, that there had been no real struggle in his mind; that, but for the grim logic of chance, he might never have felt the need of any justification. If the woman, after the manner of such baffled huntresses, had wandered off in search of fresh prey, he might, quite sincerely, have congratulated himself on having saved a decent name and an honest fortune from her talons. It was the price she had paid to establish her claim that for the first time brought him to a startled sense of its justice. His conscience responded only to the concrete pressure of facts.

It was with the anguish of this discovery that Kate Orme locked herself in at the end of their talk. How the talk had ended, how at length she had got him from the room and the house, she recalled but confusedly. The tragedy of the woman's death, and of his own share in it, were as nothing in the disaster of his bright irreclaimableness. Once, when she had cried out, "You would have married me and said nothing," and he groaned back, "But I *have* told you," she felt like a trainer with a lash above some bewildered animal.

But she persisted savagely. "You told me because you had to; because your nerves gave way; because you knew it couldn't hurt you to tell." The perplexed appeal of his gaze had almost checked her. "You told me because it was a relief; but nothing will really relieve you—nothing will really help you—till you have told someone who—who *will* hurt you."

"Who will hurt me—?"

"Till you have told the truth as—as openly as you lied."

He started up, ghastly with fear. "I don't understand you."

"You must confess, then—publicly—openly—you must go to the judge. I don't know how it's done."

"To the judge? When they're both dead? When everything is at an end? What good could that do?" he groaned.

"Everything is not at an end for you—everything is just beginning. You must clear yourself of this guilt; and there is only one way—to confess it. And you must give back the money."

This seemed to strike him as conclusive proof of her irrelevance. "I wish I had never heard of the money! But to whom would you have me give it back? I tell you she was a waif out of the gutter. I don't believe any one knew her real name—I don't believe she had one."

"She must have had a mother and father."

"Am I to devote my life to hunting for them through the slums of California? And how shall I know when I have found them? It's impossible to make you understand. I did wrong—I did horribly wrong—but that is not the way to repair it."

"What is, then?"

He paused, a little askance at the question. "To do better—to do my best," he said, with a sudden flourish of firmness. "To take warning by this dreadful—"

"Oh, be silent," she cried out, and hid her face. He looked at her hopelessly.

At last he said: "I don't know what good it can do to go on talking. I have only one more thing to say. Of course you know that you are free."

He spoke simply, with a sudden return to his old voice and accent, at which she weakened as under a caress. She lifted her head and gazed at him. "Am I?" she said musingly.

"Kate!" burst from him; but she raised a silencing hand.

"It seems to me," she said, "that I am imprisoned—imprisoned with you in this dreadful thing. First I must help you to get out—then it will be time enough to think of myself."

His face fell and he stammered: "I don't understand you."

"I can't say what I shall do—or how I shall feel—till I know what you are going to do and feel."

"You must see how I feel—that I'm half dead with it."

"Yes—but that is only half."

He turned this over for a perceptible space of time before asking slowly: "You mean that you'll give me up, if I don't do this crazy thing you propose?"

She paused in turn. "No," she said; "I don't want to bribe you. You must feel the need of it yourself."

"The need of proclaiming this thing publicly?"

"Yes."

He sat staring before him. "Of course you realize what it would mean?" he began at length.

"To you?" she returned.

"I put that aside. To others—to you. I should go to prison."

"I suppose so," she said simply.

"You seem to take it very easily—I'm afraid my mother wouldn't."

"Your mother?" This produced the effect he had expected.

"You hadn't thought of her, I suppose? It would probably kill her.

"It would have killed her to think that you could do what you have done!"

"It would have made her very unhappy; but there's a difference."

Yes: there was a difference; a difference which no rhetoric could disguise. The secret sin would have made Mrs. Peyton wretched, but it would not have killed her. And she would have taken precisely Denis's view of the elasticity of atonement: she would have accepted private regrets as the genteel equivalent of open expiation. Kate could even imagine her extracting a "lesson" from the providential fact that her son had not been found out.

"You see it's not so simple," he broke out, with a tinge of doleful triumph.

"No: it's not simple," she assented.

"One must think of others," he continued, gathering faith in his argument as he saw her reduced to acquiescence.

She made no answer, and after a moment he rose to go. So far, in retrospect, she could follow the course of their talk; but when, in the act of parting, argument lapsed into entreaty, and renunciation into the passionate appeal to give him at least one more hearing, her memory lost itself in a tumult of pain, and she recalled only that, when the door closed on him, he took with him her promise to see him once again.

※ IV ※

She had promised to see him again; but the promise did not imply that she had rejected his offer of freedom. In the first rush of misery she had not fully repossessed herself, had felt herself entangled in his fate by a hundred meshes of association and habit; but after a sleepless night spent with the thought of him— that dreadful bridal of their souls—she woke to a morrow in which he had no part. She had not sought her freedom, nor had he given it; but a chasm had opened at their feet, and they found themselves on different sides.

Now she was able to scan the disaster from the melancholy vantage of her independence. She could even draw a solace from the fact that she had ceased to love Denis. It was inconceivable that an emotion so interwoven with every fibre of consciousness should cease as suddenly as the flow of sap in an uprooted plant; but she had never allowed herself to be tricked by the current phraseology of sentiment, and there were no stock axioms to protect her from the truth.

It was probably because she had ceased to love him that she could look forward with a kind of ghastly composure to seeing him again. She had stipulated, of course, that the wedding should be put off, but she had named no other condition beyond asking for two days to herself—two days during which he was not even to write. She wished to shut herself in with her misery, to accustom herself to it as she had accustomed herself to happiness. But actual seclusion was impossible: the subtle reactions of life almost at once began to break down her defences. She could no more have her wretchedness to herself than any other emotion: all the lives about her were so many unconscious factors in her sensations. She tried to concentrate herself on the thought as to how she could best help poor Denis; for love, in ebbing, had laid bare an unsuspected depth of pity. But she found it more and more difficult to consider his situation in the abstract light of right and wrong. Open expiation still seemed to her the only possible way of healing; but she tried vainly to think of Mrs. Peyton as taking such a view. Yet Mrs. Peyton ought at least to know what had happened: was it not, in the last resort, she who should pronounce on her son's course? For a moment Kate was fascinated by this evasion of responsibility; she had nearly decided to tell Denis that he must begin by confessing everything to his mother. But almost at once she began to shrink from the consequences. There was nothing she so dreaded for him as that anyone should take a light view of his act: should turn its irremediableness into an excuse. And this, she foresaw, was what Mrs. Peyton would do. The first burst of misery over, she would envelop the whole situation in a mist of expediency. Brought to the bar of Kate's judgment, she at once revealed herself incapable of higher action.

Kate's conception of her was still under arraignment when the actual Mrs. Peyton fluttered in. It was the afternoon of the second day, as the girl phrased it in the dismal re-creation of her universe. She had been thinking so hard of Mrs. Peyton that the lady's silvery insubstantial presence seemed hardly more than a projection of the thought; but as Kate collected herself, and regained contact with the outer world, her preoccupation yielded to surprise. It was unusual for Mrs. Peyton to pay visits. For years she had remained enthroned in a semi-invalidism which prohibited effort while it did not preclude diversion; and the girl at once divined a special purpose in her coming.

Mrs. Peyton's traditions would not have permitted any direct method of attack; and Kate had to sit through the usual prelude of ejaculation and anecdote. Presently, however, the elder lady's voice gathered significance, and laying her hand on Kate's she murmured: "I have come to talk to you of this sad affair."

Kate began to tremble. Was it possible that Denis had after all spoken? A rising hope checked her utterance, and she saw in a flash that it still lay with him to regain his hold on her. But Mrs. Peyton went on delicately: "It has been a great shock to my poor boy. To be brought in contact with Arthur's past was in itself inexpressibly painful; but this last dreadful business—that woman's wicked act—"

"Wicked?" Kate exclaimed.

Mrs. Peyton's gentle stare reproved her. "Surely religion teaches us that suicide is a sin? And to murder her child! I ought not to speak to you of such things, my dear. No one has ever mentioned anything so dreadful in my presence: my dear husband used to screen me so carefully from the painful side of life. Where there is so much that is beautiful to dwell upon, we should try to ignore the existence of such horrors. But nowadays everything is in the papers; and Denis told me he thought it better that you should hear the news first from him."

Kate nodded without speaking.

"He felt how *dreadful* it was to have to tell you. But I tell him he takes a morbid view of the case. Of course one is shocked at the woman's crime—but, if one looks a little deeper, how can one help seeing that it may have been designed as the means of rescuing that poor child from a life of vice and misery? That is the view I want Denis to take: I want him to see how all the difficulties of life disappear when one has learned to look for a divine purpose in human sufferings."

Mrs. Peyton rested a moment on this period, as an

experienced climber pauses to be overtaken by a less agile companion; but presently she became aware that Kate was still far below her, and perhaps needed a stronger incentive to the ascent.

"My dear child," she said adroitly, "I said just now that I was sorry you had been obliged to hear of this sad affair; but after all it is only you who can avert its consequences."

Kate drew an eager breath. "Its consequences?" she faltered.

Mrs. Peyton's voice dropped solemnly. "Denis has told me everything," she said.

"Everything?"

"That you insist on putting off the marriage. Oh, my dear, I do implore you to reconsider that!"

Kate sank back with the sense of having passed again into a region of leaden shadow. "Is that all he told you?"

Mrs. Peyton gazed at her with arch raillery. "All? Isn't it everything—to him?"

"Did he give you my reason, I mean?"

"He said you felt that, after this shocking tragedy, there ought, in decency, to be a delay; and I quite understand the feeling. It does seem too unfortunate that the woman should have chosen this particular time! But you will find as you grow older that life is full of such sad contrasts."

Kate felt herself slowly petrifying under the warm drip of Mrs. Peyton's platitudes.

"It seems to me," the elder lady continued, "that there is only one point from which we ought to consider the question—and that is, its effect on Denis. But for that we ought to refuse to know anything about it. But it has made my boy so unhappy. The law-suit was a cruel ordeal to him—the dreadful notoriety, the revelation of poor Arthur's infirmities. Denis is as sensitive as a woman; it is his unusual refinement of feeling that makes him so worthy of being loved by you. But such sensitiveness may be carried to excess. He ought not to let this unhappy incident prey on him: it shows a lack of trust in the divine ordering of things.

That is what troubles me: his faith in life has been shaken. And —you must forgive me, dear child—you *will* forgive me, I know— but I can't help blaming you a little—"

Mrs. Peyton's accent converted the accusation into a caress, which prolonged itself in a tremulous pressure of Kate's hand.

The girl gazed at her blankly. "You blame *me*——?"

"Don't be offended, my child. I only fear that your excessive sympathy with Denis, your own delicacy of feeling, may have led you to encourage his morbid ideas. He tells me you were very much shocked—as you naturally would be—as any girl must be —I would not have you otherwise, dear Kate! It is *beautiful* that you should both feel so; most beautiful; but you know religion teaches us not to yield too much to our grief. Let the dead bury their dead; the living owe themselves to each other. And what had this wretched woman to do with either of you? It is a misfortune for Denis to have been connected in any way with a man of Arthur Peyton's character; but after all, poor Arthur did all he could to atone for the disgrace he brought on us, by making Denis his heir—and I am sure I have no wish to question the decrees of Providence." Mrs. Peyton paused again, and then softly absorbed both of Kate's hands. "For my part," she continued, "I see in it another instance of the beautiful ordering of events. Just after dear Denis's inheritance has removed the last obstacle to your marriage, this sad incident comes to show how desperately he needs you, how cruel it would be to ask him to defer his happiness."

She broke off, shaken out of her habitual placidity by the abrupt withdrawal of the girl's hands. Kate sat inertly staring, but no answer rose to her lips.

At length Mrs. Peyton resumed, gathering her draperies about her with a tentative hint of leave-taking: "I may go home and tell him that you will not put off the wedding?"

Kate was still silent, and her visitor looked at her with the mild surprise of an advocate unaccustomed to plead in vain.

"If your silence means refusal, my dear, I think you ought to realize the responsibility you assume." Mrs. Peyton's voice had acquired an edge of righteous asperity. "If Denis has a fault it is that he is too gentle, too yielding, too readily influenced by those he cares for. Your influence is paramount with him now—but if you turn from him just when he needs your help, who can say what the result will be?"

The argument, though impressively delivered, was hardly of a nature to carry conviction to its hearer; but it was perhaps for that very reason that she suddenly and unexpectedly replied to it by sinking back into her seat with a burst of tears. To Mrs. Peyton, however, tears were the signal of surrender, and, at Kate's side in an instant she hastened to temper her triumph with magnanimity.

"Don't think I don't feel with you; but we must both forget ourselves for our boy's sake. I told him I should come back with your promise."

The arm she had slipped about Kate's shoulder fell back with the girl's start. Kate had seen in a flash what capital would be made of her emotion.

"No, no, you misunderstand me. I can make no promise," she declared.

The older lady sat a moment irresolute; then she restored her arm to the shoulder from which it had been so abruptly displaced.

"My dear child," she said, in a tone of tender confidence, "if I have misunderstood you, ought you not to enlighten me? You asked me just now if Denis had given me your reason for this strange postponement. He gave me one reason, but it seems hardly sufficient to explain your conduct. If there is any other,—and I know you well enough to feel sure there is,—will you not trust me with it? If my boy has been unhappy enough to displease you, will you not give his mother the chance to plead his cause? Remember, no one should be condemned unheard. As Denis's mother, I have the right to ask for your reason."

"My reason? My reason?" Kate stammered, panting with the

exhaustion of the struggle. Oh, if only Mrs. Peyton would release her! "If you have the right to know it, why doesn't he tell you?" she cried.

Mrs. Peyton stood up, quivering. "I will go home and ask him," she said. "I will tell him he had your permission to speak."

She moved toward the door, with the nervous haste of a person unaccustomed to decisive action. But Kate sprang before her.

"No, no; don't ask him! I implore you not to ask him," she cried.

Mrs. Peyton turned on her with sudden authority of voice and gesture. "Do I understand you?" she said. "You admit that you have a reason for putting off your marriage, and yet you forbid me—me, Denis's mother—to ask him what it is? My poor child, I needn't ask, for I know already. If he has offended you, and you refuse him the chance to defend himself, I needn't look farther for your reason: it is simply that you have ceased to love him."

Kate fell back from the door which she had instinctively barricaded.

"Perhaps that is it," she murmured, letting Mrs. Peyton pass.

❈ V ❈

Mr. Orme's returning carriage-wheels crossed Mrs. Peyton's indignant flight; and an hour later Kate, in the bland candle-light of the dinner-hour, sat listening with practised fortitude to her father's comments on the venison.

She had wondered, as she awaited him in the drawing-room, if he would notice any change in her appearance. It seemed to her that the flagellation of her thoughts must have left visible traces. But Mr. Orme was not a man of subtle perceptions, save where his personal comfort was affected: though his egoism was clothed in the finest feelers, he did not suspect a similar surface in others. His daughter, as part of himself, came within the normal range of his solicitude; but she was an outlying region, a subject province; and Mr. Orme's was a highly centralized polity.

News of the painful incident—he often used Mrs. Peyton's vocabulary—had reached him at his club, and to some extent disturbed the assimilation of a carefully ordered breakfast; but since then two days had passed, and it did not take Mr. Orme forty-eight hours to resign himself to the misfortunes of others. It was all very nasty, of course, and he wished to heaven it hadn't happened to anyone about to be connected with him; but he viewed it with the transient annoyance of a gentleman who has been splashed by the mud of a fatal runaway.

Mr. Orme affected, under such circumstances, a bluff and hearty stoicism as remote as possible from Mrs. Peyton's deprecating evasion of facts. It was a bad business; he was sorry Kate should have been mixed up with it; but she would be married soon now, and then she would see that life wasn't exactly a Sunday-school story. Everybody was exposed to such disagreeable accidents: he remembered a case in their own family—oh, a distant cousin whom Kate wouldn't have heard of—a poor fellow who had got entangled with just such a woman, and having (most properly) been sent packing by his father, had justified the latter's course by promptly forging his name—a very nasty affair altogether; but luckily the scandal had been hushed up, the woman bought off, and the prodigal, after a season of probation, safely married to a nice girl with a good income, who was told by the family that the doctors recommended his settling in California.

Luckily the scandal was hushed up: the phrase blazed out against the dark background of Kate's misery. That was doubtless what most people felt—the words represented the consensus of respectable opinion. The best way of repairing a fault was to hide it: to tear up the floor and bury the victim at night. Above all, no coroner and no autopsy!

She began to feel a strange interest in her distant cousin. "And his wife—did she know what he had done?"

Mr. Orme stared. His moral pointed, he had returned to the contemplation of his own affairs.

"His wife? Oh, of course not. The secret has been most admirably kept; but her property was put in trust, so she's quite safe with him."

Her property! Kate wondered if her faith in her husband had also been put in trust, if her sensibilities had been protected from his possible inroads.

"Do you think it quite fair to have deceived her in that way?"

Mr. Orme gave her a puzzled glance: he had no taste for the by-paths of ethical conjecture.

"His people wanted to give the poor fellow another chance; they did the best they could for him."

"And—he has done nothing dishonourable since?"

"Not that I know of: the last I heard was that they had a little boy, and that he was quite happy. At that distance he's not likely to bother *us*, at all events."

Long after Mr. Orme had left the topic, Kate remained lost in its contemplation. She had begun to perceive that the fair surface of life was honeycombed by a vast system of moral sewage. Every respectable household had its special arrangements for the private disposal of family scandals; it was only among the reckless and improvident that such hygienic precautions were neglected. Who was she to pass judgment on the merits of such a system? The social health must be preserved: the means devised were the result of long experience and the collective instinct of self-preservation. She had meant to tell her father that evening that her marriage had been put off; but she now abstained from doing so, not from any doubt of Mr. Orme's acquiescence—he could always be made to feel the force of conventional scruples —but because the whole question sank into insignificance beside the larger issue which his words had raised.

In her own room, that night, she passed through that travail of the soul of which the deeper life is born. Her first sense was of a great moral loneliness—an isolation more complete, more impenetrable, than that in which the discovery of Denis's act had plunged her. For she had vaguely leaned, then, on a collective sense of justice that should respond to her own ideas of right and wrong: she still believed in the logical correspondence of theory and practice. Now she saw that, among those nearest her, there was no one who recognized the moral need of expiation. She saw that to take her father or Mrs. Peyton into her confidence would be but to widen the circle of sterile misery in which she and Denis moved. At first the aspect of life thus revealed to her seemed simply mean and base—a world where honour was a pact of silence between adroit accomplices. The network of circumstance had tightened round her, and every effort to escape drew its meshes closer. But as her struggles subsided she felt the spiritual release which comes with acceptance: not connivance in dishonour, but recognition of evil. Out of that dark vision light was to come, the shaft of cloud turning to the pillar of fire. For here, at last, life lay before her as it was: not brave, garlanded and victorious, but naked, grovelling and diseased, dragging its maimed limbs through the mud, yet lifting piteous hands to the stars. Love itself, once throned aloft on an altar of dreams, how it stole to her now, storm-beaten and scarred, pleading for the shelter of her breast! Love, indeed, not in the old sense in which she had conceived it, but a graver, austerer presence—the charity of the mystic three. She thought she had ceased to love Denis—but what had she loved in him but her happiness and his? Their affection had been the *garden enclosed* of the Canticles, where they were to walk forever in a delicate isolation of bliss. But now love appeared to her as something more than this—something wider, deeper, more enduring than the selfish passion of a man and a woman. She saw it in all its far-reaching issues, till the first meeting of two pairs of young eyes kindled a light which might be a high-lifted beacon across dark waters of humanity.

All of this did not come to her clearly, consecutively, but in a series of blurred and shifting images. Marriage had meant to her, as it means to girls brought up in ignorance of life, simply the exquisite prolongation of wooing. If she had looked beyond, to the vision of wider ties, it was as a traveller gazes over a land veiled in golden haze, and so far distant that the imagination delays to explore it. But now through the blur of sensations one image strangely persisted—the image of Denis's child. Had she ever before thought of their having a child? She could not remember. She was like one who wakens from a long fever: she recalled nothing of her former self or of her former feelings. She knew only that the vision persisted—the vision of the child whose mother she was not to be. It was impossible that she should marry Denis—her inmost soul rejected him . . . but it was just because she was not to be the child's mother that its image followed her so pleadingly. For she saw with perfect clearness the inevitable course of events. Denis would marry someone else—he was one of the men who are fated to marry, and she needed not his mother's reminder that her abandonment of him at an emotional crisis would fling him upon the first sympathy within reach. He would marry a girl who knew nothing of his secret—for Kate was intensely aware that he would never again willingly confess himself—he would marry a girl who trusted him and leaned on him, as she, Kate Orme—the earlier Kate Orme—had done but two days since! And with this deception between them their child would be born: born to an inheritance of secret weakness, a vice of the moral fibre, as it might be born with some hidden physical taint which would destroy it before the cause should be detected. . . . Well, and what of it? Was she to hold herself responsible? Were not thousands of children born with some such unsuspected taint? . . . Ah, but if here was one that she could save? What if she, who had had so exquisite a vision of wifehood, should reconstruct from its ruins this vision of protecting maternity—if her love for her lover should be, not lost, but transformed, enlarged, into this passion of charity for his race? If she might expiate and redeem his fault by becoming a refuge from its consequences? Before this strange extension of her love all the old limitations seemed to fall. Something had cleft the surface of self, and there welled up the mysterious primal influences, the sacrificial instinct of her sex, a passion of spiritual motherhood that made her long to fling herself between the unborn child and its fate.

She never knew, then or after, how she reached this mystic climax of effacement; she was only conscious, through her anguish, of that lift of the heart which made one of the saints declare that joy was the inmost core of sorrow. For it was indeed a kind of joy she felt, if old names must serve for such new meanings; a surge of liberating faith in life, the old *credo quia absurdum* which is the secret cry of all supreme endeavour.

D OES it look nice, mother?"

Dick Peyton met her with the question on the threshold, drawing her gaily into the little square room, and adding, with a laugh with a blush in it: "You know she's an uncommonly noticing person, and little things tell with her."

He swung round on his heel to follow his mother's smiling inspection of the apartment.

"She seems to have *all* the qualities," Mrs. Denis Peyton remarked, as her circuit finally brought her to the prettily appointed tea-table.

"*All,*" he declared, taking the sting from her emphasis by his prompt adoption of it. Dick had always had a wholesome way of thus appropriating to his own use such small shafts of maternal irony as were now and then aimed at him.

Kate Peyton laughed and loosened her furs. "It looks charmingly," she pronounced, ending her survey by an approach to the window, which gave, far below, the oblique perspective of a long side-street leading to Fifth Avenue.

The high-perched room was Dick Peyton's private office, a retreat partitioned off from the larger enclosure in which, under a north light and on a range of deal tables, three or four young draughtsmen were busily engaged in elaborating his architectural projects. The outer door of the office bore the sign: *Peyton and Gill, Architects;* but Gill was an utilitarian person, as unobtrusive as his name, who contented himself with a desk in the work-room, and left Dick to lord it alone in the small apartment

114

to which clients were introduced, and where the social part of
the business was carried on.

It was to serve, on this occasion, as the scene of a tea designed, as Kate Peyton was vividly aware, to introduce a certain
young lady to the scene of her son's labours. Mrs. Peyton had
been hearing a great deal lately about Clemence Verney. Dick
was naturally expansive, and his close intimacy with his mother
—an intimacy fostered by his father's early death—if it had
suffered some natural impairment in his school and college days,
had of late been revived by four years of comradeship in Paris,
where Mrs. Peyton, in a tiny apartment off the Rue de Varennes,
had kept house for him during his course of studies at the Beaux
Arts. There were indeed not lacking critics of her own sex who
accused Kate Peyton of having figured too largely in her son's
life; of having failed to efface herself at a period when it is agreed
that young men are best left free to try conclusions with the
world. Mrs. Peyton, had she cared to defend herself, might have
said that Dick, if communicative, was not impressionable, and
that the closeness of texture which enabled him to throw off her
sarcasms preserved him also from the infiltration of her prejudices. He was certainly no knight of the apron-string, but a seemingly resolute and self-sufficient young man, whose romantic
friendship with his mother had merely served to throw a veil of
suavity over the hard angles of youth.

But Mrs. Peyton's real excuse was after all one which she
would never have given. It was because her intimacy with her
son was the one need of her life that she had, with infinite tact
and discretion, but with equal persistency, clung to every step of
his growth, dissembling herself, adapting herself, rejuvenating
herself in the passionate effort to be always within reach, but
never in the way.

Denis Peyton had died after seven years of marriage, when
his boy was barely six. During those seven years he had managed
to squander the best part of the fortune he had inherited from
his step-brother; so that, at his death, his widow and son were

left with a scant competence. Mrs. Peyton, during her husband's life, had apparently made no effort to restrain his expenditure. She had even been accused by those judicious persons who are always ready with an estimate of their neighbours' motives, of having encouraged poor Denis's improvidence for the gratification of her own ambition. She had in fact, in the early days of their marriage, tried to launch him in politics, and had perhaps drawn somewhat heavily on his funds in the first heat of the contest; but the experiment ending in failure, as Denis Peyton's experiments were apt to end, she had made no farther demands on his exchequer. Her personal tastes were in fact unusually simple, but her outspoken indifference to money was not, in the opinion of her critics, designed to act as a check upon her husband; and it resulted in leaving her, at his death, in straits from which it was impossible not to deduce a moral.

Her small means, and the care of the boy's education, served the widow as a pretext for secluding herself in a socially remote suburb, where it was inferred that she was expiating, on queer food and in ready-made boots, her rash defiance of fortune. Whether or not Mrs. Peyton's penance took this form, she hoarded her substance to such good purpose that she was not only able to give Dick the best of schooling, but to propose, on his leaving Harvard, that he should prolong his studies by another four years at the Beaux Arts. It had been the joy of her life that her boy had early shown a marked bent for a special line of work. She could not have borne to see him reduced to a mere money-getter, yet she was not sorry that their small means forbade the cultivation of an ornamental leisure. In his college days Dick had troubled her by a superabundance of tastes, a restless flitting from one form of artistic expression to another. Whatever art he enjoyed he wished to practise, and he passed from music to painting, from painting to architecture, with an ease which seemed to his mother to indicate lack of purpose rather than excess of talent. She had observed that these changes were usually due, not to self-criticism, but to some external discouragement.

Any depreciation of his work was enough to convince him of the uselessness of pursuing that special form of art, and the reaction produced the immediate conviction that he was really destined to shine in some other line of work. He had thus swung from one calling to another till, at the end of his college career, his mother took the decisive step of transplanting him to the Beaux Arts, in the hope that a definite course of study, combined with the stimulus of competition, might fix his wavering aptitudes. The result justified her expectation, and their four years in the Rue de Varennes yielded the happiest confirmation of her belief in him. Dick's ability was recognized not only by his mother, but by his professors. He was engrossed in his work, and his first successes developed his capacity for application. His mother's only fear was that praise was still too necessary to him. She was uncertain how long his ambition would sustain him in the face of failure. He gave lavishly where he was sure of a return; but it remained to be seen if he were capable of production without recognition. She had brought him up in a wholesome scorn of material rewards, and nature seemed, in this direction, to have seconded her training. He was genuinely indifferent to money, and his enjoyment of beauty was of that happy sort which does not generate the wish for possession. As long as the inner eye had food for contemplation, he cared very little for the deficiencies in his surroundings; or, it might rather be said, he felt, in the sum-total of beauty about him, an ownership of appreciation that left him free from the fret of personal desire. Mrs. Peyton had cultivated to excess this disregard of material conditions; but she now began to ask herself whether, in so doing, she had not laid too great a strain on a temperament naturally exalted. In guarding against other tendencies she had perhaps fostered in him too exclusively those qualities which circumstances had brought to an unusual development in herself. His enthusiasms and his disdains were alike too unqualified for that happy mean of character which is the best defence against the surprises of fortune. If she had taught him to set an exaggerated value on ideal rewards, was not that but a shifting of the danger-point on which her fears had always hung? She trembled sometimes to think how little love and a lifelong vigilance had availed in the deflecting of inherited tendencies.

Her fears were in a measure confirmed by the first two years of their life in New York, and the opening of his career as a professional architect. Close on the easy triumphs of his studentships there came the chilling reaction of public indifference. Dick, on his return from Paris, had formed a partnership with an architect who had had several years of practical training in a New York office; but the quiet and industrious Gill, though he attracted to the new firm a few small jobs which overflowed from the business of his former employer, was not able to infect the public with his own faith in Peyton's talents, and it was trying to a genius who felt himself capable of creating palaces to have to restrict his efforts to the building of suburban cottages or the planning of cheap alterations in private houses.

Mrs. Peyton expended all the ingenuities of tenderness in keeping up her son's courage; and she was seconded in the task by a friend whose acquaintance Dick had made at the Beaux Arts, and who, two years before the Peytons, had returned to New York to start on his own career as an architect. Paul Darrow was a young man full of crude seriousness, who, after a youth of struggling work and study in his native northwestern state, had won a scholarship which sent him abroad for a course at the Beaux Arts. His two years there coincided with the first part of Dick's residence, and Darrow's gifts had at once attracted the younger student. Dick was unstinted in his admiration of rival talent, and Mrs. Peyton, who was romantically given to the cultivation of such generosities, had seconded his enthusiasm by the kindest offers of hospitality to the young student. Darrow thus became the grateful frequenter of their little *salon;* and after their return to New York the intimacy between the young men was renewed, though Mrs. Peyton found it more difficult to coax Dick's friend to her New York drawing-room than to the informal surroundings of the Rue de Varennes. There, no doubt, secluded and absorbed in her son's work, she had seemed to Darrow almost a fellow-student; but seen among her own associates she became once more the woman of fashion, divided from him by the whole breadth of her ease and his awkwardness. Mrs. Peyton, whose tact had divined the cause of his estrangement, would not for an instant let it affect the friendship of the two young men. She encouraged Dick to frequent Darrow, in whom she divined a persistency of effort, an artistic self-confidence, in curious contrast to his social hesitancies. The example of his obstinate capacity for work was just the influence her son needed, and if Darrow would not come to them she insisted that Dick must seek him out, must never let him think that any social discrepancy could affect a friendship based on deeper things. Dick, who had all the loyalties, and who took an honest pride in his friend's growing success, needed no urging to maintain the intimacy; and his copious reports of midnight colloquies in Darrow's lodgings showed Mrs. Peyton that she had a strong ally in her invisible friend.

It had been, therefore, somewhat of a shock to learn in the course of time that Darrow's influence was being shared, if not counteracted, by that of a young lady in whose honour Dick was now giving his first professional tea. Mrs. Peyton had heard a great deal about Miss Clemence Verney, first from the usual purveyors of such information, and more recently from her son, who, probably divining that rumour had been before him, adopted his usual method of disarming his mother by taking her into his confidence. But, ample as her information was, it remained perplexing and contradictory, and even her own few meetings with the girl had not helped her to a definite opinion. Miss Verney, in conduct and ideas, was patently of the "new school": a young woman of feverish activities and broad-cast judgments, whose very versatility made her hard to define. Mrs. Peyton was shrewd enough to allow for the accidents of environment; what she wished to get at was the residuum of character beneath Miss Verney's shifting surface.

"It looks charmingly," Mrs. Peyton repeated, giving a loosening touch to the chrysanthemums in a tall vase on her son's desk.

Dick laughed, and glanced at his watch.

"They won't be here for another quarter of an hour. I think I'll tell Gill to clean out the work-room before they come."

"Are we to see the drawings for the competition?" his mother asked.

He shook his head smilingly. "Can't—I've asked one or two of the Beaux Arts fellows, you know; and besides, old Darrow's actually coming."

"Impossible!" Mrs. Peyton exclaimed.

"He swore he would last night." Dick laughed again, with a tinge of self-satisfaction. "I've an idea he wants to see Miss Verney."

"Ah," his mother murmured. There was a pause before she added: "Has Darrow really gone in for this competition?"

"Rather! I should say so! He's simply working himself to the bone."

Mrs. Peyton sat revolving her muff on a meditative hand; at length she said: "I'm not sure I think it quite nice of him."

Her son halted before her with an incredulous stare. "*Mother!*" he exclaimed.

The rebuke sent a blush to her forehead. "Well—considering your friendship—and everything."

"Everything? What do you mean by everything? The fact that he had more ability than I have and is therefore more likely to succeed? The fact that he needs the money and the success a deuced sight more than any of us? Is that the reason you think he oughtn't to have entered? Mother! I never heard you say an ungenerous thing before."

The blush deepened to crimson, and she rose with a nervous laugh. "It *was* ungenerous," she conceded. "I suppose I'm jealous for you. I hate these competitions!"

Her son smiled reassuringly. "You needn't. I'm not afraid: I think I shall pull it off this time. In fact, Paul's the only man I'm afraid of—I'm always afraid of Paul—but the mere fact that he's in the thing is a tremendous stimulus."

His mother continued to study him with an anxious tenderness. "Have you worked out the whole scheme? Do you *see* it yet?"

"Oh, broadly, yes. There's a gap here and there—a hazy bit, rather—it's the hardest problem I've ever had to tackle; but then it's my biggest opportunity, and I've simply *got* to pull it off!"

Mrs. Peyton sat silent, considering his flushed face and illumined eye, which were rather those of the victor nearing the goal than of the runner just beginning the race. She remembered something that Darrow had once said of him: "Dick always sees the end too soon."

"You haven't too much time left," she murmured.

"Just a week. But I shan't go anywhere after this. I shall renounce the world." He glanced smilingly at the festal tea-table and the embowered desk. "When I next appear, it will either be with my heel on Paul's neck—poor old Paul—or else—or else— being dragged lifeless from the arena!"

His mother nervously took up the laugh with which he ended. "Oh, not lifeless," she said.

His face clouded. "Well, maimed for life, then," he muttered.

Mrs. Peyton made no answer. She knew how much hung on the possibility of his winning the competition which for weeks past had engrossed him. It was a design for the new museum of sculpture, for which the city had recently voted half a million. Dick's taste ran naturally to the grandiose, and the erection of public buildings had always been the object of his ambition. Here was an unmatched opportunity, and he knew that, in a competition of the kind, the newest man had as much chance of success as the firm of most established reputation, since every competitor entered on his own merits, the designs being submitted to a jury of architects who voted on them without knowing the names of the contestants. Dick, characteristically, was not afraid of the older firms; indeed, as he had told his mother, Paul Darrow was the only rival he feared. Mrs. Peyton knew that, to a certain point, self-confidence was a good sign; but somehow her son's did not strike her as being of the right substance—it seemed to have no dimension but extent. Her fears were complicated by a suspicion that, under his professional eagerness for success, lay the knowledge that Miss Verney's favour hung on the victory. It was that, perhaps, which gave a feverish touch to his ambition; and Mrs. Peyton, surveying the future from the height of her material apprehensions, divined that the situation depended mainly on the girl's view of it. She would have given a great deal to know Clemence Verney's conception of success.

❊ II ❊

MISS VERNEY, when she presently appeared, in the wake of the impersonal and exclamatory young married woman who served as a background to her vivid outline, seemed competent to impart at short notice any information required of her. She had never struck Mrs. Peyton as more alert and efficient. A melting grace of line and colour tempered her edges with the charming haze of youth; but it occurred to her critic that she might emerge from this morning mist as a dry and metallic old woman.

If Miss Verney suspected a personal application in Dick's hospitality, it did not call forth in her the usual tokens of self-consciousness. Her manner may have been a shade more vivid than usual, but she preserved all her bright composure of glance and speech, so that one guessed, under the rapid dispersal of words, an undisturbed steadiness of perception. She was lavishly but not indiscriminately interested in the evidences of her host's industry, and as the other guests assembled, straying with vague ejaculations through the labyrinth of scale drawings and blue prints, Mrs. Peyton noted that Miss Verney alone knew what these symbols stood for.

To his visitors' requests to be shown his plans for the competition, Peyton had opposed a laughing refusal, enforced by the
presence of two fellow-architects, young men with lingering
traces of the Beaux Arts in their costume and vocabulary, who
stood about in Gavarni attitudes and dazzled the ladies by allusions to fenestration and entasis. The party had already drifted
back to the tea-table when a hesitating knock announced Darrow's approach. He entered with his usual air of having blun-
dered in by mistake, embarrassed by his hat and great-coat, and
thrown into deeper confusion by the necessity of being introduced to the ladies grouped about the urn. To the men he threw
a gruff nod of fellowship, and Dick having relieved him of his
encumbrances, he retreated behind the shelter of Mrs. Peyton's
welcome. The latter judiciously gave him time to recover, and
when she turned to him he was engaged in a surreptitious inspection of Miss Verney, whose dusky slenderness, relieved
against the bare walls of the office, made her look like a young
St. John of Donatello's. The girl returned his look with one of her
clear glances, and the group having presently broken up again,
Mrs. Peyton saw that she had drifted to Darrow's ride. The visitors at length wandered back to the work-room to see a portfolio
of Dick's water-colours; but Mrs. Peyton remained seated behind
the urn, listening to the interchange of talk through the open
door while she tried to coordinate her impressions.

She saw that Miss Verney was sincerely interested in Dick's
work: it was the nature of her interest that remained in doubt.
As if to solve this doubt, the girl presently reappeared alone on
the threshold, and discovering Mrs. Peyton, advanced toward
her with a smile.

"Are you tired of hearing us praise Mr. Peyton's things?" she
asked, dropping into a low chair beside her hostess. "Unintelligent admiration must be a bore to people who know, and Mr.
Darrow tells me you are almost as learned as your son."

Mrs. Peyton returned the smile, but evaded the question. "I
should be sorry to think your admiration unintelligent," she said.

"I like to feel that my boy's work is appreciated by people who understand it."

"Oh, I have the usual smattering," said Miss Verney carelessly. "I *think* I know why I admire his work; but then I am sure I see more in it when someone like Mr. Darrow tells me how remarkable it is."

"Does Mr. Darrow say that?" the mother exclaimed, losing sight of her object in the rush of maternal pleasure.

"He has said nothing else: it seems to be the only subject which loosens his tongue. I believe he is more anxious to have your son win the competition than to win it himself."

"He is a very good friend," Mrs. Peyton assented. She was struck by the way in which the girl led the topic back to the special application of it which interested her. She had none of the artifices of prudery.

"He feels sure that Mr. Peyton *will* win," Miss Verney continued. "It was very interesting to hear his reasons. He is an extraordinarily interesting man. It must be a tremendous incentive to have such a friend."

Mrs. Peyton hesitated. "The friendship is delightful; but I don't know that my son needs the incentive. He is almost too ambitious."

Miss Verney looked up brightly. "Can one be?" she said. "Ambition is so splendid! It must be so glorious to be a man and go crashing through obstacles, straight up to the thing one is after. I'm afraid I don't care for people who are superior to success. I like marriage by capture!" She rose with her wandering laugh, and stood flushed and sparkling above Mrs. Peyton, who continued to gaze at her gravely.

"What do you call success?" the latter asked. "It means so many different things."

"Oh, yes, I know—the inward approval, and all that. Well, I'm afraid I like the other kind: the drums and wreaths and acclamations. If I were Mr. Peyton, for instance, I'd much rather win the competition than—than be as disinterested as Mr. Darrow."

Mrs. Peyton smiled. "I hope you won't tell him so," she said half seriously. "He is over-stimulated already; and he is so easily influenced by anyone who—whose opinion he values."

She stopped abruptly, hearing herself, with a strange inward shock, reëcho the words which another man's mother had once spoken to her. Miss Verney did not seem to take the allusion to herself, for she continued to fix on Mrs. Peyton a gaze of impartial sympathy.

"But we can't help being interested!" she declared.

"It's very kind of you; but I wish you would all help him to feel that his competition is after all of very little account compared with other things—his health and his peace of mind, for instance. He is looking horribly used up."

The girl glanced over her shoulder at Dick, who was just reëntering the room at Darrow's side.

"Oh, do you think so?" she said. "I should have thought it was his friend who was used up."

Mrs. Peyton followed the glance with surprise. She had been too preoccupied to notice Darrow, whose crudely modelled face was always of a dull pallour, to which his slow-moving grey eye lent no relief except in rare moments of expansion. Now the face had the fallen lines of a death-mask, in which only the smile he turned on Dick remained alive; and the sight smote her with compunction. Poor Darrow! He did look horribly fagged out: as if he needed care and petting and good food. No one knew exactly how he lived. His rooms, according to Dick's report, were fireless and ill kept, but he stuck to them because his landlady, whom he had fished out of some financial plight, had difficulty in obtaining other lodgers. He belonged to no clubs, and wandered out alone for his meals, mysteriously refusing the hospitality which his friends pressed on him. It was plain that he was very poor, and Dick conjectured that he sent what he earned to an aunt in his native village; but he was so silent about such matters that, outside of his profession, he seemed to have no personal life.

Miss Verney's companion having presently advised her of the lapse of time, there ensued a general leave-taking, at the close of which Dick accompanied the ladies to their carriage. Darrow was meanwhile blundering into his great-coat, a process which always threw him into a state of perspiring embarrassment; but Mrs. Peyton, surprising him in the act, suggested that he should defer it and give her a few moments' talk.

"Let me make you some fresh tea," she said, as Darrow blushingly shed the garment, "and when Dick comes back we'll all walk home together. I've not had a chance to say two words to you this winter."

Darrow sank into a chair at her side and nervously contemplated his boots. "I've been tremendously hard at work," he said.

"I know: *too* hard at work, I'm afraid. Dick tells me you have been wearing yourself out over your competition plans."

"Oh, well, I shall have time to rest now," he returned. "I put the last stroke to them this morning."

Mrs. Peyton gave him a quick look. "You're ahead of Dick, then."

"In point of time only," he said smiling.

"That is in itself an advantage," she answered with a tinge of asperity. In spite of an honest effort for impartiality she could not, at the moment, help regarding Darrow as an obstacle in her son's path.

"I wish the competition were over!" she exclaimed, conscious that her voice had betrayed her. "I hate to see you both looking so fagged."

Darrow smiled again, perhaps at her studied inclusion of himself.

"Oh, *Dick's* all right," he said. "He'll pull himself together in no time."

He spoke with an emphasis which might have struck her, if

her sympathies had not again been deflected by the allusion to her son.

"Not if he doesn't win," she exclaimed.

Darrow took the tea she had poured for him, knocking the spoon to the floor in his eagerness to perform the feat gracefully. In bending to recover the spoon he struck the tea-table with his shoulder, and set the cups dancing. Having regained a measure of composure, he took a swallow of the hot tea and set it down with a gasp, precariously near the edge of the tea-table. Mrs. Peyton rescued the cup, and Darrow, apparently forgetting its existence, rose and began to pace the room. It was always hard for him to sit still when he talked.

"You mean he's so tremendously set on it?" he broke out.

Mrs. Peyton hesitated. "You know him almost as well as I do," she said. "He's capable of anything where there is a possibility of success; but I'm always afraid of the reaction."

"Oh, well, Dick's a man," said Darrow bluntly. "Besides, he's going to succeed."

"I wish he didn't feel so sure of it. You mustn't think I'm afraid for him. He's a man, and I want him to take his chances with other men; but I wish he didn't care so much about what people think."

"People?"

"Miss Verney, then: I suppose you know."

Darrow paused in front of her. "Yes: he's talked a good deal about her. You think she wants him to succeed?"

"At any price!"

He drew his brows together. "What do you call any price?"

"Well—herself, in this case, I believe."

Darrow bent a puzzled stare on her. "You mean she attached that amount of importance to this competition?"

"She seems to regard it as symbolical: that's what I gather. And I'm afraid she's given him the same impression."

Darrow's sunken face was suffused by his rare smile. "Oh, well, he'll pull it off then!" he said.

Mrs. Peyton rose with a distracted sigh. "I half hope he won't, for such a motive," she exclaimed.

"The motive won't show in his work," said Darrow. He added, after a pause probably devoted to the search for the right word: "He seems to think a great deal of her."

Mrs. Peyton fixed him thoughtfully. "I wish I knew what *you* think of her."

"Why, I never saw her before."

"No; but you talked with her today. You've formed an opinion: I think you came here on purpose."

He chuckled joyously at her discernment: she had always seemed to him gifted with supernatural insight. "Well, I did want to see her," he owned.

"And what do you think?"

He took a few vague steps and then halted before Mrs. Peyton. "I think," he said, smiling, "that she likes to be helped first, and to have everything on her plate at once."

※ III ※

AT dinner, with a rush of contrition, Mrs. Peyton remembered that she had after all not spoken to Darrow about his health. He had distracted her by beginning to talk to Dick; and besides, much as Darrow's opinions interested her, his personality had never fixed her attention. He always seemed to her simply a vehicle for the transmission of ideas.

It was Dick who recalled her to a sense of her omission by asking if she hadn't thought that old Paul looked rather more ragged than usual.

"He did look tired," Mrs. Peyton conceded. "I meant to tell him to take care of himself."

Dick laughed at the futility of the measure. "Old Paul is never tired: he can work twenty-five hours out of the twenty-four. The trouble with him is that he's ill. Something wrong with the machinery, I'm afraid."

"Oh, I'm sorry. Has he seen a doctor?"

"He wouldn't listen to me when I suggested it the other day; but he's so deuced mysterious that I don't know what he may have done since." Dick rose, putting down his coffee-cup and half-smoked cigarette. "I've half a mind to pop in on him tonight and see how he's getting on."

"But he lives at the other end of the earth; and you're tired yourself."

"I'm not tired; only a little strung-up," he returned, smiling. "And besides, I'm going to meet Gill at the office by and by and put in a night's work. It won't hurt me to take a look at Paul first."

Mrs. Peyton was silent. She knew it was useless to contend with her son about his work, and she tried to fortify herself with the remembrance of her own words to Darrow: Dick was a man and must take his chance with other men.

But Dick, glancing at his watch, uttered an exclamation of annoyance. "Oh, by Jove, I shan't have time after all. Gill is waiting for me now; we must have dawdled over dinner." He went to give his mother a caressing tap on the cheek. "Now don't worry," he adjured her; and as she smiled back at him he added with a sudden happy blush: "She doesn't, you know: she's so sure of me."

Mrs. Peyton's smile faded, and laying a detaining hand on his, she said with sudden directness: "Sure of you, or of your success?"

He hesitated. "Oh, she regards them as synonymous. She thinks I'm bound to get on."

"But if you don't?"

He shrugged laughingly, but with a slight contraction of his confident brows. "Why, I shall have to make way for someone else, I suppose. That's the law of life."

Mrs. Peyton sat upright, gazing at him with a kind of solemnity. "Is it the law of love?" she asked.

He looked down on her with a smile that trembled a little. "My dear romantic mother, I don't want her pity, you know!"

Dick, coming home the next morning shortly before daylight, left the house again after a hurried breakfast, and Mrs. Peyton heard nothing of him till nightfall. He had promised to be back for dinner, but a few moments before eight, as she was coming down to the drawing-room, the parlour-maid handed her a hastily pencilled note.

"Don't wait for me," it ran. "Darrow is ill and I can't leave him. I'll send a line when the doctor has seen him."

Mrs. Peyton, who was a woman of rapid reactions, read the words with a pang. She was ashamed of the jealous thoughts she had harboured of Darrow, and of the selfishness which had made her lose sight of his troubles in the consideration of Dick's welfare. Even Clemence Verney, whom she secretly accused of a want of heart, had been struck by Darrow's ill looks, while she had had eyes only for her son. Poor Darrow! How cold and self-engrossed he must have thought her! In the first rush of penitence her impulse was to drive at once to his lodgings; but the infection of his own shyness restrained her. Dick's note gave no details; the illness was evidently grave, but might not Darrow regard her coming as an intrusion? To repair her negligence of yesterday by a sudden invasion of his privacy might be only a greater failure in tact; and after a moment of deliberation she resolved on sending to ask Dick if he wished her to go to him.

The reply, which came late, was what she had expected. "No, we have all the help we need. The doctor has sent a good nurse, and is coming again later. It's pneumonia, but of course he doesn't say much yet. Let me have some beef-juice as soon as the cook can make it."

The beef-juice ordered and dispatched, she was left to a vigil in melancholy contrast to that of the previous evening. Then she had been enclosed in the narrow limits of her maternal interests; now the barriers of self were broken down, and her personal preoccupations swept away on the current of a wider sympathy. As she sat there in the radius of lamp-light which, for so many evenings, had held Dick and herself in a charmed circle of tenderness, she saw that her love for her boy had come to be merely a kind of extended egotism. Love had narrowed instead of widening her, had rebuilt between herself and life the very walls which, years and years before, she had laid low with bleeding fingers. It was horrible, how she had come to sacrifice everything to the one passion of ambition for her boy.

At daylight she sent another messenger, one of her own servants, who returned without having seen Dick. Mr. Peyton had sent word that there was no change. He would write later; he wanted nothing. The day wore on drearily. Once Kate found herself computing the precious hours lost to Dick's unfinished task. She blushed at her ineradicable selfishness, and tried to turn her mind to poor Darrow. But she could not master her impulses; and now she caught herself indulging the thought that his illness would at least exclude him from the competition. But no—she remembered that he had said his work was finished. Come what might, he stood in the path of her boy's success. She hated herself for the thought, but it would not down.

Evening drew on, but there was no note from Dick. At length, in the shamed reaction from her fears, she rang for a carriage and went upstairs to dress. She could stand aloof no longer: she must go to Darrow, if only to escape from her wicked thoughts of him. As she came down again she heard Dick's key in the door. She hastened her steps, and as she reached the hall he stood before her without speaking.

She looked at him and the question died on her lips. He nodded, and walked slowly past her.

"There was no hope from the first," he said.

The next day Dick was taken up with the preparations for the funeral. The distant aunt, who appeared to be Darrow's only relation, had been duly notified of his death; but no answer having been received from her, it was left to his friend to fulfil the customary duties. He was again absent for the best part of the day; and when he returned at dusk Mrs. Peyton, looking up from the tea-table behind which she awaited him, was startled by the deep-lined misery of his face.

Her own thoughts were too painful for ready expression, and they sat for a while in a mute community of wretchedness.

"Is everything arranged?" she asked at length.

"Yes. Everything."

"And you have not heard from the aunt?"

He shook his head.

"Can you find no trace of any other relations?"

"None. I went over all his papers. There were very few, and I found no address but the aunt's." He sat thrown back in his chair, disregarding the cup of tea she had mechanically poured for him. "I found this, though," he added, after a pause, drawing a letter from his pocket and holding it out to her.

She took it doubtfully. "Ought I to read it?"

"Yes."

She saw then that the envelope, in Darrow's hand, was addressed to her son. Within were a few pencilled words, dated on the first day of his illness, the morrow of the day on which she had last seen him.

"Dear Dick," she read, "I want you to use my plans for the museum if you can get any good out of them. Even if I pull out of this I want you to. I shall have other chances, and I have an idea this one means a lot to you."

Mrs. Peyton sat speechless, gazing at the date of the letter, which she had instantly connected with her last talk with Darrow. She saw that he had understood her, and the thought scorched her to the soul.

"Wasn't it glorious of him?" Dick said.

She dropped the letter, and hid her face in her hands.

❀ IV ❀

THE funeral took place the next morning, and on the return
from the cemetery Dick told his mother that he must go and look
over things at Darrow's office. He had heard the day before from
his friend's aunt, a helpless person to whom telegraphy was
difficult and travel inconceivable, and who, in eight pages of un-
punctuated eloquence, made over to Dick what she called the
melancholy privilege of winding up her nephew's affairs.

Mrs. Peyton looked anxiously at her son. "Is there no one
who can do this for you? He must have had a clerk or someone
who knows about his work."

Dick shook his head. "Not lately. He hasn't had much to do
this winter, and these last months he had chucked everything to
work alone over his plans."

The word brought a faint colour to Mrs. Peyton's cheek. It
was the first allusion that either of them had made to Darrow's
bequest.

"Oh, of course you must do all you can," she murmured,
turning alone into the house.

The emotions of the morning had stirred her deeply, and she
sat at home during the day, letting her mind dwell, in a kind of
retrospective piety, on the thought of poor Darrow's devotion.
She had given him too little time while he lived, had acquiesced
too easily in his growing habits of seclusion; and she felt it as a
proof of insensibility that she had not been more closely drawn
to the one person who had loved Dick as she loved him. The evidence of that love, as shown in Darrow's letter, filled her with a
vain compunction. The very extravagance of his offer lent it a
deeper pathos. It was wonderful that, even in the urgency of
affection, a man of his almost morbid rectitude should have
overlooked the restrictions of professional honour, should have

implied the possibility of his friend's overlooking them. It seemed to make his sacrifice the more complete that it had, unconsciously, taken the form of a subtle temptation.

The last word arrested Mrs. Peyton's thoughts. A temptation? To whom? Not, surely, to one capable, as her son was capable, of rising to the height of his friend's devotion. The offer, to Dick, would mean simply, as it meant to her, the last touching expression of an inarticulate fidelity: the utterance of a love which at last had found its formula. Mrs. Peyton dismissed as morbid any other view of the case. She was annoyed with herself for supposing that Dick could be ever so remotely affected by the possibility at which poor Darrow's renunciation hinted. The nature of the offer removed it from practical issues to the idealizing region of sentiment.

Mrs. Peyton had been sitting alone with these thoughts for the greater part of the afternoon, and dusk was falling when Dick entered the drawing-room. In the dim light, with his pallour heightened by the sombre effect of his mourning, he came upon her almost startlingly, with a revival of some long-effaced impression which, for a moment, gave her the sense of struggling among shadows. She did not, at first, know what had produced the effect; then she saw that it was his likeness to his father.

"Well—is it over?" she asked, as he threw himself into a chair without speaking.

"Yes: I've looked through everything." He leaned back, crossing his hands behind his head, and gazing past her with a look of utter lassitude.

She paused a moment, and then said tentatively: "Tomorrow you will be able to go back to your work."

"Oh—my work," he exclaimed, as if to brush aside an ill-timed pleasantry.

"Are you too tired?"

"No." He rose and began to wander up and down the room. "I'm not tired.—Give me some tea, will you?" He paused before her while she poured the cup, and then, without taking it, turned away to light a cigarette.

"Surely there is still time?" she suggested, with eyes on him.

"Time? To finish my plans? Oh, yes—there's time. But they're not worth it."

"Not worth it?" She started up, and then dropped back into her seat, ashamed of having betrayed her anxiety. "They are worth as much as they were last week," she said with an attempt at cheerfulness.

"Not to me," he returned. "I hadn't seen Darrow's then."

There was a long silence. Mrs. Peyton sat with her eyes fixed on her clasped hands, and her son paced the room restlessly.

"Are they so wonderful?" she asked at length.

"Yes."

She paused again, and then said, lifting a tremulous glance to his face: "That makes his offer all the more beautiful."

Dick was lighting another cigarette, and his face was turned from her. "Yes—I suppose so," he said in a low tone.

"They were quite finished, he told me," she continued, unconsciously dropping her voice to the pitch of his.

"Yes."

"Then they will be entered, I suppose?"

"Of course—why not?" he answered almost sharply.

"Shall you have time to attend to all that and to finish yours too?"

"Oh, I suppose so. I've told you it isn't a question of time. I see now that mine are not worth bothering with."

She rose and approached him, laying her hands on his shoulders. "You are tired and unstrung; how can you judge? Why not let me look at both designs tomorrow?"

Under her gaze he flushed abruptly and drew back with a half-impatient gesture.

"Oh, I'm afraid that wouldn't help me; you'd be sure to think mine best," he said with a laugh.

"But if I could give you good reasons?" she pressed him.

He took her hand, as if ashamed of his impatience. "Dear mother, if you had any reasons their mere existence would prove that they were bad."

His mother did not return his smile. "You won't let me see the two designs then?" she said with a faint tinge of insistence.

"Oh, of course—if you want to—if you only won't talk about it now! Can't you see that I am pretty nearly dead-beat?" he burst out uncontrollably; and as she stood silent, he added with a weary fall in his voice, "I think I'll go upstairs and see if I can't get a nap before dinner."

Though they had separated upon the assurance that she should see the two designs if she wished it, Mrs. Peyton knew they would not be shown to her. Dick, indeed, would not again deny her request; but had he not reckoned on the improbability of her renewing it? All night she lay confronted by that question. The situation shaped itself before her with that hallucinating distinctness which belongs to the midnight vision. She knew now why Dick had suddenly reminded her of his father; had she not once before seen the same thought moving behind the same eyes? She was sure it had occurred to Dick to use Darrow's drawings. As she lay awake in the darkness she could hear him, long after midnight, pacing the floor overhead: she held her breath, listening to the recurring beat of his foot, which seemed that of an imprisoned spirit revolving wearily in the cage of the same thought. She felt in every fibre that a crisis in her son's life had been reached, that the act now before him would have a determining effect on his whole future. The circumstances of her past had raised to clairvoyance her natural insight into human motive, had made of her a moral barometer responding to the faintest fluctuations of atmosphere, and years of anxious meditation had familiarized her with the form which her son's temptations were likely to take. The peculiar misery of her situation was that she could not, except indirectly, put this intuition, this foresight, at his service. It was a part of her discernment to

be aware that life is the only real counsellor, that wisdom unfil-
tered through personal experience does not become a part of the
moral tissues. Love such as hers had a great office, the office of
preparation and direction; but it must know how to hold its hand
and keep its counsel, how to attend upon its object as an invisible
influence rather than as an active interference.

All this Kate Peyton had told herself again and again, during
those hours of anxious calculation in which she had tried to cast
Dick's horoscope; but not in her moments of most fantastic foreboding had she figured so cruel a test of her courage. If her
prayers for him had taken precise shape, she might have asked
that he should be spared the spectacular, the dramatic appeal to
his will-power: that his temptations should slip by him in a dull
disguise. She had secured him against all ordinary forms of baseness; the vulnerable point lay higher, in that region of idealizing
egotism which is the seat of life in such natures.

Years of solitary foresight gave her mind a singular alertness
in dealing with such possibilities. She saw at once that the peril
of the situation lay in the minimum of risk it involved. Darrow
had employed no assistant in working out his plans for the competition, and his secluded life made it almost certain that he had
not shown them to anyone, and that she and Dick alone knew
them to have been completed. Moreover, it was a part of Dick's
duty to examine the contents of his friend's office, and in doing
this nothing would be easier than to possess himself of the drawings and make use of any part of them that might serve his purpose. He had Darrow's authority for doing so; and though the act
involved a slight breach of professional probity, might not his
friend's wishes be invoked as a secret justification? Mrs. Peyton
found herself almost hating poor Darrow for having been the unconscious instrument of her son's temptation. But what right had
she, after all, to suspect Dick of considering, even for a moment,
the act of which she was so ready to accuse him? His unwillingness to let her see the drawings might have been the accidental
result of lassitude and discouragement. He was tired and troubled, and she had chosen the wrong moment to make the

request. His want of readiness might even be due to the wish to conceal from her how far his friend had surpassed him. She knew his sensitiveness on this point, and reproached herself for not having foreseen it. But her own arguments failed to convince her. Deep beneath her love for her boy and her faith in him there lurked a nameless doubt. She could hardly now, in looking back, define the impulse upon which she had married Denis Peyton: she knew only that the deeps of her nature had been loosened, and that she had been borne forward on their current to the very fate from which her heart recoiled. But if in one sense her marriage remained a problem, there was another in which her motherhood seemed to solve it. She had never lost the sense of having snatched her child from some dim peril which still lurked and hovered; and he became more closely hers with every effort of her vigilant love. For the act of rescue had not been accomplished once and for all in the moment of immolation: it had not been by a sudden stroke of heroism, but by ever-renewed and indefatigable effort, that she had built up for him the miraculous shelter of her love. And now that it stood there, a hallowed refuge against failure, she could not even set a light in the pane, but must let him grope his way to it unaided.

※ V ※

Mrs. Peyton's midnight musings summed themselves up in the conclusion that the next few hours would end her uncertainty. She felt the day to be decisive. If Dick offered to show her the drawings, her fears would be proved groundless; if he avoided the subject, they were justified.

She dressed early in order not to miss him at breakfast; but as she entered the dining-room the parlour-maid told her that Mr. Peyton had overslept himself, and had rung to have his breakfast sent upstairs. Was it a pretext to avoid her? She was vexed at her own readiness to see a portent in the simplest incident; but while she blushed at her doubts she let them govern her. She left the dining-room door open, determined not to miss him if he came downstairs while she was at breakfast; then she went back to the drawing-room and sat down at her writing-table, trying to busy herself with some accounts while she listened for his step. Here too she had left the door open; but presently even this slight departure from her daily usage seemed a deviation from the passive attitude she had adopted, and she rose and shut the door. She knew that she could still hear his step on the stairs—he had his father's quick swinging gait—but as she sat listening, and vainly trying to write, the closed door seemed to symbolize a refusal to share in his trial, a hardening of herself against his need of her. What if he should come down intending to speak, and should be turned from his purpose? Slighter obstacles have deflected the course of events in those indeterminate moments when the soul floats between two tides. She sprang up quickly, and as her hand touched the latch she heard his step on the stairs.

When he entered the drawing-room she had regained the writing-table and could lift a composed face to his. He came in hurriedly, yet with a kind of reluctance beneath his haste: again it was his father's step. She smiled, but looked away from him as he approached her; she seemed to be re-living her own past as one re-lives things in the distortion of fever.

"Are you off already?" she asked, glancing at the hat in his hand.

"Yes; I'm late as it is. I overslept myself." He paused and looked vaguely about the room. "Don't expect me till late—don't wait dinner for me."

She stirred impulsively. "Dick, you're overworking—you'll make yourself ill."

"Nonsense. I'm as fit as ever this morning. Don't be imagining things."

He dropped his habitual kiss on her forehead, and turned to go. On the threshold he paused, and she felt that something in him sought her and then drew back. "Good-bye," he called to her as the door closed on him.

She sat down and tried to survey the situation divested of her midnight fears. He had not referred to her wish to see the drawings: but what did the omission signify? Might he not have forgotten her request? Was she not forcing the most trivial details to fit in with her apprehensions? Unfortunately for her own reassurance, she knew that her familiarity with Dick's processes was based on such minute observation, and that, to such intimacy as theirs, no indications were trivial. She was as certain as if he had spoken, that when he had left the house that morning he was weighing the possibility of using Darrow's drawings, of supplementing his own incomplete design from the fulness of his friend's invention. And with a bitter pang she divined that he was sorry he had shown her Darrow's letter.

It was impossible to remain face to face with such conjectures, and though she had given up all her engagements during the few days since Darrow's death, she now took refuge in the thought of a concert which was to take place at a friend's house that morning. The music-room, when she entered, was thronged with acquaintances, and she found transient relief in that dispersal of attention which makes society an anesthetic for some forms of wretchedness. Contact with the pressure of busy indifferent life often gives remoteness to questions which have clung as close as the flesh to the bone; and if Mrs. Peyton did not find such complete release, she at least interposed between herself and her anxiety the obligation to dissemble it. But the relief was only momentary, and when the first bars of the overture turned from her the smiles of recognition among which she had tried to lose herself, she felt a deeper sense of isolation. The music, which at another time would have swept her away on some rich current of emotion, now seemed to island her in her own thoughts, to create an artificial solitude in which she found herself more immitigably face to face with her fears. The silence, the *recueillement*, about her gave resonance to the inner voices, lucidity to the inner vision, till she seemed enclosed in a luminous empty horizon against which every possibility took the sharp edge of accomplished fact. With relentless precision the course of events was unrolled before her: she saw Dick yielding to his opportunity, snatching victory from dishonour, winning love, happiness and success in the act by which he lost himself. It was all so simple, so easy, so inevitable, that she felt the futility of struggling or hoping against it. He would win the competition, would marry Miss Verney, would press on to achievement through the opening which the first success had made for him.

As Mrs. Peyton reached this point in her forecast, she found her outward gaze arrested by the face of the young lady who so dominated her inner vision. Miss Verney, a few rows distant, sat intent upon the music, in that attitude of poised motion which was her nearest approach to repose. Her slender brown profile with its breezy hair, her quick eye, and the lips which seemed to listen as well as speak, all betokened to Mrs. Peyton a nature through which the obvious energies blew free, a bare open stretch of consciousness without shelter for tenderer growths. She shivered to think of Dick's frail scruples exposed to those rustling airs. And then, suddenly, a new thought struck her. What if she might turn this force to her own use, make it serve, unconsciously to Dick, as the means of his deliverance? Hitherto she had assumed that her son's worst danger lay in the chance of his confiding his difficulty to Clemence Verney; and she had, in her own past, a precedent which made her think such a confidence not unlikely. If he did carry his scruples to the girl, she argued, the latter's imperviousness, her frank inability to understand them, would have the effect of dispelling them like mist; and he was acute enough to know this and profit by it. So she had hitherto reasoned; but now the girl's presence seemed to clarify her perceptions, and she told herself that something in Dick's nature, something which she herself had put there, would resist this short cut to safety, would make him take the more tortuous way to his goal rather than gain it through the privacies of the heart he loved. For she had lifted him thus far above his father, that it would be a disenchantment to him to find that Clemence Verney did not share his scruples. On this much, his mother now exultingly felt, she could count in her passive struggle for supremacy. No, he would never, never tell Clemence Verney—and his one hope, his sure salvation, therefore lay in someone else's telling her.

The excitement of this discovery had nearly, in mid-concert, swept Mrs. Peyton from her seat to the girl's side. Fearing to miss the latter in the throng at the entrance, she slipped out during the last number and, lingering in the farther drawing-room, let the dispersing audience drift her in Miss Verney's direction. The girl shone sympathetically on her approach, and in a moment they had detached themselves from the crowd and taken refuge in the perfumed emptiness of the conservatory.

The girl, whose sensations were always easily set in motion, had at first a good deal to say of the music, for which she claimed, on her hearer's part, an active show of approval or dissent; but this dismissed, she turned a melting face on Mrs. Peyton and said with one of her rapid modulations of tone: "I was so sorry about poor Mr. Darrow."

Mrs. Peyton uttered an assenting sigh. "It was a great grief to us—a great loss to my son."

"Yes—I know. I can imagine what you must have felt. And then it was so unlucky that it should have happened just now."

Mrs. Peyton shot a reconnoitering glance at her profile. "His dying, you mean, on the eve of success?"

Miss Verney turned a frank smile upon her. "One ought to feel that, of course—but I'm afraid I am very selfish where my friends are concerned, and I was thinking of Mr. Peyton's having to give up his work at such a critical moment." She spoke without a note of deprecation: there was a pagan freshness in her opportunism.

Mrs. Peyton was silent, and the girl continued after a pause: "I suppose now it will be almost impossible for him to finish his drawings in time. It's a pity he hadn't worked out the whole scheme a little sooner. Then the details would have come of themselves."

Mrs. Peyton felt a contempt strangely mingled with exultation. If only the girl would talk in that way to Dick!

"He has hardly had time to think of himself lately," she said, trying to keep the coldness out of her voice.

"No, of course not," Miss Verney assented; "but isn't that all the more reason for his friends to think of him? It was very dear of him to give up everything to nurse Mr. Darrow—but, after all, if a man is going to get on in his career there are times when he must think first of himself."

Mrs. Peyton paused, trying to choose her words with deliberation. It was quite clear now that Dick had not spoken, and she felt the responsibility that devolved upon her.

"Getting on in a career—is that always the first thing to be considered?" she asked, letting her eyes rest musingly on the girl's.

The glance did not disconcert Miss Verney, who returned it with one of equal comprehensiveness. "Yes," she said quickly, and with a slight blush. "With a temperament like Mr. Peyton's I believe it is. Some people can pick themselves up after any number of bad falls: I am not sure that he could. I think discouragement would weaken instead of strengthening him."

Both women had forgotten external conditions in the quick reach for each other's meanings. Mrs. Peyton flushed, her maternal pride in revolt; but the answer was checked on her lips by the sense of the girl's unexpected insight. Here was someone who knew Dick as well as she did—should she say a partisan or an accomplice? A dim jealousy stirred beneath Mrs. Peyton's other emotions: she was undergoing the agony which the mother feels at the first intrusion on her privilege of judging her child; and her voice had a flutter of resentment.

"You must have a poor opinion of his character," she said.

Miss Verney did not remove her eyes, but her blush deepened beautifully. "I have, at any rate," she said, "a high one of his talent. I don't suppose many men have an equal amount of moral and intellectual energy."

"And you would cultivate the one at the expense of the other?"

"In certain cases—and up to a certain point." She shook out

the long fur of her muff, one of those silvery flexible furs which clothe a woman with a delicate sumptuousness. Everything about her, at the moment, seemed rich and cold—everything, as Mrs. Peyton quickly noted, but the blush lingering under her dark skin; and so complete was the girl's self-command that the blush seemed to be there only because it had been forgotten.

"I dare say you think me strange," she continued. "Most people do, because I speak the truth. It's the easiest way of concealing one's feelings. I can, for instance, talk quite openly about Mr. Peyton under shelter of your inference that I shouldn't do so if I were what is called 'interested' in him. And as I *am* interested in him, my method has its advantages!" She ended with one of the fluttering laughs which seemed to flit from point to point of her expressive person.

Mrs. Peyton leaned toward her. "I believe you are interested," she said quietly; "and since I suppose you allow others the privilege you claim for yourself, I am going to confess that I followed you here in the hope of finding out the nature of your interest."

Miss Verney shot a glance at her, and drew away in a soft subsidence of undulating furs.

"Is this an embassy?" she asked smiling.

"No: not in any sense."

The girl leaned back with an air of relief. "I'm glad; I should have disliked—" She looked again at Mrs. Peyton. "You want to know what I mean to do?"

"Yes."

"Then I can only answer that I mean to wait and see what he does."

"You mean that everything is contingent on his success?"

"*I* am—if I'm everything," she admitted gaily.

The mother's heart was beating in her throat, and her words seemed to force themselves out through the throbs.

"I—I don't quite see why you attach such importance to this special success."

"Because he does," the girl returned instantly. "Because to

him it is the final answer to his self-questioning—the questioning whether he is ever to amount to anything or not. He says if he has anything in him it ought to come out now. All the conditions are favourable—it is the chance he has always prayed for. You see," she continued, almost confidentially, but without the least loss of composure—"you see he has told me a great deal about himself and his various experiments—his phrases of indecision and disgust. There are lots of tentative talents in the world, and the sooner they are crushed out by circumstances the better. But it seems as though he really had it in him to do something distinguished—as though the uncertainty lay in his character and not in his talent. That is what interests, what attracts me. One can't teach a man to have genius, but if he has it one may show him how to use it. That is what I should be good for, you see—to keep him up to his opportunities."

Mrs. Peyton had listened with an intensity of attention that left her reply unprepared. There was something startling and yet half attractive in the girl's avowal of principles which are oftener lived by than professed.

"And you think," she began at length, "that in this case he has fallen below his opportunity?"

"No one can tell, of course; but his discouragement, his *abattement,* is a bad sign. I don't think he has any hope of succeeding."

The mother again wavered a moment. "Since you are so frank," she then said, "will you let me be equally so, and ask how lately you have seen him?"

The girl smiled at the circumlocution. "Yesterday afternoon," she said simply.

"And you thought him—"

"Horribly down on his luck. He said himself that his brain was empty."

Again Mrs. Peyton felt the throb in her throat, and a slow blush rose to her cheek. "Was that all he said?"

"About himself—was there anything else?" said the girl quickly.

"He didn't tell you of—of an opportunity to make up for the time he has lost?"

"An opportunity? I don't understand."

"He didn't speak to you, then, of Mr. Darrow's letter?"

"He said nothing of any letter."

"There *was* one, which was found after poor Darrow's death. In it he gave Dick leave to use his design for the competition. Dick says the design is wonderful—it would give him just what he needs."

Miss Verney sat listening raptly, with a rush of colour that suffused her like light.

"But when was this? Where was the letter found? He never said a word of it!" she exclaimed.

"The letter was found on the day of Darrow's death."

"But I don't understand! Why has he never told me? Why should he seem so hopeless?" She turned an ignorant appealing face on Mrs. Peyton. It was prodigious, but it was true—she felt nothing, saw nothing, but the crude fact of the opportunity.

Mrs. Peyton's voice trembled with the completeness of her triumph. "I suppose his reason for not speaking is that he has scruples."

"Scruples?"

"He feels that to use the design would be dishonest."

Miss Verney's eyes fixed themselves on her in a commiserating stare. "Dishonest? When the poor man wished it himself? When it was his last request? When the letter is there to prove it? Why, the design belongs to your son! No one else had any right to it."

"But Dick's right does not extend to passing it off as his own —at least that is his feeling, I believe. If he won the competition he would be winning it on false pretenses."

"Why should you call them false pretenses? His design might have been better than Darrow's if he had had time to carry it out. It seems to me that Mr. Darrow must have felt this—must have felt that he owed his friend some compensation for the time he took from him. I can imagine nothing more natural than his wishing to make this return for your son's sacrifice."

She positively glowed with the force of her conviction, and Mrs. Peyton, for a strange instant, felt her own resistance wavering. She herself had never considered the question in that light—the light of Darrow's viewing his gift as a justifiable compensation. But the glimpse she caught of it drove her shuddering behind her retrenchments.

"That argument," she said coldly, "would naturally be more convincing to Darrow than to my son."

Miss Verney glanced up, struck by the change in Mrs. Peyton's voice.

"Ah, then you agree with him? You think it *would* be dishonest?"

Mrs. Peyton saw that she had slipped into self-betrayal. "My son and I have not spoken of the matter," she said evasively. She caught the flash of relief in Miss Verney's face.

"You haven't spoken? Then how do you know how he feels about it?"

"I only judge from—well, perhaps from his not speaking."

The girl drew a deep breath. "I see," she murmured. "That is the very reason that prevents his speaking."

"The reason?"

"Your knowing what he thinks—and his knowing that you know."

Mrs. Peyton was startled at her subtlety. "I assure you," she said, rising, "that I have done nothing to influence him."

The girl gazed at her musingly. "No," she said with a faint smile, "nothing except to read his thoughts."

※ VI ※

MRS. PEYTON reached home in the state of exhaustion which follows on a physical struggle. It seemed to her as though her talk with Clemence Verney had been an actual combat, a measuring of wrist and eye. For a moment she was frightened at what she had done—she felt as though she had betrayed her son to the enemy. But before long she regained her moral balance, and saw that she had merely shifted the conflict to the ground on which it could best be fought out—since the prize fought for was the natural battlefield. The reaction brought with it a sense of helplessness, a realization that she had let the issue pass out of her hold; but since, in the last analysis, it had never lain there, since it was above all needful that the determining touch should be given by any hand but hers, she presently found courage to subside into inaction. She had done all she could—even more, perhaps, than prudence warranted—and now she could but await passively the working of the forces she had set in motion.

For two days after her talk with Miss Verney she saw little of Dick. He went early to his office and came back late. He seemed less tired, more self-possessed, than during the first days after Darrow's death; but there was a new inscrutableness in his manner, a note of reserve, of resistance almost, as though he had barricaded himself against her conjectures. She had been struck by Miss Verney's reply to the anxious asseveration that she had done nothing to influence Dick—"Nothing," the girl had answered, "except to read his thoughts." Mrs. Peyton shrank from this detection of a tacit interference with her son's liberty of action. She longed—how passionately he would never know—to stand apart from him in this struggle between his two destinies, and it was almost a relief that he on his side should hold aloof, should, for the first time in their relation, seem to feel her tenderness as an intrusion.

Only four days remained before the date fixed for the sending in of the designs, and still Dick had not referred to his work. Of Darrow, also, he had made no mention. His mother longed to know if he had spoken to Clemence Verney—or rather if the girl had forced his confidence. Mrs. Peyton was almost certain that Miss Verney would not remain silent—there were times when Dick's renewed application to his work seemed an earnest of her having spoken, and spoken convincingly. At the thought Kate's heart grew chill. What if her experiment should succeed in a sense she had not intended? If the girl should reconcile Dick to his weakness, should pluck the sting from his temptation? In this round of uncertainties the mother revolved for two interminable days; but the second evening brought an answer to her question.

Dick, returning earlier than usual from the office, had found, on the hall-table, a note which, since morning, had been under his mother's observation. The envelope, fashionable in tint and texture, was addressed in a rapid staccato hand which seemed the very imprint of Miss Verney's utterance. Mrs. Peyton did not know the girl's writing; but such notes had of late lain often enough on the hall-table to make their attribution easy. This communication Dick, as his mother poured his tea, looked over with a face of shifting lights; then he folded it into his note-case, and said, with a glance at his watch: "If you haven't asked any-one for this evening I think I'll dine out."

"Do, dear; the change will be good for you," his mother assented.

He made no answer, but sat leaning back, his hands clasped behind his head, his eyes fixed on the fire. Every line of his body expressed a profound physical lassitude, but the face remained alert and guarded. Mrs. Peyton, in silence, was busying herself with the details of the tea-making, when suddenly, inexplicably, a question forced itself to her lips.

"And your work—?" she said, strangely hearing herself speak.

"My work—?" He sat up, on the defensive almost, but with-out a tremor of the guarded face.

"You're getting on well? You've made up for lost time?"

"Oh, yes: things are going better." He rose, with another glance at his watch. "Time to dress," he said, nodding to her as he turned to the door.

It was an hour later, during her own solitary dinner, that a ring at the door was followed by the parlour-maid's announce-ment that Mr. Gill was there from the office. In the hall, in fact,

Kate found her son's partner, who explained apologetically that he had understood Peyton was dining at home, and had come to consult him about a difficulty which had arisen since he had left the office. On hearing that Dick was out, and that his mother did not know where he had gone, Mr. Gill's perplexity became so manifest that Mrs. Peyton, after a moment, said hesitatingly: "He may be at a friend's house; I could give you the address."

The architect caught up his hat. "Thank you; I'll have a try for him."

Mrs. Peyton hesitated again. "Perhaps," she suggested, "it would be better to telephone."

She led the way into the little study behind the drawing-room, where a telephone stood on the writing-table. The folding doors between the two rooms were open: should she close them as she passed back into the drawing-room? On the threshold she wavered an instant; then she walked on and took her usual seat by the fire.

Gill, meanwhile, at the telephone, had "rung up" the Verney house, and inquired if his partner were dining there. The reply was evidently affirmative; and a moment later Kate knew that he was in communication with her son. She sat motionless, her hands clasped on the arms of her chair, her head erect, in an attitude of avowed attention. If she listened she would listen openly: there should be no suspicion of eavesdropping. Gill, engrossed in his message, was probably hardly conscious of her presence; but if he turned his head he should at least have no difficulty in seeing her, and in being aware that she could hear what he said. Gill, however, as she was quick to remember, was doubtless ignorant of any need for secrecy in his communication to Dick. He had often heard the affairs of the office discussed openly before Mrs. Peyton, had been led to regard her as familiar with all the details of her son's work. He talked on unconcernedly, and she listened.

Ten minutes later, when he rose to go, she knew all that she had wanted to find out. Long familiarity with the technicalities of her son's profession made it easy for her to translate the steno-graphic jargon of the office. She could lengthen out all Gill's ab-breviations, interpret all his allusions, and reconstruct Dick's an-swers from the questions addressed to him. And when the door closed on the architect she was left face to face with the fact that her son, unknown to anyone but herself, was using Darrow's drawings to complete his work.

Mrs. Peyton, left alone, found it easier to continue her vigil by the drawing-room fire than to carry up to the darkness and si-lence of her own room the truth she had been at such pains to acquire. She had no thought of sitting up for Dick. Doubtless, his dinner over, he would rejoin Gill at the office, and prolong through the night the task in which she now knew him to be en-gaged. But it was less lonely by the fire than in the wide-eyed darkness which awaited her upstairs. A mortal loneliness enveloped her. She felt as though she had fallen by the way, spent and broken in a struggle of which even its object had been unconscious. She had tried to deflect the natural course of events, she had sacrificed her personal happiness to a fantastic ideal of duty, and it was her punishment to be left alone with her failure, outside the normal current of human strivings and regrets.

She had no wish to see her son just then: she would have preferred to let the inner tumult subside, to repossess herself in this new adjustment to life, before meeting his eyes again. But as she sat there, far adrift on her misery, she was aroused by the turning of his key in the latch. She started up, her heart sounding a retreat, but her faculties too dispersed to obey it; and while she stood wavering, the door opened and he was in the room.

In the room, and with face illumined: a Dick she had not seen since the strain of the contest had cast its shade on him. Now he shone as in a sunrise of victory, holding out exultant hands from which she hung back instinctively.

"Mother! I knew you'd be waiting for me!" He had her on his breast now, and his kisses were in her hair. "I've always said

you knew everything that was happening to me, and now you've
guessed that I wanted you tonight."

She was struggling faintly against the dear endearments.
"What *has* happened?" she murmured, drawing back for a dazzled look at him.

He had drawn her to the sofa, had dropped beside her, regaining his hold of her in the boyish need that his happiness
should be touched and handled.

"My engagement has happened!" he cried out to her. "You
stupid dear, do you need to be told?"

※ VII ※

SHE had indeed needed to be told: the surprise was complete
and overwhelming. She sat silent under it, her hands trembling
in his, till the blood mounted to his face and she felt his confident grasp relax.

"You didn't guess it, then?" he exclaimed, starting up and
moving away from her.

"No; I didn't guess it," she confessed in a dead-level voice.

He stood above her, half challenging, half defensive. "And
you haven't a word to say to me? Mother!" he adjured her.

She rose too, putting her arms about him with a kiss. "Dick!
Dear Dick!" she murmured.

"She imagines you don't like her; she says she's always felt it.
And yet she owns you've been delightful, that you've tried to
make friends with her. And I thought you knew how much it
would mean to me, just now, to have this uncertainty over, and
that you'd actually been trying to help me, to put in a good word
for me. I thought it was you who had made her decide."

"I?"

"By your talk with her the other day. She told me of your
talk with her."

His mother's hands slipped from his shoulders and she sank
back into her seat. She felt the cruelty of her silence, but only an

inarticulate murmur found a way to her lips. Before speaking she must clear a space in the suffocating rush of her sensations. For the moment she could only repeat inwardly that Clemence Verney had yielded before the final test, and that she herself was somehow responsible for this fresh entanglement of fate. For she saw in a flash how the coils of circumstance had tightened; and as her mind cleared it was filled with the perception that this, precisely, was what the girl intended, that this was why she had conferred the crown before the victory. By pledging herself to Dick she had secured his pledge in return: had put him on his honour in a cynical inversion of the term. Kate saw the succession of events spread out before her like a map, and the astuteness of the girl's policy frightened her. Miss Verney had conducted the campaign like a strategist. She had frankly owned that her interest in Dick's future depended on his capacity for success, and in order to key him up to his first achievement she had given him a foretaste of its results.

So much was almost immediately clear to Mrs. Peyton; but in a moment her inferences had carried her a point farther. For it was now plain to her that Miss Verney had not risked so much without first trying to gain her point at less cost: that if she had had to give herself as a prize, it was because no other bribe had been sufficient. This then, as the mother saw with a throb of hope, meant that Dick, who since Darrow's death had held to his purpose unwaveringly, had been deflected from it by the first hint of Clemence Verney's connivance. Kate had not miscalculated: things had happened as she had foreseen. In the light of the girl's approval his act had taken an odious look. He had recoiled from it, and it was to revive his flagging courage that she had had to promise herself, to take him in the meshes of her surrender.

Kate, looking up, saw above her the young perplexity of her boy's face, the suspended happiness waiting to brim over. With a fresh touch of misery she said to herself that this was his hour, his one irrecoverable moment, and that she was darkening it by her silence. Her memory went back to the same hour in her own life: she could feel its heat in her pulses still. What right had she to stand in Dick's light? Who was she to decide between his code and hers? She put out her hand and drew him down to her.

"She'll be the making of me, you know, mother," he said, as they leaned together. "She'll put new life in me—she'll help me get my second wind. Her talk is like a fresh breeze blowing away the fog in my head. I never knew anyone who saw so straight to the heart of things, who had such a grip on values. She goes straight up to life and catches hold of it, and you simply can't make her let go."

He got up and walked the length of the room; then he came back and stood smiling above his mother.

"You know you and I are rather complicated people," he said. "We're always walking around things to get new views of them—we're always rearranging the furniture. And somehow she simplifies life so tremendously." He dropped down beside her with a deprecating laugh. "Not that I mean, dear, that it hasn't been good for me to argue things out with myself, as you've taught me to—only the man who stops to talk is apt to get shoved aside nowadays, and I don't believe Milton's archangels would have had much success in active business."

He had begun in a strain of easy confidence, but as he went on she detected an effort to hold the note, she felt that his words were being poured out in a vain attempt to fill the silence which was deepening between them. She longed, in her turn, to pour something into that menacing void, to bridge it with a reconciling word or look; but her soul hung back, and she had to take refuge in a vague murmur of tenderness.

"My boy! My boy!" she repeated; and he sat beside her without speaking, their hand-clasp alone spanning the distance which had widened between their thoughts.

The engagement, as Kate subsequently learned, was not to be made known till later. Miss Verney had even stipulated that for the present there should be no recognition of it in her own family or in Dick's. She did not wish to interfere with his final work for the competition, and had made him promise, as he laughingly owned, that he would not see her again till the drawings were sent in. His mother noticed that he made no other allusion to his work; but when he bade her good-night he added that he might not see her the next morning, as he had to go to the office early. She took this as a hint that he wished to be left alone, and kept her room the next day till the closing door told her that he was out of the house.

She herself had waked early, and it seemed to her that the day was already old when she came downstairs. Never had the house appeared so empty. Even in Dick's longest absences something of his presence had always hung about the rooms: a fine dust of memories and associations, which wanted only the evocation of her thought to float into a palpable semblance of him. But now he seemed to have taken himself quite away, to have broken every fibre by which their lives had hung together. Where the sense of him had been there was only a deeper emptiness: she felt as if a strange man had gone out of her house.

She wandered from room to room, aimlessly, trying to adjust herself to their solitude. She had known such loneliness before, in the years when most women's hearts are fullest; but that was long ago, and the solitude had after all been less complete, because of the sense that it might still be filled. Her son had come: her life had brimmed over; but now the tide ebbed again, and she was left gazing over a bare stretch of wasted years. Wasted! There was the mortal pang, the stroke from which there was no healing. Her faith and hope had been marsh-lights luring her to the wilderness, her love a vain edifice reared on shifting ground.

In her round of the rooms she came at last to Dick's study upstairs. It was full of his boyhood: she could trace the history of his past in its quaint relics and survivals, in the school-books lingering on his crowded shelves, the school-photographs and college-trophies hung among his later treasures. All his successes and failures, his exaltations and inconsistencies, were recorded in the warm huddled heterogeneous room. Everywhere she saw the touch of her own hand, the vestiges of her own steps. It was she alone who held the clue to the labyrinth, who could thread a way through the confusions and contradictions of his past; and her soul rejected the thought that his future could ever escape from her. She dropped down into his shabby college armchair and hid her face in the papers on his desk.

※ VIII ※

THE day dwelt in her memory as a long stretch of aimless hours: blind alleys of time that led up to a dead wall of inaction.

Toward afternoon she remembered that she had promised to dine out and go to the opera. At first she felt that the contact of life would be unendurable; then she shrank from shutting herself up with her misery. In the end she let herself drift passively on the current of events, going through the mechanical routine of the day without much consciousness of what was happening.

At twilight, as she sat in the drawing-room, the evening paper was brought in, and in glancing over it her eye fell on a paragraph which seemed printed in more vivid type than the rest. It was headed, *The New Museum of Sculpture,* and underneath she read: "The artist and architects selected to pass on the competitive designs for the new Museum will begin their sittings on Monday, and tomorrow is the last day on which designs may be sent in to the committee. Great interest is felt in the competition, as the conspicuous site chosen for the new building, and the exceptionally large sum voted by the city for its erection, offer an unusual field for the display of architectural ability."

She leaned back, closing her eyes. It was as though a clock had struck, loud and inexorably, marking off some irrecoverable hour. She was seized by a sudden longing to seek Dick out, to fall on her knees and plead with him: it was one of those physical obsessions against which the body has to stiffen its muscles as well as the mind its thoughts. Once she even sprang up to ring for a cab; but she sank back again, breathing as if after a struggle, and gripping the arms of her chair to keep herself down.

"I can only wait for him—only wait for him—" she heard herself say; and the words loosened the sobs in her throat.

At length she went upstairs to dress for dinner. A ghost-like self looked back at her from her toilet-glass: she watched it performing the mechanical gestures of the toilet, dressing her, as it appeared, without help from her actual self. Each little act stood out sharply against the blurred background of her brain: when she spoke to her maid her voice sounded extraordinarily loud. Never had the house been so silent; or, stay—yes, once she had felt the same silence, once when Dick, in his school-days, had been ill of a fever, and she had sat up with him on the decisive night. The silence had been as deep and as terrible then; and as she dressed she had before her the vision of his room, of the cot in which he lay, of his restless head working a hole in the pillow, his face so pinched and alien under the familiar freckles. It might be his death-watch she was keeping: the doctors had warned her to be ready. And in the silence her soul had fought for her boy, her love had hung over him like wings, her abundant useless hateful life had struggled to force itself into his empty veins. And she had succeeded, she had saved him, she had poured her life into him; and in place of the strange child she had watched all night, at daylight she held her own boy to her breast.

That night had once seemed to her the most dreadful of her life; but she knew now that it was one of the agonies which enrich, that the passion thus spent grows fourfold from its ashes. She could not have borne to keep this new vigil alone. She must escape from its sterile misery, must take refuge in other lives till she regained courage to face her own. At the opera, in the illumination of the first *entr'acte,* as she gazed about the house, wondering through the numb ache of her wretchedness how others could talk and smile and be indifferent, it seemed to her that all the jarring animation about her was suddenly focussed in the face of Clemence Verney. Miss Verney sat opposite, in the front of a crowded box, a box in which, continually, the black-coated background shifted and renewed itself. Mrs. Peyton felt a throb of anger at the girl's bright air of unconcern. She forgot that she

too was talking, smiling, holding out her hand to newcomers, in a
studied mimicry of life, while her real self played out its tragedy
behind the scenes. Then it occurred to her that, to Clemence
Verney, there was no tragedy in the situation. According to the
girl's calculations, Dick was virtually certain of success; and un-
success was to her the only conceivable disaster.

All through the opera the sense of that opposing force, that
negation of her own beliefs, burned itself into Mrs. Peyton's consciousness. The space between herself and the girl seemed to
vanish, the throng about them to disperse, till they were face to
face and alone, enclosed in their mortal enmity. At length the
feeling of humiliation and defeat grew unbearable to Mrs.
Peyton. The girl seemed to flout her in the insolence of victory,
to sit there as the visible symbol of her failure. It was better after
all to be at home alone with her thoughts.

As she drove away from the opera she thought of that other
vigil which, only a few streets away, Dick was perhaps still keeping. She wondered if his work were over, if the final stroke had
been drawn. And as she pictured him there, signing his pact with
evil in the loneliness of the conniving night, an uncontrollable
impulse possessed her. She must drive by his windows and see if
they were still alight. She would not go up to him,—she dared
not,—but at least she would pass near to him, would invisibly
share his watch and hover on the edge of his thoughts. She lowered the window and called out the address to the coachman.

The tall office-building loomed silent and dark as she approached it; but presently, high up, she caught a light in the familiar windows. Her heart gave a leap, and the light swam on
her through tears. The carriage drew up, and for a moment she
sat motionless. Then the coachman bent down toward her, and
she saw that he was asking if he should drive on. She tried to
shape a yes, but her lips refused it, and she shook her head. He
continued to lean down perplexedly, and at length, under the interrogation of his attitude, it became impossible to sit still, and
she opened the door and stepped out. It was equally impossible
to stand on the sidewalk, and her next steps carried her to the

door of the building. She groped for the bell and rang it, feeling
still dimly accountable to the coachman for some consecutiveness
of action, and after a moment the night watchman opened the
door, drawing back amazed at the shining apparition which confronted him. Recognizing Mrs. Peyton, whom he had seen about
the building by day, he tried to adapt himself to the situation by
a vague stammer of apology.

"I came to see if my son is still here," she faltered.

"Yes, ma'am, he's here. He's been here most nights lately till
after twelve."

"And is Mr. Gill with him?"

"No: Mr. Gill he went away just after I come on this
evening."

She glanced up into the cavernous darkness of the stairs.

"Is he alone up there, do you think?"

"Yes, ma'am, I know he's alone, because I seen his men leaving soon after Mr. Gill."

Kate lifted her head quickly. "Then I will go up to him," she
said.

The watchman apparently did not think it proper to offer
any comment on this unusual proceeding, and a moment later
she was fluttering and rustling up through the darkness, like a
night-bird hovering among rafters. There were ten flights to
climb: at every one her breath failed her, and she had to stand
still and press her hands against her heart. Then the weight on
her breast lifted, and she went on again, upward and upward,
the great dark building dropping away from her, in tier after tier
of mute doors and mysterious corridors. At last she reached
Dick's floor, and saw the light shining down the passage from his
door. She leaned against the wall, her breath coming short, the
silence throbbing in her ears. Even now it was not too late to
turn back. She bent over the stairs, letting her eyes plunge into
the nether blackness, with the single glimmer of the watchman's
lights in its depths; then she turned and stole toward her son's
door.

There again she paused and listened, trying to catch,

through the hum of her pulses, any noise that might come to her from within. But the silence was unbroken—it seemed as though the office must be empty. She pressed her ear to the door, straining for a sound. She knew he never sat long at his work, and it seemed unaccountable that she should not hear him moving about the drawing-board. For a moment she fancied he might be sleeping; but sleep did not come to him readily after prolonged mental effort—she recalled the restless straying of his feet above her head for hours after he returned from his night work in the office.

She began to fear that he might be ill. A nervous trembling seized her, and she laid her hand on the latch, whispering "Dick!"

Her whisper sounded loudly through the silence, but there was no answer, and after a pause she called again. With each call the hush seemed to deepen: it closed in on her, mysterious and impenetrable. Her heart was beating in short frightened leaps: a moment more and she would have cried out. She drew a quick breath and turned the door-handle.

The outer room, Dick's private office, with its red carpet and easy-chairs, stood in pleasant lamp-lit emptiness. The last time she had entered it, Darrow and Clemence Verney had been there, and she had sat behind the urn observing them. She paused a moment, struck now by a faint sound from beyond; then she slipped noiselessly across the carpet, pushed open the swinging door, and stood on the threshold of the work-room. Here the gas-lights hung a green-shaded circle of brightness over the great draughting-table in the middle of the floor. Table and floor were strewn with a confusion of papers—torn blue-prints and tracings, crumpled sheets of tracing-paper wrenched from the draughting-boards in a sudden fury of destruction; and in the centre of the havoc, his arms stretched across the table and his face hidden in them, sat Dick Peyton.

He did not seem to hear his mother's approach, and she stood looking at him, her breast tightening with a new fear.

"Dick!" she said, "Dick!—" and he sprang up, staring with dazed eyes. But gradually, as his gaze cleared, a light spread in it, a mounting brightness of recognition.

"You've come—you've come—" he said, stretching his hands to her; and all at once she had him in her breast as in a shelter.

"You wanted me?" she whispered as she held him.

He looked up at her, tired, breathless, with the white radiance of the runner near the goal.

"I *had* you, dear!" he said, smiling strangely on her; and her heart gave a great leap of understanding.

Her arms had slipped from his neck, and she stood leaning on him, deep-suffused in the shyness of her discovery. For it might still be that he did not wish her to know what she had done for him.

But he put his arm about her, boyishly, and drew her toward one of the hard seats between the tables; and there, on the bare floor, he knelt before her, and hid his face in her lap. She sat motionless, feeling the dear warmth of his head against her knees, letting her hands stray in faint caresses through his hair.

Neither spoke for awhile; then he raised his head and looked at her. "I suppose you know what has been happening to me," he said.

She shrank from seeming to press into his life a hair's-breadth farther than he was prepared to have her go. Her eyes turned from him toward the scattered drawings on the table.

"You have given up the competition?" she said.

"Yes—and a lot more." He stood up, the wave of emotion ebbing, yet leaving him nearer, in his recovered calmness, than in the shock of their first moment.

"I didn't know, at first, how much you guessed," he went on quietly. "I was sorry I'd shown you Darrow's letter; but it didn't worry me much because I didn't suppose you'd think it possible that I should—take advantage of it. It's only lately that I've understood that you knew everything." He looked at her with a smile. "I don't know yet how I found it out, for you're wonderful about keeping things to yourself, and you never made a sign. I simply felt it in a kind of nearness—as if I couldn't get away from you.—Oh, there were times when I should have preferred not having you about—when I tried to turn my back on you, to see things from other people's standpoint. But you were always there—you wouldn't be discouraged. And I got tired of trying to explain things to you, of trying to bring you round to my way of thinking. You wouldn't go away and you wouldn't come any nearer—you just stood there and watched everything that I was doing."

He broke off, taking one of his restless turns down the long room. Then he drew up a chair beside her, and dropped into it with a great sigh.

"At first, you know, I hated it most awfully. I wanted to be let alone and to work out my own theory of things. If you'd said a word—if you'd tried to influence me—the spell would have been broken. But just because the actual *you* kept apart and didn't meddle or pry, the other, the you in my heart, seemed to get a tighter hold on me. I don't know how to tell you,—it's all mixed up in my head—but old things you'd said and done kept coming back to me, crowding between me and what I was trying for, looking at me without speaking, like old friends I'd gone back on, till I simply couldn't stand it any longer. I fought it off till tonight, but when I came back to finish the work there you were again—and suddenly, I don't know how, you weren't an obstacle any longer, but a refuge—and I crawled into your arms as I used to when things went against me at school."

His hands stole back into hers, and he leaned his head against her shoulder like a boy.

"I'm an abysmally weak fool, you know," he ended; "I'm not worth the fight you've put up for me. But I want you to know that it's your doing—that if you had let go an instant I should have gone under—and that if I'd gone under I should never have come up again alive."

Madame de Treymes

❦[1907]❦

JOHN DURHAM, while he waited for Madame de Malrive to draw on her gloves, stood in the hotel doorway looking out across the Rue de Rivoli at the afternoon brightness of the Tuileries gardens.

His European visits were infrequent enough to have kept unimpaired the freshness of his eye, and he was always struck anew by the vast and consummately ordered spectacle of Paris: by its look of having been boldly and deliberately planned as a background for the enjoyment of life, instead of being forced into grudging concessions to the festive instincts, or barricading itself against them in unenlightened ugliness, like his own lamentable New York.

But today, if the scene had never presented itself more alluringly, in that moist spring bloom between showers, when the horse-chestnuts dome themselves in unreal green against a gauzy sky, and the very dust of the pavement seems the fragrance of lilac made visible—today for the first time the sense of a personal stake in it all, of having to reckon individually with its effects and influences, kept Durham from an unrestrained yielding to the spell. Paris might still be—to the unimplicated it doubtless still was—the most beautiful city in the world; but whether it were the most lovable or the most detestable depended for him, in the last analysis, on the buttoning of the white glove over which Fanny de Malrive still lingered.

The mere fact of her having forgotten to draw on her gloves as they were descending in the hotel lift from his mother's drawing-room was, in this connection, charged with significance to Durham. She was the kind of woman who always presents herself to the mind's eye as completely equipped, as made up of exquisitely cared for and finely related details; and that the heat of her parting with his family should have left her unconscious that she was emerging gloveless into Paris, seemed, on the whole, to speak hopefully for Durham's future opinion of the city.

Even now, he could detect a certain confusion, a desire to draw breath and catch up with life, in the way she dawdled over the last buttons in the dimness of the porte-cochère, while her footman, outside, hung on her retarded signal.

When at length they emerged, it was to learn from that functionary that Madame la Marquise's carriage had been obliged to yield its place at the door, but was at the moment in the act of regaining it. Madame de Malrive cut the explanation short. "I shall walk home. The carriage this evening at eight."

As the footman turned away, she raised her eyes for the first time to Durham's.

"Will you walk with me? Let us cross the Tuileries. I should like to sit a moment on the terrace."

She spoke quite easily and naturally, as if it were the most commonplace thing in the world for them to be straying afoot together over Paris; but even his vague knowledge of the world she lived in—a knowledge mainly acquired through the perusal of yellow-backed fiction—gave a thrilling significance to her naturalness. Durham, indeed, was beginning to find that one of the charms of a sophisticated society is that it lends point and perspective to the slightest contact between the sexes. If, in the old unrestricted New York days, Fanny Frisbee, from a brownstone door-step, had proposed that they should take a walk in the Park, the idea would have presented itself to her companion as agreeable but unimportant; whereas Fanny de Malrive's suggestion that they should stroll across the Tuileries was obviously fraught with unspecified possibilities.

He was so throbbing with the sense of these possibilities that he walked beside her without speaking down the length of the wide alley which follows the line of the Rue de Rivoli, suffering her even, when they reached its farthest end, to direct him in silence up the steps to the terrace of the Feuillants. For, after all, the possibilities were double-faced, and her bold departure from custom might simply mean that what she had to say was so dreadful that it needed all the tenderest mitigation of circumstance.

There was apparently nothing embarrassing to her in his silence: it was a part of her long European discipline that she had learned to manage pauses with ease. In her Frisbee days she might have packed this one with a random fluency; now she was content to let it widen slowly before them like the spacious prospect opening at their feet. The complicated beauty of this prospect, as they moved toward it between the symmetrically clipped limes of the lateral terrace, touched him anew through her nearness, as with the hint of some vast impersonal power, controlling and regulating her life in ways he could not guess, putting between himself and her the whole width of the civilization into which her marriage had absorbed her. And there was such fear in the thought—he read such derision of what he had to offer in the splendour of the great avenues tapering upward to the sunset glories of the Arch—that all he had meant to say when he finally spoke compressed itself at last into an abrupt unmitigated: "Well?"

She answered at once—as though she had only awaited the call of the national interrogation—"I don't know when I have been so happy."

"So happy?" The suddenness of his joy flushed up through his fair skin.

"As I was just now—taking tea with your mother and sisters."

Durham's "Oh!" of surprise betrayed also a note of disillusionment, which she met only by the reconciling murmur: "Shall we sit down?"

He found two of the springy yellow chairs indigenous to the spot, and placed them under the tree near which they had paused, saying reluctantly, as he did so: "Of course it was an immense pleasure to *them* to see you again."

"Oh, not in the same way. I mean—" she paused, sinking into the chair, and betraying, for the first time, a momentary inability to deal becomingly with the situation. "I mean," she resumed, smiling, "that it was not an event for them, as it was for me."

"An event?"—he caught her up again, eagerly; for what, in the language of any civilization, could that word mean but just the one thing he most wished it to?

"To be with dear, good, sweet, simple, real Americans again!" she burst out, heaping up her epithets with reckless prodigality.

Durham's smile once more faded to impersonality, as he rejoined, just a shade on the defensive: "If it's merely our Americanism you enjoyed—I've no doubt we can give you all you want in that line."

"Yes, it's just that! But if you knew what the word means to me! It means—it means—" she paused as if to assure herself that they were sufficiently isolated from the desultory groups beneath the other trees—"it means that I'm *safe* with them; as safe as in a bank!"

Durham felt a sudden warmth behind his eyes and in his throat. "I think I do know——"

"No, you don't, really; you can't know how dear and strange and familiar it all sounded: the old New York names that kept coming up in your mother's talk, and her charming quaint ideas about Europe—their all regarding it as a great big innocent pleasure ground and shop for Americans; and your mother's missing the homemade bread and preferring the American asparagus— I'm so tired of Americans who despise even their own asparagus! And then your married sister's spending her summers at—where is it?—the Kittawittany House on Lake Pohunk——"

A vision of earnest women in Shetland shawls, with spectacles and thin knobs of hair, eating blueberry-pie at unwholesome hours in a shingled dining-room on a bare New England hilltop, rose pallidly between Durham and the verdant brightness of the Champs Elysées, and he protested with a slight smile: "Oh, but my married sister is the black sheep of the family—the rest of us never sank as low as that."

"Low? I think it's beautiful—fresh and innocent and simple. I remember going to such a place once. They have early dinner —rather late—and go off in buckboards over terrible roads, and bring back goldenrod and autumn leaves, and read nature books aloud on the piazza; and there is always one shy young man in flannels—only one—who has come to see the prettiest girl (though how he can choose among so many!) and who takes her off in a buggy for hours and hours——" She paused and summed up with a long sigh: "It is fifteen years since I was in America."

"And you're still so good an American."

"Oh, a better and better one every day!"

He hesitated. "Then why did you never come back?"

Her face altered instantly, exchanging its retrospective light for the look of slightly shadowed watchfulness which he had known as most habitual to it.

"It was impossible—it has always been so. My husband would not go; and since—since our separation—there have been family reasons."

Durham sighed impatiently. "Why do you talk of reasons? The truth is, you have made your life here. You could never give all this up!" He made a discouraged gesture in the direction of the Place de la Concorde.

"Give it up! I would go tomorrow! But it could never, now, be for more than a visit. I must live in France on account of my boy."

Durham's heart gave a quick beat. At last the talk had neared the point toward which his whole mind was straining, and he began to feel a personal application in her words. But that made him all the more cautious about choosing his own.

"It is an agreement—about the boy?" he ventured.

"I gave my word. They knew that was enough," she said proudly; adding, as if to put him in full possession of her reasons: "It would have been much more difficult for me to obtain complete control of my son if it had not been understood that I was to live in France."

"That seems fair," Durham assented after a moment's reflection: it was his instinct, even in the heat of personal endeavour, to pause a moment on the question of "fairness." The personal claim reasserted itself as he added tentatively: "But when he *is* brought up—when he's grown up: then you would feel freer?"

She received this with a start, as a possibility too remote to have entered into her view of the future. "He is only eight years old!" she objected.

"Ah, of course it would be a long way off?"

"A long way off, thank heaven! French mothers part late with their sons, and in that one respect I mean to be a French mother."

"Of course—naturally—since he has only you," Durham again assented.

He was eager to show how fully he took her point of view, if only to dispose her to the reciprocal fairness of taking his when the time came to present it. And he began to think that the time had now come; that their walk would not have thus resolved itself, without excuse or pretext, into a tranquil session beneath the trees, for any purpose less important than that of giving him his opportunity.

He took it, characteristically, without seeking a transition. "When I spoke to you, the other day, about myself—about what I felt for you—I said nothing of the future, because, for the moment, my mind refused to travel beyond its immediate hope of happiness. But I felt, of course, even then, that the hope involved various difficulties—that we can't, as we might once have done, come together without any thought but for ourselves; and whatever your answer is to be, I want to tell you now that I am ready to accept my share of the difficulties." He paused, and then added explicitly: "If there's the least chance of your listening to me, I'm willing to live over here as long as you can keep your boy with you."

❋ II ❋

WHATEVER Madame de Malrive's answer was to be, there could be no doubt as to her readiness to listen. She received Durham's words without sign of resistance, and took time to ponder them gently before she answered, in a voice touched by emotion: "You are very generous—very unselfish; but when you fix a limit—no matter how remote—to my remaining here, I see how wrong it is to let myself consider for a moment such possibilities as we have been talking of."

"Wrong? Why should it be wrong?"

"Because I shall want to keep my boy always! Not, of course, in the sense of living with him, or even forming an important part of his life; I am not deluded enough to think that possible. But I do believe it possible never to pass wholly out of his life; and while there is a hope of that, how can I leave him?" She paused, and turned on him a new face, a face in which the past of which he was still so ignorant showed itself like a shadow suddenly darkening a clear pane. "How can I make you understand?" she went on urgently. "It is not only because of my love for him—not only, I mean, because of my own happiness in being with him; that I can't, in imagination, surrender even the remotest hour of his future; it is because, the moment he passes out of my influence, he passes under that other—the influence I have been fighting against every hour since he was born!—I don't mean, you know," she added, as Durham, with bent head, continued to offer her the silent fixity of his attention, "I don't mean the special personal influence—except inasmuch as it represents something wider, more general, something that encloses and circulates through the whole world in which he belongs. That is what I meant when I said you could never understand! There is nothing in your experience—in any American experience—to correspond with that far-reaching family organization, which is itself a part of the larger system, and which encloses a young man of my son's position in a network of accepted prejudices and opinions. Everything is prepared in advance—his political and religious convictions, his judgments of people, his sense of honour, his ideas of women, his whole view of life. He is taught to see vileness and corruption in everyone not of his own way of thinking, and in every idea that does not directly serve the religious and political purposes of his class. The truth isn't a fixed thing: it's not used to test actions by, it's tested by them, and made to fit in with them. And this forming of the mind begins with the child's first consciousness; it's in his nursery stories, his baby prayers, his very games with his playmates! Already he is only half mine, because the Church has the other half, and will be reaching out for my share as soon as his education begins. But that other half is still mine, and I mean to make it the strongest and most living half of the two, so that, when the inevitable conflict begins, the energy and the truth and the endurance shall be on my side and not on theirs!"

She paused, flushing with the repressed fervour of her utterance, though her voice had not been raised beyond its usual discreet modulations; and Durham felt himself tingling with the transmitted force of her resolve. Whatever shock her words brought to his personal hope, he was grateful to her for speaking them so clearly, for having so sure a grasp of her purpose.

Her decision strengthened his own, and after a pause of deliberation he said quietly: "There might be a good deal to urge on the other side—the ineffectualness of your sacrifice, the probability that when your son marries he will inevitably be absorbed back into the life of his class and his people; but I can't look at it in that way, because if I were in your place I believe I should feel just as you do about it. As long as there was a fighting chance I should want to keep hold of my half, no matter how much the struggle cost me. And one reason why I understand your feeling about your boy is that I have the same feeling about *you:* as long as there's a fighting chance of keeping my half of you—the half he is willing to spare me—I don't see how I can ever give it up." He waited again, and then brought out firmly: "If you'll marry me, I'll agree to live out here as long as you want, and we'll be two instead of one to keep hold of your half of him."

He raised his eyes as he ended, and saw that hers met them through a quick clouding of tears.

"Ah, I am glad to have had this said to me! But I could never accept such an offer."

He caught instantly at the distinction. "That doesn't mean that you could never accept *me?*"

"Under such conditions——"

"But if I am satisfied with the conditions? Don't think I am speaking rashly, under the influence of the moment. I have expected something of this sort, and I have thought out my side of the case. As far as material circumstances go, I have worked long enough and successfully enough to take my ease and take it where I choose. I mention that because the life I offer you is offered to your boy as well." He let this sink into her mind before summing up gravely: "The offer I make is made deliberately, and at least I have a right to a direct answer."

She was silent again, and then lifted a cleared gaze to his. "My direct answer then is: if I were still Fanny Frisbee I would marry you."

He bent toward her persuasively. "But you will be—when the divorce is pronounced."

"Ah, the divorce——" She flushed deeply, with an instinctive shrinking back of her whole person which made him straighten himself in his chair.

"Do you so dislike the idea?"

"The idea of divorce? No—not in my case. I should like anything that would do away with the past—obliterate, it all—make everything new in my life!"

"Then what——?" he began again, waiting with the patience of a wooer on the uneasy circling of her tormented mind.

"Oh, don't ask me; I don't know; I am frightened."

Durham gave a deep sigh of discouragement. "I thought your coming here with me today—and above all your going with me just now to see my mother—was a sign that you were *not* frightened!"

"Well, I was not when I was with your mother. She made everything seem easy and natural. She took me back into that clear American air where there are no obscurities, no mysteries——"

"What obscurities, what mysteries, are you afraid of?"

She looked about her with a faint shiver. "I am afraid of everything!" she said.

"That's because you are alone; because you've no one to turn to. I'll clear the air for you fast enough if you'll let me."

He looked forth defiantly, as if flinging his challenge at the great city which had come to typify the powers contending with him for her possession.

"You say that so easily! But you don't know; none of you know."

"Know what?"

"The difficulties——"

"I told you I was ready to take my share of the difficulties—and my share naturally includes yours. You know Americans are great hands at getting over difficulties." He drew himself up confidently. "Just leave that to me—only tell me exactly what you're afraid of."

She paused again, and then said: "The divorce, to begin with—they will never consent to it."

He noticed that she spoke as though the interests of the whole clan, rather than her husband's individual claim, were to be considered; and the use of the plural pronoun shocked his free individualism like a glimpse of some dark feudal survival.

"But you are absolutely certain of your divorce! I've consulted—of course without mentioning names——"

She interrupted him, with a melancholy smile: "Ah, so have I. The divorce would be easy enough to get, if they ever let it come into the courts."

"How on earth can they prevent that?"

"I don't know; my never knowing how they will do things is one of the secrets of their power."

"Their power? What power?" he broke in with irrepressible contempt. "Who are these bogeys whose machinations are going to arrest the course of justice in a—comparatively—civilized country? You've told me yourself that Monsieur de Malrive is the least likely to give you trouble; and the others are his uncle the abbé, his mother and sister. That kind of a syndicate doesn't scare me much. A priest and two women *contra mundum!*"

She shook her head. "Not *contra mundum,* but with it, their whole world is behind them. It's that mysterious solidarity that you can't understand. One doesn't know how far they may reach, or in how many directions. I have never known. They have always cropped up where I least expected them."

Before this persistency of negation Durham's buoyancy began to flag, but his determination grew the more fixed.

"Well, then, supposing them to possess these supernatural powers; do you think it's to people of that kind that I'll ever consent to give you up?"

She raised a half-smiling glance of protest. "Oh, they're not wantonly wicked. They'll leave me alone as long as——"

"As I do?" he interrupted. "Do you want me to leave you alone? Was that what you brought me here to tell me?"

The directness of the challenge seemed to gather up the scattered strands of her hesitation, and lifting her head she turned on him a look in which, but for its underlying shadow, he might have recovered the full free beam of Fanny Frisbee's gaze.

"I don't know why I brought you here," she said gently, "except from the wish to prolong a little the illusion of being once more an American among Americans. Just now, sitting there with your mother and Katy and Nannie, the difficulties seemed to vanish; the problems grew as trivial to me as they are to you. And I wanted them to remain so a little longer; I wanted to put off going back to them. But it was of no use—they were waiting for me here. They are over there now in that house across the river." She indicated the grey skyline of the Faubourg, shining in the splintered radiance of the sunset beyond the long sweep of the quays. "They are a part of me—I belong to them. I must go back to them!" she sighed.

She rose slowly to her feet, as though her metaphor had expressed an actual fact and she felt herself bodily drawn from his side by the influences of which she spoke.

Durham had risen too. "Then I go back with you!" he exclaimed energetically; and as she paused, wavering a little under the shock of his resolve: "I don't mean into your house—but into your life!" he said.

She suffered him, at any rate, to accompany her to the door of the house, and allowed their debate to prolong itself through the almost monastic quiet of the quarter which led thither. On the way, he succeeded in wresting from her the confession that, if it were possible to ascertain in advance that her husband's family would not oppose her action, she might decide to apply for a divorce. Short of a positive assurance on this point, she made it clear that she would never move in the matter; there must be no scandal, no *retentissement*, nothing which her boy, necessarily brought up in the French tradition of scrupulously preserved appearances, could afterward regard as the faintest blur on his much-quartered escutcheon. But even this partial concession again raised fresh obstacles; for there seemed to be no one to whom she could entrust so delicate an investigation, and to apply directly to the Marquis de Malrive or his relatives appeared, in the light of her past experience, the last way of learning their intentions.

"But," Durham objected, beginning to suspect a morbid fixity of idea in her perpetual attitude of distrust—"but surely you have told me that your husband's sister—what is her name? Madame de Treymes?—was the most powerful member of the group, and that she has always been on your side."

She hesitated. "Yes, Christiane has been on my side. She dislikes her brother. But it would not do to ask her."

"But could no one else ask her? Who are her friends?"

"She has a great many; and some, of course, are mine. But in a case like this they would be all hers; they wouldn't hesitate a moment between us."

"Why should it be necessary to hesitate between you? Suppose Madame de Treymes sees the reasonableness of what you ask; suppose, at any rate, she sees the hopelessness of opposing you? Why should she make a mystery of your opinion?"

"It's not that; it is that, if I went to her friends, I should never get her real opinion from them. At least I should never know if it *was* her real opinion; and therefore I should be no farther advanced. Don't you see?"

Durham struggled between the sentimental impulse to soothe her, and the practical instinct that it was a moment for unmitigated frankness.

"I'm not sure that I do; but if you can't find out what Madame de Treymes thinks, I'll see what I can do myself."

"Oh—*you!*" broke from her in mingled terror and admiration; and pausing on her doorstep to lay her hand in his before she touched the bell, she added with a half-whimsical flash of regret: "Why didn't this happen to Fanny Frisbee?"

❊ III ❊

WHY had it not happened to Fanny Frisbee?

Durham put the question to himself as he walked back along the quays, in a state of inner commotion which left him, for once, insensible to the ordered beauty of his surroundings. Propinquity had not been lacking: he had known Miss Frisbee since his college days. In unsophisticated circles, one family is apt to quote another; and the Durham ladies had always quoted the Frisbees. The Frisbees were bold, experienced, enterprising: they had what the novelists of the day called "dash." The beautiful Fanny was especially dashing; she had the showiest national attributes, tempered only by a native grace of softness, as the beam of her eyes was subdued by the length of their lashes. And yet young Durham, though not unsusceptible to such charms, had remained content to enjoy them from a safe distance of good-fellowship. If he had been asked why, he could not have told; but the Durham of forty understood. It was because there were, with minor modifications, many other Fanny Frisbees; whereas never before, within his ken, had there been a Fanny de Malrive.

He had felt it in a flash, when, the autumn before, he had run across her one evening in the dining-room of the Beaurivage at Ouchy; when, after a furtive exchange of glances, they had simultaneously arrived at recognition, followed by an eager pressure of hands, and a long evening of reminiscence on the starlit terrace. She was the same, but so mysteriously changed! And it was the mystery, the sense of unprobed depths of initiation, which drew him to her as her freshness had never drawn him. He had not hitherto attempted to define the nature of the change: it remained for his sister Nannie to do that when, on his return to the Rue de Rivoli, where the family were still sitting in conclave upon their recent visitor, Miss Durham summed up their groping comments in the phrase: "I never saw anything so French!"

Durham, understanding what his sister's use of the epithet implied, recognized it instantly as the explanation of his own feelings. Yes, it was the finish, the modelling, which Madame de Malrive's experience had given her that set her apart from the fresh uncomplicated personalities of which she had once been simply the most charming type. The influences that had lowered her voice, regulated her gestures, toned her down to harmony with the warm dim background of a long social past—these influences had lent to her natural fineness of perception a command of expression adapted to complex conditions. She had moved in surroundings through which one could hardly bounce and bang on the genial American plan without knocking the angles off a number of sacred institutions; and her acquired dexterity of movement seemed to Durham a crowning grace. It was a shock, now that he knew at what cost the dexterity had been acquired, to acknowledge this even to himself; he hated to think that she could owe anything to such conditions as she had been placed in. And it gave him a sense of the tremendous strength of the organization into which she had been absorbed, that in spite of her horror, her moral revolt, she had not reacted against its external forms. She might abhor her husband, her marriage, and the world to which it had introduced her, but she had become a product of that world in its outward expression, and no better proof of the fact was needed than her exotic enjoyment of Americanism.

The sense of the distance to which her American past had been removed was never more present to him than when, a day or two later, he went with his mother and sisters to return her visit. The region beyond the river existed, for the Durham ladies, only as the unmapped environment of the Bon Marché; and Nannie Durham's exclamation on the pokiness of the streets and the dulness of the houses showed Durham, with a start, how far he had already travelled from the family point of view.

"Well, if this is all she got by marrying a Marquis!" the young lady summed up as they paused before the small sober hotel in its high-walled court; and Katy, following her mother through the stone-vaulted and stone-floored vestibule, murmured: "It must be simply freezing in winter."

In the softly faded drawing-room, with its old pastels in old frames, its windows looking on the damp green twilight of a garden sunk deep in blackened walls, the American ladies might have been even more conscious of the insufficiency of their friend's compensations, had not the warmth of her welcome precluded all other reflections. It was not till she had gathered them about her in the corner beside the tea-table, that Durham identified the slender dark lady loitering negligently in the background, and introduced in a comprehensive murmur to the American group, as the redoubtable sister-in-law to whom he had declared himself ready to throw down his challenge.

There was nothing very redoubtable about Madame de Treymes, except perhaps the kindly yet critical observation which she bestowed on her sister-in-law's visitors: the unblinking attention of a civilized spectator observing an encampment of aborigines. He had heard of her as a beauty, and was surprised to find her, as Nannie afterward put it, a mere stick to hang clothes on (but they *did* hang!), with a small brown glancing face, like that of a charming little inquisitive animal. Yet before she had addressed ten words to him—nibbling at the hard English consonants like nuts—he owned the justice of the epithet. She was a beauty, if beauty, instead of being restricted to the cast of the face, is a pervasive attribute informing the hands, the voice, the gestures, the very fall of a flounce and tilt of a feather. In this impalpable *aura* of grace Madame de Treymes' dark meagre presence unmistakably moved, like a thin flame in a wide quiver of light. And as he realized that she looked much handsomer than she was, so, while they talked, he felt that she understood a great deal more than she betrayed. It was not through the groping speech which formed their apparent medium of communication that she imbibed her information: she found it in the air, she extracted it from Durham's look and manner, she caught it in the turn of her sister-in-law's defenceless eyes—for in her presence Madame de Malrive became Fanny Frisbee again!—she put it together, in short, out of just such unconsidered indescribable trifles as differentiated the quiet felicity of her dress from Nannie and Katy's "handsome" haphazard clothes.

Her actual converse with Durham moved, meanwhile, strictly in the conventional ruts: had he been long in Paris, which of the new plays did he like best, was it true that American *jeunes filles* were sometimes taken to the Boulevard theatres? And she threw an interrogative glance at the young ladies beside the tea-table. To Durham's reply that it depended on how much French they knew, she shrugged and smiled, replying that his compatriots all spoke French like Parisians, enquiring, after a moment's thought, if they learned it, *là bas, des nègres,* and laughing heartily when Durham's astonishment revealed her blunder.

When at length she had taken leave—enveloping the Durham ladies in a last puzzled penetrating look—Madame de Malrive turned to Mrs. Durham with a faintly embarrassed smile.

"My sister-in-law was much interested; I believe you are the first Americans she has ever known."

"Good gracious!" ejaculated Nannie, as though such social darkness required immediate missionary action on someone's part.

"Well, she knows *us,*" said Durham, catching, in Madame de Malrive's rapid glance, a startled assent to his point.

"After all," reflected the accurate Katy, as though seeking an excuse for Madame de Treymes' unenlightenment, "*we* don't know many French people, either."

To which Nannie promptly if obscurely retorted: "Ah! but we couldn't and *she* could!"

※ IV ※

MADAME DE TREYMES' friendly observation of her sister-in-law's visitors resulted in no expression on her part of a desire to renew her study of them. To all appearances, she passed out of their lives when Madame de Malrive's door closed on her; and Durham felt that the arduous task of making her acquaintance was still to be begun.

He felt also, more than ever, the necessity of attempting it; and in his determination to lose no time, and his perplexity how to set most speedily about the business, he bethought himself of applying to his cousin Mrs. Boykin.

Mrs. Elmer Boykin was a small plump woman, to whose vague prettiness the lines of middle age had given no meaning: as though whatever had happened to her had merely added to the sum total of her inexperience. After a Parisian residence of twenty-five years, spent in a state of feverish servitude to the great artists of the Rue de la Paix, her dress and hair still retained a certain rigidity in keeping with the directness of her gaze and the unmodulated candour of her voice. Her very drawing-room had the hard bright atmosphere of her native skies, and one felt that she was still true at heart to the national ideals in electric lighting and plumbing.

She and her husband had left America owing to the impossibility of living there with the finish and decorum which the Boykin standard demanded; but in the isolation of their exile they had created about them a kind of phantom America, where the national prejudices continued to flourish unchecked by the national progressiveness: a little world sparsely peopled by compatriots in the same attitude of chronic opposition toward a society chronically unaware of them. In this uncontaminated air Mr. and Mrs. Boykin had preserved the purity of simpler conditions, and Elmer Boykin, returning rakishly from a Sunday's racing at

Chantilly, betrayed, under his "knowing" coat and the racing-glasses slung ostentatiously across his shoulder, the unmistakable cut of the American business man coming "up town" after a long day in the office.

It was a part of the Boykins' uncomfortable but determined attitude—and perhaps a last expression of their latent patriotism—to live in active disapproval of the world about them, fixing in memory with little stabs of reprobation innumerable instances of what the abominable foreigner was doing; so that they reminded Durham of persons peacefully following the course of a horrible war by pricking red pins in a map. To Mrs. Durham, with her gentle tourist's view of the European continent, as a vast Museum in which the human multitudes simply furnished the element of costume, the Boykins seemed abysmally instructed, and darkly expert in forbidden things; and her son, without sharing her simple faith in their omniscience, credited them with an ample supply of the kind of information of which he was in search.

Mrs. Boykin, from the corner of an intensely modern Gobelin sofa, studied her cousin as he balanced himself insecurely on one of the small gilt chairs which always look surprised at being sat in.

"Fanny de Malrive? Oh, of course: I remember you were all very intimate with the Frisbees when they lived in West Thirty-third Street. But she has dropped all her American friends since her marriage. The excuse was that de Malrive didn't like them; but as she's been separated for five or six years, I can't see—. You say she's been very nice to your mother and the girls? Well, I dare say she is beginning to feel the need of friends she can really trust; for as for her French relations——! That Malrive set is the worst in the Faubourg. Of course you know what *he* is; even the family, for decency's sake, had to back her up, and urge her to get a separation. And Christiane de Treymes——"

Durham seized his opportunity. "Is she so very reprehensible too?"

Mrs. Boykin pursed up her small colourless mouth. "I can't

speak from personal experience. I know Madame de Treymes slightly—I have met her at Fanny's—but she never remembers the fact except when she wants me to go to one of her *ventes de charité*. They all remember us then; and some American women are silly enough to ruin themselves at the smart bazaars, and fancy they will get invitations in return. They say Mrs. Addison G. Pack followed Madame d'Alglade around for a whole winter, and spent a hundred thousand francs at her stalls; and at the end of the season Madame d'Alglade asked her to tea, and when she got there she found *that* was for a charity too, and she had to pay a hundred francs to get in."

Mrs. Boykin paused with a smile of compassion. "That is not *my* way," she continued. "Personally I have no desire to thrust myself into French society—I can't see how any American woman can do so without loss of self-respect. But anyone can tell you about Madame de Treymes."

"I wish you would, then," Durham suggested.

"Well, I think Elmer had better," said his wife mysteriously, as Mr. Boykin, at this point, advanced across the wide expanse of Aubusson on which his wife and Durham were islanded in a state of propinquity without privacy.

"What's that, Bessy? Hah, Durham, how are you? Didn't see you at Auteuil this afternoon. You don't race? Busy sight-seeing, I suppose? What was that my wife was telling you? Oh, about Madame de Treymes."

He stroked his pepper-and-salt moustache with a gesture intended rather to indicate than to conceal the smile of experience beneath it. "Well, Madame de Treymes has not been like a happy country—she's had a history: several of 'em. Someone said she constituted the *feuilleton* of the Faubourg daily news. *La suite au prochain numéro*—you see the point? Not that I speak from personal knowledge. Bessy and I have never cared to force our way"——He paused, reflecting that his wife had probably anticipated him in the expression of this familiar sentiment, and added with a significant nod: "Of course you know the Prince d'Armillac by sight? No? I'm surprised at that. Well, he's one of the choicest ornaments of the Jockey Club: very fascinating to the ladies, I believe, but the deuce and all at baccarat. Ruined his mother and a couple of maiden aunts already—and now Madame de Treymes has put the family pearls up the spout, and is wearing imitation for love of him."

"I had that straight from my maid's cousin, who is employed by Madame d'Armillac's jeweller," said Mrs. Boykin with conscious pride.

"Oh, it's straight enough—more than *she* is!" retorted her husband, who was slightly jealous of having his facts reinforced by any information not of his own gleaning.

"Be careful of what you say, Elmer," Mrs. Boykin interposed with archness. "I suspect John of being seriously smitten by the lady."

Durham let this pass unchallenged, submitting with a good grace to his host's low whistle of amusement, and the sardonic enquiry: "Ever do anything with the foils? D'Armillac is what they call over here a *fine lame.*"

"Oh, I don't mean to resort to bloodshed unless it's absolutely necessary; but I mean to make the lady's acquaintance," said Durham, falling into his key.

Mrs. Boykin's lips tightened to the vanishing point. "I am afraid you must apply for an introduction to more fashionable people than *we* are. Elmer and I so thoroughly disapprove of French society that we have always declined to take any part in it. But why should not Fanny de Malrive arrange a meeting for you?"

Durham hesitated. "I don't think she is on very intimate terms with her husband's family——"

"You mean that she's not allowed to introduce *her* friends to them," Mrs. Boykin interjected sarcastically; while her husband added, with an air of portentous initiation: "Ah, my dear fellow, the way they treat the Americans over here—that's another chapter, you know."

"How some people can *stand* it!" Mrs. Boykin chimed in; and as the footman, entering at that moment, tendered her a large coronetted envelope, she held it up as if in illustration of the indignities to which her countrymen were subjected.

"Look at that, my dear John," she exclaimed—"another card to one of their everlasting bazaars! Why, it's at Madame d'Armillac's, the Prince's mother. Madame de Treymes must have sent it, of course. The brazen way in which they combine religion and immorality! Fifty francs admission—*rein que cela!*—to see some of the most disreputable people in Europe. And if you're an American, you're expected to leave at least a thousand behind you. Their own people naturally get off cheaper." She tossed over the card to her cousin. "There's your opportunity to see Madame de Treymes."

"Make it two thousand, and she'll ask you to tea," Mr. Boykin scathingly added.

※ V ※

In the monumental drawing-room of the Hôtel de Malrive— it had been a surprise to the American to read the name of the house emblazoned on black marble over its still more monumental gateway—Durham found himself surrounded by a buzz of feminine tea-sipping oddly out of keeping with the wigged and cuirassed portraits frowning high on the walls, the majestic attitude of the furniture, the rigidity of great gilt consoles drawn up like lords-in-waiting against the tarnished panels.

It was the old Marquise de Malrive's "day," and Madame de Treymes, who lived with her mother, had admitted Durham to the heart of the enemy's country by inviting him, after his prodigal disbursements at the charity bazaar, to come in to tea on a Thursday. Whether, in thus fulfilling Mr. Boykin's prediction, she had been aware of Durham's purpose, and had her own reasons for falling in with it; or whether she simply wished to reward his lavishness at the fair, and permit herself another glimpse of an American so picturesquely embodying the type familiar to French fiction—on these points Durham was still in doubt.

Meanwhile, Madame de Treymes being engaged with a venerable Duchess in a black shawl—all the older ladies present had the sloping shoulders of a generation of shawl-wearers—her American visitor, left in the isolation of his unimportance, was using it as a shelter for a rapid survey of the scene.

He had begun his study of Fanny de Malrive's situation without any real understanding of her fears. He knew the repugnance to divorce existing in the French Catholic world, but since the French laws sanctioned it, and in a case so flagrant as his injured friend's, would inevitably accord it with the least possible delay and exposure, he could not take seriously any risk of opposition on the part of the husband's family. Madame de Malrive had not become a Catholic, and since her religious scruples could not be played on, the only weapon remaining to the enemy—the threat of fighting the divorce—was one they could not wield without self-injury. Certainly, if the chief object were to avoid scandal, common sense must counsel Monsieur de Malrive and his friends not to give the courts an opportunity of exploring his past; and since the echo of such explorations, and their ultimate transmission to her son, were what Madame de Malrive most dreaded, the opposing parties seemed to have a common ground for agreement, and Durham could not but regard his friend's fears as the result of over-taxed sensibilities. All this had seemed evident enough to him as he entered the austere portals of the Hôtel de Malrive and passed, between the faded liveries of old family servants, to the presence of the dreaded dowager above. But he had not been ten minutes in that presence before he had arrived at a faint intuition of what poor Fanny meant. It was not in the exquisite mildness of the old Marquise, a little grey-haired bunch of a woman in dowdy mourning, or in the small neat pres-

ence of the priestly uncle, the Abbé who had so obviously just
stepped down from one of the picture-frames overhead: it was
not in the aspect of these chief protagonists, so outwardly unfor-
midable, that Durham read an occult danger to his friend. It was
rather in their setting, their surroundings, the little company of
elderly and dowdy persons—so uniformly clad in weeping blacks
and purples that they might have been assembled for some mor-
tuary anniversary—it was in the remoteness and the solidarity of
this little group that Durham had his first glimpse of the social
force of which Fanny de Malrive had spoken. All these amiably
chatting visitors, who mostly bore the stamp of personal insignificance on their mildly sloping or aristocratically beaked faces,
hung together in a visible closeness of tradition, dress, attitude
and manner, as different as possible from the loose aggregation
of a roomful of his own countrymen. Durham felt, as he observed
them, that he had never before known what "society" meant; nor
understood that, in an organized and inherited system, it exists
full-fledged where two or three of its members are assembled.

Upon this state of bewilderment, this sense of having entered a room in which the lights had suddenly been turned out,
even Madame de Treymes' intensely modern presence threw no
illumination. He was conscious, as she smilingly rejoined him,
not of her points of difference from the others, but of the myriad
invisible threads by which she held to them; he even recognized
the audacious slant of her little brown profile in the portrait of a
powdered ancestress beneath which she had paused a moment in
advancing. She was simply one particular facet of the solid, glittering, impenetrable body which he had thought to turn in his
hands and look through like a crystal; and when she said, in her
clear staccato English, "Perhaps you will like to see the other
rooms," he felt like crying out his blindness: "If I could only be
sure of seeing *anything* here!" Was she conscious of his blindness, and was he as remote and unintelligible to her as she was to
him? This possibility, as he followed her through the nobly
unfolding rooms of the great house, gave him his first hope of

recoverable advantage. For, after all, he had some vague traditional lights on her world and its antecedents; whereas to her he was a wholly new phenomenon, as unexplained as a fragment of meteorite dropped at her feet on the smooth gravel of the garden-path they were pacing.

She had led him down into the garden, in response to his admiring exclamation, and perhaps also because she was sure that, in the chill spring afternoon, they would have its embowered privacies to themselves. The garden was small, but intensely rich and deep—one of those wells of verdure and fragrance which everywhere sweeten the air of Paris by wafts blown above old walls on quiet streets; and as Madame de Treymes paused against the ivy bank masking its farther boundary, Durham felt more than ever removed from the normal bearings of life.

His sense of strangeness was increased by the surprise of his companion's next speech.

"You wish to marry my sister-in-law?" she asked abruptly; and Durham's start of wonder was followed by an immediate feeling of relief. He had expected the preliminaries of their interview to be as complicated as the bargaining in an Eastern bazaar, and had feared to lose himself at the first turn in a labyrinth of "foreign" intrigue.

"Yes, I do," he said with equal directness; and they smiled together at the sharp report of question and answer.

The smile put Durham more completely at his ease, and after waiting for her to speak, he added with deliberation: "So far, however, the wishing is entirely on my side." His scrupulous conscience felt itself justified in this reserve by the conditional nature of Madame de Malrive's consent.

"I understand; but you have been given reason to hope——"

"Every man in my position gives himself his own reasons for hoping," he interposed with a smile.

"I understand that too," Madame de Treymes assented. "But still—you spent a great deal of money the other day at our bazaar."

"Yes: I wanted to have a talk with you, and it was the readiest—if not the most distinguished—means of attracting your attention."

"I understand," she once more reiterated, with a gleam of amusement.

"It is because I suspect you of understanding everything that I have been so anxious for this opportunity."

She bowed her acknowledgement, and said: "Shall we sit a moment?" adding, as he drew their chairs under a tree: "You permit me, then, to say that I believe I understand also a little of our good Fanny's mind?"

"On that point I have no authority to speak. I am here only to listen."

"Listen, then: you have persuaded her that there would be no harm in divorcing my brother—since I believe your religion does not forbid divorce?"

"Madame de Malrive's religion sanctions divorce in such a case as——"

"As my brother has furnished? Yes, I have heard that your race is stricter in judging such *écarts*. But you must not think," she added, "that I defend my brother. Fanny must have told you that we have always given her our sympathy."

"She has let me infer it from her way of speaking of you."

Madame de Treymes arched her dramatic eyebrows. "How cautious you are! I am so straightforward that I shall have no chance with you."

"You will be quite safe, unless you are so straightforward that you put me on my guard."

She met this with a low note of amusement.

"At this rate we shall never get any farther; and in two minutes I must go back to my mother's visitors. Why should we go on fencing? The situation is really quite simple. Tell me just what you wish to know. I have always been Fanny's friend, and that disposes me to be yours."

Durham, during this appeal, had had time to steady his thoughts; and the result of his deliberation was that he said, with a return to his former directness: "Well, then, what I wish to know is, what position your family would take if Madame de Malrive should sue for a divorce." He added, without giving her time to reply: "I naturally wish to be clear on this point before urging my cause with your sister-in-law."

Madame de Treymes seemed in no haste to answer; but after a pause of reflection she said, not unkindly: "My poor Fanny might have asked me that herself."

"I beg you to believe that I am not acting as her spokesman," Durham hastily interposed. "I merely wish to clear up the situation before speaking to her in my own behalf."

"You are the most delicate of suitors! But I understand your feeling. Fanny also is extremely delicate: it was a great surprise to us at first. Still, in this case—" Madame de Treymes paused— "since she has no religious scruples, and she had no difficulty in obtaining a separation, why should she fear any in demanding a divorce?"

"I don't know that she does: but the mere fact of possible opposition might be enough to alarm the delicacy you have observed in her."

"Ah—yes: on her boy's account."

"Partly, doubtless, on her boy's account."

"So that, if my brother objects to a divorce, all he has to do is to announce his objection? But, my dear sir, you are giving your case into my hands!" She flashed an amused smile on him.

"Since you say you are Madame de Malrive's friend, could there be a better place for it?"

As she turned her eyes on him he seemed to see, under the flitting lightness of her glance, the sudden concentrated expression of the ancestral will. "I am Fanny's friend, certainly. But with us family considerations are paramount. And our religion forbids divorce."

"So that, inevitably, your brother will oppose it?"

She rose from her seat, and stood fretting with her slender boot-tip the minute red pebbles of the path.

"I must really go in: my mother will never forgive me for deserting her."

"But surely you owe me an answer?" Durham protested, rising also.

"In return for your purchases at my stall?"

"No: in return for the trust I have placed in you."

She mused on this, moving slowly a step or two toward the house.

"Certainly I wish to see you again; you interest me," she said smiling. "But it is so difficult to arrange. If I were to ask you to come here again, my mother and uncle would be surprised. And at Fanny's——"

"Oh, not there!" he exclaimed.

"Where then? Is there any other house where we are likely to meet?"

Durham hesitated; but he was goaded by the flight of the precious minutes. "Not unless you'll come and dine with me," he said boldly.

"Dine with you? *Au cabaret?* Ah, that would be diverting—but impossible!"

"Well, dine with my cousin, then—I have a cousin, an American lady, who lives here," said Durham, with suddenly soaring audacity.

She paused with puzzled brows. "An American lady whom I know?"

"By name, at any rate. You send her cards for all your charity bazaars."

She received the thrust with a laugh. "We do exploit your compatriots."

"Oh, I don't think she has ever gone to the bazaars."

"But she might if I dined with her?"

"Still less, I imagine."

She reflected on this, and then said with acuteness: "I like that, and I accept—but what is the lady's name?"

❋ VI ❋

On the way home, in the first drop of exaltation, Durham had said to himself: "But why on earth should Bessy invite her?"

He had, naturally, no very cogent reasons to give Mrs. Boykin in support of his astonishing request, and could only, marvelling at his own growth in duplicity, suffer her to infer that he was really, shamelessly "smitten" with the lady he thus proposed to thrust upon her hospitality. But, to his surprise, Mrs. Boykin hardly gave herself time to pause upon his reasons. They were swallowed up in the fact that Madame de Treymes wished to dine with her, as the lesser luminaries vanish in the blaze of the sun.

"I am not surprised," she declared, with a faint smile intended to check her husband's unruly wonder. "I wonder *you* are, Elmer. Didn't you tell me that Armillac went out of his way to speak to you the other day at the races? And at Madame d'Alglade's sale—yes, I went there after all, just for a minute, because I found Katy and Nannie were so anxious to be taken— well, that day I noticed that Madame de Treymes was quite *empressée* when we went up to her stall. Oh, I didn't buy anything: I merely waited while the girls chose some lampshades. They thought it would be interesting to take home something painted by a real Marquise, and of course I didn't tell them that those women *never* make the things they sell at their stalls. But I repeat I'm not surprised: I suspected that Madame de Treymes had heard of our little dinners. You know they're really horribly bored in that poky old Faubourg. My poor John, I see now why she's been making up to you! But on one point I am quite determined, Elmer; whatever you say, I shall *not* invite the Prince d'Armillac."

Elmer, as far as Durham could observe, did not say much;
but, like his wife, he continued in a state of pleasantly agitated
activity till the momentous evening of the dinner.

The festivity in question was restricted in numbers, either
owing to the difficulty of securing suitable guests, or from a
desire not to have it appear that Madame de Treymes' hosts attached any special importance to her presence; but the smallness
of the company was counterbalanced by the multiplicity of the
courses.

The national determination not be "downed" by the despised
foreigner, to show a wealth of material resource obscurely felt to
compensate for the possible lack of other distinctions—this resolve had taken, in Mrs. Boykin's case, the shape—or rather the
multiple shapes—of a series of culinary feats, of gastronomic
combinations, which would have commanded her deep respect
had she seen them on any other table, and which she naturally
relied on to produce the same effect on her guest. Whether or not
the desired result was achieved, Madame de Treymes' manner
did not specifically declare; but it showed a general complai-
sance, a charming willingness to be amused, which made Mr.
Boykin, for months afterward, allude to her among his compatriots as "an old friend of my wife's—takes potluck with us, you
know. Of course there's not a word of truth in any of those
ridiculous stories."

It was only when, to Durham's intense surprise, Mr. Boykin
hazarded to his neighbour the regret that they had not been so
lucky as to "secure the Prince"—it was then only that the lady
showed, not indeed anything so simple and unprepared as embarrassment, but a faint play of wonder, an under-flicker of
amusement, as though recognizing that, by some odd law of social compensation, the crudity of the talk might account for the
complexity of the dishes.

But Mr. Boykin was tremulously alive to hints, and the conversation at once slid to safer topics, easy generalizations which

left Madame de Treymes ample time to explore the table, to use her narrowed gaze like a knife slitting open the unsuspicious personalities about her. Nannie and Katy Durham, who, after much discussion (to which their hostess candidly admitted them), had been included in the feast, were the special objects of Madame de Treymes' observation. During dinner she ignored in their favour the other carefully selected guests—the fashionable art-critic, the old Legitimist general, the beauty from the English Embassy, the whole impressive marshalling of Mrs. Boykin's social resources— and when the men returned to the drawing-room, Durham found her still fanning in his sisters the flame of an easily kindled enthusiasm. Since she could hardly have been held by the intrinsic interest of their converse, the sight gave him another swift intuition of the working of those hidden forces with which Fanny de Malrive felt herself encompassed. But when Madame de Treymes, at his approach, let him see that it was for him she had been reserving herself, he felt that so graceful an impulse needed no special explanation. She had the art of making it seem quite natural that they should move away together to the remotest of Mrs. Boykin's far-drawn salons, and that there, in a glaring privacy of brocade and ormolu, she should turn to him with a smile which avowed her intentional quest of seclusion.

"Confess that I have done a great deal for you!" she exclaimed, making room for him on a sofa judiciously screened from the observation of the other rooms.

"In coming to dine with my cousin?" he enquired, answering her smile.

"Let us say, in giving you this half hour."

"For that I am duly grateful—and shall be still more so when I know what it contains for me."

"Ah, I am not sure. You will not like what I am going to say."

"Shall I not?" he rejoined, changing colour.

She raised her eyes from the thoughtful contemplation of

her painted fan. "You appear to have no idea of the difficulties."

"Should I have asked your help if I had not had an idea of them?"

"But you are still confident that with my help you can surmount them?"

"I can't believe you have come here to take that confidence from me?"

She leaned back, smiling at him through her lashes. "And all this I am to do for your *beaux yeux*?"

"No—for your own: that you may see with them what happiness you are conferring."

"You are extremely clever, and I like you." She paused, and then brought out with lingering emphasis: "But my family will not hear of a divorce."

She threw into her voice such an accent of finality that Durham, for the moment, felt himself brought up against an insurmountable barrier, but, almost at once, his fear was mitigated by the conviction that she would not have put herself out so much to say so little.

"When you speak of your family, do you include yourself?" he suggested.

She threw a surprised glance at him. "I thought you understood that I am simply their mouthpiece."

At this he rose quietly to his feet with a gesture of acceptance. "I have only to thank you, then, for not keeping me longer in suspense."

His air of wishing to put an immediate end to the conversation seemed to surprise her. "Sit down a moment longer," she commanded him kindly; and as he leaned against the back of his chair, without appearing to hear her request, she added in a low voice: "I am very sorry for you and Fanny—but you are not the only persons to be pitied."

"The only persons?"

"In our unhappy family." She touched her breast with a sudden tragic gesture. "I, for instance, whose help you ask—if you could guess how I need help myself!"

She had dropped her light manner as she might have tossed aside her fan, and he was startled at the intimacy of misery to which her look and movement abruptly admitted him. Perhaps no Anglo-Saxon fully understands the fluency in self-revelation which centuries of the confessional have given to the Latin races, and to Durham, at any rate, Madame de Treymes' sudden avowal gave the shock of a physical abandonment.

"I am so sorry," he stammered—"is there any way in which I can be of use to you?"

She sat before him with her hands clasped, her eyes fixed on his in a terrible intensity of appeal. "If you would—if you would! Oh, there is nothing I would not do for you. I have still a great deal of influence with my mother, and what my mother commands we all do. I could help you—I am sure I could help you; but not if my own situation were known. And if nothing can be done it must be known in a few days."

Durham had reseated himself at her side. "Tell me what I can do," he said in a low tone, forgetting his own preoccupations in his genuine concern for her distress.

She looked up at him through tears. "How dare I? Your race is so cautious, so self-controlled—you have so little indulgence for the extravagances of the heart. And my folly has been incredible—and unrewarded." She paused, and as Durham waited in a silence which she guessed to be compassionate, she brought out below her breath: "I have lent money—my husband's, my brother's—money that was not mine, and now I have nothing to repay it with."

Durham gazed at her in genuine astonishment. The turn the conversation had taken led quite beyond his uncomplicated experiences with the other sex. She saw his surprise, and extended her hands in deprecation and entreaty. "Alas, what must you think of me? How can I explain my humiliating myself before a stranger? Only by telling you the whole truth—the fact that I am not alone in this disaster, that I could not confess my situation to my family without ruining myself, and involving in my ruin someone who, however undeservedly, has been as dear to me as —as you are to——"

Durham pushed his chair back with a sharp exclamation.

"Ah, even that does not move you!" she said.

The cry restored him to his senses by the long shaft of light it sent down the dark windings of the situation. He seemed suddenly to know Madame de Treymes as if he had been brought up with her in the inscrutable shades of the Hôtel de Malrive.

She, on her side, appeared to have a startled but uncomprehending sense of the fact that his silence was no longer completely sympathetic, but her touch called forth no answering vibration; and she made a desperate clutch at the one chord she could be certain of sounding.

"You have asked a great deal of me—much more than you can guess. Do you mean to give me nothing—not even your sympathy—in return? Is it because you have heard horrors of me? When are they not said of a woman who is married unhappily? Perhaps not in your fortunate country, where she may seek liberation without dishonour. But here—! You who have seen the consequences of our disastrous marriages—you who may yet be the victim of our cruel and abominable system; have you no pity for one who has suffered in the same way, and without the possibility of release?" She paused, laying her hand on his arm with a smile of deprecating irony. "It is not because you are not rich. At such times the crudest way is the shortest, and I don't pretend to deny that I know I am asking you a trifle. You Americans, when you want a thing, always pay ten times what it is worth, and I am giving you the wonderful chance to get what you most want at a bargain."

Durham sat silent, her little gloved hand burning his coat-sleeve as if it had been a hot iron. His brain was tingling with the shock of her confession. She wanted money, a great deal of money: that was clear, but it was not the point. She was ready to sell her influence, and he fancied she could be counted on to fulfil her side of the bargain. The fact that he could so trust her seemed only to make her more terrible to him—more supernaturally dauntless and baleful. For what was it that she exacted of him? She had said she must have money to pay her debts; but he knew that was only a pretext which she scarcely expected him to believe. She wanted the money for someone else; that was what her allusion to a fellow-victim meant. She wanted it to pay the Prince's gambling debts—it was at that price that Durham was to buy the right to marry Fanny de Malrive.

Once the situation had worked itself out in his mind, he found himself unexpectedly relieved of the necessity of weighing the arguments for and against it. All the traditional forces of his blood were in revolt, and he could only surrender himself to their pressure, without thought of compromise or parley.

He stood up in silence, and the abruptness of his movement caused Madame de Treymes' hand to slip from his arm.

"You refuse?" she exclaimed; and he answered with a bow: "Only because of the return you propose to make me."

She stood staring at him, in a perplexity so genuine and profound that he could almost have smiled at it through his disgust.

"Ah, you are all incredible," she murmured at last, stooping to repossess herself of her fan; and as she moved past him to rejoin the group in the farther room, she added in an incisive undertone: "You are quite at liberty to repeat our conversation to your friend!"

❊ VII ❊

DURHAM did not take advantage of the permission thus strangely flung at him. Of his talk with her sister-in-law he gave to Madame de Malrive only that part which concerned her.

Presenting himself for this purpose, the day after Mrs. Boykin's dinner, he found his friend alone with her son; and the sight of the child had the effect of dispelling whatever illusive hopes had attended him to the threshold. Even after the governess's descent upon the scene had left Madame de Malrive and her visitor alone, the little boy's presence seemed to hover admonishingly between them, reducing to a bare statement of fact Durham's confession of the total failure of his errand.

Madame de Malrive heard the confession calmly; she had been too prepared for it not to have prepared a countenance to receive it. Her first comment was: "I have never known them to declare themselves so plainly——" and Durham's baffled hopes fastened themselves eagerly on the words. Had she not always warned him that there was nothing so misleading as their plainness? And might it not be that, in spite of his advisedness, he had suffered too easy a rebuff? But second thoughts reminded him that the refusal had not been as unconditional as his necessary reservations made it seem in the repetition; and that, furthermore, it was his own act, and not that of his opponents, which had determined it. The impossibility of revealing this to Madame de Malrive only made the difficulty shut in more darkly around him, and in the completeness of his discouragement he scarcely needed her reminder of his promise to regard the subject as closed when once the other side had defined its position.

He was secretly confirmed in this acceptance of his fate by the knowledge that it was really he who had defined the position. Even now that he was alone with Madame de Malrive, and subtly aware of the struggle under her composure, he felt no temptation to abate his stand by a jot. He had not yet formulated a reason for his resistance: he simply went on feeling, more and more strongly with every precious sign of her participation in his unhappiness, that he could neither owe his escape from it to such a transaction, nor suffer her, innocently, to owe hers.

The only mitigating effect of his determination was in an increase of helpless tenderness toward her; so that, when she exclaimed, in answer to his announcement that he meant to leave

Paris the next night: "Oh, give me a day or two longer!" he at once resigned himself to saying: "If I can be of the least use, I'll give you a hundred."

She answered sadly that all he could do would be to let her feel that he was there—just for a day or two, till she had readjusted herself to the idea of going on in the old way; and on this note of renunciation they parted.

But Durham, however pledged to the passive part, could not long sustain it without rebellion. To "hang round" the shut door of his hopes seemed, after two long days, more than even his passion required of him; and on the third he despatched a note of good-bye to his friend. He was going off for a few weeks, he explained—his mother and sisters wished to be taken to the Italian lakes: but he would return to Paris, and say his real farewell to her, before sailing for America in July.

He had not intended his note to act as an ultimatum: he had no wish to surprise Madame de Malrive into unconsidered surrender. When, almost immediately, his own messenger returned with a reply from her, he even felt a pang of disappointment, a momentary fear lest she should have stooped a little from the high place where his passion had preferred to leave her; but her first words turned his fear into rejoicing.

"Let me see you before you go: something extraordinary has happened," she wrote.

What had happened, as he heard from her a few hours later —finding her in a tremor of frightened gladness, with her door boldly closed to all the world but himself—was nothing less extraordinary than a visit from Madame de Treymes, who had come, officially delegated by the family, to announce that Monsieur de Malrive had decided not to oppose his wife's suit for divorce. Durham, at the news, was almost afraid to show himself too amazed; but his small signs of alarm and wonder were swallowed up in the flush of Madame de Malrive's incredulous joy.

"It's the long habit, you know, of not believing them—of looking for the truth always in what they *don't* say. It took me hours and hours to convince myself that there's no trick under it, that there can't be any," she explained.

"Then you *are* convinced now?" escaped from Durham; but the shadow of his question lingered no more than the flit of a wing across her face.

"I am convinced because the facts are there to reassure me. Christiane tells me that Monsieur de Malrive has consulted his lawyers, and that they have advised him to free me. Maître Enguerrand has been instructed to see my lawyer whenever I wish it. They quite understand that I never should have taken the step in face of any opposition on their part—I am so thankful to you for making that perfectly clear to them!—and I suppose this is the return their pride makes to mine. For they *can* be proud collectively——" She broke off, and added, with happy hands outstretched: "And I owe it all to you—Christiane said it was your talk with her that had convinced them."

Durham, at this statement, had to repress a fresh sound of amazement; but with her hands in his, and, a moment after, her whole self drawn to him in the first yielding of her lips, doubt perforce gave way to the lover's happy conviction that such love was after all too strong for the powers of darkness.

It was only when they sat again in the blissful after-calm of their understanding, that he felt the pricking of an unappeased distrust.

"Did Madame de Treymes give you any reason for this change of front?" he risked asking, when he found the distrust was not otherwise to be quelled.

"Oh, yes: just what I've said. It was really her admiration of *you*—of your attitude—your delicacy. She said that at first she hadn't believed in it: they're always looking for a hidden motive. And when she found that yours was staring at her in the actual words you said: that you really respected my scruples, and would never, never try to coerce or entrap me—something in her —poor Christiane!—answered to it, she told me, and she wanted to prove to us that she was capable of understanding us too. If you knew her history you'd find it wonderful and pathetic that she can!"

Durham thought he knew enough of it to infer that Madame de Treymes had not been the object of many conscientious scruples on the part of the opposite sex; but this increased rather his sense of the strangeness than of the pathos of her action. Yet Madame de Malrive, whom he had once inwardly taxed with the morbid raising of obstacles, seemed to see none now; and he could only infer that her sister-in-law's actual words had carried more conviction than reached him in the repetition of them. The mere fact that he had so much to gain by leaving his friend's faith undisturbed was no doubt stirring his own suspicions to unnatural activity; and this sense gradually reasoned him back into acceptance of her view, as the most normal as well as the pleasantest he could take.

❈ VIII ❈

THE uneasiness thus temporarily repressed slipped into the final disguise of hoping he should not again meet Madame de Treymes; and in this wish he was seconded by the decision, in which Madame de Malrive concurred, that it would be well for him to leave Paris while the preliminary negotiations were going on. He committed her interests to the best professional care, and his mother, resigning her dream of the lakes, remained to fortify Madame de Malrive by her mild unimaginative view of the transaction, as an uncomfortable but commonplace necessity, like house-cleaning or dentistry. Mrs. Durham would doubtless have preferred that her only son, even with his hair turning grey, should have chosen a Fanny Frisbee rather than a Fanny de Malrive; but it was a part of her acceptance of life on a general basis of innocence and kindliness, that she entered generously into his dream of rescue and renewal, and devoted herself without afterthought to keeping up Fanny's courage with so little to spare for herself.

The process, the lawyers declared, would not be a long one, since Monsieur de Malrive's acquiescence reduced it to a formality; and when, at the end of June, Durham returned from Italy with Katy and Nannie, there seemed no reason why he should not stop in Paris long enough to learn what progress had been made.

But before he could learn this he was to hear, on entering Madame de Malrive's presence, news more immediate if less personal. He found her, in spite of her gladness in his return, so evidently preoccupied and distressed that his first thought was one of fear for their own future. But she read and dispelled this by saying, before he could put his question: "Poor Christiane is here. She is very unhappy. You have seen in the papers——?"

"I have seen no papers since we left Turin. What has happened?"

"The Prince d'Armillac has come to grief. There has been some terrible scandal about money and he has been obliged to leave France to escape arrest."

"And Madame de Treymes has left her husband?"

"Ah, no, poor creature: they don't leave their husbands—they can't. But de Treymes has gone down to their place in Brittany, and as my mother-in-law is with another daughter in Auvergne, Christiane came here for a few days. With me, you see, she need not pretend—she can cry her eyes out."

"And that is what she is doing?"

It was so unlike his conception of the way in which, under the most adverse circumstances, Madame de Treymes would be likely to occupy her time, that Durham was conscious of a note of scepticism in his query.

"Poor thing—if you saw her you would feel nothing but pity. She is suffering so horribly that I reproach myself for being happy under the same roof."

Durham met this with a tender pressure of her hand; then he said, after a pause of reflection: "I should like to see her."

He hardly knew what prompted him to utter the wish, unless it were a sudden stir of compunction at the memory of his own dealings with Madame de Treymes. Had he not sacrificed the poor creature to a purely fantastic conception of conduct? She had said that she knew she was asking a trifle of him; and the fact that, materially, it would have been a trifle, had seemed at the moment only an added reason for steeling himself in his moral resistance to it. But now that he had gained his point—and through her own generosity, as it still appeared—the largeness of her attitude made his own seem cramped and petty. Since conduct, in the last resort, must be judged by its enlarging or diminishing effect on character, might it not be that the zealous weighing of the moral anise and cummin was less important than the unconsidered lavishing of the precious ointment? At any rate, he could enjoy no peace of mind under the burden of Madame de Treymes' magnanimity, and when he had assured himself that his own affairs were progressing favourably, he once more, at the risk of surprising his betrothed, brought up the possibility of seeing her relative.

Madame de Malrive evinced no surprise. "It is natural, knowing what she has done for us, that you should want to show her your sympathy. The difficulty is that it is just the one thing you *can't* show her. You can thank her, of course, for ourselves, but even that at the moment——"

"Would seem brutal? Yes, I recognize that I should have to choose my words," he admitted, guiltily conscious that his capability of dealing with Madame de Treymes extended far beyond her sister-in-law's conjecture.

Madame de Malrive still hesitated. "I can tell her; and when you come back tomorrow——"

It had been decided that, in the interests of discretion—the interests, in other words, of the poor little future Marquis de Malrive—Durham was to remain but two days in Paris, withdrawing then with his family till the conclusion of the divorce proceedings permitted him to return in the acknowledged character of Madame de Malrive's future husband. Even on this occasion, he had not come to her alone; Nannie Durham, in the adjoining room, was chatting conspicuously with the little Marquis, whom she could with difficulty be restrained from teaching to call her "Aunt Nannie." Durham thought her voice had risen unduly once or twice during his visit, and when, on taking leave, he went to summon her from the inner room, he found the higher note of ecstasy had been evoked by the appearance of Madame de Treymes, and that the little boy, himself absorbed in a new toy of Durham's bringing, was being bent over by an actual as well as a potential aunt.

Madame de Treymes raised herself with a slight start at Durham's approach: she had her hat on, and had evidently paused a moment on her way out to speak with Nannie, without expecting to be surprised by her sister-in-law's other visitor. But her surprises never wore the awkward form of embarrassment, and she smiled beautifully on Durham as he took her extended hand.

The smile was made the more appealing by the way in which it lit up the ruin of her small dark face, which looked seared and hollowed as by a flame that might have spread over it from her fevered eyes. Durham, accustomed to the pale inward grief of the inexpressive races, was positively startled by the way in which she seemed to have been openly stretched on the pyre; he almost felt an indelicacy in the ravages so tragically confessed.

The sight caused an involuntary readjustment of his whole view of the situation, and made him, as far as his own share in it went, more than ever inclined to extremities of self-disgust. With him such sensations required, for his own relief, some immediate penitential escape, and as Madame de Treymes turned toward the door he addressed a glance of entreaty to his betrothed.

Madame de Malrive, whose intelligence could be counted on at such moments, responded by laying a detaining hand on her sister-in-law's arm.

"Dear Christiane, may I leave Mr. Durham in your charge for two minutes? I have promised Nannie that she shall see the boy put to bed."

Madame de Treymes made no audible response to this request, but when the door had closed on the other ladies, she said, looking quietly at Durham: "I don't think that, in this house, your time will hang so heavy that you need my help in supporting it."

Durham met her glance frankly. "It was not for that reason that Madame de Malrive asked you to remain with me."

"Why, then? Surely not in the interest of preserving appearances, since she is safely upstairs with your sister?"

"No; but simply because I asked her to. I told her I wanted to speak to you."

"How you arrange things! And what reason can you have for wanting to speak to me?"

He paused a moment. "Can't you imagine? The desire to thank you for what you have done."

She stirred restlessly, turning to adjust her hat before the glass above the mantelpiece.

"Oh, as for what I have done——!"

"Don't speak as if you regretted it," he interposed.

She turned back to him with a flash of laughter lighting up the haggardness of her face. "Regret working for the happiness of two such excellent persons? Can't you fancy what a charming change it is for me to do something so innocent and beneficent?"

He moved across the room and went up to her, drawing down the hand which still flitted experimentally about her hat.

"Don't talk in that way, however much one of the persons of whom you speak may have deserved it."

"One of the persons? Do you mean me?"

He released her hand, but continued to face her resolutely. "I mean myself, as you know. You have been generous—extraordinarily generous."

"Ah, but I was doing good in a good cause. You have made me see that there is a distinction."

He flushed to the forehead. "I am here to let you say whatever you choose to me."

"Whatever I choose?" She made a slight gesture of deprecation. "Has it never occurred to you that I may conceivably choose to say nothing?"

Durham paused, conscious of the increasing difficulty of the advance. She met him, parried him, at every turn: he had to take his baffled purpose back to another point of attack.

"Quite conceivably," he said: "so much so that I am aware I must make the most of this opportunity, because I am not likely to get another."

"But what remains of your opportunity, if it isn't one to me?"

"It still remains, for me, an occasion to abase myself—" He broke off, conscious of a grossness of allusion that seemed, on a close approach, the real obstacle to full expression. But the moments were flying, and for his self-esteem's sake he must find some way of making her share the burden of his repentance.

"There is only one thinkable pretext for detaining you: it is that I may still show my sense of what you have done for me."

Madame de Treymes, who had moved toward the door, paused at this and faced him, resting her thin brown hands on a slender sofa-back.

"How do you propose to show that sense?" she enquired.

Durham coloured still more deeply: he saw that she was determined to save her pride by making what he had to say of the utmost difficulty. Well! he would let his expiation take that form, then—it was as if her slender hands held out to him the fool's cap he was condemned to press down on his own ears.

"By offering in return—in any form, and to the utmost—any service you are forgiving enough to ask of me."

She received this with a low sound of laughter that scarcely rose to her lips. "You are princely. But, my dear sir, does it not occur to you that I may, meanwhile, have taken my own way of repaying myself for any service I have been fortunate enough to render you?"

Durham, at the question, or still more, perhaps, at the tone in which it was put, felt, through his compunction, a vague faint chill of apprehension. Was she threatening him or only mocking him? Or was this barbed swiftness of retort only the wounded creature's way of defending the privacy of her own pain? He looked at her again, and read his answer in the last conjecture.

"I don't know how you can have repaid yourself for anything so disinterested—but I am sure, at least, that you have given me no chance of recognizing, ever so slightly, what you have done."

She shook her head, with the flicker of a smile on her melancholy lips. "Don't be too sure! You have given me a chance and I have taken it—taken it to the full. So fully," she continued, keeping her eyes fixed on his, "that if I were to accept any farther service you might choose to offer, I should simply be robbing you—robbing you shamelessly." She paused, and added in an undefinable voice: "I was entitled, wasn't I, to take something in return for the service I had the happiness of doing you?"

Durham could not tell whether the irony of her tone was self-directed or addressed to himself—perhaps it comprehended them both. At any rate, he chose to overlook his own share in it in replying earnestly: "So much so, that I can't see how you can have left me nothing to add to what you say you have taken."

"Ah, but you don't know what that is!" She continued to smile, elusively, ambiguously. "And what's more, you wouldn't believe me if I told you."

"How do you know?" he rejoined.

"You didn't believe me once before; and this is so much more incredible."

He took the taunt full in the face. "I shall go away unhappy unless you tell me—but then perhaps I have deserved to," he confessed.

She shook her head again, advancing toward the door with the evident intention of bringing their conference to a close; but on the threshold she paused to launch her reply.

"I can't send you away unhappy, since it is in the contemplation of your happiness that I have found my reward."

※ IX ※

THE next day Durham left with his family for England, with the intention of not returning till after the divorce should have been pronounced in September.

To say that he left with a quiet heart would be to overstate the case: the fact that he could not communicate to Madame de Malrive the substance of his talk with her sister-in-law still hung upon him uneasily. But of definite apprehensions the lapse of time gradually freed him, and Madame de Malrive's letters, addressed more frequently to his mother and sisters than to himself, reflected, in their reassuring serenity, the undisturbed course of events.

There was to Durham something peculiarly touching—as of an involuntary confession of almost unbearable loneliness—in the way she had regained, with her re-entry into the clear air of American associations, her own fresh trustfulness of view. Once she had accustomed herself to the surprise of finding her divorce unopposed, she had been, as it now seemed to Durham, in almost too great haste to renounce the habit of weighing motives and calculating chances. It was as though her coming liberation had already freed her from the garb of a mental slavery, as though she could not too soon or too conspicuously cast off the ugly badge of suspicion. The fact that Durham's cleverness had achieved so easy a victory over forces apparently impregnable, merely raised her estimate of that cleverness to the point of let-

ting her feel that she could rest in it without farther demur. He
had even noticed in her, during his few hours in Paris, a
tendency to reproach herself for her lack of charity, and a desire,
almost as fervent as his own, to expiate it by exaggerated recognition of the disinterestedness of her opponents—if opponents
they could still be called. This sudden change in her attitude was
peculiarly moving to Durham. He knew she would hazard herself lightly enough wherever her heart called her; but that, with
the precious freight of her child's future weighing her down, she
should commit herself so blindly to his hand stirred in him the
depths of tenderness. Indeed, had the actual course of events
been less auspiciously regular, Madame de Malrive's confidence
would have gone far toward unsettling his own; but with the
process of law going on unimpeded, and the other side making
no sign of open or covert resistance, the fresh air of good faith
gradually swept through the inmost recesses of his distrust.

   It was expected that the decision in the suit would be
reached by mid-September; and it was arranged that Durham
and his family should remain in England till a decent interval
after the conclusion of the proceedings. Early in the month,
however, it became necessary for Durham to go to France to
confer with a business associate who was in Paris for a few days,
and on the point of sailing for Cherbourg. The most zealous ob-
servance of appearances could hardly forbid Durham's return for
such a purpose; but it had been agreed between himself and Madame de Malrive—who had once more been left alone by Madame de Treymes' return to her family—that, so close to the frui-
tion of their wishes, they would propitiate fate by a scrupulous
adherence to usage, and communicate only, during his hasty
visit, by a daily interchange of notes.

   The ingenuity of Madame de Malrive's tenderness found,
however, the day after his arrival, a means of tempering their
privation. "Christiane," she wrote, "is passing through Paris on
her way from Trouville, and has promised to see you for me if
you will call on her today. She thinks there is no reason why you

should not go to the Hôtel de Malrive, as you will find her there alone, the family having gone to Auvergne. She is really our friend and understands us."

In obedience to this request—though perhaps inwardly regretting that it should have been made—Durham that afternoon presented himself at the proud old house beyond the Seine. More than ever, in the semi-abandonment of the *morte saison*, with reduced service, and shutters closed to the silence of the high-walled court, did it strike the American as the incorruptible custodian of old prejudices and strange social survivals. The thought of what he must represent to the almost human consciousness which such old houses seem to possess, made him feel like a barbarian desecrating the silence of a temple of the earlier faith. Not that there was anything venerable in the attestations of the Hôtel de Malrive, except in so far as, to a sensitive imagination, every concrete embodiment of a past order of things testifies to real convictions once suffered for. Durham, at any rate, always alive in practical issues to the view of the other side, had enough sympathy left over to spend it sometimes, whimsically, on such perceptions of difference. Today, especially, the assurance of success —the sense of entering like a victorious beleaguerer receiving the keys of the stronghold—disposed him to a sentimental perception of what the other side might have to say for itself, in the language of old portraits, old relics, old usages, dumbly outraged by his mere presence.

On the appearance of Madame de Treymes, however, such considerations gave way to the immediate act of wondering how she meant to carry off her share of the adventure. Durham had not forgotten the note on which their last conversation had closed: the lapse of time serving only to give more precision and perspective to the impression he had then received.

Madame de Treymes' first words implied a recognition of what was in his thoughts.

"It is extraordinary, my receiving you here, but *que voulez vous?* There was no other place, and I would do more than this for our dear Fanny."

Durham bowed. "It seems to me that you are also doing a great deal for me."

"Perhaps you will see later that I have my reasons," she returned, smiling. "But before speaking for myself I must speak for Fanny."

She signed to him to take a chair near the sofa-corner in which she had installed herself, and he listened in silence while she delivered Madame de Malrive's message, and her own report of the progress of affairs.

"You have put me still more deeply in your debt," he said as she concluded; "I wish you would make the expression of this feeling a large part of the message I send back to Madame de Malrive."

She brushed this aside with one of her light gestures of deprecation. "Oh, I told you I had my reasons. And since you are here—and the mere sight of you assures me that you are as well as Fanny charged me to find you—with all these preliminaries disposed of, I am going to relieve you, in a small measure, of the weight of your obligation."

Durham raised his head quickly. "By letting me do something in return?"

She made an assenting motion. "By asking you to answer a question."

"That seems very little to do."

"Don't be so sure! It is never very little to your race." She leaned back, studying him through half-dropped lids.

"Well, try me," he protested.

She did not immediately respond; and when she spoke, her first words were explanatory rather than interrogative.

"I want to begin by saying that I believe I once did you an injustice, to the extent of misunderstanding your motive for a certain action."

Durham's uneasy flush confessed his recognition of her meaning. "Ah, if we must go back to *that*——"

"You withdraw your assent to my request?"

"By no means; but nothing consolatory you can find to say on that point can really make any difference."

"Will not the difference in my view of you perhaps make a difference in your own?"

She looked at him earnestly, without a trace of irony in her eyes or on her lips. "It is really I who have an *amende* to make, as I now understand the situation. I once turned to you for help in a painful extremity, and I have only now learned to understand your reasons for refusing to help me."

"Oh, my reasons——" groaned Durham.

"I have learned to understand them," she persisted, "by being so much, lately, with Fanny."

"But I never told her!" he broke in.

"Exactly. That was what told *me*. I understood you through her, and through your dealings with her. There she was—the woman you adored and longed to save; and you would not lift a finger to make her yours by means which would have seemed—I see it now—a desecration of your feeling for each other." She paused, as if to find the exact words for meanings she had never before had occasion to formulate. "It came to me first—a light on your attitude—when I found you had never breathed to her a word of our talk together. She had confidently commissioned you to find a way for her, as the mediaeval lady sent a prayer to her knight to deliver her from captivity, and you came back, confessing you had failed, but never justifying yourself by so much as a hint of the reason why. And when I had lived a little in Fanny's intimacy—at a moment when circumstances helped to bring us extraordinarily close—I understood why you had done this; why you had let her take what view she pleased of your failure, your passive acceptance of defeat, rather than let her suspect the alternative offered you. You couldn't, even with my permission, betray to anyone a hint of my miserable secret, and you couldn't,

for your life's happiness, pay the particular price that I asked."
She leaned toward him in the intense, almost childlike, effort at
full expression. "Oh, we are of different races, with a different
point of honour; but I understand, I see, that you are good people—just simply, courageously *good!*"

She paused, and then said slowly: "Have I understood you?
Have I put my hand on your motive?"

Durham sat speechless, subdued by the rush of emotion
which her words set free.

"That, you understand, is my question," she concluded with
a faint smile; and he answered hesitatingly: "What can it matter,
when the upshot is something I infinitely regret?"

"Having refused me? Don't!" She spoke with deep seriousness, bending her eyes full on his: "Ah, I have suffered—suffered!
But I have learned also—my life has been enlarged. You see how
I have understood you both. And that is something I should have
been incapable of a few months ago."

Durham returned her look. "I can't think that you can ever
have been incapable of any generous interpretation."

She uttered a slight exclamation, which resolved itself into a
laugh of self-directed irony.

"If you knew into what language I have always translated
life! But that," she broke off, "is not what you are here to learn."

"I think," he returned gravely, "that I am here to learn the
measure of Christian charity."

She threw him a new, odd look. "Ah, no—but to show it!"
she exclaimed.

"To show it? And to whom?"

She paused for a moment, and then rejoined, instead of answering: "Do you remember that day I talked with you at
Fanny's? The day after you came back from Italy?"

He made a motion of assent, and she went on: "You asked
me then what return I expected for my service to you, as you
called it; and I answered, the contemplation of your happiness.
Well, do you know what that meant in my old language—the

language I was still speaking then? It meant that I knew there was horrible misery in store for you, and that I was waiting to feast my eyes on it: that's all!"

She had flung out the words with one of her quick bursts of self-abandonment, like a fevered sufferer stripping the bandage from a wound. Durham received them with a face blanching to the pallor of her own.

"What misery do you mean?" he exclaimed.

She leaned forward, laying her hand on his with just such a gesture as she had used to enforce her appeal in Mrs. Boykin's boudoir. The remembrance made him shrink slightly from her touch, and she drew back with a smile.

"Have you never asked yourself," she enquired, "why our family consented so readily to a divorce?"

"Yes, often," he replied, all his unformed fears gathering in a dark throng about him. "But Fanny was so reassured, so convinced that we owed it to your good offices——"

She broke into a laugh. "My good offices! Will you never, you Americans, learn that we do not act individually in such cases? That we are all obedient to a common principle of authority?"

"Then it was not you——"

She made an impatient shrugging motion. "Oh, you are too confiding—it is the other side of your beautiful good faith!"

"The side you have taken advantage of, it appears?"

"I—we—all of us, I especially!" she confessed.

※ X ※

THERE was another pause, during which Durham tried to steady himself against the shock of the impending revelation. It was an odd circumstance of the case, that though Madame de Treymes' avowal of duplicity was fresh in his ears, he did not for a moment believe that she would deceive him again. Whatever passed between them now would go to the root of the matter.

The first thing that passed was the long look they exchanged: searching on his part, tender, sad, undefinable on hers. As the result of it he said: "Why, then, did you consent to the divorce?"

"To get the boy back," she answered instantly; and while he sat stunned by the unexpectedness of the retort, she went on: "Is it possible you never suspected? It has been our whole thought from the first. Everything was planned with that object."

He drew a sharp breath of alarm. "But the divorce—how could that give him back to you?"

"It was the only thing that could. We trembled lest the idea should occur to you. But we were reasonably safe, for there has only been one other case of the same kind before the courts." She leaned back, the sight of his perplexity checking her quick rush of words. "You didn't know," she began again, "that in that case, on the remarriage of the mother, the courts instantly restored the child to the father, though he had—well, given as much cause for divorce as my unfortunate brother?"

Durham gave an ironic laugh. "Your French justice takes a grammar and dictionary to understand."

She smiled. "*We* understand it—and it isn't necessary that you should."

"So it would appear!" he exclaimed bitterly.

"Don't judge us too harshly—or not, at least, till you have taken the trouble to learn our point of view. You consider the individual—we think only of the family."

"Why don't you take care to preserve it, then?"

"Ah, that's what we do; in spite of every aberration of the individual. And so, when we saw it was impossible that my brother and his wife should live together, we simply transferred our allegiance to the child—we constituted *him* the family."

"A precious kindness you did him! If the result is to give him back to his father."

"That, I admit, is to be deplored; but his father is only a fraction of the whole. What we really do is to give him back to his race, his religion, his true place in the order of things."

"His mother never tried to deprive him of any of those inestimable advantages!"

Madame de Treymes unclasped her hands with a slight gesture of deprecation.

"Not consciously, perhaps; but silences and reserves can teach so much. His mother has another point of view——"

"Thank heaven!" Durham interjected.

"Thank heaven for *her*—yes—perhaps; but it would not have done for the boy."

Durham squared his shoulders with the sudden resolve of a man breaking through a throng of ugly phantoms.

"You haven't yet convinced me that it won't have to do for him. At the time of Madame de Malrive's separation, the court made no difficulty about giving her the custody of her son; and you must pardon me for reminding you that the father's unfitness was the reason alleged."

Madame de Treymes shrugged her shoulders. "And my poor brother, you would add, has not changed; but the circumstances have, and that proves precisely what I have been trying to show you: that, in such cases, the general course of events is considered, rather than the action of any one person."

"Then why is Madame de Malrive's action to be considered?"

"Because it breaks up the unity of the family."

"*Unity*——!" broke from Durham; and Madame de Treymes gently suffered his smile.

"Of the family tradition, I mean: it introduces new elements. You are a new element."

"Thank heaven!" said Durham again.

She looked at him singularly. "Yes—you may thank heaven. Why isn't it enough to satisfy Fanny?"

"Why isn't what enough?"

"Your being, as I say, a new element; taking her so completely into a better air. Why shouldn't she be content to begin a new life with you, without wanting to keep the boy too?"

Durham stared at her dumbly. "I don't know what you mean," he said at length.

"I mean that in her place——" she broke off, dropping her eyes. "She may have another son—the son of the man she adores."

Durham rose from his seat and took a quick turn through the room. She sat motionless, following his steps through her lowered lashes, which she raised again slowly as he stood before her.

"Your idea, then, is that I should tell her nothing?" he said.

"Tell her *now?* But, my poor friend, you would be ruined!"

"Exactly." He paused. "Then why have you told *me?*"

Under her dark skin he saw the faint colour stealing. "We see things so differently—but can't you conceive that, after all that has passed, I felt it a kind of loyalty not to leave you in ignorance?"

"And you feel no such loyalty to her?"

"Ah, I leave her to you," she murmured, looking down again.

Durham continued to stand before her, grappling slowly with his perplexity, which loomed larger and darker as it closed in on him.

"You don't leave her to me; you take her from me at a stroke! I suppose," he added painfully, "I ought to thank you for doing it before it's too late."

She stared. "I take her from you? I simply prevent your going to her unprepared. Knowing Fanny as I do, it seemed to me necessary that you should find a way in advance—a way of tiding over the first moment. That, of course, is what we had planned that you shouldn't have. We meant to let you marry, and then—. Oh, there is no question about the result: we are certain of our case—our measures have been taken *de loin*." She broke off, as if oppressed by his stricken silence. "You will think me stupid, but my warning you of this is the only return I know how to make for your generosity. I could not bear to have you say afterward that I had deceived you twice."

"Twice?" He looked at her perplexedly, and her colour rose.

"I deceived you once—that night at your cousin's, when I tried to get you to bribe me. Even then we meant to consent to the divorce—it was decided the first day that I saw you." He was silent, and she added, with one of her mocking gestures: "You see from what a *milieu* you are taking her!"

Durham groaned. "She will never give up her son!"

"How can she help it? After you are married there will be no choice."

"No—but there is one now."

"*Now?*" She sprang to her feet, clasping her hands in dismay. "Haven't I made it clear to you? Haven't I shown you your course?" She paused, and then brought out with emphasis: "I love Fanny, and I am ready to trust her happiness to you."

"I shall have nothing to do with her happiness," he repeated doggedly.

She stood close to him, and with a look intently fixed on his face. "Are you afraid?" she asked with one of her mocking flashes.

"Afraid?"

"Of not being able to make it up to her——?"

Their eyes met, and he returned her look steadily.

"No; if I had the chance, I believe I could."

"I know you could!" she exclaimed.

"That's the worst of it," he said with a cheerless laugh.

"The worst——?"

"Don't you see that I can't deceive her? Can't trick her into marrying me now?"

Madame de Treymes continued to hold his eyes for a puzzled moment after he had spoken; then she broke out despairingly: "Is happiness never more to you, then, than this abstract standard of truth?"

Durham reflected. "I don't know—it's an instinct. There doesn't seem to be any choice."

"Then I am a miserable wretch for not holding my tongue!"

He shook his head sadly. "That would not have helped me; and it would have been a thousand times worse for her."

"Nothing can be as bad for her as losing you! Aren't you moved by seeing her need?"

"Horribly—are not *you?*" he said, lifting his eyes to hers suddenly.

She started under his look. "You mean, why don't I help you? Why don't I use my influence? Ah, if you knew how I have tried!"

"And you are sure that nothing can be done?"

"Nothing, nothing: what arguments can I use? We abhor divorce—we go against our religion in consenting to it—and nothing short of recovering the boy could possibly justify us."

Durham turned slowly away. "Then there is nothing to be done," he said, speaking more to himself than to her.

He felt her light touch on his arm. "Wait! There is one thing more——" She stood close to him, with entreaty written on her small passionate face. "There is one thing more," she repeated. "And that is, to believe that I am deceiving you again."

He stopped short with a bewildered stare. "That you are deceiving me—about the boy?"

"Yes—yes; why shouldn't I? You're so credulous—the temptation is irresistible."

"Ah, it would be too easy to find out——"

"Don't try, then! Go on as if nothing had happened. I have been lying to you," she declared with vehemence.

"Do you give me your word of honour?" he rejoined.

"A liar's? I haven't any! Take the logic of the facts instead. What reason have you to believe any good of me? And what reason have I to do any to you? Why on earth should I betray my family for your benefit? Ah, don't let yourself be deceived to the end!" She sparkled up at him, her eyes suffused with mockery; but on the lashes he saw a tear.

He shook his head sadly. "I should first have to find a reason for your deceiving me."

"Why, I gave it to you long ago. I wanted to punish you— and now I've punished you enough."

"Yes, you've punished me enough," he conceded.

The tear gathered and fell down her thin cheek. "It's you who are punishing me now. I tell you I'm false to the core. Look back and see what I've done to you!"

He stood silent, with his eyes fixed on the ground. Then he took one of her hands and raised it to his lips.

"You poor, good woman!" he said gravely.

Her hand trembled as she drew it away. "You're going to her —straight from here?"

"Yes—straight from here."

"To tell her everything—to renounce your hope?"

"That is what it amounts to, I suppose."

She watched him cross the room and lay his hand on the door.

"Ah, you poor, good man!" she said with a sob.

Bunner Sisters

❧[1916]❧

IN the days when New York's traffic moved at the pace of the
drooping horse-car, when society applauded Christine Nilsson
at the Academy of Music and basked in the sunsets of the Hud-
son River School on the walls of the National Academy of Design,
an inconspicuous shop with a single show-window was intimately
and favourably known to the feminine population of the quarter
bordering on Stuyvesant Square.

It was a very small shop, in a shabby basement, in a side-
street already doomed to decline; and from the miscellaneous
display behind the window-pane, and the brevity of the sign sur-
mounting it (merely "Bunner Sisters" in blotchy gold on a black
ground) it would have been difficult for the uninitiated to guess
the precise nature of the business carried on within. But that was
of little consequence, since its fame was so purely local that the
customers on whom its existence depended were almost congeni-
tally aware of the exact range of "goods" to be found at Bunner
Sisters'.

The house of which Bunner Sisters had annexed the basement was a private dwelling with a brick front, green shutters on
weak hinges, and a dressmaker's sign in the window above the
shop. On each side of its modest three stories stood higher buildings, with fronts of brown stone, cracked and blistered, cast-iron
balconies and cat-haunted grass-patches behind twisted railings.
These houses too had once been private, but now a cheap lunch-
room filled the basement of one, while the other announced itself, above the knotty wistaria that clasped its central balcony, as
the Mendoza Family Hotel. It was obvious from the chronic cluster of refuse-barrels at its area-gate and the blurred surface of its
curtainless windows, that the families frequenting the Mendoza
Hotel were not exacting in their tastes; though they doubtless in-

dulged in as much fastidiousness as they could afford to pay for, and rather more than their landlord thought they had a right to express.

These three houses fairly exemplified the general character of the street, which, as it stretched eastward, rapidly fell from shabbiness to squalor, with an increasing frequency of projecting sign-boards, and of swinging doors that softly shut or opened at the touch of red-nosed men and pale little girls with broken jugs. The middle of the street was full of irregular depressions, well adapted to retain the long swirls of dust and straw and twisted paper that the wind drove up and down its sad untended length; and toward the end of the day, when traffic had been active, the fissured pavement formed a mosaic of coloured handbills, lids of tomato-cans, old shoes, cigar-stumps and banana skins, cemented together by a layer of mud, or veiled in a powdering of dust, as the state of the weather determined.

The sole refuge offered from the contemplation of this depressing waste was the sight of the Bunner Sisters' window. Its panes were always well-washed, and though their display of artificial flowers, bands of scalloped flannel, wire hat-frames, and jars of homemade preserves, had the undefinable greyish tinge of objects long preserved in the show-case of a museum, the window revealed a background of orderly counters and white-washed walls in pleasant contrast to the adjoining dinginess.

The Bunner sisters were proud of the neatness of their shop and content with its humble prosperity. It was not what they had once imagined it would be, but though it presented but a shrunken image of their earlier ambitions it enabled them to pay their rent and keep themselves alive and out of debt; and it was long since their hopes had soared higher.

Now and then, however, among their greyer hours there came one not bright enough to be called sunny, but rather of the silvery twilight hue which sometimes ends a day of storm. It was such an hour that Ann Eliza, the elder of the firm, was soberly enjoying as she sat one January evening in the back room which served as bedroom, kitchen and parlour to herself and her sister Evelina. In the shop the blinds had been drawn down, the counters cleared and the wares in the window lightly covered with an old sheet; but the shop-door remained unlocked till Evelina, who had taken a parcel to the dyer's, should come back.

In the back room a kettle bubbled on the stove, and Ann Eliza had laid a cloth over one end of the centre table, and placed near the green-shaded sewing lamp two tea-cups, two plates, a sugar-bowl and a piece of pie. The rest of the room remained in a greenish shadow which discreetly veiled the outline of an old-fashioned mahogany bedstead surmounted by a chromo of a young lady in a nightgown who clung with eloquently rolling eyes to a crag described in illuminated letters as the Rock of Ages; and against the unshaded windows two rocking-chairs and a sewing-machine were silhouetted on the dusk.

Ann Eliza, her small and habitually anxious face smoothed to unusual serenity, and the streaks of pale hair on her veined temples shining glossily beneath the lamp, had seated herself at the table, and was tying up, with her usual fumbling deliberation, a knotty object wrapped in paper. Now and then, as she struggled with the string, which was too short, she fancied she heard the click of the shop-door, and paused to listen for her sister; then, as no one came, she straightened her spectacles and entered into renewed conflict with the parcel. In honour of some event of obvious importance, she had put on her double-dyed and triple-turned black silk. Age, while bestowing on this garment a *patine* worthy of a Renaissance bronze, had deprived it of whatever curves the wearer's pre-Raphaelite figure had once been able to impress on it; but this stiffness of outline gave it an air of sacerdotal state which seemed to emphasize the importance of the occasion.

Seen thus, in her sacramental black silk, a wisp of lace turned over the collar and fastened by a mosaic brooch, and her face smoothed into harmony with her apparel, Ann Eliza looked ten years younger than behind the counter, in the heat and burden of the day. It would have been as difficult to guess her approximate age as that of the black silk, for she had the same worn and glossy aspect as her dress; but a faint tinge of pink still lingered on her cheek-bones, like the reflection of sunset which sometimes colours the west long after the day is over.

When she had tied the parcel to her satisfaction, and laid it with furtive accuracy just opposite her sister's plate, she sat down, with an air of obviously assumed indifference, in one of the rocking-chairs near the window; and a moment later the shop-door opened and Evelina entered.

The younger Bunner sister, who was a little taller than her elder, had a more pronounced nose, but a weaker slope of mouth and chin. She still permitted herself the frivolity of waving her pale hair, and its tight little ridges, stiff as the tresses of an Assyrian statue, were flattened under a dotted veil which ended at the tip of her cold-reddened nose. In her scant jacket and skirt of black cashmere she looked singularly nipped and faded; but it seemed possible that under happier conditions she might still warm into relative youth.

"Why, Ann Eliza," she exclaimed, in a thin voice pitched to chronic fretfulness, "what in the world you got your best silk on for?"

Ann Eliza had risen with a blush that made her steel-bowed spectacles incongruous.

"Why, Evelina, why shouldn't I, I sh'ld like to know? Ain't it your birthday, dear?" She put out her arms with the awkwardness of habitually repressed emotion.

Evelina, without seeming to notice the gesture, threw back the jacket from her narrow shoulders.

"Oh, pshaw," she said, less peevishly. "I guess we'd better give up birthdays. Much as we can do to keep Christmas nowadays."

"You hadn't oughter say that, Evelina. We ain't so badly off as all that. I guess you're cold and tired. Set down while I take the kettle off: it's right on the boil."

She pushed Evelina toward the table, keeping a sideward eye on her sister's listless movements, while her own hands were busy with the kettle. A moment later came the exclamation for which she waited.

"Why, Ann Eliza!" Evelina stood transfixed by the sight of the parcel beside her plate.

Ann Eliza, tremulously engaged in filling the teapot, lifted a look of hypocritical surprise.

"Sakes, Evelina! What's the matter?"

The younger sister had rapidly untied the string, and drawn from its wrappings a round nickel clock of the kind to be bought for a dollar-seventy-five.

"Oh, Ann Eliza, how could you?" She set the clock down, and the sisters exchanged agitated glances across the table.

"Well," the elder retorted, "*ain't* it your birthday?"

"Yes, but—"

"Well, and ain't you had to run round the corner to the Square every morning, rain or shine, to see what time it was, ever since we had to sell mother's watch last July? Ain't you, Evelina?"

"Yes, but—"

"There ain't any buts. We've always wanted a clock and now we've got one: that's all there is about it. Ain't she a beauty, Evelina?" Ann Eliza, putting back the kettle on the stove, leaned over her sister's shoulder to pass an approving hand over the circular rim of the clock. "Hear how loud she ticks. I was afraid you'd hear her soon as you come in."

"No. I wasn't thinking," murmured Evelina.

"Well, ain't you glad now?" Ann Eliza gently reproached her. The rebuke had no acerbity, for she knew that Evelina's seeming indifference was alive with unexpressed scruples.

"I'm real glad, sister; but you hadn't oughter. We could have got on well enough without."

"Evelina Bunner, just you sit down to your tea. I guess I know what I'd oughter and what I'd hadn't oughter just as well as you do—I'm old enough!"

"You're real good, Ann Eliza; but I know you've given up something you needed to get me this clock."

"What do I need, I'd like to know? Ain't I got a best black silk?" the elder sister said with a laugh full of nervous pleasure.

She poured out Evelina's tea, adding some condensed milk from the jug, and cutting for her the largest slice of pie; then she drew up her own chair to the table.

The two women ate in silence for a few moments before Evelina began to speak again. "The clock is perfectly lovely and I don't say it ain't a comfort to have it; but I hate to think what it must have cost you."

"No, it didn't, neither," Ann Eliza retorted. "I got it dirt cheap, if you want to know. And I paid for it out of a little extra work I did the other night on the machine for Mrs. Hawkins."

"The baby-waists?"

"Yes."

"There, I knew it! You swore to me you'd buy a new pair of shoes with that money."

"Well, and s'posin' I didn't want 'em—what then? I've patched up the old ones as good as new—and I do declare, Eve-lina Bunner, if you ask me another question you'll go and spoil all my pleasure."

"Very well, I won't," said the younger sister.

They continued to eat without further words. Evelina yielded to her sister's entreaty that she should finish the pie, and poured out a second cup of tea, into which she put the last lump of sugar; and between them, on the table, the clock kept up its sociable tick.

"Where'd you get it, Ann Eliza?" asked Evelina fascinated.

"Where'd you s'pose? Why, right round here, over acrost the

Square, in the queerest little store you ever laid eyes on. I saw it in the window as I was passing, and I stepped right in and asked how much it was, and the store-keeper he was real pleasant about it. He was just the nicest man. I guess he's a German. I told him I couldn't give much, and he said, well, he knew what hard times was too. His name's Ramy—Herman Ramy: I saw it written up over the store. And he told me he used to work at Tiff'ny's, oh, for years, in the clock-department, and three years ago he took sick with some kinder fever, and lost his place, and when he got well they'd engaged somebody else and didn't want him, and so he started this little store by himself. I guess he's real smart, and he spoke quite like an educated man—but he looks sick."

Evelina was listening with absorbed attention. In the narrow lives of the two sisters such an episode was not to be under-rated.

"What you say his name was?" she asked as Ann Eliza paused.

"Herman Ramy."

"How old is he?"

"Well, I couldn't exactly tell you, he looked so sick—but I don't b'lieve he's much over forty."

By this time the plates had been cleared and the teapot emp-tied, and the two sisters rose from the table. Ann Eliza, tying an apron over her black silk, carefully removed all traces of the meal; then, after washing the cups and plates, and putting them away in a cupboard, she drew her rocking-chair to the lamp and sat down to a heap of mending. Evelina, meanwhile, had been roaming about the room in search of an abiding-place for the clock. A rosewood what-not with ornamental fret-work hung on the wall beside the devout young lady in dishabille, and after much weighing of alternatives the sisters decided to dethrone a broken china vase filled with dried grasses which had long stood on the top shelf, and to put the clock in its place; the vase, after farther consideration, being relegated to a small table covered with blue and white bead-work, which held a Bible and prayer-book, and an illustrated copy of Longfellow's poems given as a school-prize to their father.

This change having been made, and the effect studied from every angle of the room, Evelina languidly put her pinking-machine on the table, and sat down to the monotonous work of pinking a heap of black silk flounces. The strips of stuff slid slowly to the floor at her side, and the clock, from its commanding altitude, kept time with the dispiriting click of the instrument under her fingers.

※ II ※

THE purchase of Evelina's clock had been a more important event in the life of Ann Eliza Bunner than her younger sister could divine. In the first place, there had been the demoralizing satisfaction of finding herself in possession of a sum of money which she need not put into the common fund, but could spend as she chose, without consulting Evelina, and then the excitement of her stealthy trips abroad, undertaken on the rare occasions when she could trump up a pretext for leaving the shop; since, as a rule, it was Evelina who took the bundles to the dyer's, and delivered the purchases of those among their customers who were too genteel to be seen carrying home a bonnet or a bundle of pinking—so that, had it not been for the excuse of having to see Mrs. Hawkins's teething baby, Ann Eliza would hardly have known what motive to allege for deserting her usual seat behind the counter.

The infrequency of her walks made them the chief events of her life. The mere act of going out from the monastic quiet of the shop into the tumult of the streets filled her with a subdued excitement which grew too intense for pleasure as she was swallowed by the engulfing roar of Broadway or Third Avenue, and began to do timid battle with their incessant cross-currents of humanity. After a glance or two into the great show-windows she usually allowed herself to be swept back into the shelter of a side-street, and finally regained her own roof in a state of breathless bewilderment and fatigue; but gradually, as her nerves were soothed by the familiar quiet of the little shop, and the click of Evelina's pinking-machine, certain sights and sounds would detach themselves from the torrent along which she had been swept, and she would devote the rest of the day to a mental reconstruction of the different episodes of her walk, till finally it took shape in her thought as a consecutive and highly coloured experience, from which, for weeks afterwards, she would detach some fragmentary recollection in the course of her long dialogues with her sister.

But when, to the unwonted excitement of going out, was added the intenser interest of looking for a present for Evelina, Ann Eliza's agitation, sharpened by concealment, actually preyed upon her rest; and it was not till the present had been given, and she had unbosomed herself of the experiences connected with its purchase, that she could look back with anything like composure to that stirring moment of her life. From that day forward, however, she began to take a certain tranquil pleasure in thinking of Mr. Ramy's small shop, not unlike her own in its countrified obscurity, though the layer of dust which covered its counter and shelves made the comparison only superficially acceptable. Still, she did not judge the state of the shop severely, for Mr. Ramy had told her that he was alone in the world, and lone men, she was aware, did not know how to deal with dust. It gave her a good deal of occupation to wonder why he had never married, or if, on the other hand, he were a widower, and had lost all his dear little children; and she scarcely knew which alternative seemed to make him the more interesting. In either case, his life was assuredly a sad one; and she passed many hours in speculating on the manner in which he probably spent his evenings. She knew he lived at the back of his shop, for she had caught, on entering, a glimpse of a dingy room with a tumbled bed; and the pervading smell of cold fry suggested that he probably did his own cooking. She wondered if he did not often make his tea with water that had not boiled, and asked herself, almost jealously, who looked after the shop while he went to market. Then it occurred to her as likely that he bought his provisions at the same market as Evelina; and she was fascinated by the thought that he and her sister might constantly be meeting in total unconsciousness of the link between them. Whenever she reached this stage in her reflexions she lifted a furtive glance to the clock, whose loud staccato tick was becoming a part of her inmost being.

The seed sown by these long hours of meditation germinated at last in the secret wish to go to market some morning in Evelina's stead. As this purpose rose to the surface of Ann Eliza's thoughts she shrank back shyly from its contemplation. A plan so steeped in duplicity had never before taken shape in her crystalline soul. How was it possible for her to consider such a step? And, besides (she did not possess sufficient logic to mark the downward trend of this "besides"), what excuse could she make that would not excite her sister's curiosity? From this second query it was an easy descent to the third: how soon could she manage to go?

It was Evelina herself, who furnished the necessary pretext by awaking with a sore throat on the day when she usually went to market. It was a Saturday, and as they always had their bit of steak on Sunday the expedition could not be postponed, and it seemed natural that Ann Eliza, as she tied an old stocking around Evelina's throat, should announce her intention of stepping round to the butcher's.

"Oh, Ann Eliza, they'll cheat you so," her sister wailed.

Ann Eliza brushed aside the imputation with a smile, and a few minutes later, having set the room to rights, and cast a last glance at the shop, she was tying on her bonnet with fumbling haste.

The morning was damp and cold, with a sky full of sulky

clouds that would not make room for the sun, but as yet dropped only an occasional snow-flake. In the early light the street looked its meanest and most neglected; but to Ann Eliza, never greatly troubled by any untidiness for which she was not responsible, it seemed to wear a singularly friendly aspect.

A few minutes' walk brought her to the market where Evelina made her purchases, and where, if he had any sense of topographical fitness, Mr. Ramy must also deal.

Ann Eliza, making her way through the outskirts of potato-barrels and flabby fish, found no one in the shop but the gory-aproned butcher who stood in the background cutting chops.

As she approached him across the tessellation of fish-scales, blood and saw-dust, he laid aside his cleaver and not unsympathetically asked: "Sister sick?"

"Oh, not very—jest a cold," she answered, as guiltily as if Evelina's illness had been feigned. "We want a steak as usual, please—and my sister said you was to be sure to give me jest as good a cut as if it was her," she added with child-like candour.

"Oh, that's all right." The butcher picked up his weapon with a grin. "Your sister knows a cut as well as any of us," he remarked.

In another moment, Ann Eliza reflected, the steak would be cut and wrapped up, and no choice left her but to turn her disappointed steps toward home. She was too shy to try to delay the butcher by such conversational arts as she possessed, but the approach of a deaf old lady in an antiquated bonnet and mantle gave her her opportunity.

"Wait on her first, please," Ann Eliza whispered. "I ain't in any hurry."

The butcher advanced to his new customer, and Ann Eliza, palpitating in the back of the shop, saw that the old lady's hesitations between liver and pork chops were likely to be indefinitely prolonged. They were still unresolved when she was interrupted by the entrance of a blowsy Irish girl with a basket on her arm.

The newcomer caused a momentary diversion, and when she had departed the old lady, who was evidently as intolerant of interruption as a professional story-teller, insisted on returning to the beginning of her complicated order, and weighing anew, with an anxious appeal to the butcher's arbitration, the relative advantages of pork and liver. But even her hesitations, and the intrusion on them of two or three other customers, were of no avail, for Mr. Ramy was not among those who entered the shop; and at last Ann Eliza, ashamed of staying longer, reluctantly claimed her steak, and walked home through the thickening snow.

Even to her simple judgment the vanity of her hopes was plain, and in the clear light that disappointment turns upon our actions she wondered how she could have been foolish enough to suppose that, even if Mr. Ramy *did* go to that particular market, he would hit on the same day and hour as herself.

There followed a colourless week unmarked by farther incident. The old stocking cured Evelina's throat, and Mrs. Hawkins dropped in once or twice to talk of her baby's teeth; some new orders for pinking were received, and Evelina sold a bonnet to the lady with puffed sleeves. The lady with puffed sleeves—a resident of "the Square," whose name they had never learned, because she always carried her own parcels home—was the most distinguished and interesting figure on their horizon. She was youngish, she was elegant (as the title they had given her implied), and she had a sweet sad smile about which they had woven many histories; but even the news of her return to town— it was her first apparition that year—failed to arouse Ann Eliza's interest. All the small daily happenings which had once sufficed to fill the hours now appeared to her in their deadly insignificance; and for the first time in her long years of drudgery she rebelled at the dullness of her life. With Evelina such fits of discontent were habitual and openly proclaimed, and Ann Eliza still excused them as one of the prerogatives of youth. Besides, Evelina had not been intended by Providence to pine in such a narrow life: in the original plan of things, she had been meant to marry and have a baby, to wear silk on Sundays, and take a leading part in a Church circle. Hitherto opportunity had played her false; and for all her superior aspirations and carefully crimped hair she had remained as obscure and unsought as Ann Eliza. But the elder sister, who had long since accepted her own fate, had never accepted Evelina's. Once a pleasant young man who taught in Sunday-school had paid the younger Miss Bunner a few shy visits. That was years since, and he had speedily vanished from their view. Whether he had carried with him any of Evelina's illusions, Ann Eliza had never discovered; but his attentions had clad her sister in a halo of exquisite possibilities.

Ann Eliza, in those days, had never dreamed of allowing herself the luxury of self-pity; it seemed as much a personal right of Evelina's as her elaborately crinkled hair. But now she began to transfer to herself a portion of the sympathy she had so long bestowed on Evelina. She had at last recognized her right to set up some lost opportunities of her own; and once that dangerous precedent established, they began to crowd upon her memory.

It was at this stage of Ann Eliza's transformation that Evelina, looking up one evening from her work, said suddenly: "My! She's stopped."

Ann Eliza, raising her eyes from a brown merino seam, followed her sister's glance across the room. It was a Monday, and they always wound the clock on Sundays.

"Are you sure you wound her yesterday, Evelina?"

"Jest as sure as I live. She must be broke. I'll go and see."

Evelina laid down the hat she was trimming, and took the clock from its shelf.

"There—I knew it! She's wound jest as *tight*—what you suppose's happened to her, Ann Eliza?"

"I dunno, I'm sure," said the elder sister, wiping her spectacles before proceeding to a close examination of the clock.

With anxiously bent heads the two women shook and turned it, as though they were trying to revive a living thing, but it remained unresponsive to their touch, and at length Evelina laid it down with a sigh.

"Seems like somethin' *dead,* don't it, Ann Eliza? How still the room is!"

"Yes, ain't it?"

"Well, I'll put her back where she belongs," Evelina continued, in the tone of one about to perform the last offices for the departed. "And I guess," she added, "you'll have to step round to Mr. Ramy's tomorrow, and see if he can fix her."

Ann Eliza's face burned. "I—yes, I guess I'll have to," she stammered, stooping to pick up a spool of cotton which had rolled to the floor. A sudden heart-throb stretched the seams of her flat alpaca bosom, and a pulse leapt to life in each of her temples.

That night, long after Evelina slept, Ann Eliza lay awake in the unfamiliar silence, more acutely conscious of the nearness of the crippled clock than when it had volubly told out the minutes. The next morning she woke from a troubled dream of having carried it to Mr. Ramy's, and found that he and his shop had vanished; and all through the day's occupations the memory of this dream oppressed her.

It had been agreed that Ann Eliza should take the clock to be repaired as soon as they had dined; but while they were still at table a weak-eyed little girl in a black apron stabbed with innumerable pins burst in on them with the cry: "Oh, Miss Bunner, for mercy's sake! Miss Mellins has been took again."

Miss Mellins was the dressmaker upstairs, and the weak-eyed child one of her youthful apprentices.

Ann Eliza started from her seat. "I'll come at once. Quick, Evelina, the cordial!"

By this euphemistic name the sisters designated a bottle of cherry brandy, the last of a dozen inherited from their grandmother, which they kept locked in their cupboard against such emergencies. A moment later, cordial in hand, Ann Eliza was hurrying upstairs behind the weak-eyed child.

Miss Mellins's "turn" was sufficiently serious to detain Ann Eliza for nearly two hours, and dusk had fallen when she took up the depleted bottle of cordial and descended again to the shop. It was empty, as usual, and Evelina sat at her pinking-machine in the back room. Ann Eliza was still agitated by her efforts to restore the dressmaker, but in spite of her preoccupation she was struck, as soon as she entered, by the loud tick of the clock, which still stood on the shelf where she had left it.

"Why, she's going!" she gasped, before Evelina could question her about Miss Mellins. "Did she start up again by herself?"

"Oh, no; but I couldn't stand not knowing what time it was, I've got so accustomed to having her round; and just after you went upstairs Mrs. Hawkins dropped in, so I asked her to tend the store for a minute, and I clapped on my things and ran right round to Mr. Ramy's. It turned out there wasn't anything the matter with her—nothin' on'y a speck of dust in the works—and he fixed her for me in a minute and I brought her right back. Ain't it lovely to hear her going again? But tell me about Miss Mellins, quick!"

For a moment Ann Eliza found no words. Not till she learned that she had missed her chance did she understand how many hopes had hung upon it. Even now she did not know why she had wanted so much to see the clock-maker again.

"I s'pose it's because nothing's ever happened to me," she thought, with a twinge of envy for the fate which gave Evelina every opportunity that came their way. "She had the Sunday-school teacher too," Ann Eliza murmured to herself; but she was well-trained in the arts of renunciation, and after a scarcely perceptible pause she plunged into a detailed description of the dressmaker's "turn."

Evelina, when her curiosity was roused, was an insatiable questioner, and it was supper-time before she had come to the end of her enquiries about Miss Mellins; but when the two sisters had seated themselves at their evening meal Ann Eliza at last found a chance to say: "So she on'y had a speck of dust in her."

Evelina understood at once that the reference was not to Miss Mellins. "Yes—at least he thinks so," she answered, helping herself as a matter of course to the first cup of tea.

"On'y to think!" murmured Ann Eliza.

"But he isn't *sure*," Evelina continued, absently pushing the teapot toward her sister. "It may be something wrong with the— I forget what he called it. Anyhow, he said he'd call round and see, day after to-morrow, after supper."

"Who said?" gasped Ann Eliza.

"Why, Mr. Ramy, of course. I think he's real nice, Ann Eliza. And I don't believe he's forty; but he *does* look sick. I guess he's pretty lonesome, all by himself in that store. He as much as told me so, and somehow"—Evelina paused and bridled—"I kinder thought that maybe his saying he'd call round about the clock was on'y just an excuse. He said it just as I was going out of the store. What you think, Ann Eliza?"

"Oh, I don't har'ly know." To save herself, Ann Eliza could produce nothing warmer.

"Well, I don't pretend to be smarter than other folks," said Evelina, putting a conscious hand to her hair, "but I guess Mr. Herman Ramy wouldn't be sorry to pass an evening here, 'stead of spending it all alone in that poky little place of his."

Her self-consciousness irritated Ann Eliza.

"I guess he's got plenty of friends of his own," she said, almost harshly.

"No, he ain't, either. He's got hardly any."

"Did he tell you that too?" Even to her own ears there was a faint sneer in the interrogation.

"Yes, he did," said Evelina, dropping her lids with a smile. "He seemed to be just crazy to talk to somebody—somebody agreeable, I mean. I think the man's unhappy, Ann Eliza."

"So do I," broke from the elder sister.

"He seems such an educated man, too. He was reading the paper when I went in. Ain't it sad to think of his being reduced to that little store, after being years at Tiff'ny's and one of the head men in their clock-department?"

"He told you all that?"

"Why, yes. I think he'd a' told me everything ever happened to him if I'd had the time to stay and listen. I tell you he's dead lonely, Ann Eliza."

"Yes," said Ann Eliza.

※ III ※

Two days afterward, Ann Eliza noticed that Evelina, before they sat down to supper, pinned a crimson bow under her collar; and when the meal was finished the younger sister, who seldom concerned herself with the clearing of the table, set about with nervous haste to help Ann Eliza in the removal of the dishes.

"I hate to see food mussing about," she grumbled. "Ain't it hateful having to do everything in one room?"

"Oh, Evelina, I've always thought we was so comfortable," Ann Eliza protested.

"Well, so we are, comfortable enough; but I don't suppose there's any harm in my saying I wisht we had a parlour, is there? Anyway, we might manage to buy a screen to hide the bed."

Ann Eliza coloured. There was something vaguely embarrassing in Evelina's suggestion.

"I always think if we ask for more what we have may be taken from us," she ventured.

"Well, whoever took it wouldn't get much," Evelina retorted with a laugh as she swept up the table-cloth.

A few moments later the back room was in its usual flawless order and the two sisters had seated themselves near the lamp. Ann Eliza had taken up her sewing, and Evelina was preparing to make artificial flowers. The sisters usually relegated this more delicate business to the long leisure of the summer months; but tonight Evelina had brought out the box which lay all winter under the bed, and spread before her a bright array of muslin petals, yellow stamens and green corollas, and a tray of little implements curiously suggestive of the dental art. Ann Eliza made no remark on this unusual proceeding; perhaps she guessed why for that evening her sister had chosen a graceful task.

Presently a knock on the outer door made them look up; but Evelina, the first on her feet, said promptly: "Sit still. I'll see who it is."

Ann Eliza was glad to sit still: the baby's petticoat that she was stitching shook in her fingers.

"Sister, here's Mr. Ramy come to look at the clock," said Evelina, a moment later, in the high drawl she cultivated before strangers; and a shortish man with a pale bearded face and upturned coat-collar came stiffly into the room.

Ann Eliza let her work fall as she stood up. "You're very welcome, I'm sure, Mr. Ramy. It's real kind of you to call."

"Nod ad all, ma'am." A tendency to illustrate Grimm's law in the interchange of his consonants betrayed the clock-maker's nationality, but he was evidently used to speaking English, or at least the particular branch of the vernacular with which the Bunner sisters were familiar. "I don't like to led any clock go out of my store without being sure it gives satisfaction," he added.

"Oh,—but we were satisfied," Ann Eliza assured him.

"But I wasn't, you see, ma'am," said Mr. Ramy looking slowly about the room, "nor I won't be, not till I see that clock's going all right."

"May I assist you off with your coat, Mr. Ramy?" Evelina interposed. She could never trust Ann Eliza to remember these opening ceremonies.

"Thank you, ma'am," he replied, and taking his thread-bare overcoat and shabby hat she laid them on a chair with the gesture she imagined the lady with the puffed sleeves might make use of on similar occasions. Ann Eliza's social sense was roused, and she felt that the next act of hospitality must be hers. "Won't you suit yourself to a seat?" she suggested. "My sister will reach down the clock; but I'm sure she's all right again. She's went beautiful ever since you fixed her."

"Dat's good," said Mr. Ramy. His lips parted in a smile which showed a row of yellowish teeth with one or two gaps in it; but in spite of this disclosure Ann Eliza thought his smile extremely pleasant: there was something wistful and conciliating in it which agreed with the pathos of his sunken cheeks and prominent eyes. As he took the clock from Evelina and bent toward the lamp, the light fell on his bulging forehead and wide skull thinly covered with grayish hair. His hands were pale and broad, with knotty joints and square finger-tips rimmed with grime; but his touch was as light as a woman's.

"Well, ladies, dat clock's all right," he pronounced.

"I'm sure we're very much obliged to you," said Evelina, throwing a glance at her sister.

"Oh," Ann Eliza murmured, involuntarily answering the admonition. She selected a key from the bunch that hung at her waist with her cutting-out scissors, and fitting it into the lock of the cupboard, brought out the cherry brandy and three old-fashioned glasses engraved with vine wreaths.

"It's a very cold night," she said, "and maybe you'd like a sip of this cordial. It was made a great while ago by our grandmother."

"It looks fine," said Mr. Ramy bowing, and Ann Eliza filled the glasses. In her own and Evelina's she poured only a few drops, but she filled their guest's to the brim. "My sister and I seldom take wine," she explained.

With another bow, which included both his hostesses, Mr. Ramy drank off the cherry brandy and pronounced it excellent.

Evelina meanwhile, with an assumption of industry intended to put their guest at ease, had taken up her instruments and was twisting a rose-petal into shape.

"You make artificial flowers, I see, ma'am," said Mr. Ramy with interest. "It's very pretty work. I had a lady-vriend in Shermany dat used to make flowers." He put out a square finger-tip to touch the petal.

Evelina blushed a little. "You left Germany long ago, I suppose?"

"Dear me yes, a goot while ago. I was only ninedeen when I come to the States."

After this the conversation dragged on intermittently till Mr. Ramy, peering about the room with the shortsighted glance of his race, said with an air of interest: "You're pleasantly fixed here; it looks real cosy." The note of wistfulness in his voice was obscurely moving to Ann Eliza.

"Oh, we live very plainly," said Evelina, with an affectation of grandeur deeply impressive to her sister. "We have very simple tastes."

"You look real comfortable, anyhow," said Mr. Ramy. His bulging eyes seemed to muster the details of the scene with a gentle envy. "I wisht I had as good a store; but I guess no blace seems homelike when you're always alone in it."

For some minutes longer the conversation moved on at this desultory pace, and then Mr. Ramy, who had been obviously nerving himself for the difficult act of departure, took his leave with an abruptness which would have startled anyone used to the subtler gradations of intercourse. But to Ann Eliza and her sister there was nothing surprising in his abrupt retreat. The long-drawn agonies of preparing to leave, and the subsequent dumb plunge through the door, were so usual in their circle that they would have been as much embarrassed as Mr. Ramy if he had tried to put any fluency into his adieux.

After he had left both sisters remained silent for a while: then Evelina, laying aside her unfinished flower, said: "I'll go and lock up."

※ IV ※

INTOLERABLY monotonous seemed now to the Bunner sisters the treadmill routine of the shop, colourless and long their evenings about the lamp, aimless their habitual interchange of words to the weary accompaniment of the sewing and pinking machines.

It was perhaps with the idea of relieving the tension of their mood that Evelina, the following Sunday, suggested inviting Miss Mellins to supper. The Bunner sisters were not in a position to be lavish of the humblest hospitality, but two or three times in the year they shared their evening meal with a friend; and Miss Mellins, still flushed with the importance of her "turn," seemed the most interesting guest they could invite.

As the three women seated themselves at the supper-table, embellished by the unwonted addition of pound cake and sweet pickles, the dressmaker's sharp swarthy person stood out vividly between the neutral-tinted sisters. Miss Mellins was a small woman with a glossy yellow face and a frizz of black hair bristling with imitation tortoise-shell pins. Her sleeves had a fashionable cut, and half a dozen metal bangles rattled on her wrists. Her voice rattled like her bangles as she poured forth a stream of anecdote and ejaculation; and her round black eyes jumped with acrobatic velocity from one face to another. Miss Mellins was always having or hearing of amazing adventures. She had surprised a burglar in her room at midnight (though how he got there, what he robbed her of, and by what means he escaped had never been quite clear to her auditors); she had been warned by anonymous letters that her grocer (a rejected suitor) was putting poison in her tea; she had a customer who was shadowed by detectives, and another (a very wealthy lady) who had been arrested in a department store for kleptomania; she had been present at a spiritualist seance where an old gentleman had died in a fit on seeing a materialization of his mother-in-law; she had escaped from two fires in her nightgown, and at the funeral of her first cousin the horses attached to the hearse had run away and smashed the coffin, precipitating her relative into an open manhole before the eyes of his distracted family.

A sceptical observer might have explained Miss Mellins's proneness to adventure by the fact that she derived her chief mental nourishment from the *Police Gazette* and the *Fireside Weekly;* but her lot was cast in a circle where such insinuations were not likely to be heard, and where the title-role in bloodcurdling drama had long been her recognized right.

"Yes," she was now saying, her emphatic eyes on Ann Eliza, "you may not believe it, Miss Bunner, and I don't know's I should myself if anybody else was to tell me, but over a year before ever I was born, my mother she went to see a gypsy fortune-teller that was exhibited in a tent on the Battery with the green-headed lady, though her father warned her not to—and what you s'pose she told her? Why, she told her these very words —says she: 'Your next child'll be a girl with jet-black curls, and she'll suffer from spasms.'"

"Mercy!" murmured Ann Eliza, a ripple of sympathy running down her spine.

"D'you ever have spasms before, Miss Mellins?" Evelina asked.

"Yes, ma'am," the dressmaker declared. "And where'd you suppose I had 'em? Why, at my cousin Emma McIntyre's wedding, her that married the apothecary over in Jersey City, though her mother appeared to her in a dream and told her she'd rue the day she done it, but as Emma said, she got more advice than she wanted from the living, and if she was to listen to spectres too she'd never be sure what she'd ought to do and what she'd oughtn't; but I will say her husband took to drink, and she never was the same woman after her fust baby—well, they had an elegant church wedding, and what you s'pose I saw as I was walkin' up the aisle with the wedding percession?"

"Well?" Ann Eliza whispered, forgetting to thread her needle.

"Why, a coffin, to be sure, right on the top step of the chancel—Emma's folks is 'piscopalians and she would have a church wedding, though *his* mother raised a terrible rumpus over it—well, there it set, right in front of where the minister stood that was going to marry 'em, a coffin, covered with a black velvet pall with a gold fringe, and a 'Gates Ajar' in white camellias atop of it."

"Goodness," said Evelina, starting, "there's a knock!"

"Who can it be?" shuddered Ann Eliza, still under the spell of Miss Mellins's hallucination.

Evelina rose and lit a candle to guide her through the shop. They heard her turn the key of the outer door, and a gust of night air stirred the close atmosphere of the back room; then there was a sound of vivacious exclamations, and Evelina returned with Mr. Ramy.

Ann Eliza's heart rocked like a boat in a heavy sea, and the dressmaker's eyes, distended with curiosity, sprang eagerly from face to face.

"I just thought I'd call in again," said Mr. Ramy, evidently somewhat disconcerted by the presence of Miss Mellins. "Just to see how the clock's behaving," he added with his hollow-cheeked smile.

"Oh, she's behaving beautiful," said Ann Eliza; "but we're real glad to see you all the same. Miss Mellins, let me make you acquainted with Mr. Ramy."

The dressmaker tossed back her head and dropped her lids in condescending recognition of the stranger's presence; and Mr. Ramy responded by an awkward bow. After the first moment of constraint a renewed sense of satisfaction filled the consciousness of the three women. The Bunner sisters were not sorry to let Miss Mellins see that they received an occasional evening visit, and Miss Mellins was clearly enchanted at the opportunity of pouring

her latest tale into a new ear. As for Mr. Ramy, he adjusted himself to the situation with greater ease than might have been expected, and Evelina, who had been sorry that he should enter the
room while the remains of supper still lingered on the table,
blushed with pleasure at his good-humored offer to help her
"glear away."

The table cleared, Ann Eliza suggested a game of cards; and
it was after eleven o'clock when Mr. Ramy rose to take leave. His
adieux were so much less abrupt than on the occasion of his first
visit that Evelina was able to satisfy her sense of etiquette by es-
corting him, candle in hand, to the outer door; and as the two
disappeared into the shop Miss Mellins playfully turned to Ann
Eliza.

"Well, well, Miss Bunner," she murmured, jerking her chin
in the direction of the retreating figures, "I'd no idea your sister
was keeping company. On'y to think!"

Ann Eliza, roused from a state of dreamy beatitude, turned
her timid eyes on the dressmaker.

"Oh, you're mistaken, Miss Mellins. We don't har'ly know
Mr. Ramy."

Miss Mellins smiled incredulously. "You go 'long, Miss Bunner. I guess there'll be a wedding somewheres round here before
spring, and I'll be real offended if I ain't asked to make the dress.
I've always seen her in a gored satin with rooshings."

Ann Eliza made no answer. She had grown very pale, and
her eyes lingered searchingly on Evelina as the younger sister
re-entered the room. Evelina's cheeks were pink, and her blue
eyes glittered; but it seemed to Ann Eliza that the coquettish tilt
of her head regrettably emphasized the weakness of her receding
chin. It was the first time that Ann Eliza had ever seen a flaw in
her sister's beauty, and her involuntary criticism startled her like
a secret disloyalty.

That night, after the light had been put out, the elder sister
knelt longer than usual at her prayers. In the silence of the darkened room she was offering up certain dreams and aspirations

whose brief blossoming had lent a transient freshness to her days. She wondered now how she could ever have supposed that Mr. Ramy's visits had another cause than the one Miss Mellins suggested. Had not the sight of Evelina first inspired him with a sudden solicitude for the welfare of the clock? And what charms but Evelina's could have induced him to repeat his visit? Grief held up its torch to the frail fabric of Ann Eliza's illusions, and with a firm heart she watched them shrivel into ashes; then, rising from her knees full of the chill joy of renunciation, she laid a kiss on the crimping pins of the sleeping Evelina and crept under the bedspread at her side.

※ V ※

DURING the months that followed, Mr. Ramy visited the sisters with increasing frequency. It became his habit to call on them every Sunday evening, and occasionally during the week he would find an excuse for dropping in unannounced as they were settling down to their work beside the lamp. Ann Eliza noticed that Evelina now took the precaution of putting on her crimson bow every evening before supper, and that she had refurbished with a bit of carefully washed lace the black silk which they still called new because it had been bought a year after Ann Eliza's.

Mr. Ramy, as he grew more intimate, became less conversational, and after the sisters had blushingly accorded him the privilege of a pipe he began to permit himself long stretches of meditative silence that were not without charm to his hostesses. There was something at once fortifying and pacific in the sense of that tranquil male presence in an atmosphere which had so long quivered with little feminine doubts and distresses; and the sisters fell into the habit of saying to each other, in moments of uncertainty: "We'll ask Mr. Ramy when he comes," and of accepting his verdict, whatever it might be, with a fatalistic readiness that relieved them of all responsibility.

When Mr. Ramy drew the pipe from his mouth and became,

in his turn, confidential, the acuteness of their sympathy grew almost painful to the sisters. With passionate participation they listened to the story of his early struggles in Germany, and of the long illness which had been the cause of his recent misfortunes. The name of the Mrs. Hochmüller (an old comrade's widow) who had nursed him through his fever was greeted with reverential sighs and an inward pang of envy whenever it recurred in his biographical monologues, and once when the sisters were alone Evelina called a responsive flush to Ann Eliza's brow by saying suddenly, without the mention of any name: "I wonder what she's like?"

One day toward spring Mr. Ramy, who had by this time become as much a part of their lives as the letter-carrier or the milkman, ventured the suggestion that the ladies should accompany him to an exhibition of stereopticon views which was to take place at Chickering Hall on the following evening.

After their first breathless "Oh!" of pleasure there was a silence of mutual consultation, which Ann Eliza at last broke by saying: "You better go with Mr. Ramy, Evelina. I guess we don't both want to leave the store at night."

Evelina, with such protests as politeness demanded, acquiesced in this opinion, and spent the next day in trimming a white chip bonnet with forget-me-nots of her own making. Ann Eliza brought out her mosaic brooch, a cashmere scarf of their mother's was taken from its linen cerements, and thus adorned Evelina blushingly departed with Mr. Ramy, while the elder sister sat down in her place at the pinking-machine.

It seemed to Ann Eliza that she was alone for hours, and she was surprised, when she heard Evelina tap on the door, to find that the clock marked only half-past ten.

"It must have gone wrong again," she reflected as she rose to let her sister in.

The evening had been brilliantly interesting, and several striking stereopticon views of Berlin had afforded Mr. Ramy the opportunity of enlarging on the marvels of his native city.

"He said he'd love to show it all to me!" Evelina declared as Ann Eliza conned her glowing face. "Did you ever hear anything so silly? I didn't know which way to look."

Ann Eliza received this confidence with a sympathetic murmur.

"My bonnet *is* becoming, isn't it?" Evelina went on irrelevantly, smiling at her reflection in the cracked glass above the chest of drawers.

"You're jest lovely," said Ann Eliza.

Spring was making itself unmistakably known to the distrustful New Yorker by an increased harshness of wind and prevalence of dust, when one day Evelina entered the back room at supper-time with a cluster of jonquils in her hand.

"I was just that foolish," she answered Ann Eliza's wondering glance, "I couldn't help buyin' 'em. I felt as if I must have something pretty to look at right away."

"Oh, sister," said Ann Eliza, in trembling sympathy. She felt that special indulgence must be conceded to those in Evelina's state since she had had her own fleeting vision of such mysterious longings as the words betrayed.

Evelina, meanwhile, had taken the bundle of dried grasses out of the broken china vase, and was putting the jonquils in their place with touches that lingered down their smooth stems and blade-like leaves.

"Ain't they pretty?" she kept repeating as she gathered the flowers into a starry circle. "Seems as if spring was really here, don't it?"

Ann Eliza remembered that it was Mr. Ramy's evening.

When he came, the Teutonic eye for anything that blooms made him turn at once to the jonquils.

"Ain't dey pretty?" he said. "Seems like as if de spring was really here."

"Don't it?" Evelina exclaimed, thrilled by the coincidence of their thought. "It's just what I was saying to my sister."

Ann Eliza got up suddenly and moved away: she remembered that she had not wound the clock the day before. Evelina was sitting at the table; the jonquils rose slenderly between herself and Mr. Ramy.

"Oh," she murmured with vague eyes, "how I'd love to get away somewheres into the country this very minute—somewheres where it was green and quiet. Seems as if I couldn't stand the city another day." But Ann Eliza noticed that she was looking at Mr. Ramy, and not at the flowers.

"I guess we might go to Cendral Park some Sunday," their visitor suggested. "Do you ever go there, Miss Evelina?"

"No, we don't very often; leastways we ain't been for a good while." She sparkled at the prospect. "It would be lovely, wouldn't it, Ann Eliza?"

"Why, yes," said the elder sister, coming back to her seat.

"Well, why don't we go next Sunday?" Mr. Ramy continued. "And we'll invite Miss Mellins too—that'll make a gosy little party."

That night when Evelina undressed she took a jonquil from the vase and pressed it with a certain ostentation between the leaves of her prayer-book. Ann Eliza, covertly observing her, felt that Evelina was not sorry to be observed, and that her own acute consciousness of the act was somehow regarded as magnifying its significance.

The following Sunday broke blue and warm. The Bunner sisters were habitual church-goers, but for once they left their prayer-books on the what-not, and ten o'clock found them, gloved and bonneted, awaiting Miss Mellins's knock. Miss Mellins presently appeared in a glitter of jet sequins and spangles, with a tale of having seen a strange man prowling under her windows till he was called off at dawn by a confederate's whistle; and shortly afterward came Mr. Ramy, his hair brushed with more than usual care, his broad hands encased in gloves of olive-green kid.

The little party set out for the nearest street-car, and a flutter of mingled gratification and embarrassment stirred Ann Eliza's bosom when it was found that Mr. Ramy intended to pay their fares. Nor did he fail to live up to this opening liberality; for after guiding them through the Mall and the Ramble he led the way to a rustic restaurant where, also at his expense, they fared idyllically on milk and lemon-pie.

After this they resumed their walk, strolling on with the slowness of unaccustomed holiday-makers from one path to another—through budding shrubberies, past grass-banks sprinkled with lilac crocuses, and under rocks on which the forsythia lay like sudden sunshine. Everything about her seemed new and miraculously lovely to Ann Eliza; but she kept her feelings to herself, leaving it to Evelina to exclaim at the hepaticas under the shady ledges, and to Miss Mellins, less interested in the vegetable than in the human world, to remark significantly on the probable history of the persons they met. All the alleys were thronged with promenaders and obstructed by perambulators; and Miss Mellins's running commentary threw a glare of lurid possibilities over the placid family groups and their romping progeny.

Ann Eliza was in no mood for such interpretations of life; but, knowing that Miss Mellins had been invited for the sole purpose of keeping her company she continued to cling to the dressmaker's side, letting Mr. Ramy lead the way with Evelina. Miss Mellins, stimulated by the excitement of the occasion, grew more and more discursive, and her ceaseless talk, and the kaleidoscopic whirl of the crowd, were unspeakably bewildering to Ann Eliza. Her feet, accustomed to the slippered ease of the shop, ached with the unfamiliar effort of walking, and her ears with the din of the dressmaker's anecdotes; but every nerve in her was aware of Evelina's enjoyment, and she was determined that no weariness of hers should curtail it. Yet even her heroism shrank from the significant glances which Miss Mellins presently began to cast at the couple in front of them: Ann Eliza could bear to connive at Evelina's bliss, but not to acknowledge it to others.

At length Evelina's feet also failed her, and she turned to suggest that they ought to be going home. Her flushed face had grown pale with fatigue, but her eyes were radiant.

The return lived in Ann Eliza's memory with the persistence of an evil dream. The horse-cars were packed with the returning throng, and they had to let a dozen go by before they could push their way into one that was already crowded. Ann Eliza had never before felt so tired. Even Miss Mellins's flow of narrative ran dry, and they sat silent, wedged between a Negro woman and a pock-marked man with a bandaged head, while the car rumbled slowly down a squalid avenue to their corner. Evelina and Mr. Ramy sat together in the forward part of the car, and Ann Eliza could catch only an occasional glimpse of the forget-me-not bonnet and the clock-maker's shiny coat-collar; but when the little party got out at their corner the crowd swept them together again, and they walked back in the effortless silence of tired children to the Bunner sisters' basement. As Miss Mellins and Mr. Ramy turned to go their various ways Evelina mustered a last display of smiles; but Ann Eliza crossed the threshold in silence, feeling the stillness of the little shop reach out to her like consoling arms.

That night she could not sleep; but as she lay cold and rigid at her sister's side, she suddenly felt the pressure of Evelina's arms, and heard her whisper: "Oh, Ann Eliza, warn't it heavenly?"

※ VI ※

For four days after their Sunday in the Park the Bunner sisters had no news of Mr. Ramy. At first neither one betrayed her disappointment and anxiety to the other; but on the fifth morning

Evelina, always the first to yield to her feelings, said, as she turned from her untasted tea: "I thought you'd oughter take that money out by now, Ann Eliza."

Ann Eliza understood and reddened. The winter had been a fairly prosperous one for the sisters, and their slowly accumulated savings had now reached the handsome sum of two hundred dollars; but the satisfaction they might have felt in this unwonted opulence had been clouded by a suggestion of Miss Mellins's that there were dark rumours concerning the savings bank in which their funds were deposited. They knew Miss Mellins was given to vain alarms; but her words, by the sheer force of repetition, had so shaken Ann Eliza's peace that after long hours of midnight counsel the sisters had decided to advise with Mr. Ramy; and on Ann Eliza, as the head of the house, this duty had devolved. Mr. Ramy, when consulted, had not only confirmed the dressmaker's report, but had offered to find some safe investment which should give the sisters a higher rate of interest than the suspected savings bank; and Ann Eliza knew that Evelina alluded to the suggested transfer.

"Why, yes, to be sure," she agreed. "Mr. Ramy said if he was us he wouldn't want to leave his money there any longer'n he could help."

"It was over a week ago he said it," Evelina reminded her.

"I know; but he told me to wait till he'd found out for sure about that other investment; and we ain't seen him since then."

Ann Eliza's words released their secret fear. "I wonder what's happened to him," Evelina said. "You don't suppose he could be sick?"

"I was wondering too," Ann Eliza rejoined; and the sisters looked down at their plates.

"I should think you'd oughter do something about that money pretty soon," Evelina began again.

"Well, I know I'd oughter. What would you do if you was me?"

"If I was *you*," said her sister, with perceptible emphasis and a rising blush, "I'd go right round and see if Mr. Ramy was sick. *You* could."

The words pierced Ann Eliza like a blade. "Yes, that's so," she said.

"It would only seem friendly, if he really *is* sick. If I was you I'd go today," Evelina continued; and after dinner Ann Eliza went.

On the way she had to leave a parcel at the dyer's, and having performed that errand she turned toward Mr. Ramy's shop. Never before had she felt so old, so hopeless and humble. She knew she was bound on a love-errand of Evelina's, and the knowledge seemed to dry the last drop of young blood in her veins. It took from her, too, all her faded virginal shyness; and with a brisk composure she turned the handle of the clock-maker's door.

But as she entered her heart began to tremble, for she saw Mr. Ramy, his face hidden in his hands, sitting behind the counter in an attitude of strange dejection. At the click of the latch he looked up slowly, fixing a lustreless stare on Ann Eliza. For a moment she thought he did not know her.

"Oh, you're sick!" she exclaimed; and the sound of her voice seemed to recall his wandering senses.

"Why, if it ain't Miss Bunner!" he said, in a low thick tone; but he made no attempt to move, and she noticed that his face was the colour of yellow ashes.

"You *are* sick," she persisted, emboldened by his evident need of help. "Mr. Ramy, it was real unfriendly of you not to let us know."

He continued to look at her with dull eyes. "I ain't been sick," he said. "Leastways not very: only one of my old turns." He spoke in a slow laboured way, as if he had difficulty in getting his words together.

"Rheumatism?" she ventured, seeing how unwillingly he seemed to move.

"Well—somethin' like, maybe. I couldn't hardly put a name to it."

"If it *was* anything like rheumatism, my grandmother used to make a tea—" Ann Eliza began: she had forgotten, in the warmth of the moment, that she had only come as Evelina's messenger.

At the mention of tea an expression of uncontrollable repugnance passed over Mr. Ramy's face. "Oh, I guess I'm getting on all right. I've just got a headache today."

Ann Eliza's courage dropped at the note of refusal in his voice.

"I'm sorry," she said gently. "My sister and me'd have been glad to do anything we could for you."

"Thank you kindly," said Mr. Ramy wearily; then, as she turned to the door, he added with an effort: "Maybe I'll step round tomorrow."

"We'll be real glad," Ann Eliza repeated. Her eyes were fixed on a dusty bronze clock in the window. She was unaware of looking at it at the time, but long afterward she remembered that it represented a Newfoundland dog with his paw on an open book.

When she reached home there was a purchaser in the shop, turning over hooks and eyes under Evelina's absentminded supervision. Ann Eliza passed hastily into the back room, but in an instant she heard her sister at her side.

"Quick! I told her I was goin' to look for some smaller hooks —how is he?" Evelina gasped.

"He ain't been very well," said Ann Eliza slowly, her eyes on Evelina's eager face; "but he says he'll be sure to be round tomorrow night."

"He will? Are you telling me the truth?"

"Why, Evelina Bunner!"

"Oh, I don't care!" cried the younger recklessly, rushing back into the shop.

Ann Eliza stood burning with the shame of Evelina's self-exposure. She was shocked that, even to her, Evelina should lay bare the nakedness of her emotion; and she tried to turn her thoughts from it as though its recollection made her a sharer in her sister's debasement.

The next evening, Mr. Ramy reappeared, still somewhat sallow and red-lidded, but otherwise like his usual self. Ann Eliza consulted him about the investment he had recommended, and after it had been settled that he should attend to the matter for her he took up the illustrated volume of Longfellow—for, as the sisters had learned, his culture soared beyond the newspapers— and read aloud, with a fine confusion of consonants, the poem on "Maidenhood." Evelina lowered her lids while he read. It was a very beautiful evening, and Ann Eliza thought afterward how different life might have been with a companion who read poetry like Mr. Ramy.

※ VII ※

DURING the ensuing weeks Mr. Ramy, though his visits were as frequent as ever, did not seem to regain his usual spirits. He complained frequently of headache, but rejected Ann Eliza's tentatively proffered remedies, and seemed to shrink from any prolonged investigation of his symptoms. July had come, with a sudden ardour of heat, and one evening, as the three sat together by the open window in the back room, Evelina said: "I dunno what I wouldn't give, a night like this, for a breath of real country air."

"So would I," said Mr. Ramy, knocking the ashes from his pipe. "I'd like to be setting in an arbour with you dis very minute."

"Oh, wouldn't it be lovely?"

"I always think it's real cool here—we'd be heaps hotter up where Miss Mellins is," said Ann Eliza.

"Oh, I daresay—but we'd be heaps cooler somewhere else,"

her sister snapped: she was not infrequently exasperated by Ann Eliza's furtive attempts to mollify Providence.

A few days later Mr. Ramy appeared with a suggestion which enchanted Evelina. He had gone the day before to see his friend, Mrs. Hochmüller, who lived in the outskirts of Hoboken, and Mrs. Hochmüller had proposed that on the following Sunday he should bring the Bunner sisters to spend the day with her.

"She's got a real garden, you know," Mr. Ramy explained, "wid trees and a real summer-house to set in; and hens and chickens too. And it's an elegant sail over on de ferry-boat."

The proposal drew no response from Ann Eliza. She was still oppressed by the recollection of her interminable Sunday in the Park; but, obedient to Evelina's imperious glance, she finally faltered out an acceptance.

The Sunday was a very hot one, and once on the ferry-boat Ann Eliza revived at the touch of the salt breeze, and the spectacle of the crowded waters; but when they reached the other shore, and stepped out in the dirty wharf, she began to ache with anticipated weariness. They got into a street-car, and were jolted from one mean street to another, till at length Mr. Ramy pulled the conductor's sleeve and they got out again; then they stood in the blazing sun, near the door of a crowded beer-saloon, waiting for another car to come; and that carried them out to a thinly settled district, past vacant lots and narrow brick houses standing in unsupported solitude, till they finally reached an almost rural region of scattered cottages and low wooden buildings that looked like village "stores." Here the car finally stopped of its own accord, and they walked along a rutty road, past a stone-cutter's yard with a high fence tapestried with theatrical advertisements, to a little red house with green blinds and a garden paling. Really, Mr. Ramy had not deceived them. Clumps of dielytra and day-lilies bloomed behind the paling, and a crooked elm hung romantically over the gable of the house.

At the gate Mrs. Hochmüller, a broad woman in brick-brown merino, met them with nods and smiles, while her daugh-

ter Linda, a flaxen-haired girl with mottled red cheeks and a
sidelong stare, hovered inquisitively behind her. Mrs. Hochmüller, leading the way into the house, conducted the Bunner sisters
the way to her bedroom. Here they were invited to spread out on
a mountainous white feather-bed the cashmere mantles under
which the solemnity of the occasion had compelled them to swel-
ter, and when they had given their black silks the necessary
twitch of readjustment, and Evelina had fluffed out her hair before a looking-glass framed in pink-shell work, their hostess led
them to a stuffy parlour smelling of ginger-bread. After another
ceremonial pause, broken by polite enquiries and shy ejaculations, they were shown into the kitchen, where the table was already spread with strange-looking spice-cakes and stewed fruits,
and where they presently found themselves seated between Mrs.
Hochmüller and Mr. Ramy, while the staring Linda bumped
back and forth from the stove with steaming dishes.

To Ann Eliza the dinner seemed endless, and the rich fare
strangely unappetizing. She was abashed by the easy intimacy of
her hostess's voice and eye. With Mr. Ramy Mrs. Hochmüller
was almost flippantly familiar, and it was only when Ann Eliza
pictured her generous form bent above his sick-bed that she
could forgive her for tersely addressing him as "Ramy." During
one of the pauses of the meal Mrs. Hochmüller laid her knife and
fork against the edges of her plate, and, fixing her eyes on the
clock-maker's face, said accusingly: "You hat one of dem turns
again, Ramy."

"I dunno as I had," he returned evasively.

Evelina glanced from one to the other. "Mr. Ramy has been
sick," she said at length, as though to show that she also was in a
position to speak with authority. "He's complained very frequently of headaches."

"Ho!—I know him," said Mrs. Hochmüller with a laugh, her
eyes still on the clock-maker. "Ain't you ashamed of yourself,
Ramy?"

Mr. Ramy, who was looking at his plate, said suddenly one

word which the sisters could not understand; it sounded to Ann Eliza like "Shwike."

Mrs. Hochmüller laughed again. "My, my," she said, "wouldn't you think he'd be ashamed to go and be sick and never dell me, me that nursed him troo dat awful fever?"

"Yes, I *should*," said Evelina, with a spirited glance at Ramy; but he was looking at the sausages that Linda had just put on the table.

When dinner was over Mrs. Hochmüller invited her guests to step out of the kitchen-door, and they found themselves in a green enclosure, half garden, half orchard. Grey hens followed by golden broods clucked under the twisted apple-boughs, a cat dozed on the edge of an old well, and from tree to tree ran the network of clothes-line that denoted Mrs. Hochmüller's calling. Beyond the apple trees stood a yellow summer-house festooned with scarlet runners; and below it, on the farther side of a rough fence, the land dipped down, holding a bit of woodland in its hollow. It was all strangely sweet and still on that hot Sunday afternoon, and as she moved across the grass under the apple-boughs Ann Eliza thought of quiet afternoons in church, and of the hymns her mother had sung to her when she was a baby.

Evelina was more restless. She wandered from the well to the summer-house and back, she tossed crumbs to the chickens and disturbed the cat with arch caresses; and at last she expressed a desire to go down into the wood.

"I guess you got to go round by the road, then," said Mrs. Hochmüller. "My Linda she goes troo a hole in de fence, but I guess you'd tear your dress if you was to dry."

"I'll help you," said Mr. Ramy; and guided by Linda the pair walked along the fence till they reached a narrow gap in its boards. Through this they disappeared, watched curiously in their descent by the grinning Linda, while Mrs. Hochmüller and Ann Eliza were left alone in the summer-house.

Mrs. Hochmüller looked at her guest with a confidential smile. "I guess dey'll be gone quite a while," she remarked, jerking her double chin toward the gap in the fence. "Folks like dat don't never remember about de dime." And she drew out her knitting.

Ann Eliza could think of nothing to say.

"Your sister she thinks a great lot of him, don't she?" her hostess continued.

Ann Eliza's cheeks grew hot. "Ain't you a teeny bit lonesome away out here sometimes?" she asked. "I should think you'd be scared nights, all alone with your daughter."

"Oh, no, I ain't," said Mrs. Hochmüller. "You see I take in washing—dat's my business—and it's a lot cheaper doing it out here dan in de city: where'd I get a drying-ground like dis in Hobucken? And den it's safer for Linda too; it geeps her outer de streets."

"Oh," said Ann Eliza, shrinking. She began to feel a distinct aversion for her hostess, and her eyes turned with involuntary annoyance to the square-backed form of Linda, still inquisitively suspended on the fence. It seemed to Ann Eliza that Evelina and her companion would never return from the wood; but they came at length, Mr. Ramy's brow pearled with perspiration, Evelina pink and conscious, a drooping bunch of ferns in her hand; and it was clear that, to her at least, the moments had been winged.

"D'you suppose they'll revive?" she asked, holding up the ferns; but Ann Eliza, rising at her approach, said stiffly: "We'd better be getting home, Evelina."

"Mercy me! Ain't you going to take your coffee first?" Mrs. Hochmüller protested; and Ann Eliza found to her dismay that another long gastronomic ceremony must intervene before politeness permitted them to leave. At length, however, they found themselves again on the ferry-boat. Water and sky were grey, with a dividing gleam of sunset that sent sleek opal waves in the boat's wake. The wind had a cool tarry breath, as though it had travelled over miles of shipping, and the hiss of the water about the paddles was as delicious as though it had been splashed into their tired faces.

Ann Eliza sat apart, looking away from the others. She had made up her mind that Mr. Ramy had proposed to Evelina in the wood, and she was silently preparing herself to receive her sister's confidence that evening.

But Evelina was apparently in no mood for confidences. When they reached home she put her faded ferns in water, and after supper, when she had laid aside her silk dress and the forget-me-not bonnet, she remained silently seated in her rocking-chair near the open window. It was long since Ann Eliza had seen her in so uncommunicative a mood.

The following Saturday Ann Eliza was sitting alone in the shop when the door opened and Mr. Ramy entered. He had never before called at that hour, and she wondered a little anxiously what had brought him.

"Has anything happened?" she asked, pushing aside the basketful of buttons she had been sorting.

"Not's I know of," said Mr. Ramy tranquilly. "But I always close up the store at two o'clock Saturdays at this season, so I thought I might as well call round and see you."

"I'm real glad, I'm sure," said Ann Eliza; "but Evelina's out."

"I know dat," Mr. Ramy answered. "I met her round de corner. She told me she got to go to dat new dyer's up in Forty-eighth Street. She won't be back for a couple of hours, har'ly, will she?"

Ann Eliza looked at him with rising bewilderment. "No, I guess not," she answered; her instinctive hospitality prompting her to add: "Won't you set down jest the same?"

Mr. Ramy sat down on the stool beside the counter, and Ann Eliza returned to her place behind it.

"I can't leave the store," she explained.

"Well, I guess we're very well here." Ann Eliza had become

suddenly aware that Mr. Ramy was looking at her with unusual intentness. Involuntarily her hand strayed to the thin streaks of hair on her temples, and thence descended to straighten the brooch beneath her collar.

"You're looking very well today, Miss Bunner," said Mr. Ramy, following her gesture with a smile.

"Oh," said Ann Eliza nervously. "I'm always well in health," she added.

"I guess you're healthier than your sister, even if you are less sizeable."

"Oh, I don't know. Evelina's a mite nervous sometimes, but she ain't a bit sickly."

"She eats heartier than you do; but that don't mean nothing," said Mr. Ramy.

Ann Eliza was silent. She could not follow the trend of his thought, and she did not care to commit herself farther about Evelina before she had ascertained if Mr. Ramy considered nervousness interesting or the reverse.

But Mr. Ramy spared her all farther indecision.

"Well, Miss Bunner," he said, drawing his stool closer to the counter, "I guess I might as well tell you fust as last what I come here for today. I want to get married."

Ann Eliza, in many a prayerful midnight hour, had sought to strengthen herself for the hearing of this avowal, but now that it had come she felt pitifully frightened and unprepared. Mr. Ramy was leaning with both elbows on the counter, and she noticed that his nails were clean and that he had brushed his hat; yet even these signs had not prepared her!

At last she heard herself say, with a dry throat in which her heart was hammering: "Mercy me, Mr. Ramy!"

"I want to get married," he repeated. "I'm too lonesome. It ain't good for a man to live all alone, and eat noding but cold meat every day."

"No," said Ann Eliza softly.

"And the dust fairly beats me."

"Oh, the dust—I know!"

Mr. Ramy stretched one of his blunt-fingered hands toward her. "I wisht you'd take me."

Still Ann Eliza did not understand. She rose hesitatingly from her seat, pushing aside the basket of buttons which lay between them; then she perceived that Mr. Ramy was trying to take her hand, and as their fingers met a flood of joy swept over her. Never afterward, though every other word of their interview was stamped on her memory beyond all possible forgetting, could she recall what he said while their hands touched; she only knew that she seemed to be floating on a summer sea, and that all its waves were in her ears.

"Me—me?" she gasped.

"I guess so," said her suitor placidly. "You suit me right down to the ground, Miss Bunner. Dat's the truth."

A woman passing along the street paused to look at the shop-window, and Ann Eliza half hoped she would come in; but after a desultory inspection she went on.

"Maybe you don't fancy me?" Mr. Ramy suggested, discountenanced by Ann Eliza's silence.

A word of assent was on her tongue, but her lips refused it. She must find some other way of telling him.

"I don't say that."

"Well, I always kinder thought we was suited to one another," Mr. Ramy continued, eased of his momentary doubt. "I always liked de quiet style—no fuss and airs, and not afraid of work." He spoke as though dispassionately cataloguing her charms.

Ann Eliza felt that she must make an end. "But, Mr. Ramy, you don't understand. I've never thought of marrying."

Mr. Ramy looked at her in surprise. "Why not?"

"Well, I don't know, har'ly." She moistened her twitching lips. "The fact is, I ain't as active as I look. Maybe I couldn't stand the care. I ain't as spry as Evelina—nor as young," she added, with a last great effort.

"But you do most of de work here, anyways," said her suitor doubtfully.

"Oh, well, that's because Evelina's busy outside; and where there's only two women the work don't amount to much. Besides, I'm the oldest; I have to look after things," she hastened on, half pained that her simple ruse should so readily deceive him.

"Well, I guess you're active enough for me," he persisted. His calm determination began to frighten her; she trembled lest her own should be less staunch.

"No, no," she repeated, feeling the tears on her lashes. "I couldn't, Mr. Ramy, I couldn't marry. I'm so surprised. I always thought it was Evelina—always. And so did everybody else. She's so bright and pretty—it seemed so natural."

"Well, you was all mistaken," said Mr. Ramy obstinately.

"I'm so sorry."

He rose, pushing back his chair.

"You'd better think it over," he said, in the large tone of a man who feels he may safely wait.

"Oh, no, no. It ain't any sorter use, Mr. Ramy. I don't never mean to marry. I get tired so easily—I'd be afraid of the work. And I have such awful headaches." She paused, racking her brain for more convincing infirmities.

"Headaches, do you?" said Mr. Ramy, turning back.

"My, yes, awful ones, that I have to give right up to. Evelina has to do everything when I have one of them headaches. She has to bring me my tea in the mornings."

"Well, I'm sorry to hear it," said Mr. Ramy.

"Thank you kindly all the same," Ann Eliza murmured. "And please don't—don't—" She stopped suddenly, looking at him through her tears.

"Oh, that's all right," he answered. "Don't you fret, Miss Bunner. Folks have got to suit themselves." She thought his tone had grown more resigned since she had spoken of her headaches.

For some moments he stood looking at her with a hesitating eye, as though uncertain how to end their conversation; and at length she found courage to say (in the words of a novel she had once read): "I don't want this should make any difference between us."

"Oh, my, no," said Mr. Ramy, absently picking up his hat.

"You'll come in just the same?" she continued, nerving herself to the effort. "We'd miss you awfully if you didn't. Evelina, she—" She paused, torn between her desire to turn his thoughts to Evelina, and the dread of prematurely disclosing her sister's secret.

"Don't Miss Evelina have no headaches?" Mr. Ramy suddenly asked.

"My, no, never—well, not to speak of, anyway. She ain't had one for ages, and when Evelina *is* sick she won't never give in to it," Ann Eliza declared, making some hurried adjustments with her conscience.

"I wouldn't have thought that," said Mr. Ramy.

"I guess you don't know us as well as you thought you did."

"Well, no, that's so; maybe I don't. I'll wish you good day, Miss Bunner;" and Mr. Ramy moved toward the door.

"Good day, Mr. Ramy," Ann Eliza answered.

She felt unutterably thankful to be alone. She knew the crucial moment of her life had passed, and she was glad that she had not fallen below her own ideals. It had been a wonderful experience, full of undreamed-of fear and fascination; and in spite of the tears on her cheeks she was not sorry to have known it. Two facts, however, took the edge from its perfection: that it had happened in the shop, and that she had not had on her black silk.

She passed the next hour in a state of dreamy ecstasy. Something had entered into her life of which no subsequent empoverishment could rob it: she glowed with the same rich sense of possessorship that once, as a little girl, she had felt when her mother had given her a gold locket and she had sat up in bed in the dark to draw it from its hiding-place beneath her nightgown.

At length a dread of Evelina's return began to mingle with these musings. How could she meet her younger sister's eye without betraying what had happened? She felt as though a visible glory lay on her, and she was glad that dusk had fallen when Evelina entered. But her fears were superfluous. Evelina, always self-absorbed, had of late lost all interest in the simple happenings of the shop, and Ann Eliza, with mingled mortification and relief, perceived that she was in no danger of being cross-questioned as to the events of the afternoon. She was glad of this; yet there was a touch of humiliation in finding that the portentous secret in her bosom did not visibly shine forth. It struck her as dull, and even slightly absurd, of Evelina not to know at last that they were equals.

※ VIII ※

MR. RAMY, after a decent interval, returned to the shop; and Ann Eliza, when they met, was unable to detect whether the emotions which seethed under her black alpaca found an echo in his bosom. Outwardly he made no sign. He lit his pipe as placidly as ever and seemed to relapse without effort into the unruffled intimacy of old. Yet to Ann Eliza's initiated eye a change became gradually perceptible. She saw that he was beginning to look at her sister as he had looked at her on that momentous afternoon: she even discerned a secret significance in the turn of his talk with Evelina. Once he asked her abruptly if she should like to travel, and Ann Eliza saw that the flush on Evelina's cheek was reflected from the same fire which had scorched her own.

So they drifted on through the sultry weeks of July. At that season the business of the little shop almost ceased, and one Saturday morning Mr. Ramy proposed that the sisters should lock up early and go with him for a sail down the bay in one of the Coney Island boats.

Ann Eliza saw the light in Evelina's eye and her resolve was instantly taken.

"I guess I won't go, thank you kindly; but I'm sure my sister will be happy to."

She was pained by the perfunctory phrase with which Evelina urged her to accompany them; and still more by Mr. Ramy's silence.

"No, I guess I won't go," she repeated, rather in answer to herself than to them. "It's dreadfully hot and I've got a kinder headache."

"Oh, well, I wouldn't then," said her sister hurriedly. "You'd better jest set here quietly and rest."

"Yes, I'll rest," Ann Eliza assented.

At two o'clock Mr. Ramy returned, and a moment later he and Evelina left the shop. Evelina had made herself another new bonnet for the occasion, a bonnet, Ann Eliza thought, almost too youthful in shape and colour. It was the first time it had ever occurred to her to criticize Evelina's taste, and she was frightened at the insidious change in her attitude toward her sister.

When Ann Eliza, in later days, looked back on that afternoon she felt that there had been something prophetic in the quality of its solitude; it seemed to distill the triple essence of loneliness in which all her after-life was to be lived. No purchasers came; not a hand fell on the door-latch; and the tick of the clock in the back room ironically emphasized the passing of the empty hours.

Evelina returned late and alone. Ann Eliza felt the coming crisis in the sound of her footstep, which wavered along as if not knowing on what it trod. The elder sister's affection had so passionately projected itself into her junior's fate that at such moments she seemed to be living two lives, her own and Evelina's; and her private longings shrank into silence at the sight of the other's hungry bliss. But it was evident that Evelina, never acutely alive to the emotional atmosphere about her, had no idea that her secret was suspected; and with an assumption of unconcern that would have made Ann Eliza smile if the pang had been less piercing, the younger sister prepared to confess herself.

"What are you so busy about?" she said impatiently, as Ann Eliza, beneath the gas-jet, fumbled for the matches. "Ain't you even got time to ask me if I'd had a pleasant day?"

Ann Eliza turned with a quiet smile. "I guess I don't have to. Seems to me it's pretty plain you have."

"Well, I don't know. I don't know *how* I feel—it's all so queer. I almost think I'd like to scream."

"I guess you're tired."

"No, I ain't. It's not that. But it all happened so suddenly, and the boat was so crowded I thought everybody'd hear what he was saying.—Ann Eliza," she broke out, "why on earth don't you ask me what I'm talking about?"

Ann Eliza, with a last effort of heroism, feigned a fond incomprehension.

"What *are* you?"

"Why, I'm engaged to be married—so there! Now it's out! And it happened right on the boat; only to think of it! Of course I wasn't exactly surprised—I've known right along he was going to sooner or later—on'y somehow I didn't think of its happening today. I thought he'd never get up his courage. He said he was so 'fraid I'd say no—that's what kep' him so long from asking me. Well, I ain't said yes *yet*—leastways I told him I'd have to think it over; but I guess he knows. Oh, Ann Eliza, I'm so happy!" She hid the blinding brightness of her face.

Ann Eliza, just then, would only let herself feel that she was glad. She drew down Evelina's hands and kissed her, and they held each other. When Evelina regained her voice she had a tale to tell which carried their vigil far into the night. Not a syllable, not a glance or gesture of Ramy's, was the elder sister spared; and with unconscious irony she found herself comparing the details of his proposal to her with those which Evelina was imparting with merciless prolixity.

The next few days were taken up with the embarrassed adjustment of their new relation to Mr. Ramy and to each other. Ann Eliza's ardour carried her to new heights of self-effacement, and she invented late duties in the shop in order to leave Evelina and her suitor longer alone in the back room. Later on, when she tried to remember the details of those first days, few came back to her: she knew only that she got up each morning with the sense of having to push the leaden hours up the same long steep of pain.

Mr. Ramy came daily now. Every evening he and his betrothed went out for a stroll around the Square, and when Evelina came in her cheeks were always pink. "He's kissed her under that tree at the corner, away from the lamp-post," Ann Eliza said to herself, with sudden insight into unconjectured things. On Sundays they usually went for the whole afternoon to the Central Park, and Ann Eliza, from her seat in the mortal hush of the back room, followed step by step their long slow beatific walk.

There had been, as yet, no allusion to their marriage, except that Evelina had once told her sister that Mr. Ramy wished them to invite Mrs. Hochmüller and Linda to the wedding. The mention of the laundress raised a half-forgotten fear in Ann Eliza, and she said in a tone of tentative appeal: "I guess if I was you I wouldn't want to be very great friends with Mrs. Hochmüller."

Evelina glanced at her compassionately. "I guess if you was me you'd want to do everything you could to please the man you loved. It's lucky," she added with glacial irony, "that I'm not too grand for Herman's friends."

"Oh," Ann Eliza protested, "that ain't what I mean—and you know it ain't. Only somehow the day we saw her I didn't think she seemed like the kinder person you'd want for a friend."

"I guess a married woman's the best judge of such matters," Evelina replied, as though she already walked in the light of her future state.

Ann Eliza, after that, kept her own counsel. She saw that Evelina wanted her sympathy as little as her admonitions, and that already she counted for nothing in her sister's scheme of life. To Ann Eliza's idolatrous acceptance of the cruelties of fate this exclusion seemed both natural and just; but it caused her the most lively pain. She could not divest her love for Evelina of its passionate motherliness; no breath of reason could lower it to the cool temperature of sisterly affection.

She was then passing, as she thought, through the novitiate of her pain; preparing, in a hundred experimental ways, for the solitude awaiting her when Evelina left. It was true that it would be a tempered loneliness. They would not be far apart. Evelina would "run in" daily from the clock-maker's; they would doubtless take supper with her on Sundays. But already Ann Eliza guessed with what growing perfunctoriness her sister would fulfill these obligations; she even foresaw the day when, to get news of Evelina, she should have to lock the shop at nightfall and go herself to Mr. Ramy's door. But on that contingency she would not dwell. "They can come to me when they want to— they'll always find me here," she simply said to herself.

One evening Evelina came in flushed and agitated from her stroll around the Square. Ann Eliza saw at once that something had happened; but the new habit of reticence checked her question.

She had not long to wait. "Oh, Ann Eliza, on'y to think what he says—" (the pronoun stood exclusively for Mr. Ramy). "I declare I'm so upset I thought the people in the Square would notice me. Don't I look queer? He wants to get married right off— this very next week."

"Next week?"

"Yes. So's we can move out to St. Louis right away."

"Him and you—move out to St. Louis?"

"Well, I don't know as it would be natural for him to want to go out there without me," Evelina simpered. "But it's all so sudden I don't know what to think. He only got the letter this morning. *Do* I look queer, Ann Eliza?" Her eye was roving for the mirror.

"No, you don't," said Ann Eliza almost harshly.

"Well, it's a mercy," Evelina pursued with a tinge of disappointment. "It's a regular miracle I didn't faint right out there in the Square. Herman's so thoughtless—he just put the letter into my hand without a word. It's from a big firm out there—the Tiff'ny of St. Louis, he says it is—offering him a place in their clock-department. Seems they heard of him through a German friend of his that's settled out there. It's a splendid opening, and if he gives satisfaction they'll raise him at the end of the year."

She paused, flushed with the importance of the situation, which seemed to lift her once for all above the dull level of her former life.

"Then you'll have to go?" came at last from Ann Eliza.

Evelina stared. "You wouldn't have me interfere with his prospects, would you?"

"No—no. I on'y meant—has it got to be so soon?"

"Right away, I tell you—next week. Ain't it awful?" blushed the bride.

Well, this was what happened to mothers. They bore it, Ann Eliza mused; so why not she? Ah, but they had their own chance first; she had had no chance at all. And now this life which she had made her own was going from her forever; had gone, already, in the inner and deeper sense, and was soon to vanish in even its outward nearness, its surface-communion of voice and eye. At that moment even the thought of Evelina's happiness refused her its consolatory ray; or its light, if she saw it, was too remote to warm her. The thirst for a personal and inalienable tie, for pangs and problems of her own, was parching Ann Eliza's soul: it seemed to her that she could never again gather strength to look her loneliness in the face.

The trivial obligations of the moment came to her aid. Nursed in idleness her grief would have mastered her; but the needs of the shop and the back room, and the preparations for Evelina's marriage, kept the tyrant under.

Miss Mellins, true to her anticipations, had been called on to aid in the making of the wedding dress, and she and Ann Eliza were bending one evening over the breadths of pearl-grey cashmere which, in spite of the dressmaker's prophetic vision of gored satin, had been judged most suitable, when Evelina came into the room alone.

Ann Eliza had already had occasion to notice that it was a bad sign when Mr. Ramy left his affianced at the door. It generally meant that Evelina had something disturbing to communicate, and Ann Eliza's first glance told her that this time the news was grave.

Miss Mellins, who sat with her back to the door and her head bent over her sewing, started as Evelina came around to the opposite side of the table.

"Mercy, Miss Evelina! I declare I thought you was a ghost, the way you crep' in. I had a customer once up in Forty-ninth Street—a lovely young woman with a thirty-six bust and a waist you could ha' put into her wedding ring—and her husband, he crep' up behind her that way jest for a joke, and frightened her into a fit, and when she come to she was a raving maniac, and had to be taken to Bloomingdale with two doctors and a nurse to hold her in the carriage, and a lovely baby on'y six weeks old—and there she is to this day, poor creature."

"I didn't mean to startle you," said Evelina.

She sat down on the nearest chair, and as the lamplight fell on her face Ann Eliza saw that she had been crying.

"You do look dead-beat," Miss Mellins resumed, after a pause of soul-probing scrutiny. "I guess Mr. Ramy lugs you round that Square too often. You'll walk your legs off if you ain't careful. Men don't never consider—they're all alike. Why, I had a cousin once that was engaged to a book-agent—"

"Maybe we'd better put away the work for tonight, Miss Mellins," Ann Eliza interposed. "I guess what Evelina wants is a good night's rest."

"That's so," assented the dressmaker. "Have you got the back breadths run together, Miss Bunner? Here's the sleeves. I'll pin 'em together." She drew a cluster of pins from her mouth, in which she seemed to secrete them as squirrels stow away nuts. "There," she said, rolling up her work, "you go right away to bed,

Miss Evelina, and we'll set up a little later tomorrow night. I guess you're a mite nervous, ain't you? I know when my turn comes I'll be scared to death."

With this arch forecast she withdrew, and Ann Eliza, returning to the back room, found Evelina still listlessly seated by the table. True to her new policy of silence, the elder sister set about folding up the bridal dress; but suddenly Evelina said in a harsh unnatural voice: "There ain't any use in going on with that."

The folds slipped from Ann Eliza's hands.

"Evelina Bunner—what you mean?"

"Jest what I say. It's put off."

"Put off—what's put off?"

"Our getting married. He can't take me to St. Louis. He ain't got money enough." She brought the words out in the monotonous tone of a child reciting a lesson.

Ann Eliza picked up another breadth of cashmere and began to smooth it out. "I don't understand," she said at length.

"Well, it's plain enough. The journey's fearfully expensive, and we've got to have something left to start with when we get out there. We've counted up, and he ain't got the money to do it —that's all."

"But I thought he was going right into a splendid place."

"So he is; but the salary's pretty low the first year, and board's very high in St. Louis. He's jest got another letter from his German friend, and he's been figuring it out, and he's afraid to chance it. He'll have to go alone."

"But there's your money—have you forgotten that? The hundred dollars in the bank."

Evelina made an impatient movement. "Of course I ain't forgotten it. On'y it ain't enough. It would all have to go into buying furniture, and if he was took sick and lost his place again we wouldn't have a cent left. He says he's got to lay by another hundred dollars before he'll be willing to take me out there."

For a while Ann Eliza pondered this surprising statement;

then she ventured: "Seems to me he might have thought of it before."

In an instant Evelina was aflame. "I guess he knows what's right as well as you or me. I'd sooner die than be a burden to him."

Ann Eliza made no answer. The clutch of an unformulated doubt had checked the words on her lips. She had meant on the day of her sister's marriage to give Evelina the other half of their common savings; but something warned her not to say so now.

The sisters undressed without farther words. After they had gone to bed, and the light had been put out, the sound of Evelina's weeping came to Ann Eliza in the darkness, but she lay motionless on her own side of the bed, out of contact with her sister's shaken body. Never had she felt so coldly remote from Evelina.

The hours of the night moved slowly, ticked off with wearisome insistence by the clock which had played so prominent a part in their lives. Evelina's sobs still stirred the bed at gradually lengthening intervals, till at length Ann Eliza thought she slept. But with the dawn the eyes of the sisters met, and Ann Eliza's courage failed her as she looked in Evelina's face.

She sat up in bed and put out a pleading hand.

"Don't cry so, dearie. Don't."

"Oh, I can't bear it, I can't bear it," Evelina moaned.

Ann Eliza stroked her quivering shoulder. "Don't, don't," she repeated. "If you take the other hundred, won't that be enough? I always meant to give it to you. On'y I didn't want to tell you till your wedding day."

※ IX ※

Evelina's marriage took place on the appointed day. It was celebrated in the evening, in the chantry of the church which the sisters attended, and after it was over the few guests who had been present repaired to the Bunner Sisters' basement, where a wedding supper awaited them. Ann Eliza, aided by Miss Mellins and Mrs. Hawkins, and consciously supported by the sentimental interest of the whole street, had expended her utmost energy on the decoration of the shop and the back room. On the table a vase of white chrysanthemums stood between a dish of oranges and bananas and an iced wedding-cake wreathed with orange-blossoms of the bride's own making. Autumn leaves studded with paper roses festooned the what-not and the chromo of the Rock of Ages, and a wreath of yellow immortelles was twined about the clock which Evelina revered as the mysterious agent of her happiness.

At the table sat Miss Mellins, profusely spangled and bangled, her head sewing-girl, a pale young thing who had helped with Evelina's outfit, Mr. and Mrs. Hawkins, with Johnny, their eldest boy, and Mrs. Hochmüller and her daughter.

Mrs. Hochmüller's large blonde personality seemed to pervade the room to the effacement of the less amply proportioned guests. It was rendered more impressive by a dress of crimson poplin that stood out from her in organ-like folds; and Linda, whom Ann Eliza had remembered as an uncouth child with a sly look about the eyes, surprised her by a sudden blossoming into feminine grace such as sometimes follows on a gawky girlhood. The Hochmüllers, in fact, struck the dominant note in the entertainment. Beside them Evelina, unusually pale in her grey cashmere and white bonnet, looked like a faintly washed sketch beside a brilliant chromo; and Mr. Ramy, doomed to the traditional insignificance of the bridegroom's part, made no attempt to rise above his situation. Even Miss Mellins sparkled and jingled in vain in the shadow of Mrs. Hochmüller's crimson bulk; and Ann Eliza, with a sense of vague foreboding, saw that the wedding feast centred about the two guests she had most wished to exclude from it. What was said or done while they all sat about the table she never afterward recalled: the long hours remained in her memory as a whirl of high colours and loud voices, from which the pale presence of Evelina now and then emerged like a drowned face on a sunset-dabbled sea.

The next morning Mr. Ramy and his wife started for St. Louis, and Ann Eliza was left alone. Outwardly the first strain of parting was tempered by the arrival of Miss Mellins, Mrs. Hawkins and Johnny, who dropped in to help in the ungarlanding and tidying up of the back room. Ann Eliza was duly grateful for their kindness, but the "talking over" on which they had evidently counted was Dead Sea fruit on her lips; and just beyond the familiar warmth of their presences she saw the form of Solitude at her door.

Ann Eliza was but a small person to harbour so great a guest, and a trembling sense of insufficiency possessed her. She had no high musings to offer to the new companion of her hearth. Every one of her thoughts had hitherto turned to Evelina and shaped itself in homely easy words; of the mighty speech of silence she knew not the earliest syllable.

Everything in the back room and the shop, on the second day after Evelina's going, seemed to have grown coldly unfamiliar. The whole aspect of the place had changed with the changed conditions of Ann Eliza's life. The first customer who opened the shop-door startled her like a ghost; and all night she lay tossing on her side of the bed, sinking now and then into an uncertain doze from which she would suddenly wake to reach out her hand for Evelina. In the new silence surrounding her the walls and furniture found voice, frightening her at dusk and midnight with strange sighs and stealthy whispers. Ghostly hands shook the window shutters or rattled at the outer latch, and once she grew cold at the sound of a step like Evelina's stealing through the dark shop to die out on the threshold. In time, of course, she found an explanation for these noises, telling herself that the bedstead was warping, that Miss Mellins trod heavily overhead, or that the thunder of passing beer-waggons shook the door-latch; but the hours leading up to these conclusions were full of the floating terrors that harden into fixed foreboding. Worst of all

were the solitary meals, when she absently continued to set aside
the largest slice of pie for Evelina, and to let the tea grow cold
while she waited for her sister to help herself to the first cup.
Miss Mellins, coming in on one of these sad repasts, suggested
the acquisition of a cat; but Ann Eliza shook her head. She had
never been used to animals, and she felt the vague shrinking of
the pious from creatures divided from her by the abyss of soul-
lessness.

At length, after ten empty days, Evelina's first letter came.

"My dear Sister," she wrote, in her pinched Spencerian hand,
"it seems strange to be in this great City so far from home alone
with him I have chosen for life, but marriage has its solemn duties
which those who are not can never hope to understand, and happier perhaps for this reason, life for them has only simple tasks
and pleasures, but those who must take thought for others must
be prepared to do their duty in whatever station it has pleased the
Almighty to call them. Not that I have cause to complain, my
dear Husband is all love and devotion, but being absent all day
at his business how can I help but feel lonesome at times, as the
poet says it is hard for they that love to live apart, and I often
wonder, my dear Sister, how you are getting along alone in the
store, may you never experience the feelings of solitude I have
underwent since I came here. We are boarding now, but soon
expect to find rooms and change our place of Residence, then I
shall have all the care of a household to bear, but such is the
fate of those who join their Lot with others, they cannot hope to
escape from the burdens of Life, nor would I ask it, I would not
live alway, but while I live would always pray for strength to do
my duty. This city is not near as large or handsome as New York,
but had my lot been cast in a Wilderness I hope I should not
repine, such never was my nature, and they who exchange their
independence for the sweet name of Wife must be prepared to
find all is not gold that glitters, nor I would not expect like you
to drift down the stream of Life unfettered and serene as a
Summer cloud, such is not my fate, but come what may will

always find in me a resigned and prayerful Spirit, and hoping
this finds you as well as it leaves me, I remain, my dear Sister,
                    "Yours truly,
                            "Evelina B. Ramy."

Ann Eliza had always secretly admired the oratorical and
impersonal tone of Evelina's letters; but the few she had pre-
viously read, having been addressed to schoolmates or distant
relatives, had appeared in the light of literary compositions
rather than as records of personal experience. Now she could not
but wish that Evelina had laid aside her swelling periods for a
style more suited to the chronicling of homely incidents. She
read the letter again and again, seeking for a clue to what her
sister was really doing and thinking; but after each reading she
emerged impressed but unenlightened from the labyrinth of Evelina's eloquence.

During the early winter she received two or three more
letters of the same kind, each enclosing in its loose husk of rhetoric a smaller kernel of fact. By dint of patient interlinear study,
Ann Eliza gathered from them that Evelina and her husband,
after various costly experiments in boarding, had been reduced
to a tenement-house flat; that living in St. Louis was more expensive than they had supposed, and that Mr. Ramy was kept out
late at night (why, at a jeweller's, Ann Eliza wondered?) and
found his position less satisfactory than he had been led to expect. Toward February the letters fell off; and finally they ceased
to come.

At first Ann Eliza wrote, shyly but persistently, entreating
for more frequent news; then, as one appeal after another was
swallowed up in the mystery of Evelina's protracted silence,
vague fears began to assail the elder sister. Perhaps Evelina was
ill, and with no one to nurse her but a man who could not even
make himself a cup of tea! Ann Eliza recalled the layer of dust in
Mr. Ramy's shop, and pictures of domestic disorder mingled with
the more poignant vision of her sister's illness. But surely if Eve-

lina were ill Mr. Ramy would have written. He wrote a small neat hand, and epistolary communication was not an insuperable embarrassment to him. The too probable alternative was that both the unhappy pair had been prostrated by some disease which left them powerless to summon her—for summon her they surely would, Ann Eliza with unconscious cynicism reflected, if she or her small economies could be of use to them! The more she strained her eyes into the mystery, the darker it grew; and her lack of initiative, her inability to imagine what steps might be taken to trace the lost in distant places, left her benumbed and helpless.

At last there floated up from some depth of troubled memory the name of the firm of St. Louis jewellers by whom Mr. Ramy was employed. After much hesitation, and considerable effort, she addressed to them a timid request for news of her brother-in-law; and sooner than she could have hoped the answer reached her

"Dear Madam,

"In reply to yours of the 29th ult. we beg to state that the party you refer to was discharged from our employ a month ago. We are sorry we are unable to furnish you with his address.

"Yours respectfully,
"LUDWIG AND HAMMERBUSCH."

Ann Eliza read and re-read the curt statement in a stupor of distress. She had lost her last trace of Evelina. All that night she lay awake, revolving the stupendous project of going to St. Louis in search of her sister; but though she pieced together her few financial possibilities with the ingenuity of a brain used to fitting odd scraps into patchwork quilts, she woke to the cold daylight fact that she could not raise the money for her fare. Her wedding gift to Evelina had left her without any resources beyond her daily earnings, and these had steadily dwindled as the winter passed. She had long since renounced her weekly visit to the butcher, and had reduced her other expenses to the narrowest measure; but the most systematic frugality had not enabled her to put by any money. In spite of her dogged efforts to maintain the prosperity of the little shop, her sister's absence had already told on its business. Now that Ann Eliza had to carry the bundles to the dyer's herself, the customers who called in her absence, finding the shop locked, too often went elsewhere. Moreover, after several stern but unavailing efforts, she had had to give up the trimming of bonnets, which in Evelina's hands had been the most lucrative as well as the most interesting part of the business. This change, to the passing female eye, robbed the shop window of its chief attraction; and when painful experience had convinced the regular customers of the Bunner Sisters of Ann Eliza's lack of millinery skill they began to lose faith in her ability to curl a feather or even "freshen up" a bunch of flowers. The time came when Ann Eliza had almost made up her mind to speak to the lady with puffed sleeves, who had always looked at her so kindly, and had once ordered a hat of Evelina. Perhaps the lady with puffed sleeves would be able to get her a little plain sewing to do; or she might recommend the shop to friends. Ann Eliza, with this possibility in view, rummaged out of a drawer the fly-blown remainder of the business cards which the sisters had ordered in the first flush of their commercial adventure; but when the lady with puffed sleeves finally appeared she was in deep mourning, and wore so sad a look that Ann Eliza dared not speak. She came in to buy some spools of black thread and silk, and in the doorway she turned back to say: "I am going away tomorrow for a long time. I hope you will have a pleasant winter." And the door shut on her.

One day not long after this it occurred to Ann Eliza to go to Hoboken in quest of Mrs. Hochmüller. Much as she shrank from pouring her distress into that particular ear; her anxiety had carried her beyond such reluctances; but when she began to think the matter over she was faced by a new difficulty. On the occasion of her only visit to Mrs. Hochmüller, she and Evelina had suffered themselves to be led there by Mr. Ramy; and Ann Eliza now perceived that she did not even know the name of the laundress's suburb, much less that of the street in which she lived. But she must have news of Evelina, and no obstacle was great enough to thwart her.

Though she longed to turn to some one for advice she disliked to expose her situation to Miss Mellins's searching eye, and at first she could think of no other confidant. Then she remembered Mrs. Hawkins, or rather her husband, who, though Ann Eliza had always thought him a dull uneducated man, was probably gifted with the mysterious masculine faculty of finding out people's addresses. It went hard with Ann Eliza to trust her secret even to the mild ear of Mrs. Hawkins, but at least she was spared the cross-examination to which the dressmaker would have subjected her. The accumulating pressure of domestic cares had so crushed in Mrs. Hawkins any curiosity concerning the affairs of others that she received her visitor's confidence with an almost masculine indifference, while she rocked her teething baby on one arm and with the other tried to check the acrobatic impulses of the next in age.

"My my," she simply said as Ann Eliza ended. "Keep still now, Arthur: Miss Bunner don't want you to jump up and down on her foot today. And what are you gaping at, Johnny? Run right off and play," she added, turning sternly to her eldest, who, because he was the least naughty, usually bore the brunt of her wrath against the others.

"Well, perhaps Mr. Hawkins can help you," Mrs. Hawkins continued meditatively, while the children, after scattering at her bidding, returned to their previous pursuits like flies settling down on the spot from which an exasperated hand has swept them. "I'll send him right round the minute he comes in, and you can tell him the whole story. I wouldn't wonder but what he can find that Mrs. Hochmüller's address in the d'rectory. I know they've got one where he works."

"I'd be real thankful if he could," Ann Eliza murmured, rising from her seat with the factitious sense of lightness that comes from imparting a long-hidden dread.

※ X ※

MR. HAWKINS proved himself worthy of his wife's faith in his capacity. He learned from Ann Eliza as much as she could tell him about Mrs. Hochmüller and returned the next evening with a scrap of paper bearing her address, beneath which Johnny (the family scribe) had written in a large round hand the names of the streets that led there from the ferry.

Ann Eliza lay awake all that night, repeating over and over again the directions Mr. Hawkins had given her. He was a kind man, and she knew he would willingly have gone with her to Hoboken; indeed she read in his timid eye the half-formed intention of offering to accompany her—but on such an errand she preferred to go alone.

The next Sunday, accordingly, she set out early, and without much trouble found her way to the ferry. Nearly a year had passed since her previous visit to Mrs. Hochmüller, and a chilly April breeze smote her face as she stepped on the boat. Most of the passengers were huddled together in the cabin, and Ann Eliza shrank into its obscurest corner, shivering under the thin black mantle which had seemed so hot in July. She began to feel a little bewildered as she stepped ashore, but a paternal policeman put her into the right car, and as in a dream she found herself retracing the way to Mrs. Hochmüller's door. She had told the conductor the name of the street at which she wished to get out, and presently she stood in the biting wind at the corner near the beer-saloon, where the sun had once beat down on her so fiercely. At length an empty car appeared, its yellow flank emblazoned with the name of Mrs. Hochmüller's suburb, and Ann Eliza was presently jolting past the narrow brick houses islanded between vacant lots like giant piles in a desolate lagoon. When the car reached the end of its journey she got out and stood for some time trying to remember which turn Mr. Ramy had taken. She had just made up her mind to ask the car-driver when he shook the reins on the backs of his lean horses, and the car, still empty, jogged away toward Hoboken.

Ann Eliza, left alone by the roadside, began to move cautiously forward, looking about for a small red house with a gable overhung by an elm-tree: but everything about her seemed unfamiliar and forbidding. One or two surly looking men slouched past with inquisitive glances, and she could not make up her mind to stop and speak to them.

At length a tow-headed boy came out of a swinging door suggestive of illicit conviviality, and to him Ann Eliza ventured to confide her difficulty. The offer of five cents fired him with an instant willingness to lead her to Mrs. Hochmüller, and he was soon trotting past the stone-cutter's yard with Ann Eliza in his wake.

Another turn in the road brought them to the little red house, and having rewarded her guide, Ann Eliza unlatched the gate and walked up to the door. Her heart was beating violently, and she had to lean against the door-post to compose her twitching lips: she had not known till that moment how much it was going to hurt her to speak of Evelina to Mrs. Hochmüller. As her agitation subsided she began to notice now much the appearance of the house had changed. It was not only that winter had stripped the elm, and blackened the flower-borders: the house itself had a debased and deserted air. The window-panes were cracked and dirty, and one or two shutters swung dismally on loosened hinges.

She rang several times before the door was opened. At length an Irish woman with a shawl over her head and a baby in her arms appeared on the threshold, and glancing past her into the narrow passage Ann Eliza saw that Mrs. Hochmüller's neat abode had deteriorated as much within as without.

At the mention of the name the woman stared. "Mrs. who, did ye say?"

"Mrs. Hochmüller. This is surely her house?"

"No, it ain't neither," said the woman turning away.

"Oh, but wait, please," Ann Eliza entreated. "I can't be mistaken. I mean the Mrs. Hochmüller who takes in washing. I came out to see her last June."

"Oh, the Dutch washerwoman is it—her that used to live here? She's been gone two months and more. It's Mike McNulty lives here now. Whisht!" to the baby, who had squared his mouth for a howl.

Ann Eliza's knees grew weak. "Mrs. Hochmüller gone? But where has she gone? She must be somewhere round here. Can't you tell me?"

"Sure an' I can't," said the woman. "She wint away before iver we come."

"Dalia Geoghegan, will ye bring the choild in out av the cowld?" cried an irate voice from within.

"Please wait—oh, please wait," Ann Eliza insisted. "You see I must find Mrs. Hochmüller."

"Why don't ye go and look for her thin?" the woman returned, slamming the door in her face.

She stood motionless on the door-step, dazed by the immensity of her disappointment, till a burst of loud voices inside the house drove her down the path and out of the gate.

Even then she could not grasp what had happened, and pausing in the road she looked back at the house, half hoping that Mrs. Hochmüller's once detested face might appear at one of the grimy windows.

She was roused by an icy wind that seemed to spring up suddenly from the desolate scene, piercing her thin dress like gauze; and turning away she began to retrace her steps. She thought of enquiring for Mrs. Hochmüller at some of the neighbouring houses, but their look was so unfriendly that she walked on without making up her mind at which door to ring. When she reached the horse-car terminus a car was just moving off toward Hoboken, and for nearly an hour she had to wait on the corner in the bitter wind. Her hands and feet were stiff with cold when the car at length loomed into sight again, and she thought of stopping somewhere on the way to the ferry for a cup of tea; but before the region of lunch-rooms was reached she had grown so sick and dizzy that the thought of food was repulsive. At length she found herself on the ferry-boat, in the soothing stuffiness of the crowded cabin; then came another interval of shivering on a street-corner, another long jolting journey in a "cross-town" car that smelt of damp straw and tobacco; and lastly, in the cold spring dusk, she unlocked her door and groped her way through the shop to her fireless bedroom.

The next morning Mrs. Hawkins, dropping in to hear the result of the trip, found Ann Eliza sitting behind the counter wrapped in an old shawl.

"Why, Miss Bunner, you're sick! You must have fever—your face is just as red!"

"It's nothing. I guess I caught cold yesterday on the ferry-boat," Ann Eliza acknowledged.

"And it's jest like a vault in here!" Mrs. Hawkins rebuked her. "Let me feel your hand—it's burning. Now, Miss Bunner, you've got to go right to bed this very minute."

"Oh, but I can't, Mrs. Hawkins." Ann Eliza attempted a wan smile. "You forget there ain't nobody but me to tend the store."

"I guess you won't tend it long neither, if you ain't careful," Mrs. Hawkins grimly rejoined. Beneath her placid exterior she cherished a morbid passion for disease and death, and the sight of Ann Eliza's suffering had roused her from her habitual indifference. "There ain't so many folks comes to the store anyhow," she went on with unconscious cruelty, "and I'll go right up and see if Miss Mellins can't spare one of her girls."

Ann Eliza, too weary to resist, allowed Mrs. Hawkins to put her to bed and make a cup of tea over the stove, while Miss Mellins, always good-naturedly responsive to any appeal for help, sent down the weak-eyed little girl to deal with hypothetical customers.

Ann Eliza, having so far abdicated her independence, sank into sudden apathy. As far as she could remember, it was the first time in her life that she had been taken care of instead of taking care, and there was a momentary relief in the surrender. She swallowed the tea like an obedient child, allowed a poultice to be applied to her aching chest and uttered no protest when a fire was kindled in the rarely used grate; but as Mrs. Hawkins bent over to "settle" her pillows she raised herself on her elbow to whisper: "Oh, Mrs. Hawkins, Mrs. Hochmüller warn't there." The tears rolled down her cheeks.

"She warn't there? Has she moved?"

"Over two months ago—and they don't know where she's gone. Oh what'll I do, Mrs. Hawkins?"

"There, there, Miss Bunner. You lay still and don't fret. I'll ask Mr. Hawkins soon as ever he comes home."

Ann Eliza murmured her gratitude, and Mrs. Hawkins, bending down, kissed her on the forehead. "Don't you fret," she repeated, in the voice with which she soothed her children.

For over a week Ann Eliza lay in bed, faithfully nursed by her two neighbours, while the weak-eyed child, and the pale sewing girl who had helped to finish Evelina's wedding dress, took turns in minding the shop. Every morning, when her friends appeared, Ann Eliza lifted her head to ask: "Is there a letter?" and at their gentle negative sank back in silence. Mrs. Hawkins, for several days, spoke no more of her promise to consult her husband as to the best way of tracing Mrs. Hochmüller; and dread of fresh disappointment kept Ann Eliza from bringing up the subject.

But the following Sunday evening, as she sat for the first time bolstered up in her rocking-chair near the stove, while Miss Mellins studied the *Police Gazette* beneath the lamp, there came a knock on the shop-door and Mr. Hawkins entered.

Ann Eliza's first glance at his plain friendly face showed her he had news to give, but though she no longer attempted to hide her anxiety from Miss Mellins, her lips trembled too much to let her speak.

"Good evening, Miss Bunner," said Mr. Hawkins in his dragging voice. "I've been over to Hoboken all day looking round for Mrs. Hochmüller."

"Oh, Mr. Hawkins—you *have?*

"I made a thorough search, but I'm sorry to say it was no use. She's left Hoboken—moved clear away, and nobody seems to know where."

"It was real good of you, Mr. Hawkins." Ann Eliza's voice struggled up in a faint whisper through the submerging tide of her disappointment.

Mr. Hawkins, in his embarrassed sense of being the bringer of bad news, stood before her uncertainly; then he turned to go. "No trouble at all," he paused to assure her from the doorway.

She wanted to speak again, to detain him, to ask him to advise her; but the words caught in her throat and she lay back silent.

The next day she got up early, and dressed and bonneted herself with twitching fingers. She waited till the weak-eyed child appeared, and having laid on her minute instructions as to the care of the shop, she slipped out into the street. It had occurred to her in one of the weary watches of the previous night that she might go to Tiffany's and make enquiries about Ramy's past. Possibly in that way she might obtain some information that would suggest a new way of reaching Evelina. She was guiltily aware that Mrs. Hawkins and Miss Mellins would be angry with her for venturing out of doors, but she knew she should never feel any better till she had news of Evelina.

The morning air was sharp, and as she turned to face the wind she felt so weak and unsteady that she wondered if she should ever get as far as Union Square; but by walking very slowly, and standing still now and then when she could do so without being noticed, she found herself at last before the jeweller's great glass doors.

It was still so early that there were no purchasers in the

shop, and she felt herself the centre of innumerable unemployed eyes as she moved forward between long lines of show-cases glittering with diamonds and silver.

She was glancing about in the hope of finding the clock-department without having to approach one of the impressive gentlemen who paced the empty aisles, when she attracted the attention of one of the most impressive of the number.

The formidable benevolence with which he enquired what he could do for her made her almost despair of explaining herself; but she finally disentangled from a flurry of wrong beginnings the request to be shown to the clock-department.

The gentleman considered her thoughtfully. "May I ask what style of clock you are looking for? Would it be for a wedding-present, or—"

The irony of the allusion filled Ann Eliza's veins with sudden strength. "I don't want to buy a clock at all. I want to see the head of the department."

"Mr. Loomis?" His stare still weighed her—then he seemed to brush aside the problem she presented as beneath his notice. "Oh, certainly. Take the elevator to the second floor. Next aisle to the left." He waved her down the endless perspective of show-cases.

Ann Eliza followed the line of his lordly gesture, and a swift ascent brought her to a great hall full of the buzzing and booming of thousands of clocks. Whichever way she looked, clocks stretched away from her in glittering interminable vistas: clocks of all sizes and voices, from the bell-throated giant of the hall-way to the chirping dressing-table toy; tall clocks of mahogany and brass with cathedral chimes; clocks of bronze, glass, porcelain, of every possible size, voice and configuration; and between their serried ranks, along the polished floor of the aisles, moved the languid forms of other gentlemanly floorwalkers, waiting for their duties to begin.

One of them soon approached, and Ann Eliza repeated her request. He received it affably.

"Mr. Loomis? Go right down to the office at the other end." He pointed to a kind of box of ground glass and highly polished panelling.

As she thanked him he turned to one of his companions and said something in which she caught the name of Mr. Loomis, and which was received with an appreciative chuckle. She suspected herself of being the object of the pleasantry, and straightened her thin shoulders under her mantle.

The door of the office stood open, and within sat a grey-bearded man at a desk. He looked up kindly, and again she asked for Mr. Loomis.

"I'm Mr. Loomis. What can I do for you?"

He was much less portentous than the others, though she guessed him to be above them in authority; and encouraged by his tone she seated herself on the edge of the chair he waved her to.

"I hope you'll excuse my troubling you, sir. I came to ask if you could tell me anything about Mr. Herman Ramy. He was employed here in the clock-department two or three years ago."

Mr. Loomis showed no recognition of the name.

"Ramy? When was he discharged?"

"I don't har'ly know. He was very sick, and when he got well his place had been filled. He married my sister last October and they went to St. Louis, I ain't had any news of them for over two months, and she's my only sister, and I'm most crazy worrying about her."

"I see." Mr. Loomis reflected. "In what capacity was Ramy employed here?" he asked after a moment.

"He—he told us that he was one of the heads of the clock-department," Ann Eliza stammered, overswept by a sudden doubt.

"That was probably a slight exaggeration. But I can tell you about him by referring to our books. The name again?"

"Ramy—Herman Ramy."

There ensued a long silence, broken only by the flutter of

leaves as Mr. Loomis turned over his ledgers. Presently he looked up, keeping his finger between the pages.

"Here it is—Herman Ramy. He was one of our ordinary workmen, and left us three years and a half ago last June."

"On account of sickness?" Ann Eliza faltered.

Mr. Loomis appeared to hesitate; then he said: "I see no mention of sickness." Ann Eliza felt his compassionate eyes on her again. "Perhaps I'd better tell you the truth. He was discharged for drug-taking. A capable workman, but we couldn't keep him straight. I'm sorry to have to tell you this, but it seems fairer, since you say you're anxious about your sister."

The polished sides of the office vanished from Ann Eliza's sight, and the cackle of the innumerable clocks came to her like the yell of waves in a storm. She tried to speak, but could not; tried to get to her feet, but the floor was gone.

"I'm very sorry," Mr. Loomis repeated, closing the ledger. "I remember the man perfectly now. He used to disappear every now and then, and turn up again in a state that made him useless for days."

As she listened, Ann Eliza recalled the day when she had come on Mr. Ramy sitting in abject dejection behind his counter. She saw again the blurred unrecognizing eyes he had raised to her, the layer of dust over everything in the shop, and the green bronze clock in the window representing a Newfoundland dog with his paw on a book. She stood up slowly.

"Thank you. I'm sorry to have troubled you."

"It was no trouble. You say Ramy married your sister last October?"

"Yes, sir; and they went to St. Louis right afterward. I don't know how to find her. I thought maybe somebody here might know about him."

"Well, possibly some of the workmen might. Leave me your name and I'll send you word if I get on his track."

He handed her a pencil, and she wrote down her address; then she walked away blindly between the clocks.

※ XI ※

Mr. LOOMIS, true to his word, wrote a few days later that he had enquired in vain in the workshop for any news of Ramy; and as she folded this letter and laid it between the leaves of her Bible, Ann Eliza felt that her last hope was gone. Miss Mellins, of course, had long since suggested the mediation of the police, and cited from her favourite literature convincing instances of the supernatural ability of the Pinkerton detective; but Mr. Hawkins, when called in council, dashed this project by remarking that detectives cost something like twenty dollars a day; and a vague fear of the law, some half-formed vision of Evelina in the clutch of a blue-coated "officer," kept Ann Eliza from invoking the aid of the police.

After the arrival of Mr. Loomis's note the weeks followed each other uneventfully. Ann Eliza's cough clung to her till late in the spring, the reflection in her looking-glass grew more bent and meagre, and her forehead sloped back farther toward the twist of hair that was fastened above her parting by a comb of black India-rubber.

Toward spring a lady who was expecting a baby took up her abode at the Mendoza Family Hotel, and through the friendly intervention of Miss Mellins the making of some of the baby-clothes was entrusted to Ann Eliza. This eased her of anxiety for the immediate future; but she had to rouse herself to feel any sense of relief. Her personal welfare was what least concerned her. Sometimes she thought of giving up the shop altogether; and only the fear that, if she changed her address, Evelina might not be able to find her, kept her from carrying out this plan.

Since she had lost her last hope of tracing her sister, all the activities of her lonely imagination had been concentrated on the possibility of Evelina's coming back to her. The discovery of Ramy's secret filled her with dreadful fears. In the solitude of the

shop and the back room she was tortured by vague pictures of
Evelina's sufferings. What horrors might not be hidden beneath
her silence? Ann Eliza's great dread was that Miss Mellins should
worm out of her what she had learned from Mr. Loomis. She was
sure Miss Mellins must have abominable things to tell about
drug-fiends—things she did not have the strength to hear. "Drug-
fiend"—the very word was Satanic: she could hear Miss Mellins
roll it on her tongue. But Ann Eliza's own imagination, left to itself, had begun to people the long hours with evil visions. Sometimes, in the night, she thought she heard herself called: the
voice was her sister's, but faint with a nameless terror. Her most
peaceful moments were those in which she managed to convince
herself that Evelina was dead. She thought of her then, mourn-
fully but more calmly, as thrust away under the neglected mound
of some unknown cemetery, where no headstone marked her
name, no mourner with flowers for another grave paused in pity
to lay a blossom on hers. But this vision did not often give Ann
Eliza its negative relief: and always, beneath its hazy lines,
lurked the dark conviction that Evelina was alive, in misery and
longing for her.

So the summer wore on. Ann Eliza was conscious that Mrs.
Hawkins and Miss Mellins were watching her with affectionate
anxiety, but the knowledge brought no comfort. She no longer
cared what they felt or thought about her. Her grief lay far beyond touch of human healing, and after a while she became
aware that they knew they could not help her. They still came in
as often as their busy lives permitted, but their visits grew
shorter, and Mrs. Hawkins always brought Arthur or the baby, so
that there should be something to talk about, and some one
whom she could scold.

The autumn came, and the winter. Business had fallen off
again, and but few purchasers came to the little shop in the basement. In January Ann Eliza pawned her mother's cashmere scarf,
her mosaic brooch, and the rosewood what-not on which the
clock had always stood; she would have sold the bedstead too,

but for the persistent vision of Evelina returning weak and weary, and not knowing where to lay her head.

The winter passed in its turn, and March reappeared with its galaxies of yellow jonquils at the windy street corners, reminding Ann Eliza of the spring day when Evelina had come home with a bunch of jonquils in her hand. In spite of the flowers which lent such a premature brightness to the streets the month was fierce and stormy, and Ann Eliza could get no warmth into her bones. Nevertheless, she was insensibly beginning to take up the healing routine of life. Little by little she had grown used to being alone, she had begun to take a languid interest in the one or two new purchasers the season had brought, and though the thought of Evelina was as poignant as ever, it was less persistently in the foreground of her mind.

Late one afternoon she was sitting behind the counter, wrapped in her shawl, and wondering how soon she might draw down the blinds and retreat into the comparative cosiness of the back room. She was not thinking of anything in particular, except perhaps in a hazy way of the lady with the puffed sleeves, who after her long eclipse had reappeared the day before in sleeves of a new cut, and bought some tape and needles. The lady still wore mourning, but she was evidently lightening it, and Ann Eliza saw in this the hope of future orders. The lady had left the shop about an hour before, walking away with her graceful step toward Fifth Avenue. She had wished Ann Eliza good day in her usual affable way, and Ann Eliza thought how odd it was that they should have been acquainted so long, and yet that she should not know the lady's name. From this consideration her mind wandered to the cut of the lady's new sleeves, and she was vexed with herself for not having noted it more carefully. She felt Miss Mellins might have liked to know about it. Ann Eliza's powers of observation had never been as keen as Evelina's, when the latter was not too self-absorbed to exert them. As Miss Mellins always said, Evelina could "take patterns with her eyes": she could have cut that new sleeve out of a folded newspaper in a trice! Musing on these things, Ann Eliza wished the lady would come back and give her another look at the sleeve. It was not unlikely that she might pass that way, for she certainly lived in or about the Square. Suddenly Ann Eliza remarked a small neat handkerchief on the counter: it must have dropped from the lady's purse, and she would probably come back to get it. Ann Eliza, pleased at the idea, sat on behind the counter and watched the darkening street. She always lit the gas as late as possible, keeping the box of matches at her elbow, so that if anyone came she could apply a quick flame to the gas-jet. At length through the deepening dusk she distinguished a slim dark figure coming down the steps to the shop. With a little warmth of pleasure about her heart she reached up to light the gas. "I do believe I'll ask her name this time," she thought. She raised the flame to its full height, and saw her sister standing in the door.

There she was at last, the poor pale shade of Evelina, her thin face blanched of its faint pink, the stiff ripples gone from her hair, and a mantle shabbier than Ann Eliza's drawn about her narrow shoulders. The glare of the gas beat full on her as she stood and looked at Ann Eliza.

"Sister—oh, Evelina! I knowed you'd come!"

Ann Eliza had caught her close with a long moan of triumph. Vague words poured from her as she laid her cheek against Evelina's—trivial inarticulate endearments caught from Mrs. Hawkins's long discourses to her baby.

For a while Evelina let herself be passively held; then she drew back from her sister's clasp and looked about the shop. "I'm dead tired. Ain't there any fire?" she asked.

"Of course there is!" Ann Eliza, holding her hand fast, drew her into the back room. She did not want to ask any questions yet: she simply wanted to feel the emptiness of the room brimmed full again by the one presence that was warmth and light to her.

She knelt down before the grate, scraped some bits of coal and kindling from the bottom of the coal-scuttle, and drew one of the rocking-chairs up to the weak flame. "There—that'll blaze up in a minute," she said. She pressed Evelina down on the faded cushions of the rocking-chair, and, kneeling beside her, began to rub her hands.

"You're stone-cold, ain't you? Just sit still and warm yourself while I run and get the kettle. I've got something you always used to fancy for supper." She laid her hand on Evelina's shoulder. "Don't talk—oh, don't talk yet!" she implored. She wanted to keep that one frail second of happiness between herself and what she knew must come.

Evelina, without a word, bent over the fire, stretching her thin hands to the blaze and watching Ann Eliza fill the kettle and set the supper table. Her gaze had the dreamy fixity of a half-awakened child's.

Ann Eliza, with a smile of triumph, brought a slice of custard pie from the cupboard and put it by her sister's plate.

"You do like that, don't you? Miss Mellins sent it down to me this morning. She had her aunt from Brooklyn to dinner. Ain't it funny it just so happened?"

"I ain't hungry," said Evelina, rising to approach the table.

She sat down in her usual place, looked about her with the same wondering stare, and then, as of old, poured herself out the first cup of tea.

"Where's the what-not gone to?" she suddenly asked.

Ann Eliza set down the teapot and rose to get a spoon from the cupboard. With her back to the room she said: "The what-not? Why, you see, dearie, living here all alone by myself it only made one more thing to dust; so I sold it."

Evelina's eyes were still travelling about the familiar room. Though it was against all the traditions of the Bunner family to sell any household possession, she showed no surprise at her sister's answer.

"And the clock? The clock's gone too."

"Oh, I gave that away—I gave it to Mrs. Hawkins. She's kep' awake so nights with that last baby."

"I wish you'd never bought it," said Evelina harshly.

Ann Eliza's heart grew faint with fear. Without answering, she crossed over to her sister's seat and poured her out a second cup of tea. Then another thought struck her, and she went back to the cupboard and took out the cordial. In Evelina's absence considerable draughts had been drawn from it by invalid neighbours; but a glassful of the precious liquid still remained.

"Here, drink this right off—it'll warm you up quicker than anything," Ann Eliza said.

Evelina obeyed, and a slight spark of colour came into her cheeks. She turned to the custard pie and began to eat with a silent voracity distressing to watch. She did not even look to see what was left for Ann Eliza.

"I ain't hungry," she said at last as she laid down her fork. "I'm only so dead tired—that's the trouble."

"Then you'd better get right into bed. Here's my old plaid dressing-gown—you remember it, don't you?" Ann Eliza laughed, recalling Evelina's ironies on the subject of the antiquated garment. With trembling fingers she began to undo her sister's cloak. The dress beneath it told a tale of poverty that Ann Eliza dared not pause to note. She drew it gently off, and as it slipped from Evelina's shoulders it revealed a tiny black bag hanging on a ribbon about her neck. Evelina lifted her hand as though to screen the bag from Ann Eliza; and the elder sister, seeing the gesture, continued her task with lowered eyes. She undressed Evelina as quickly as she could, and wrapping her in the plaid dressing-gown put her to bed, and spread her own shawl and her sister's cloak above the blanket.

"Where's the old red comfortable?" Evelina asked, as she sank down on the pillow.

"The comfortable? Oh, it was so hot and heavy I never used it after you went—so I sold that too. I never could sleep under much clothes."

She became aware that her sister was looking at her more attentively.

"I guess you've been in trouble too," Evelina said.

"Me? In trouble? What do you mean, Evelina?"

"You've had to pawn the things, I suppose," Evelina continued in a weary unmoved tone. "Well, I've been through worse than that. I've been to hell and back."

"Oh, Evelina—don't say it, sister!" Ann Eliza implored, shrinking from the unholy word. She knelt down and began to rub her sister's feet beneath the bed-clothes.

"I've been to hell and back—if I *am* back," Evelina repeated. She lifted her head from the pillow and began to talk with a sudden feverish volubility. "It began right away, less than a month after we were married. I've been in hell all that time, Ann Eliza." She fixed her eyes with passionate intentness on Ann Eliza's face. "He took opium. I didn't find it out till long afterward—at first, when he acted so strange, I thought he drank. But it was worse, much worse than drinking."

"Oh, sister, don't say it—don't say it yet! It's so sweet just to have you here with me again."

"I must say it," Evelina insisted, her flushed face burning with a kind of bitter cruelty. "You don't know what life's like— you don't know anything about it—setting here safe all the while in this peaceful place."

"Oh, Evelina—why didn't you write and send for me if it was like that?"

"That's why I couldn't write. Didn't you guess I was ashamed?"

"How could you be? Ashamed to write to Ann Eliza?"

Evelina raised herself on her thin elbow, while Ann Eliza, bending over, drew a corner of the shawl about her shoulder.

"Do lay down again. You'll catch your death."

"My death? That don't frighten me! You don't know what I've been through." And sitting upright in the old mahogany bed, with flushed cheeks and chattering teeth, and Ann Eliza's trembling arm clasping the shawl about her neck, Evelina poured out her story. It was a tale of misery and humiliation so remote from the elder sister's innocent experiences that much of it was hardly intelligible to her. Evelina's dreadful familiarity with it all, her fluency about things which Ann Eliza half-guessed and quickly shuddered back from, seemed even more alien and terrible than the actual tale she told. It was one thing—and heaven knew it was bad enough!—to learn that one's sister's husband was a drug-fiend; it was another, and much worse thing, to learn from that sister's pallid lips what vileness lay behind the word.

Evelina, unconscious of any distress but her own, sat upright, shivering in Ann Eliza's hold, while she piled up, detail by detail, her dreary narrative.

"The minute we got out there, and he found the job wasn't as good as he expected, he changed. At first I thought he was sick—I used to try to keep him home and nurse him. Then I saw it was something different. He used to go off for hours at a time, and when he came back his eyes kinder had a fog over them. Sometimes he didn't har'ly know me, and when he did he seemed to hate me. Once he hit me here." She touched her breast. "Do you remember, Ann Eliza, that time he didn't come to see us for a week—the time after we all went to Central Park together— and you and I thought he must be sick?"

Ann Eliza nodded.

"Well, that was the trouble—he'd been at it then. But nothing like as bad. After we'd been out there about a month he disappeared for a whole week. They took him back at the store, and gave him another chance; but the second time they discharged him, and he drifted round for ever so long before he could get another job. We spent all our money and had to move to a cheaper place. Then he got something to do, but they hardly paid him anything, and he didn't stay there long. When he found out about the baby—"

"The baby?" Ann Eliza faltered.

"It's dead—it only lived a day. When he found out about it, he got mad, and said he hadn't any money to pay doctors' bills, and I'd better write to you to help us. He had an idea you had money hidden away that I didn't know about." She turned to her sister with remorseful eyes. "It was him that made me get that hundred dollars out of you."

"Hush, hush. I always meant it for you anyhow."

"Yes, but I wouldn't have taken it if he hadn't been at me the whole time. He used to make me do just what he wanted. Well, when I said I wouldn't write to you for more money he said I'd better try and earn some myself. That was when he struck me. . . . Oh, you don't know what I'm talking about yet! . . . I tried to get work at a milliner's, but I was so sick I couldn't stay. I was sick all the time. I wisht I'd ha' died, Ann Eliza."

"No, no, Evelina."

"Yes, I do. It kept getting worse and worse. We pawned the furniture, and they turned us out because we couldn't pay the rent; and so then we went to board with Mrs. Hochmüller."

Ann Eliza pressed her closer to dissemble her own tremor. "Mrs. Hochmüller?"

"Didn't you know she was out there? She moved out a month after we did. She wasn't bad to me, and I think she tried to keep him straight—but Linda—"

"Linda—?"

"Well, when I kep' getting worse, and he was always off, for days at a time, the doctor had me sent to a hospital."

"A hospital? Sister—sister!"

"It was better than being with him; and the doctors were real kind to me. After the baby was born I was very sick and had to stay there a good while. And one day when I was laying there Mrs. Hochmüller came in as white as a sheet, and told me him and Linda had gone off together and taken all her money. That's the last I ever saw of him." She broke off with a laugh and began to cough again.

Ann Eliza tried to persuade her to lie down and sleep, but the rest of her story had to be told before she could be soothed into consent. After the news of Ramy's flight she had had brain fever, and had been sent to another hospital where she stayed a long time—how long she couldn't remember. Dates and days meant nothing to her in the shapeless ruin of her life. When she left the hospital she found that Mrs. Hochmüller had gone too. She was penniless, and had no one to turn to. A lady visitor at the hospital was kind, and found her a place where she did housework; but she was so weak they couldn't keep her. Then she got a job as waitress in a down-town lunch-room, but one day she fainted while she was handing a dish, and that evening when they paid her they told her she needn't come again.

"After that I begged in the streets"—(Ann Eliza's grasp again grew tight)—"and one afternoon last week, when the matinées was coming out, I met a man with a pleasant face, something like Mr. Hawkins, and he stopped and asked me what the trouble was. I told him if he'd give me five dollars I'd have money enough to buy a ticket back to New York, and he took a good look at me and said, well, if that was what I wanted he'd go straight to the station with me and give me the five dollars there. So he did—and he bought the ticket, and put me in the cars."

Evelina sank back, her face a sallow wedge in the white cleft of the pillow. Ann Eliza leaned over her, and for a long time they held each other without speaking.

They were still clasped in this dumb embrace when there was a step in the shop and Ann Eliza, starting up, saw Miss Mellins in the doorway.

"My sakes, Miss Bunner! What in the land are you doing? Miss Evelina—Mrs. Ramy—it ain't you?"

Miss Mellins's eyes, bursting from their sockets, sprang from Evelina's pallid face to the disordered supper table and the heap of worn clothes on the floor; then they turned back to Ann Eliza, who had placed herself on the defensive between her sister and the dressmaker.

"My sister Evelina has come back—come back on a visit. She was taken sick in the cars on the way home—I guess she caught cold—so I made her go right to bed as soon as ever she got here."

Ann Eliza was surprised at the strength and steadiness of her voice. Fortified by its sound she went on, her eyes on Miss Mellins's baffled countenance: "Mr. Ramy has gone west on a trip—a trip connected with his business; and Evelina is going to stay with me till he comes back."

※ XII ※

WHAT measure of belief her explanation of Evelina's return obtained in the small circle of her friends Ann Eliza did not pause to enquire. Though she could not remember ever having told a lie before, she adhered with rigid tenacity to the consequences of her first lapse from truth, and fortified her original statement with additional details whenever a questioner sought to take her unawares.

But other and more serious burdens lay on her startled conscience. For the first time in her life she dimly faced the awful problem of the inutility of self-sacrifice. Hitherto she had never thought of questioning the inherited principles which had guided her life. Self-effacement for the good of others had always seemed to her both natural and necessary; but then she had taken it for granted that it implied the securing of that good. Now she perceived that to refuse the gifts of life does not ensure their transmission to those for whom they have been surrendered; and her familiar heaven was unpeopled. She felt she could no longer trust in the goodness of God, and that if he was not good he was not God, and there was only a black abyss above the roof of Bunner Sisters.

But there was little time to brood upon such problems. The care of Evelina filled Ann Eliza's days and nights. The hastily summoned doctor had pronounced her to be suffering from pneumonia, and under his care the first stress of the disease was relieved. But her recovery was only partial, and long after the doctor's visits had ceased she continued to lie in bed, too weak to move, and seemingly indifferent to everything about her.

At length one evening, about six weeks after her return, she said to her sister: "I don't feel's if I'd ever get up again."

Ann Eliza turned from the kettle she was placing on the stove. She was startled by the echo the words woke in her own breast.

"Don't you talk like that, Evelina! I guess you're on'y tired out—and disheartened."

"Yes, I'm disheartened," Evelina murmured.

A few months earlier Ann Eliza would have met the confession with a word of pious admonition; now she accepted it in silence.

"Maybe you'll brighten up when your cough gets better," she suggested.

"Yes—or my cough'll get better when I brighten up," Evelina retorted with a touch of her old tartness.

"Does your cough keep on hurting you jest as much?"

"I don't see's there's much difference."

"Well, I guess I'll get the doctor to come round again," Ann Eliza said, trying for the matter-of-course tone in which one might speak of sending for the plumber or the gas-fitter.

"It ain't any use sending for the doctor—and who's going to pay him?"

"I am," answered the elder sister. "Here's your tea, and a mite of toast. Don't that tempt you?"

Already, in the watches of the night, Ann Eliza had been tormented by that same question—who was to pay the doctor?—and a few days before she had temporarily silenced it by borrowing twenty dollars of Miss Mellins. The transaction had cost her one of the bitterest struggles of her life. She had never borrowed a penny of any one before, and the possibility of having to do so had always been classed in her mind among those shameful extremities to which Providence does not let decent people come. But nowadays she no longer believed in the personal supervision of Providence; and had she been compelled to steal the money instead of borrowing it, she would have felt that her conscience was the only tribunal before which she had to answer. Nevertheless, the actual humiliation of having to ask for the money was no less bitter; and she could hardly hope that Miss Mellins would view the case with the same detachment as herself. Miss Mellins was very kind; but she not unnaturally felt that her kindness should be rewarded by according her the right to ask questions; and bit by bit Ann Eliza saw Evelina's miserable secret slipping into the dressmaker's possession.

When the doctor came she left him alone with Evelina, busying herself in the shop that she might have an opportunity of seeing him alone on his way out. To steady herself she began to sort a trayful of buttons, and when the doctor appeared she was reciting under her breath: "Twenty-four horn, two and a half cards fancy pearl. . . ." She saw at once that his look was grave.

He sat down on the chair beside the counter, and her mind travelled miles before he spoke.

"Miss Bunner, the best thing you can do is to let me get a bed for your sister at St. Luke's."

"The hospital?"

"Come now, you're above that sort of prejudice, aren't you?" The doctor spoke in the tone of one who coaxes a spoiled child. "I know how devoted you are—but Mrs. Ramy can be much better cared for there than here. You really haven't time to look after her and attend to your business as well. There'll be no expense, you understand—"

Ann Eliza made no answer. "You think my sister's going to be sick a good while, then?" she asked.

"Well, yes—possibly."

"You think she's very sick?"

"Well, yes. She's very sick."

His face had grown still graver; he sat there as though he had never known what it was to hurry.

Ann Eliza continued to separate the pearl and horn buttons.

Suddenly she lifted her eyes and looked at him. "Is she going to die?"

The doctor laid a kindly hand on hers. "We never say that, Miss Bunner. Human skill works wonders—and at the hospital Mrs. Ramy would have every chance."

"What is it? What's she dying of?"

The doctor hesitated, seeking to substitute a popular phrase for the scientific terminology which rose to his lips.

"I want to know," Ann Eliza persisted.

"Yes, of course; I understand. Well, your sister has had a hard time lately, and there is a complication of causes, resulting in consumption—rapid consumption. At the hospital—"

"I'll keep her here," said Ann Eliza quietly.

After the doctor had gone she went on for some time sorting the buttons; then she slipped the tray into its place on a shelf behind the counter and went into the back room. She found Evelina propped upright against the pillows, a flush of agitation on her cheeks. Ann Eliza pulled up the shawl which had slipped from her sister's shoulders.

"How long you've been! What's he been saying?"

"Oh, he went long ago—he on'y stopped to give me a prescription. I was sorting out that tray of buttons. Miss Mellins's girl got them all mixed up."

She felt Evelina's eyes upon her.

"He must have said something: what was it?"

"Why, he said you'd have to be careful—and stay in bed—and take this new medicine he's given you."

"Did he say I was going to get well?"

"Why, Evelina!"

"What's the use, Ann Eliza? You can't deceive me. I've just been up to look at myself in the glass; and I saw plenty of 'em in the hospital that looked like me. They didn't get well, and I ain't going to." Her head dropped back. "It don't much matter—I'm about tired. On'y there's one thing—Ann Eliza—"

The elder sister drew near to the bed.

"There's one thing I ain't told you. I didn't want to tell you yet because I was afraid you might be sorry—but if he says I'm going to die I've got to say it." She stopped to cough, and to Ann Eliza it now seemed as though every cough struck a minute from the hours remaining to her.

"Don't talk now—you're tired."

"I'll be tireder tomorrow, I guess. And I want you should know. Sit down close to me—there."

Ann Eliza sat down in silence, stroking her shrunken hand.

"I'm a Roman Catholic, Ann Eliza."

"Evelina—oh, Evelina Bunner! A Roman Catholic—*you?* Oh, Evelina, did *he* make you?"

Evelina shook her head. "I guess he didn't have no religion; he never spoke of it. But you see Mrs. Hochmüller was a Catholic, and so when I was sick she got the doctor to send me to a Roman Catholic hospital, and the sisters was so good to me there —and the priest used to come and talk to me; and the things he said kep' me from going crazy. He seemed to make everything easier."

"Oh, sister, how could you?" Ann Eliza wailed. She knew little of the Catholic religion except that "Papists" believed in it—in itself a sufficient indictment. Her spiritual rebellion had not freed her from the formal part of her religious belief, and apostasy had always seemed to her one of the sins from which the pure in mind avert their thoughts.

"And then when the baby was born," Evelina continued, "he christened it right away, so it could go to heaven; and after that, you see, I had to be a Catholic."

"I don't see—"

"Don't I have to be where the baby is? I couldn't ever ha' gone there if I hadn't been made a Catholic. Don't you understand that?"

Ann Eliza sat speechless, drawing her hand away. Once more she found herself shut out of Evelina's heart, an exile from her closest affections.

"I've got to go where the baby is," Evelina feverishly insisted.

Ann Eliza could think of nothing to say; she could only feel that Evelina was dying, and dying as a stranger in her arms. Ramy and the day-old baby had parted her forever from her sister.

Evelina began again. "If I get worse I want you to send for a priest. Miss Mellins'll know where to send—she's got an aunt that's a Catholic. Promise me faithful you will."

"I promise," said Ann Eliza.

After that they spoke no more of the matter; but Ann Eliza now understood that the little black bag about her sister's neck, which she had innocently taken for a memento of Ramy, was some kind of sacrilegious amulet, and her fingers shrank from its contact when she bathed and dressed Evelina. It seemed to her the diabolical instrument of their estrangement.

※ XIII ※

SPRING had really come at last. There were leaves on the ailanthus-tree that Evelina could see from her bed, gentle clouds floated over it in the blue, and now and then the cry of a flower-seller sounded from the street.

One day there was a shy knock on the back-room door, and Johnny Hawkins came in with two yellow jonquils in his fist. He was getting bigger and squarer, and his round freckled face was growing into a smaller copy of his father's. He walked up to Evelina and held out the flowers.

"They blew off the cart and the fellow said I could keep 'em. But you can have 'em," he announced.

Ann Eliza rose from her seat at the sewing-machine and tried to take the flowers from him.

"They ain't for you; they're for her," he sturdily objected; and Evelina held out her hand for the jonquils.

After Johnny had gone she lay and looked at them without speaking. Ann Eliza, who had gone back to the machine, bent her head over the seam she was stitching; the click, click, click of the machine sounded in her ear like the tick of Ramy's clock, and it seemed to her that life had gone backward, and that Evelina, radiant and foolish, had just come into the room with the yellow flowers in her hand.

When at last she ventured to look up, she saw that her sister's head had drooped against the pillow, and that she was sleeping quietly. Her relaxed hand still held the jonquils, but it was evident that they had awakened no memories; she had dozed off almost as soon as Johnny had given them to her. The discovery gave Ann Eliza a startled sense of the ruins that must be piled upon her past. "I don't believe I could have forgotten that day, though," she said to herself. But she was glad that Evelina had forgotten.

Evelina's disease moved on along the usual course, now lifting her on a brief wave of elation, now sinking her to new depths of weakness. There was little to be done, and the doctor came only at lengthening intervals. On his way out he always repeated his first friendly suggestion about sending Evelina to the hospital; and Ann Eliza always answered: "I guess we can manage."

The hours passed for her with the fierce rapidity that great joy or anguish lends them. She went through the days with a sternly smiling precision, but she hardly knew what was happening, and when nightfall released her from the shop, and she could carry her work to Evelina's bedside, the same sense of unreality accompanied her, and she still seemed to be accomplishing a task whose object had escaped her memory.

Once, when Evelina felt better, she expressed a desire to make some artificial flowers, and Ann Eliza, deluded by this awakening interest, got out the faded bundles of stems and petals and the little tools and spools of wire. But after a few minutes the work dropped from Evelina's hands and she said: "I'll wait till tomorrow.

She never again spoke of the flower-making, but one day, after watching Ann Eliza's laboured attempt to trim a spring hat for Mrs. Hawkins, she demanded impatiently that the hat should be brought to her, and in a trice had galvanized the lifeless bow and given the brim the twist it needed.

These were rare gleams; and more frequent were the days of speechless lassitude, when she lay for hours silently staring at the window, shaken only by the hard incessant cough that sounded to Ann Eliza like the hammering of nails into a coffin.

At length one morning Ann Eliza, starting up from the mattress at the foot of the bed, hastily called Miss Mellins down, and ran through the smoky dawn for the doctor. He came back with her and did what he could to give Evelina momentary relief; then he went away, promising to look in again before night. Miss Mellins, her head still covered with curl-papers, disappeared in his wake, and when the sisters were alone Evelina beckoned to Ann Eliza.

"You promised," she whispered, grasping her sister's arm; and Ann Eliza understood. She had not yet dared to tell Miss Mellins of Evelina's change of faith; it had seemed even more difficult than borrowing the money; but now it had to be done. She ran upstairs after the dressmaker and detained her on the landing.

"Miss Mellins, can you tell me where to send for a priest—a Roman Catholic priest?"

"A priest, Miss Bunner?"

"Yes. My sister became a Roman Catholic while she was away. They were kind to her in her sickness—and now she wants a priest." Ann Eliza faced Miss Mellins with unflinching eyes.

"My aunt Dugan'll know. I'll run right round to her the minute I get my papers off," the dressmaker promised; and Ann Eliza thanked her.

An hour or two later the priest appeared. Ann Eliza, who was watching, saw him coming down the steps to the shop-door and went to meet him. His expression was kind, but she shrank from his peculiar dress, and from his pale face with its bluish chin and enigmatic smile. Ann Eliza remained in the shop. Miss Mellins's girl had mixed the buttons again and she set herself to sort them. The priest stayed a long time with Evelina. When he again carried his enigmatic smile past the counter, and Ann Eliza rejoined her sister, Evelina was smiling with something of the same mystery; but she did not tell her secret.

After that it seemed to Ann Eliza that the shop and the back room no longer belonged to her. It was as though she were there on sufferance, indulgently tolerated by the unseen power which hovered over Evelina even in the absence of its minister. The priest came almost daily; and at last a day arrived when he was called to administer some rite of which Ann Eliza but dimly grasped the sacramental meaning. All she knew was that it meant that Evelina was going, and going, under this alien guidance, even farther from her than to the dark places of death.

When the priest came, with something covered in his hands, she crept into the shop, closing the door of the back room to leave him alone with Evelina.

It was a warm afternoon in May, and the crooked ailanthus-tree rooted in a fissure of the opposite pavement was a fountain of tender green. Women in light dresses passed with the languid step of spring; and presently there came a man with a hand-cart full of pansy and geranium plants who stopped outside the window, signalling to Ann Eliza to buy.

An hour went by before the door of the back room opened and the priest reappeared with that mysterious covered something in his hands. Ann Eliza had risen, drawing back as he passed. He had doubtless divined her antipathy, for he had hitherto only bowed in going in and out; but today he paused and looked at her compassionately.

"I have left your sister in a very beautiful state of mind," he said in a low voice like a woman's. "She is full of spiritual consolation."

Ann Eliza was silent, and he bowed and went out. She has-

tened back to Evelina's bed, and knelt down beside it. Evelina's
eyes were very large and bright; she turned them on Ann Eliza
with a look of inner illumination.

"I shall see the baby," she said; then her eyelids fell and she
dozed.

The doctor came again at nightfall, administering some last
palliatives; and after he had gone Ann Eliza, refusing to have her
vigil shared by Miss Mellins or Mrs. Hawkins, sat down to keep
watch alone.

It was a very quiet night. Evelina never spoke or opened her
eyes, but in the still hour before dawn Ann Eliza saw that the
restless hand outside the bed-clothes had stopped its twitching.
She stooped over and felt no breath on her sister's lips.

The funeral took place three days later. Evelina was buried
in Calvary Cemetery, the priest assuming the whole care of the
necessary arrangements, while Ann Eliza, a passive spectator, be-
held with stony indifference this last negation of her past.

A week afterward she stood in her bonnet and mantle in the
doorway of the little shop. Its whole aspect had changed. Counter and shelves were bare, the window was stripped of its familiar miscellany of artificial flowers, note-paper, wire hat-frames,
and limp garments from the dyer's; and against the glass pane of
the doorway hung a sign: "This store to let."

Ann Eliza turned her eyes from the sign as she went out and
locked the door behind her. Evelina's funeral had been very expensive, and Ann Eliza, having sold her stock-in-trade and the
few articles of furniture that remained to her, was leaving the
shop for the last time. She had not been able to buy any
mourning, but Miss Mellins had sewed some crape on her old
black mantle and bonnet, and having no gloves she slipped her
bare hands under the folds of the mantle.

It was a beautiful morning, and the air was full of a warm
sunshine that had coaxed open nearly every window in the street,
and summoned to the window-sills the sickly plants nurtured in-

doors in winter. Ann Eliza's way lay westward, toward Broadway; but at the corner she paused and looked back down the familiar length of the street. Her eyes rested a moment on the
blotched "Bunner Sisters" above the empty window of the shop;
then they travelled on to the overflowing foliage of the Square,
above which was the church tower with the dial that had marked
the hours for the sisters before Ann Eliza had bought the nickel
clock. She looked at it all as though it had been the scene of
some unknown life, of which the vague report had reached her:
she felt for herself the only remote pity that busy people accord
to the misfortunes which come to them by hearsay.

She walked to Broadway and down to the office of the
house-agent to whom she had entrusted the sub-letting of the
shop. She left the key with one of his clerks, who took it from her
as if it had been any one of a thousand others, and remarked that
the weather looked as if spring was really coming; then she
turned and began to move up the great thoroughfare, which was
just beginning to wake to its multitudinous activities.

She walked less rapidly now, studying each shop window as
she passed, but not with the desultory eye of enjoyment: the
watchful fixity of her gaze overlooked everything but the object
of its quest. At length she stopped before a small window
wedged between two mammoth buildings, and displaying, behind its shining plate-glass festooned with muslin, a varied assort-
ment of sofa-cushions, tea-cloths, pen-wipers, painted calendars
and other specimens of feminine industry. In a corner of the window she had read, on a slip of paper pasted against the pane:
"Wanted, a Saleslady," and after studying the display of fancy
articles beneath it, she gave her mantle a twitch, straightened her
shoulders and went in.

Behind a counter crowded with pincushions, watch-holders
and other needlework trifles, a plump young woman with smooth
hair sat sewing bows of ribbon on a scrap basket. The little shop
was about the size of the one on which Ann Eliza had just closed
the door; and it looked as fresh and gay and thriving as she and

Evelina had once dreamed of making Bunner Sisters. The friendly air of the place made her pluck up courage to speak.

"Saleslady? Yes, we do want one. Have you anyone to recommend?" the young woman asked, not unkindly.

Ann Eliza hesitated, disconcerted by the unexpected question; and the other, cocking her head on one side to study the effect of the bow she had just sewed on the basket, continued: "We can't afford more than thirty dollars a month, but the work is light. She would be expected to do a little fancy sewing between times. We want a bright girl: stylish, and pleasant manners. You know what I mean. Not over thirty, anyhow; and nice-looking. Will you write down the name?"

Ann Eliza looked at her confusedly. She opened her lips to explain, and then, without speaking, turned toward the crisply curtained door.

"Ain't you going to leave the *ad*-dress?" the young woman called out after her. Ann Eliza went out into the thronged street. The great city, under the fair spring sky, seemed to throb with the stir of innumerable beginnings. She walked on, looking for another shop window with a sign in it.